Travel Page

Every publication from Rippple Books has this special page to document where the book travels, who has it and when.

Quintus Huntley

Botany

Royce Leville

Rippple
Books

Copyright © 2025 Royce Leville
All rights reserved

The right of Royce Leville to be identified as the Author of the Work has been asserted in accordance with the Copyright, Designs and Patents Act 1988.

Cover design: Claudia Bode
Editor: Jeff Kavanagh

The author would like to thank Susan Bradley-Smith for entertaining discussions about solving crimes with poetry.

Perth skyline image designed by Sky and Glass / Freepik.

This publication may only be reproduced, stored or transmitted, in any form, or by any means, with prior permission in writing from the publisher or, in accordance with the provisions of the Copyright Act 1956 (amended).

This book is sold subject to the conditions that it shall not, by way of trade or otherwise, be lent, re-sold, hired out, or otherwise circulated without the publisher's prior consent in any form of binding or cover other than that which it is published and without a similar condition including this condition being imposed on the subsequent purchaser.

Rippple Books
Rippple Media
Postfach 304263
20325 Hamburg
Germany
www.rippplemedia.com

A CIP catalogue record for this book is available from the British Library.

ISBN: 978-3-9826144-2-7

The Green Neck of the Violinist

May the intense want for something
That someone else envisions
As theirs
Lead you down a troubled path
Of disastrously poor decisions
All yours
To that precipitous point
From where there's no return
To ours
While wrongly thinking such action
Will deliver what I've earned
To me

    The body is still warm, but that isn't much of an indicator of how long it's been there, as outside it's pushing 40 and inside the air-con isn't on. The two uniformed cops stand perfectly still in the living room, hands on hips, top shirt-buttons down, faces glistening. They look around the room, and at each other; anything to keep from staring at the very pretty girl lying on the floor, slim body askew. When the detectives enter, both cops turn to them, sending a few droplets of sweat from their brows that land on the light blue carpet and form perfect circles.

    Detective Elenore Everest, also pushing 40, nods to the cops as she snaps on a pair of latex gloves. She goes to the body, bends down and touches the young woman's neck, close to the mortal wound, made by a fountain pen jammed into the jugular. She doesn't crouch down, but bends at the waist, elbows on knees, so she's looking right over the wound. She sees that blood has trickled down the victim's neck and onto the floor, where it's been absorbed by the plush, and has darkened it. This makes it seem there's far less blood than there would otherwise be, as slashing important arteries below the head normally results in a lot of blood. But it also makes her wonder if bleeding out was the actual cause of death. The fountain pen is broken, likely from the impact, its green ink all over the victim's neck and nape, giving the body a ghoulish look.

"Wow, she's beautiful. Is that ink? Is it dry?"

This from Everest's partner, Justin Booth, mid-20s, whose good looks, shaggy surfer's hair and toothy smile make him the poster boy for Perth's affluent western suburbs. Booth's questions tend to annoy Everest, though she's the first to admit to preferring Booth's good-natured inquisitiveness to the usual know-it-all-ness, or sneering disinterest, of his generation.

"Was she playing the violin at the time? She's holding the bow, but why is the violin in its case?"

Everest finds this an interesting observation, but doesn't reply.

Booth gets on his haunches and into Everest's eyeline. "What's with the yellow?" he asks, pointing at the neck with gloveless hands.

"Don't touch her."

"Come on. It's not my first day."

"Sometimes we all need reminding of that."

Offended, Booth tries to assert himself. "This stuff around the wound. Is it some kind of jaundice?"

Everest, amused with how pleased Booth is with himself for using that word, keeps looking at the victim, staring into her lifeless eyes, almost the same blue as the carpet, wondering what was the last thing she saw.

"Maybe it's the mix of green and red?"

"Oh, yeah," Everest says. "You paint. Don't you?"

"When I can. Do you like art? It started out as a mindfulness exercise, one that my dad got me onto. Then I saw I was good at it. Beach scenes. Sunsets. Mostly."

Everest stands up, wishing that Booth would stop his upbeat patter. Despite being his superior, she can't really say things like, "Shut the fuck up, Justin" because of who his father is.

"Do you like that sort of stuff?" Booth asks, standing up as well. "I'm part of an exhibition at the Cottesloe Civic Centre. On Friday. Why don't you come along?"

She continues working, trying to see everything while not getting caught up in the excitement of the moment. A murder case like this in swanky Peppermint Grove is rare and solving it could be the kind of thing that helps her climb the food chain and away from guys like Booth; it might even land her a partner she can actually exert authority over.

"Don't think of it as an obligation. Because it's not. Only come if you want. Okay?"

"It's Monday morning, Justin. I've got all week to decide."

"Shall I put you on the list?"

"Sure," Everest says, hoping it will stop him from pressing. "Put me on the list."

On inspection, the victim's hands show no signs of struggle. No attempt at defending herself. No nails broken. No visible bruising. Everest admires what beautiful hands the woman has, the fingers unusually long and slender, pink and smooth. A musician's fingers, only the tips calloused; they're dexterous, strong and precious.

"Great. That's really supportive of you. Plus one?"

Everest looks around the room, which is furnished like a bland holiday rental. Nothing knocked over or broken. No sign of forced entry. It all leads her to conclude the victim was taken by surprise; stabbed in the neck while playing the sheet music, now stained with a thin slash of blood, on the stand. Something classical, she assumes, old and good. Having learned to play the drums entirely by ear and feel, and without a clue about notations – because, as she believes, rock and roll is played, not read – she marvels at how this violinist managed to turn those lifeless squiggles, dots and lines into something remotely soulful.

Her eyes fall on the violin. "You're right, Justin. It's interesting the violin is in the case."

"You think she was playing when it happened? And the killer put it back?"

Everest points: "As you said, she's still holding the bow."

"Maybe she was getting ready to play?"

They both stand over the case. The violin looks old and well-travelled, but its surface gleams and the strings look new.

"The murderer a music lover, you think?" Booth asks. "They put the violin back."

"Or someone who understands the value of instruments. They couldn't stand to see it on the floor, wherever it fell."

"Yeah. This looks valuable. If she was playing at the time, it would open up one side of her neck, right?"

"The bow's in her right hand, so her head would be tilted left. But the pen is in the right side of her neck."

"So, not playing?" Booth extends his hands to lift the violin out of the case. "But the big question is, was she playing for someone?"

"Come on, Justin," Everest says, stopping him. "There could prints on it. Put some gloves on or put your hands in your pockets."

"I hate those gloves. They're always a bit slimy inside. It's like wearing a condom on every finger."

"And don't even think about turning the air-con on."

"Things will get ripe in here quickly, in this heat. Can I open a window?"

"Forensics will be here in a minute. Why don't you find out who she is?"

Over the last few months, Everest has garnered that the best way to get Booth to do something is to frame orders as suggestions, usually in question form. Booth lopes towards the one remaining uniformed cop, who's lingering in the room and sweating even more than before. The cop has the narrowed eyes and serious look of someone harbouring CSI ambitions.

"Got an ID on the girl?" Booth asks him.

"I found this in the bedroom," the cop says, handing Booth a bulging wallet. He gestures towards the body. "Have you checked for prints and DNA? There could be skin fragments on the pen, and under her nails."

Looking in the wallet, and frowning, Booth asks, "Anything else you think we might miss?"

"There could be hair. Bits of clothing. And dirt from shoes."

"You know a lot about this."

"I didn't mean to …"

"No worries, mate. It's good you're onto this sort of stuff. You've got the right attention to detail. The forensic team will take care of all the dirty work. Maybe you stick to what you're on shift for, yeah?"

The cop nods and wipes the beading sweat from his temples with his shirt sleeves.

"Can we turn the air-con on?"

Booth thumbs behind him. "My partner says no. I have no idea why."

"I'm cooking in here."

"Why don't you get some fresh air? Find out who owns this place?"

"You don't think she does?"

"This place is furnished like a hotel. You didn't pick up on that? There are no books on the shelves. No personal touches. Nothing that really says this is her place."

"Maybe she just moved in?"

"Doubtful. This is a transit lounge."

The cop looks around a bit, and sweats some more. "Yeah, no. Right. I'm seeing that now."

"Plus, the cleaning lady found her, which most likely means it's a serviced apartment. We need to find the owner."

"I'm on it." The cop leaves the room with purpose.

Booth continues to finger through the wallet as he walks back to Everest, who's still contemplating the violin.

"I suggest you try not to do that," she says, retying her brown hair into the severe ponytail she favours. The hairband catches in one glove, tearing the plastic. "These things are so flimsy."

"Do what? My job?"

"Make your colleagues feel like idiots."

"Is that how you saw it? You're way off. We engaged. It was a professional exchange. Anyway, he's just a street cop."

"Worth remembering that whenever you get yourself in a hole you can't get out of, and you will, because we all do, it'll be a uniform who comes to your rescue. You shouldn't ever give them a reason not to."

"Relax. I'm covered."

"Your dad won't always be there to help you ... up."

"What are you implying? You think I only got this far because of my name?"

Everest reminds herself to choose her words wisely, as anything she says could be repeated over the Booth dining table. "No. Not at all. I'm simply advising you to treat your colleagues with a little more respect."

Booth shakes his head, then sits down on the floor, cross-legged, back hunched, like a told-off toddler. He starts dealing the contents of the wallet onto the carpet.

"What do the cards say?"

"Her name is Ekaterina Valoskiya," Booth says, holding up a bank card. "Did I say that right? Doesn't sound like a local."

Having tossed away the broken right glove, Everest checks the woman's pockets with her gloved left hand.

"Russian maybe?" Booth continues. "All these cards are local though. Is she fresh off the boat?"

"Her pockets are empty. She must have her passport in the apartment somewhere. Is there a foreign driver's license in the wallet?"

"Nuh. A credit card. Local bank. Gym membership, for a place around the corner. Some kind of keycard with PSO on it. Holy shit."

"What?"

"Check it out." Booth unfurls a strip of red-packaged condoms.

"Are those the ones that are slimy inside?"

Booth laughs, rather childishly. "You think she got around?"

"As an adult, she could do whatever she wanted."

"Not anymore." Booth looks intently at the condoms. "Maybe this had something to do with her downfall."

Everest moves to stand over Booth. "You think it's that simple?"

"I'm just surveying the evidence at hand."

"The condoms being the biggest clue?"

"Yeah. They certainly stand out. Crime of passion? A rejected lover? What's that stat about 90-something per cent of murders being committed by someone the victim knows?"

Everest would prefer it not to be that straightforward, but she thinks the broken pen is looking very phallic, combined with all the envy-coloured ink that was inside it.

"You think her lover did it?" she asks.

They both look at the wallet's contents, now arranged on the carpet in an orderly fashion.

"Looks like she had more than one. I'm guessing something more lurid?"

"What do you mean?"

"You know, neon-flavoured. We're not in the right part of the city for that, but someone could've been running her out of this place. It's not her apartment."

"A prostitute who plays the violin."

"Maybe she catered to a very discerning clientele." He holds up the condoms, like they're exhibit A in a courtroom. "She's well-prepared. A Russian girl, young, beautiful. Just arrived. No passport, because her pimp's got it."

Everest bends down and picks up the card with PSO on it. "This may not be her place, but it's hardly a love nest. Anyway, she's got musician hands."

"Good point. About the apartment. And, I mean, what prostitute plays Brahms on the violin?"

"Is that what the sheet music is?"

Booth nods. "Religious stuff. Churchy hymns. Bog-standard Brahms."

"More benefits of a private school education. What instrument did you play?"

"Clarinet. I was good too."

Everest can't help smiling. "Like you are at painting. Such a talent."

Booth seems genuinely hurt. "Sarcasm really is the cheapest form of humour."

"What inspirational calendar did you pull that from?"

"As usual, you've got me all wrong. I chose the clarinet, and I learned how to read music. But I was never in the school band. Competition was tough. There were two clarinets ahead of me. Way better. Both of them practised a lot more than me. As those types of kids did. As they still do."

"Those types of kids? Easy, Justin. There's no need for that."

"For what? I'm just talking about the kids who think school matters. They get pushed by their, uh, ha, their tiger parents to be the best at everything."

"I think that's enough."

"What? I didn't say anything? It's not like it's a secret. Those kids end up at the top of every school in Perth. They want it more. Good for them."

Everest, keen to change the subject before Booth says something he deserves to be punched for, holds up the keycard. "I'm assuming this PSO has something to do with music. Any ideas?"

"It's the Perth Symphony Orchestra."

"You knew that from the start, yet you still thought the condoms said more about her."

"All that red was eye-catching. Like a ... red flag."

"They must own this place. Or there's some benefactor. She's in the orchestra. Maybe even brought out here specifically for that purpose."

"Shall we go there and talk to people? That's our next move, right?"

"It is. Can you bag all the stuff from her wallet?"

"I didn't bring any plastic bags."

"Then keep the PSO card and leave the rest for forensics."

As Booth gets to his feet, two guys enter the living room, carrying a long, dark-blue body transporter. Everest gestures for them to put it down.

"What's the problem?" one of them asks. "With this heat, we need to get this body on ice."

"You're too early," Everest says.

Booth attempts to take charge. "We still need to do a massive sweep of the apartment."

"We'll wait outside. Too bloody hot in here. Gonna be ripe soon too."

"Good idea," Booth says. "Thanks, fellas."

"So, you're nice to them, but not to street cops," Everest says.

Booth flashes a winning smile. "I'm nice to everybody."

Everest can't help but smile back.

"So, are we done here?" Booth asks.

"One more thing. There was something about the violin."

Everest goes back to the case and looks around. She carefully lifts the violin with her left hand, surprised to find that underneath is a book, titled *The Ragged Claws of Ravensthorpe*.

Booth reaches across and picks the book up.

"Don't touch that."

Booth looks at the cover and asks, "Who the fuck is Quintus Huntley?"

<>

His office is in the – previously temporary – annexe next to the Arts and Humanities building. Said annexe is a collection of white containers, the kind seen at large construction or mining sites. Here, they've been given some street cred, with murals and graffiti adorning their outsides. And it's not the usual egocentric spray painting of names; it's serious artwork, animals mostly, impressively done, and good enough for the University of WA's Cultural Collections Board to vote on keeping the containers where they are, much to the dismay of the Arts and Humanities faculty. That is, those who have offices in the main building and who refer to the containers as a "rusting trailer park". The part-timers, tutors, researchers and PhD candidates holed up in the containers, with two or three to each sweltering metal box, consider themselves outcasts; a kind of counter-revolutionary group sticking it to the established, fusty and dinosaurial A&H faculty, who sit in the main building in air-conditioned comfort and sleepwalk through the same old lectures and courses, semester after semester, trudging slowly towards academically honoured graves. But nothing changes, because there is a high turnover of people in the containers, as the best among the part-timers and researchers get head-hunted for positions at other universities, and they're only too happy to leave, which means UWA's insistence on holding onto its established professors has resulted in a continual drain of talent matched by the slowly dwindling numbers of students seeking an A&H degree.

One of the first to take an office in half a container was Quintus Huntley, and his longevity means he holds a quasi-leadership position among the group, though his tendency to miss important faculty meetings results in that group rarely having a say in matters. Huntley doesn't want to be a leader, and he doesn't think of the group as counter-revolutionary. He claims they're mercenaries; a small troupe of artists and contrary thinkers, here for the money, biding their time until a better offer comes along. For Huntley, such an offer has yet to be forthcoming, which means for him and the other long-termers, being stuck in these containers is testimony to, and a daily reminder of, their artistic and academic failures. Years ago, Huntley reached just enough acclaim with his one and only poetry collection to secure a part-time lecturer position, but has never been able to go further than that. He continues to work for hourly wages running the tutorials and workshops the tenured professors consider beneath them, while occasionally getting the chance to lead a semester course if one of the poetry professors goes on sabbatical or has a long-term illness.

Huntley, sweating, lies on the sofa in the middle of the container. The sofa acts as a two-boys-in-a-room border, demarcating his section from Miguel's; the Colombian poet's been there almost as long as Huntley, and removing either of them would require an extraction team. Over the years, the two of them have barely developed a relationship, as their part-time hours and dedicated office times never coincide. The closest they get to communicating is an annual exchange of Christmas cards.

It's incredibly hot in the container. It feels like the metal walls are melting. The oscillating fan on the floor does little more than spin the hot air anew. It drones slowly from side to side, like it's suffering.

Huntley stays perfectly still, silently praying no student will bang on the door today. Lying prone on the sofa blocks out any view of the chaotic mess of Miguel's half, thus preventing Huntley from having to fight the incredible urge to clean it all up and put everything in its proper place. It's hard enough just knowing it's there, even if it's out of his eye-line.

The fan gives maximum effort to complete another stuttering crescent course; the breeze hits the side of Huntley's face like a sick person breathing on him.

At 42, he feels old. Yet though divorced and with a daughter in her early teens, and having spent nearly two decades in this container, he still has the sense that life hasn't really begun and that there's plenty of time to do great things. Miguel has ten years on him, but somehow seems younger, with that head of sublime black curls, the lithe build of a South American soccer player and the spring in his step that reflects his full appreciation for even being here; for even being alive. He lost every member of his immediate family to drug-related violence and escaped Colombia with a bounty on his head, having witnessed some of those murders.

Huntley, rumpled and starting to let himself go, is less grateful, and he hates himself for it. Sure, he'll talk enthusiastically about being a mercenary and how poetry can change the world and that structure is everything, but he'd gladly swap all of that for a smidgen of Miguel's chaotic glee. That Miguel has had a way harder life and had to overcome so much trauma to get to a place that Huntley doesn't want to be just makes him feel worse about it all. Not to mention the fame Miguel has in Colombia, which he rejected years ago in favour of being a lowly university tutor in the world's most isolated big city, where he hoped to disappear. In certain sections of Bogota and Medellin, Miguel was well known, and his ongoing exile has only made him more famous. A revered person of letters, to those who think magical realism poetry is important and that Miguel has something impressive and/or beautiful to say.

Back in his early 20s, Huntley thought he had something impressive and/or beautiful to say. It was hard work, initially, finding it and nailing his style and voice, but once he had that, in what was a pristine moment where everything coalesced, the words flowed with such ease it was as if they were already written and he was just the vessel for them; a sensation he hasn't experienced since and the absence of which gnaws away at his soul with greater intensity with every passing year. But that debut collection thrust him into the Perth literary limelight, such as it is, and briefly made him a revered person of letters, for the small minority of locals who cared about that sort of stuff. There he was, young, rugged and good-looking, a home-schooled country boy who grew up on a commune, suddenly a shooting star of the local writing scene. As some people said, his poems had the verve, humour and energy that was in stark contrast to the usual misery-guts prose and poetry that had been churned out by local writers for decades and which no one wanted to read. All those dire books driven by plots where one bad thing happened after another and everyone was awful. Huntley changed the game. He wrote of revenge, family, love and misunderstandings in ways that people could relate to, and still be surprised by. He was bold, irreverent and funny, and determinedly local, brilliant at capturing the state's country-city contrasts and unique character. For a moment, albeit fleeting, he made poetry popular and put Ravensthorpe on the map.

But that was a long time ago, and during that time, misery-guts prose and poetry had well and truly retaken its hold as the main method of local storytelling. Nothing good had come to him since, though not for a lack of trying. He has composed thousands of poems over the years, mostly in his head, but also tried putting some on paper. Nothing measured up. He has become an absolute expert at starting, then scrunching up the paper and lobbing it into the bin. He tried replicating his initial success, by going back to Ravensthorpe and staying at the commune, but rather than supplying new magic, it only reminded him of the magic that was missing and plunged him further into the hole. And then, doubt fully took hold and hasn't let go. Now, he can't even make a shopping list without questioning its merit.

Huntley would be the first to say that confidence is integral to writing; having the belief that the stories are there and can be told and deserved to be told and only you are the one who can tell them. Without it, there's only doubt, and that fucker festers and grows like a parasite, consuming every morsel of creativity that comes its way. With a head, heart and stomach full of doubt, there's no way to write anything.

Now, he's lived with doubt so long, he wonders how he ever had any confidence to begin with.

The fan whirrs on, unhelpfully.

A hot toddy would take the edge off, he thinks, provide the illusion of balance, his body temperature matched to the air, and just enough of a kick to get his mind off things; try to drown the doubt in rum. But he's all out of cinnamon, honey and lemon, and drinking black tea with rum seems desperate; more a way to keep the tremors at bay than enjoy the drink. Making it would also mean moving, and he's kind of sweated himself stuck to the sofa.

All of which means, when there's a knock on the metal from outside, he doesn't get up. He yells, "What?"

The door opens and he lifts his head just enough to see which student is ruining his morning solitude. But the woman in the pantsuit with the tight ponytail doesn't look like a student. The shaggy-haired guy with her could almost pass for one, though.

"Mr Huntley?"

"Who are you?"

"I'm Detective Elenore Everest."

"That's a lot of E's, rolling easily off the tongue. A beautifully poetic name."

Everest, slightly taken aback, adds, "This is Detective Booth. Are you Quintus Huntley?"

Huntley stays lying. "In the melting flesh. If this is about those parking tickets, I can explain."

"It's cooking in here," Booth says. He looks around for a window to open. There isn't one, so he goes to the door and props this open with a chair.

"Any breeze yet?" Huntley asks. "Please tell me the doctor's in."

Booth stands next to Everest. Huntley finds it amusing that the two of them are almost exactly the same height.

"Is something funny?" Booth asks.

"Nothing. Detective."

"No breeze yet," Everest says. "Maybe down the beach, but it hasn't reached this part of town."

"I bet it's sublime down at Trigg right now," Booth says, glancing towards the doorway. "The water like glass."

"Not that it matters. The wind doesn't get in here anyway. I'm fine with it. My office hours are useful for helping me shed a few kilos. An educational sauna."

Booth laughs a little, then snaps his fingers. "Hey, I remember you now. I took one of your courses."

Huntley turns his head to look at Booth. "I've had a lot of students."

"It was around ten years ago. I was studying Criminal Psychology, but I did a few arts electives, to fill out my schedule, like your poetry course."

"Post-modern poetry course. At least get it right. Though it makes me assume it left no impression on you."

"Hah. Not really. I was high most of the time. Probably why I can't remember it. But I do remember you had clever ways of saying things."

Huntley sits up. He leans forward and lifts the fan towards him. "You sound like a very capable detective. What's your name again?"

"Justin Booth."

Huntley shrugs.

"I wrote an essay about hip-hop being modern poetry," Booth brags. "You remember that, right?"

"Like that narrows it down. Do you have any idea how many essays like that I've read over the years? All these kids convinced that Eminem is a modern-day Dante and Kendrick Lamar is better than Shakespeare."

Everest steps towards the sofa. "If you two are done reminiscing," she says, "we can get down to business."

"Great word that. Business. Perfectly describes our local constabulary. You're looking to get more funds for a police force already profiting from parking fines and speeding tickets."

"Settle down," Booth says. "This is much more serious."

Everest grabs a chair, moves it towards the sofa and sits down opposite Huntley, the fan between them. "We're investigating a murder."

"Now that's interesting. Real police work. Let me say how glad I am to come across cops actually out on the job trying to solve a crime."

"Geez, will you give it a rest?" Booth asks.

"Mr Huntley," Everest begins, "we'd like to ask you a few questions about a case we're working on."

"I didn't do it. Whatever it is, Detective Everest, I'm innocent." Huntley snaps his fingers. "Hang on. Everest. I know that name. Are you Ellie Everest?"

Booth scoffs. "Oh, so she rings a bell, but I don't. Did she study here too, and leave more of an impression?"

"I do not like what you're implying there, Detective Booth," Huntley says.

"I skipped university," Everest interjects. "I spent several years working the streets. You know, out there generating revenue from speed traps and cameras."

"There's good money in that. But not from me. I drive slowly."

"But you do have trouble parking, by the sounds of it."

"Parking's easy. It's where I park that's the problem, and what you lot think about it. But no speeding. You'll never get me speeding. I've always thought it weird that people here are in such a hurry. It was really clever of the police to tap into that."

Booth paces around a little. "We're getting off track. Stop beating this drum about money."

"That's it," Huntley says, pointing at Everest. "Drums. Salty Lemonade. Giorgie loved you guys. You're Ellie Everest, the drummer."

"For real?" Booth asks. "I never heard of them."

"Too busy listening to hip-hop and getting high? Salty Lemonade were absolutely killing it about 20 years ago. Maybe more."

"Okay. Way before my time."

Huntley turns to Everest. "Giorgie wanted to get you to play at our wedding, but the band had split by then."

"What happened?"

"It doesn't matter, Justin," Everest says. "It's ancient history."

"The leader singer died. Tragic. She was so young. What was her name?"

"Charlene." Everest swallows, then manages to add, "We couldn't go on after that."

"Understandable. She OD'ed, didn't she? Such a talent. She had real presence. You know? But talent can be tough to live with, day after day. You're always wondering if what you're doing is any good. So much ... doubt. It's awful."

"I guess you'd know all about that." Booth holds up Huntley's book. "Remember this?"

"Also ancient history. Where'd you find that? Recycling bin?"

"At the crime scene."

"I didn't even know it was still in print."

Everest, struggling a little, stands up and walks to the open door, to get some air.

"The book was in the victim's possession," Booth says.

"Really? This victim had a book, and it's mine? And that means I did it?"

"I didn't say that. I'm sure she had other books. But yours was in her violin case."

"Violin? What kind of murder is this? You think I put my book in there?"

"Did you?" Booth takes out his phone and holds the screen in front of Huntley. "Do you recognise this woman?"

Huntley looks away. "Come on, mate. Don't just show that kind of stuff to people. At least give me some warning."

"So, you do know who she is?"

"I don't. Really. But that image is burned onto my eyes like sun glare." Huntley shakes his head. "Who is she? And what's with all the green?"

"She was stabbed with a fountain pen. That's the ink that was inside."

"Then it must've been a writer." Huntley holds out his hands. "Take me away. Wait. I don't seem to have any green on my hands."

"You washed it off."

"Justin," Everest says. "Why don't we stick to the facts, okay?"

"But how else did the book get there if he didn't plant it?"

Everest steps away from the door. "He would have to be the world's dumbest murderer, to put his own book at the scene of his crime. Are you the world's dumbest murderer, Mr Huntley?"

"No. I'd be happy to take an IQ test. Or you can hook me up to a lie detector."

"There's no need for that," Everest says.

Huntley rubs his eyes, trying to remove the remnant of the girl, so beautiful and so dead. "How do you kill someone with a pen?"

"Most likely by driving it into the throat right at the point where a person can bleed out."

"You say that so blandly," Huntley says. "Like you don't believe it yourself."

"There's no other possibility," Booth says. "There was so much blood."

"You'd need a medical degree to get that kind of wound right, especially with a blunt instrument like a pen." Huntley stands up and goes to the little kitchenette he shares with Miguel and which Huntley keeps orderly and clean. "I can't help you there."

"Do you think that's worth exploring?" Booth asks Everest. "Potential suspects with medical backgrounds?"

"Make a note of it."

Huntley puts the kettle on and moves the kitchenette's containers and jars into alignment. "Death by pen. How creative is that? The pen is mightier than the sword after all."

"That makes two," Everest says.

"Two what?"

"People who have made that joke," Booth says, clearly thinking it not funny. "We'll probably hear it many more times before the day is out."

"Who beat me to it?"

"Leiland Taverton."

"The PSO dictator? I bet he thought himself real clever saying that."

"Do you know him?" Booth asks.

"A bit. How's he messed up in this? Giorgie knows him pretty well, but she knows everyone. God, Perth is such a small town sometimes. Two random detectives come into my office ..."

"You call this an office?" Booth interjects.

"... And I know both of them. Somehow. I also know the last person they spoke to. Dig deep enough and we're probably all distantly related."

"I had a girlfriend who turned out to be my second cousin, once."

"Small gene pool in this town. What were you doing talking to Leiland?"

"The victim was third violin in the orchestra. Our investigation started there."

"Justin, please," Everest says. "He doesn't need to know that. Stop blurting out everything about the case."

"Third violin?" Huntley pours the tea. "Help me out. I'm just a country hick. Does that mean she's part of a group of violinists, within the orchestra? Or is she the third best, and the pecking order matters?"

Booth looks at Everest. "Can I answer that?"

"Of course. And there's no need to take that tone."

"Sorry. It's just so hot in here." Booth turns to Huntley, who's sipping tea. "You could say that both are correct. But it's more related to the pecking order. That's important in the orchestra. Who plays what and when. For violins and other instruments."

"Like clarinets?" Everest asks.

"Yes. For clarinets as well. Stop making fun of me."

"I'm not."

After a few sips of tea, Huntley decides to add some rum; first a little bit, then a lot. He gives the cup a swirl, then drinks and smiles.

Everest and Booth exchange a look.

"Bit early for that, isn't it?" Booth asks.

Huntley shrugs his shoulders. "It's afternoon tea for pirates somewhere in the world right now. It's helping to calm my nerves from that gruesome pic you showed me."

"That is the weirdest thing to drink on a hot day," Booth says.

"Actually, it's surprisingly refreshing. I'm surprised every time I have one. You want to try it?"

"No. I'm working."

Huntley turns to Everest. "Surely you will, Miss Detective Rock'n'roll?"

"Also working."

"Are you two together?" Huntley asks. "I love the way you interact. Very natural, with just a slight hint of the passive-aggression that's the essential glue of so many relationships."

Booth scoffs so loudly that it echoes in the container. "We're not together. Come on. Geez, god, together?"

"Steady on, junior. There's no reason to be so dismissive. I thought people of your generation were embracing this whole thing of relationships taking many different forms. Are you saying your work partner's not young enough to be your after-hours partner?"

"That's not what I ..."

"Look who you're dealing with," Huntley continues, the rum loosening his tongue. "This dynamite detective was once the drummer for one of Perth's hottest bands. How cool is that?"

"It's cool." Booth holds up his hands apologetically, but also offers a nice-guy smile. "Very cool. And she's definitely attractive."

"I think that's enough, Justin," Everest says. She turns her attention to Huntley. "You claim not to know the victim. You don't know why she had your, let's say, obscure book in her violin case. And you're increasingly not in any condition to help us."

"Hey, I'd be happy to help, if you stop treating me like a suspect."

"Can you account for your whereabouts last night and early this morning?" Booth asks.

"I was at home. In North Freo."

"Maybe you got so drunk you don't remember what you did last night."

"Yeah, let's go with that. You know, I always wanted to be the fifth-best triangle player, but this encounter has me thinking I should shelve that ambition."

"This is no time for humour, Mr Huntley," Everest says.

"You're right. Look, I don't know who she is and I don't know why my book was in her violin case. I can't help you. I'm sorry."

"Her name is Ekaterina Valoskiya. Does that sound familiar?"

Huntley shakes his head.

"Oh, so you can share any information you want," Booth says to Everest.

"I'm sure he'll be discreet about it, or I might follow up on those parking tickets."

"I won't tell a soul," Huntley says, sipping some more. "Russian?"

"Ukrainian, according to Mr Taverton."

"That's Dr Taverton." Huntley smiles. "He'll be the first to correct you on that. Loves a title, does Leiland."

"Does her name mean anything to you?"

"Apart from it sounding poetic, like yours, no. That's the kind of name you'd find in a Tolstoy book." Huntley sits back down on the sofa. "Tell me about her. Maybe I can help."

"How can you help?" Booth asks.

"I dunno. Maybe I can fill in the gaps. Who would want to kill a Ukrainian girl who plays the violin, third violin, in a nothing orchestra? Why does she have my book? And most importantly, why was she killed with a pen?"

"None of this concerns you." Booth walks towards Everest. "I think we're done here, don't you, Ellie?"

"Don't ever call me that, Justin."

"What kind of a name for a band is Salty Lemonade?"

"A good one," Huntley says. "And they rocked. Detective E's, how did you go from rock goddess to the police? That is a massive shift."

"The universe told me to quit music and I listened."

"Fair." Huntley has another drink. "This thing with the pen is fascinating. Why a pen? And this girl, this case, it's like a story. We need to flesh it out. The girl is a character, and she has a back story that can provide insight into what happened and who killed her and why. Stories are driven by conflict. No conflict, no story. So what's the conflict that's central to this story? Then, there's the killer's back story and the motive and what the killer was trying to achieve. Because it sounds to me like this murder had a purpose. It's not just some random killing. It's not improvised. There's a method behind this, and planning. Where did you say it happened?"

"In Peppermint Grove," Everest says, intrigued.

"That's a swanky place to be killed."

"It was in an apartment."

"One of the complexes on Stirling Highway? Yeah, must be, because the majority of Peppermint Grove is little gated communities. Have you ever seen it from the air? Every second house has a tennis court and a pool, and a huge wall around it. The money there is obscene. It must have the most beautiful collection of fences and gates of any suburb in the world."

"How do you know it so well?" Booth asks.

"According to you, I go there to murder girls with fountain pens."

"So, you confess?"

"Not even close. I lived there, with Giorgie, my wife. Ex-wife. And Verity. That's my daughter. But you're detectives and you probably know all that already. The Gifford house is enormous. Verity and I used to roller-skate through it. Drove Giorgie mad, because we left marks on the precious Jarrah floorboards, which were put in by her great-grandfather. I hated living in that place. Ugh. Is there anything more disgusting than old money? Old Perth money at that, earned on the broken backs and stolen lands of others. And now, all of it inherited and all of it tainted.

But that's all from Giorgie's side of the family. My father was a hippy down south."

Booth holds up the book. "In Ravensthorpe?"

"Yep. Write what you know."

Booth opens the book and starts flipping through the pages.

"I thought it was all motorheads and bikers down there," Everest says.

"That's insulting." Huntley drains the last of the tea. The rum is really kicking in now, and he wants more. As always, the first drink is just a tap on the shoulder, inviting him for another. "You're way wrong. You've probably never even been there. So many people in Perth have no clue about the folks in country towns. It's like you all live in a big bubble here, with very little sense of the outside world."

"You live in this bubble too. You could just go back to your wonderful country town."

"It's not perfect, but it's a community. Here, I get the sense we're all one wrong word from heading out to the carpark to duke it out."

"Mr Huntley," Booth says, his eyes still on the book, "there's no reason to get aggressive."

"I'm calm. I'm perfectly calm. You're the ones who marched in here ready to call me a killer. Then, when it's clear I'm not your guy, you insult where I come from. My heritage. And you should both know, you don't do that in this very proud state."

"We'll leave," Everest says. "Come on, Justin."

Huntley waves towards the door. "Do that."

Booth snaps the book shut. "We wouldn't want to interrupt your boozy morning more than we already have."

"Thank you for your time, Mr Huntley," Everest says.

"Yeah. Whatever. Salty Lemonade. You guys were great. Seems long ago now."

"Like a lot of things, the view from inside wasn't nearly as good as the view from outside."

Huntley nods. "Having talent can be brutal. A burden not everyone is fit to carry."

Booth moves the chair that's propping the door open.

As the two detectives leave, Huntley asks, "What are you going to do with my book?"

"We'll keep it for now, as evidence," Everest says, letting the door fall shut with a clang.

Huntley sits back and lets the fan waft over him. "Evidence of what?"

He closes his eyes and sees the girl with the green ink on her neck, and her story starts to unfold before him.

<>

The outside world looks like it's baking.

Sitting in the corner of the crowded, air-conditioned meeting room, next to the big window, Aphra Massey looks down on the Swan River, the broad expanse, pure blue from this distance, funnelling towards the Narrows Bridge. She thinks the bridge needs renaming, as it isn't narrow anymore; it's ten lanes wide, with a double railroad track down the middle, and busy with traffic. It sparks a memory, of being in the car as a six-year-old with her parents, driving over that bridge and then listening to them debate, all the way to Joondalup, about how the bridge got its name. Her father claimed it was because the bridge was initially very narrow when it was first built. Her mother stood firm that the bridge was placed at the narrowest point of the river. That was 25 years ago and she still doesn't know who was right. The safe bet is her mother, because her father has always had a quiet propensity for idiocy. Once, when he was drunk while grieving a mate who had died down in the hole, he blurted out some remark about the world being flat with a little too much seriousness.

Looking at the river now, she sees the bridge definitely spans its narrowest part.

It's a glorious view, from the 34th floor of downtown Perth's second tallest skyscraper. The river is calm, so crisp and clear it looks good enough to drink. A ferry is chugging over to South Perth. A dozen surf-cats, most likely helmed by schoolkids from the nearby Wesley or Trinity colleges, are racing in a large triangle. One surf-cat has gone over, and the two kids in the water, as tiny as they are from this distance, seem perfectly happy there, lying on their backs, their lifejackets keeping them afloat. Down at the bridge, traffic continues to stream across in both directions, the cars seemingly traversing a giant circuit around the city, marking each lap when crossing the bridge. Further out, the river widens again and curves into a bay near the University of WA, then winds past acreages of luxury homes all the way to Fremantle. Her parents live in one of them, on the relatively cheaper and downscale south side, in Applecross; a five-and-four that's way too big for them, but appropriately bespeaks the wealth attained through twin careers of fly-in-fly-out mining work up north.

The meeting pushes into its second hour. Aphra's already onto her third sheet of BS-bingo. All the watchwords and catchphrases that get crossed off on her self-made bingo sheets are what will need to go into Blair Blake-Stendahl's next speech. Blair gives Aphra the liberty to write any speech as she sees fit, as long as the keywords are in there and Blair gets the final edit. So, she can listen with one ear – Blair has been speaking uninterrupted for well over half an hour, pausing only to sip mineral water – mark down the essentials and enjoy the view. She also does this safe in the knowledge that any Perth politician's speech, including one by Premier wannabe BBS, will inevitably be about one of the three R's: roads, reassurance or real estate. Best is getting all three. Reassurance is Blair's favourite.

When pursuing her literature degree at Murdoch ten years ago, Aphra never imagined she would end up here, in a political party's "situation room". Of course, she'd much rather be sitting in a café in Northbridge, writing poetry or even a novel, but there's no money in that. While her creative acumen has little in common with her hard-working, hands-dirty, deeply-tanned parents, she did inherit their enjoyment of money. There's plenty to be made in mining for people with strong work ethics, and plenty in politics for creatives with relatively loose ethics. Aphra's freelance speechwriting, combined with a lucrative side hustle of ad copywriting, results in her banking a lawyer-level income each month, something many prize-winning writers could only dream of. It financed an extravagant lifestyle, replete with a condo in North Cottesloe that she was diligently paying off, a wardrobe full of clothes handmade by a friend who had a boutique in Subiaco, and annual European escapades enjoying business class flights and top-shelf hotels. The only thing holding her back from launching towards a big career in political writing is that she's not fully local. It's also why she's on the freelance payroll, and truth be told, why Blair Blake-Stendahl treats Aphra rather badly, despite her extraordinary ability to turn clichéd straw into PR gold. Aphra's not old Perth, something that's an unwritten prerequisite for working in local politics. Here, the farther a family tree goes back, the more credibility that person has, especially in a party that wants WA to be its own country. Sure, Aphra grew up here and considers herself West Australian, but she was born in Launceston; some of the people she worked with had the nasty habit of referring to her, behind her back, as their backwards Tasmanian cousin, like she was an in-bred yokel. Aphra knew this, and mostly let it go. Yet she also harboured a little bit of anger, because her parents had moved over to WA when she was a toddler, to chase the kind of mining boom dollars that buy riverside five-bedroom and four-bathroom homes in Applecross, and she had zero recollection of or connection to Tasmania.

Aphra loves Perth. This is her hometown. She's travelled enough to know that in no other city in the world could she have the life she has here. Only in Perth can she start every day walking her dog on a stunning stretch of powder-sand beach, from the Swanbourne Surf Lifesaving Club to the point far enough north where she can legally swim nude. Then walk back and grab a coffee from the Shorehouse before strolling along the headland to North Cott. It's 25 degrees and not yet 8am, the air gloriously fresh. The sky at that time of the morning is a blue so pale and pristine it seems fake. Post-shower, she's into a tailor-made dress, then scooting on her electric Vespa between the lines of traffic, en route downtown to spend the day in air-conditioned comfort essentially doing creative writing exercises for stupid amounts of cash. When that's done, often in the early afternoon, because as a freelancer she's not beholden to any specific work hours, it's back to North Cott, with time enough to hit the gym before meeting friends for some seafood and a few icy chasers at a place on Marine Parade. On evenings when the wind drops early enough, she likes to swim at Cottesloe Beach at sunset, within the safety of the industrial-strength shark net. With Perth being that unique place where the desert meets the ocean, there's a high chance the sun will be out again tomorrow, and she can dreamily execute the exact same routine, all with a solid appreciation that this is paradise.

Blair, droning on, uses the word "localisation" for at least the fourth time. Aphra writes it down, as it wasn't on any of her bingo sheets; a new addition to BBS's vernacular, perhaps attained, Aphra thinks, through a late-night search for an antonym of "globalisation". She wonders if Perth people will understand it, and decides "local" is more palatable and relatable. Localisation sounds far too corporate, the kind of word that alienates common people. She makes more notes, to ensure Blair gets the right message across: "Perth jobs for Perth people," and "Keep hard-earned wages for local spending," and "Think local, win global." Because, as Aphra knows, even if WA becomes its own country, with an emphasis on localisation, it will still need the rest of the world. Carnarvon bananas have to go somewhere for profit, along with all the goodies extracted from the massive holes up north.

The knock on the door stops Blair, momentarily, causing Aphra to look up.

"I clearly stated we're not to be disturbed," Blair says.

The door opens anyway.

"Who are you?"

"I'm Detective Everest. This is Detective Booth."

"This better be very good," Blair says, using this interruption to check her phone. "You have no idea the schedule I'm on today."

Everest's ponytail swishes a little as she looks around the room. "We're after Aphra Massey. We tried calling her, but there was no answer."

"All phones get checked at the door before anyone enters my situation room." Blair taps and swipes at her phone. "We focus in here. No distractions."

"We mean no disrespect," Booth says, and with that simple sentence, delivered with a certain cagey reverence, he discloses, unknowingly, to this room full of very clever and attentive people, who have built their careers on being exceptionally good at reading between the lines, his agreement with their mandate.

"Someone get his email address," Blair says, eyes on her phone's screen. "Add him to our newsletter list."

"We're here for Ms Massey. She hasn't done anything wrong. Just some questions. Purely routine."

Blair Blake-Stendahl, attractive in her late 40s and always looking her best when in public, lowers her large purple-framed spectacles to look in Booth's direction. "A, take care of these two, if you please. Outside. And make it quick. I'm in top form today. Smacking aces with every serve. Straight down the line."

Aphra crosses "smacking aces" from the third bingo sheet and stands up. She goes to the door, taking her sheets with her.

"Follow me, please," she says to Everest. "And close the door."

Aphra strides down the hallway in a billowing black dress punctuated with large yellow flowers. Booth is close behind, so close he almost steps on the heels of her sandals, made from upcycled car tyres. They end up in the kitchen, where Aphra sets up the elaborate coffee machine, cranking levers and flicking switches like she's readying a helicopter for take-off.

"What do you want?" she asks.

"No coffee for me, thanks," Booth says. "I'm caffeine-free this week."

"That's for me. Why are you here? The police only visit when they're looking for, you know, our support. But they never ask for me."

"Don't worry," Booth says. "You're not in any trouble."

"I didn't think I was. So, can you put your gun away then? You're showing that sidearm like you want the whole world to see it."

Booth pulls his shirt over his sidearm. The espresso machine gets going, with the kind of noisy flourishes that bespeak expense.

"Ms Massey," Everest says, "we appreciate your time. Do you know Ekaterina Valoskiya?"

"Katie? Sure."

"How well do you know her?"

"We've been friends for years. Why?"

"So, you didn't meet her here, in Perth?"

"We met in Kyiv. Look, what's this all about? Is Katie okay?"

Booth clears his throat. "What is the, uh, the nature of your relationship?"

"Are you asking me if we're fucking?"

"Of course not. I mean, yeah, no, maybe."

"You're listed as her next of kin, according to her PSO file," Everest says.

"She lost her family in the war," Aphra says. "I'm the only person she knows here, apart from the people in the orchestra, but they've been ignoring her. Not quite accepting of foreigners, even talented ones."

The sound of the steady trickle of coffee from the machine stops. Aphra waits for the last remaining drops to fall before reaching for the espresso, blowing on it and taking a sip.

"I'm sorry to hear that," Everest says.

"She messed with the localisation of the orchestra." Aphra smiles to herself as she has another sip. "What's going on? Is Katie alright?"

Everest looks at Booth, but he shakes his head slightly, not wanting to be the one to say it, or thinking it's not his responsibility.

"There's no easy way to tell you this," Everest says. "She's dead. I'm sorry."

Aphra puts the espresso cup on the counter. She stares at Everest.

"Ms Massey?" Everest lays a hand on Aphra's forearm.

"Dead?"

"I'm so sorry."

"What happened?" Aphra shrugs off Everest's hand. "I don't know what you've been told, but I sure as hell had nothing to do with it. She was my friend." Then, to Booth, "My no-sex friend."

"She had plenty of sex, that's for sure," Booth says under his breath.

"We never said she was murdered." Everest crosses her arms. "What makes you think she was?"

"It must be something criminal, otherwise they would've sent uniforms. Detectives mean a serious crime has been committed."

"True," Booth says, smiling with admiration.

"You're not here to notify me. You're here to question me. You're not even giving me any chance to process this."

Everest takes out her notebook. "We're just doing our jobs. When did you last see Ms Valoskiya?"

"Saturday night. The PSO sent an all-female quartet to provide background music for a reception at Parliament House. A visiting trade delegation from Indonesia, all of them men. Katie was asked to be in the quartet, as one of the few women in the orchestra."

"Any contact since then?"

"We messaged each other, as friends do. She's only been here a few weeks. Still finding her feet."

"Is this her first time in Perth?"

"Shouldn't you know that already? Look, how did she die? Do you know who did it? No, you don't know. You don't look like you know anything."

"It's an ongoing investigation," Booth says.

"That's an admission you know very little at all. Did it happen today? God, I can't believe she's dead. After everything she went through."

"What did she go through?" Everest asks.

"Seriously? Apart from losing her whole family in the war?"

"How did she end up here?" Booth asks.

"That's ... my fault. She grew up really poor in Ukraine, where every family wants their daughter, no, needs their daughter to become an Olympic gymnast or a music prodigy. Like it's the only way out of poverty. Then, her apartment building got bombed when she was on tour in Romania, with no survivors. Just awful. All of it. Perth was supposed to be a new start for her."

Everest is thoughtful for a moment, studying the flowers on Aphra's dress. "You helped her with that. Right? The new start? You got her a place in the PSO in order to get her out of Ukraine."

Aphra nods.

"You would need to know the right people to pull off something like that."

"Favours and connections are the foundations on which this city was built, as I'm sure you know," Aphra says. "Yeah, I know

Leiland Taverton. And I know he didn't think Katie was good enough for his precious band. But I also know some things about Leiland that he'd really like to keep quiet. So, he was more than happy to welcome her on board. Now, she's dead, and it's all on me."

"It's not your fault," Booth says, moving to pat Aphra on the shoulder. She sees him coming and takes a step backwards. It's awkward for Booth, who runs his dangling hand back through his hair.

"If you don't mind," Aphra says, "I'm going to blame myself for as long as I want. Unless you give me a name, so I can get a very Ukrainian-style revenge."

"There's no need for that." Booth is sounding very much like someone trying to lead a support group. "Let's just take a moment to breathe and reassess."

"Don't patronise me. Don't tell me to breathe like I'm some woman with frazzled nerves. Do you want to sit me down and offer me some brandy?"

"No, no."

"I'm angry. My friend is dead. Murdered. I'm allowed to be really fucking angry."

"You're right," Everest says. "But maybe you can help us. Fill in some blanks. Get us looking in the right direction."

"That's more like it. You're the senior detective here, right?"

"I am. So?"

"So, you should give your junior partner a maximum of a dozen spoken words each day. Every time he opens his mouth, he says something idiotic."

"Now, hang on a minute," Booth says.

"Be quiet." Aphra points at Everest. "You can ask me something. Go. If at any point I can't continue, this stops."

"Understood. Was she seeing anyone?"

"Lots of people."

"Can you give us their names?" Booth asks.

"I recall you're not allowed to talk. I don't know any names. She's a very pretty girl away from home and starting out a new life. She made it clear she wanted to experience all the joy that kind of freedom brings. Sure. Maybe she was using casual sex to fill a few emotional holes, after losing everyone close to her. Who could blame her for that?"

Everest holds up a hand to stop Booth from talking. "Did you help? Take her out and introduce her to people? That is, people in your circle of friends."

"She didn't need my help. She could walk into any bar on her own and some guy would go up to her and offer to buy her a drink. But she was very selective and smart. I also told her to never take a drink that a guy tried to hand to her. She didn't go home with just anyone."

Everest makes some notes.

"I think she was still figuring out who she is," Aphra continues. "What kind of guy she likes, and what she wants. You need to keep in mind this is a woman who spent over half her waking life playing the violin. Maybe more than that. Since she could walk. Then she lost everything. I convince her to come to Perth, and she lands here and is completely overwhelmed. You need to remember this city feels for foreigners like it's a million miles from anywhere. We might as well be on the moon. Anyway, she decided to embrace that and try out different versions of herself."

"What version did she settle on?"

"Excuse me?"

"How did she reinvent herself?"

"Into a corpse, according to you two." Aphra rinses the espresso cup. "Now, are you going to tell me who did it? Or do I have to find out for myself?"

"You think you can do that?" Booth asks.

"It's just a matter of following the trail of conflict breadcrumbs. Find the person with the most motivation."

Booth laughs a little. "That's not how it works. But out of interest, how did you two meet? In Keef?"

"Kyiv."

"Right. What were you doing there?"

"You really should do your research before questioning people. I was on a book tour. I published a collection of poetry when I was at university, and it did reasonably well. It was a revenge story, gruesome, when horror was all the rage, and very satisfying to write. It turned out Russians and Ukrainians and other eastern Europeans like that sort of thing, so it was translated and I went over to do some readings. I met Katie at an embassy event, because she was playing at it."

"What happened to the book?" Booth asks. "How did you end up working here?"

"End up here? What? Like I failed?"

"That's not what I ..."

"How much money do you think poets make? Or any writer for that matter?"

Everest steps in front of Booth, to stop him from talking, and hands Aphra a business card in the process. "If you have any information to share, please contact me."

"Of course. I expect you to do the same."

Everest gestures for Booth to leave the kitchen. She follows him, then stops.

"Do you happen to know Quintus Huntley?" she asks.

"Why? What has that got to do with anything?"

"I'm just curious. Not many poets in Perth."

"Not personally, no. I think we've been at some events together. His ex-wife, Giorgina Gifford, is a big supporter of Blair. Has been ever since she won the seat for Nedlands."

"Is that right?"

"How is he connected to Katie? She never mentioned him, and he's too old for her anyway."

"We found his book at the crime scene," Booth blurts out from the doorway. "In her violin case."

"Come on, Justin," Everest says. "That's enough."

Aphra smiles. "Next time, Justin, please come on your own. I'd love to see what you would say without your minder."

"She's not my minder," Booth says.

"The book isn't a big deal."

"Why not?" Everest asks.

"It was probably there to keep the violin secure. Katie always had a book in the case, to stop the violin from moving around and getting damaged. The book had to be just the right size. I guess Huntley's was."

"Good to know," Everest says. "So his connection is possibly just random."

"Maybe. But know this. The book is awesome. The kind of heady stuff that feels lived, that you could never make up."

"Thank you, Ms Massey. Again, I'm really sorry we had to bring you this news."

"What happens now?"

"We'll be in touch when the body is released. So you can make the necessary arrangements."

"What do you mean? What arrangements?"

Everest smiles sympathetically. "The responsibility of being next of kin."

The detectives leave. With them gone, and with no one in the kitchen, Aphra can finally let go. She pulls the door closed behind them, turns to the machine and fires it up for another espresso so the extravagant gurgling can drown out her crying.

<>

Ten minutes before his scheduled office hours end, Huntley decides he's had enough. After the detectives left, he sat around for another hour, drinking hot toddies without the necessary sweetness and flavour, until all the rum was gone. He was visited briefly by two students: a wild-haired woman in her 60s who spoke with a Spanish accent, was looking for Miguel, openly criticised Huntley's day drinking, and who Huntley, in his drunk state, thought could well have been a well-disguised Colombian assassin; and by a boy barely out of high school whose voice was still breaking, who was lost and trying to find the Student Guild. In between, as he shuffled between the sofa and the kitchenette, he could only think of the girl with the green ink on her neck. He worked through the hot toddies, trying to remove the dead girl and all of her story from his head. When she wouldn't leave, he tried writing it down as poetry, but it sucked and pieces of scrunched-up paper were lobbed with honed precision into the waste bin.

What he needs, he decides, is the ending. So, he stumbles out into the daylight, with the mission of finding it.

With the ending, his addled mind concludes, the poem might improve. It would give him the scope to work backwards, create a stronger character arc and figure out the central conflict. And a girl's dead; someone has to do something about it. Plus, the best way to stop being considered a suspect is to find the culprit.

"Conflict's the heart of any story," he mutters to himself, trying to get the key into the lock of the container door.

He finally gets the key in line, but it doesn't fit. Wrong key.

"Too many bloody keys."

He picks out the right one. Getting it into the lock and securing the door seems like a monumental achievement. But it presents him with the next obstacle: remembering where he parked the Landy.

Identify the conflict, he thinks, then put challenges in the way to prevent its resolution, because without the conflict or its resolution, nothing will happen, nothing will change and nothing will be learned, and it will just be a bunch of people moving around.

"Dull."

Or, as is the case with so much local writing, it's a bunch of miserable people moving around who have bad things happen to them, for no real reason.

"This girl had something bad happen to her, and there must be a reason."

As he staggers between the containers, which now seem assembled in a labyrinth designed to entrap him, it dawns on him that it's not the ending he should be searching for: it's the conflict. The versus. The who against who. Because the ending's already there. Ekaterina is dead. The end. But the conflict that resulted in her murder, that's what he needs to find. That's the story. But then he thinks the ending may in fact be the beginning, and the story is about the killer and the associated conflicts. And then, none of these stories could be interesting enough to write about. The swirling doubts turn his stomach over, almost to the point of making him sick.

"You freaking beast."

Aware of his own slurring voice echoing off the containers, he stuffs his keys into his pants pockets and gives up trying to find his car.

"Too risky."

Out of the shadows of the containers, finally, the sunlight stings his eyes. He has to use his hand as a shield, like a celebrity warding off the flashes of paparazzi cameras, until he locates his sunglasses and gets them on.

Students stare at him.

It's cooler now, the sea breeze brisk and vaguely sobering. It will take far more than that to blow away his rum-tea fog, but at least it's drying the sweat on his forehead and neck.

"Green neck," he says, making a few students turn to him and give him judging glances. They talk behind their hands like children, but have the scathing eyes of adults. So they should, he thinks: be critical, question the behaviour of others, search for conflict, because everyone is open to interpretation, and those grey areas between what you know, what you think you know and what you know that's actually wrong are fascinating places to explore.

He wants to tell the students this, encourage them to embrace the grey, to dig deep into it, but he has just enough facility to keep his mouth shut. He would look like a weirdo if he used this bus stop he now finds himself at as a small stage from which to deliver a soliloquy of storytelling wisdom. To wax lyrical about conflict. To let loose a tirade about the bowel-twisting agony of doubt.

He manages to sit down and keep it all to himself. Because he's not that drunk. Close, but not quite. Not that kind of filterless, no consequence, fearless, losing yourself completely in the moment kind of drunk. He's at the precipice of that, but is maintaining just enough balance to keep from falling over it.

He leans back against the glass wall and lets the cool breeze pass over him.

Next thing he knows, he's on the air-conditioned bus, barrelling southbound on Stirling Highway, towards Freo. He's achieved this, somehow, and it feels like another obstacle overcome, with a high degree of difficulty. It's enough to lift his spirits and make him more aware of his surroundings.

They go through Nedlands, past the library where his book was launched, all those years ago; where there were so many people, with Giorgie and Lydette having pulled in all the favours they could, the party spilling out onto the lawns at the front and back. That night when he felt like he'd conquered Perth; the humble country boy who had shown all these snobs and elitists what real poetry was. Now, it was so long ago, it seemed like stuff that had happened to someone else.

Further along, school's out in Claremont, and a ridiculous number of kids are vaping as they slouch across the road in a fog of their own making. He changes to the other side of the bus to look at the girls in their Methodist Ladies' College uniforms, flowing out towards Stirling, hoping to spot Verity among them. But the school-issued dresses, knee socks, bags and hats make them all look the same, and the rum isn't helping his ability to focus. He can't pick her out, and doesn't want to, because they all look like clones, mass-produced by the school. And his daughter is no clone. Still, he wants to get off, to find Verity and tell her he loves her and misses her, and that he's sorry things didn't work out as they'd hoped. But he's slumped in the seat, the bell out of reach. The bus speeds on, only stopping when required, which is just about never, because there's only a handful of people on the bus and practically no one is waiting at any of the stops along Stirling Highway.

They go up and over the long hill of Claremont and start careening down the other side towards Cottesloe, where there's another library that holds a distant memory of status and fame belonging to someone else. The bus gets caught at a red light at Leake Street, making the driver bang the steering wheel with his hand, as if he was on track to break some kind of Perth to Freo record, until this hold up.

Huntley looks at the Grove Library, trying not to recall the readings and events held for him there. He sees two police cars followed by a white van come down Leake Street and turn onto Stirling Highway. He stares at the white van.

"Green neck?"

The bus starts moving forward again, with the flow of traffic. Huntley pulls himself forward unsteadily and hits the bell with a fist. The bus lurches to a halt at the next stop. Huntley exits at the back, almost falling.

Outside, the wind is really blowing now, swirling dirt and debris up into the air. It's cool against his back as he crosses Stirling, weaving between the slow-moving cars and enjoying the chorus of horns, and heads up Leake.

He regrets not having asked Everest for the address. But he doesn't need it, because a few hundred metres up Leake is a police van parked outside a small apartment block. A guy who must be cooking in the white jumpsuit he's wearing goes down a flight of steps and puts a plastic box in the back of the van.

Forensics, Huntley concludes. He continues walking purposefully up the street, so as not to arouse suspicion. At View Street, he fights the temptation to keep the wind at his back and pass the Gifford estate, once his home. No, not true, he thinks. It was never home. Not even during their happiest days. He was always temporary. A lodger.

He circles the block at Forrest Street, then gets on narrow Hurtsford Close, where he can come at the apartment block from the rear.

Once there, scoping the scene from behind a tree, he marvels at how sobering activity can be. As if purpose dilutes the alcohol in his system.

"Got to stop drinking at work," he says to himself.

The van is gone.

An old man is slowly wheeling in a bin from the street towards the apartment building. The codger's small shuffles fill Huntley with empathy, and he'd like to help, but can't risk exposure.

"Sorry, mate."

The bin gets parked with the row of others, scaring a ginger cat out from behind one. Then the codger starts heading up the stairs, slowly, one at a time, left hand pulling hard at the railing.

Huntley thinks: getting old looks like the hardest thing to do in life.

Which is essentially paraphrasing his father, who aged gracefully, until the end, when his last few months became one long complaint about the trials and tribulations of ageing. One thing he didn't do was complain about dying, even though that was what he was doing, right before Huntley's eyes, fading away into a mist of his own derision. Because, as Huntley senior had said, dying was something everyone did, at some point, so there was nothing to complain about. But growing old, becoming an invalid, and especially getting very old, was far more exclusive and difficult. Huntley's father passed away a few weeks before he would've turned 100. To be fair, Huntley senior had lived his entire life in good spirits, and it was only at the end, when each day something inside of him stopped working properly, that he became cantankerous. He remained all there in the head, right up to the end, which gave him the facility and vocabulary to graphically detail how horrible it all was.

The old codger has made it to the turnaround point of the stairs, and there he stands, a hand on the wall, breathing. Huntley half expects him to keel over right there, but the stoic old-timer gets moving and tackles the remaining stairs. Huntley's empathy turns into admiration.

Still behind the tree, Huntley now has a strong urge to use the bathroom; the purpose and activity of the last 15 minutes really supporting a body-wide detox that has sent all the rum to his bladder for expulsion. It's tempting to go where he's standing, against the tree, and he's certain he'd be finished before the codger reaches the first-floor landing. But this is the suburbs, affluent at that, and some busybody will surely see him through a window and make a scene.

So, he holds it, distracting himself by thinking of his father, who he misses dearly.

Huntley's unconventional childhood growing up on a hippy commune near Ravensthorpe was compounded by an equally unconventional familial situation. His father was 67 when he impregnated a visiting Swiss girl, 45 years younger, who, young Quintus would soon learn, took the neutrality favoured by her homeland to its absolute extreme, having no strong feelings for or attachment to anything, including her offspring. She floated in and out of the commune over the years, going only by the moniker of Soleil, French for sunlight, sometimes staying for a while but never attempting anything remotely like motherly affection. Which was weird, because a handful of times she rocked up very pregnant, had the baby and left, each time barely saying a word, as if speaking would violate her neutrality. These small living gifts that she left behind and was entirely distant towards formed a tight family unit of their own, led by Quintus's father, even though he had no obligation. Huntley senior couldn't turn these amazingly beautiful and abandoned children away, and he also held no grudge towards Soleil, who had chosen her own path. If anything, he was grateful to her for enabling him to have this special family so late in his life. All the children would eventually move away from the commune, starting with Quintus, to pursue their respective lives, though Jonty, the youngest, returned to live there. They all remained very close, in the ways makeshift families often do more so than standard nuclear ones. When Huntley senior died, they were all there at the end, crowded into the caravan and holding each other's hands as the old patriarch became increasingly rabid about how awful getting old is, and the caravan shook with laughter, because he was always very funny when mad.

Huntley wonders what happened to Soleil; it had been nearly a decade since she last surfaced at the commune.

He also wonders, not for the first time, how many other children she may have left at selected places around Australia and the world, on top of the five left in Ravensthorpe.

An idea forms: *The Neutrality of Sunlight*, a collection of narrative poems about all those children, with the overarching theme of Soleil always darkening the family door.

No, he thinks. Don't go there.

The old codger has made it to the landing. He walks towards apartment 9.

Huntley moves out from behind the tree, with economical steps so as not to disturb his bladder. He sneaks up the stairs, pausing just before the turnaround to hear the door to apartment 9 close.

Finding the Ukrainian girl's apartment, number 10, turns out to be easy, as there's a police seal just above the door's keyhole. He really wants to get into the apartment, but breaking that seal is out of the question, and pissing in the toilet could potentially leave strands of unwanted DNA at the crime scene. He needs to find another way in, and, urgently, another bathroom.

He goes to number 9 and knocks on the door. It takes a while, but the locks click and the door is opened. The old codger squints at him through a pair of surprisingly stylish spectacles. Huntley thinks he seems younger up close.

"Can I help you?"

"Yeah, hi, mate," Huntley says, as friendly and sober as he can muster. "Sorry to bother you. Have you, ah, seen a ginger cat around here?"

The old man moves his head slightly sideways and narrows his eyes. "There was one nosing around the bins. I scared it away."

"That sounds like her. Always a nose for trouble."

"The cat taking after her owner, perhaps?"

"Hah, yeah, no. Maybe a bit."

"I didn't see a collar on her. You should get one. So people can contact you. Or better, get one of those pet trackers, with GPS."

"Right. Good idea. I'll do that."

"She's probably back at the bins. Cats are territorial like that."

"They are indeed." Huntley is almost at the point of crossing his legs. "Look, sorry, mate, I hate to be a bother, but I've been out all afternoon, looking for her. I really need a leak. Middle-aged prostate and all that."

The old man lowers his pants a little to show he's wearing a man nappy. "Be warned. The worst is yet to come."

"Not much fun, is it? Getting old."

"There's plenty that's good about it, if you put the bodily stuff aside. The gaining of a bit more knowledge and wisdom is well worth wearing a secure undergarment when needed."

"That's a good way of looking at it."

"I'm glad to still be kicking on. I've finally had the time, in my old age, to write the book I've always wanted to write."

"Book?"

"Family history. One of my ancestors was convict number 26 on the first boat that landed here."

"How about that?"

"The story starts with him, but you can tell just about the entire history of WA using my family."

"Must be a big book."

"Let's hope I live long enough to finish it." The old man steps out of the doorway. "Come in and I'll tell you about it. The lav's just here on the right. Sit down, please. I don't like my bathroom reeking of urine."

"Smart."

"Or rum. There's mouthwash in case you want to freshen yourself up a bit."

"Thanks."

Huntley enters the apartment expecting it to be messy and sad, in typical lonely old-man fashion. But it's well-kept, modern and clean. There are lots of photos, in standing frames and hanging on the walls, of families and children, a collaged testimony to all those originating from the spawn of convict number 26. The sparse interior, like something out of a Swedish holiday cabin, helps Huntley picture the old man's story: a long marriage that recently ended with his wife's death, resulting in a downsizing from the large house they raised their children in, with all the possessions sold off or distributed to family members, because the old man couldn't bear to live with all the memories tied to them. This apartment is a fresh start, and a home office for writing his book. Or he's got it all wrong and the family callously sold off everything for profit and dumped the old man here, as a waypoint before shelving him for good in a seniors' home. Or there was no marriage, and he's lived here the whole time. All the photos are fakes. Or.

Huntley goes into the bathroom and closes the door. "Damn."

He sits and pees, trying his hardest to stop all the alternate stories from unfolding before him. There are so many possibilities. Every story seems like it has potential, until another follows, causing him to question the one before. And then another comes along that makes him doubt the efficacy of its predecessor. And on and on.

He flushes, then washes his hands with purple soap shaped like a duck and rinses his mouth with mouthwash that looks and tastes like pool water.

"Green neck," he says to his reflection. "Focus on her."

In the living room, he finds the old fella asleep at his desk, chin on his chest, stylish spectacles slowly sliding down his nose. Huntley catches them and puts them on the desk, which is a piece of glass resting on two black wooden horses. On it is a fancy laptop, very large and not exactly portable, a Word document open, cursor flashing. The old man has two smartphones, lined up side by side. Huntley's tempted to read what's on the laptop's screen, as convict number 26 surely had a hell of a tale to tell, but he doesn't want to plant yet another story seed in his own head. He moves to the balcony and gently slides the screen door open, careful not to rouse the old man.

He's lucky. Apartments 9 and 10 share the same balcony, divided by a wall made from strung-together bamboo sticks. They're easy enough to move aside and push through, but, on the other side, the locked balcony door presents an actual problem.

"Oh, come on."

The limited options open to Huntley are all bad, consisting mainly of throwing something heavy at the glass, which looks pretty thick, and making the kind of noise that attracts busybodies and that will very likely wake the old man. He presses his nose to the glass and cups his hands around his temples. It's hard to see anything between the almost closed vertical blinds.

He needs to get inside. He can't walk away from this, because not knowing what happened to the girl, after all his suppositions, will gnaw at his brain and keep him awake at night, not to mention the matter of his own accused involvement.

The folded metal chair seems the most viable option. He picks it by the legs. It's surprisingly heavy, but that's good, because it should have the weight needed to shatter the glass. He looks around to see if anyone is watching. The trees that shade the balcony help obscure the view of it, but he's certain there are bored Peppermint Grovers out there just waiting to stick their upturned noses into the business of others.

He raises the chair and is about to swing it when the old man appears in the gap between the bamboo partition.

"All right, mate?"

Huntley lowers the chair. "It's not what you think."

"It never is."

"I'm investigating. The girl's death."

"You don't look like an investigator."

"I'm private." Huntley puts the chair against the balcony wall. "Freelance, so to speak."

"You're certainly not looking for a ginger cat. And you still smell far more like a pirate than a cop."

Huntley laughs.

"You need to explain this, mate," the old man continues. "It's been a really rough day so far. I'm not in the mood for this."

"You know about ..." Huntley thumbs towards the balcony door. "The girl and all?"

The old man nods.

"Just awful. I'm trying to find out who did it."

"Did you know her?"

"Ah, sort of. We're ... connected. Look, this is going to sound weird, but I'll level with you. I'm a poet."

"You better come back to this side. So you can fully explain what you're up to."

Huntley complies, but not before having another look through the gaps in the blinds. From what he can see, the apartment looks bland, though the open violin case catches his eye. The case that had his book in it, for whatever reason. He wants to hold the case in his hands and let it speak to him.

It seems harder to get through the gap in the bamboo. Some of the pieces break. What remains is a large hole that looks like someone charged through to make.

He wonders how a violin might be used metaphorically. Control? Manipulation? Pulling the strings? Playing someone like a violin?

"Too obvious."

"What is?"

Huntley, inside apartment 9 now, says, "Oh, that pathetic cat story. Sorry about that. Need to work on my cover."

"Listen, you need to stop lying. If you tell me what you're doing here, without any more lies, then I'll decide what to do with you." The old man lowers himself into his desk chair. "I was a high school English teacher for 31 years. I've seen every kind of lying known to the human race. So don't think you can get anything by me."

"I hear you. If lying was a sport, my daughter could go to the Olympics."

"Sit down. Let's have your honesty."

Huntley sits on the very modern charcoal sofa. "I am actually a poet. That much is true."

"I know."

Huntley is taken slightly aback. "And I am trying to find out who did it."

"Why?"

"Because ... you see ... I didn't do it. Really. Full honesty. It wasn't me."

The old man takes off his glasses and gives them a polish. "Sounds like someone thinks it was. And now you're here to clear your name."

"I thought that if I could get into the apartment, I might figure out the story. Get the poetry of it. You know, what happened and how and why. You do know what actually happened, right?"

"The police were here already. They returned my keys."

"Your keys?"

"I own the whole apartment block. Don't look so surprised. The land's been in my family for generations. Not from convict number 26. He died penniless, from scurvy, of all things. But other forebears did well. A few years ago, I decided to tear down the old house and build these apartments. I thought that was better than another monstrous mansion."

"The Grove's got enough of them already."

"It helped me move on too. To start again, without completely forgetting. It was my wife's idea. Her last request. Get rid of the house and build something practical that will benefit more people."

"Smart woman. Must've been hard though, letting all that go."

"It's only stuff. People put far too much stock in things and possessions. Letting go of Christa has been much harder. Still is."

"I'm sorry for your loss."

"Thank you. Another downside of getting old. It can pile on the losses. I feel like I'm in a perpetual cycle of taking my best suit to the dry cleaners and picking it up in time to wear it again."

"Rough."

"With wisdom and knowledge comes man nappies and grief." The old man smiles sadly. "You're Quintus Huntley, aren't you?"

"Ah, yeah. I am. Have we met?"

"Let me see if I remember. 'May I grind his bones into a fine powder, and snort it, to get high on him all over again.' I always liked that. Primal and disgusting and committed. Everything that love is. Messy too."

Huntley doesn't know how to reply to this. It's been years since anyone quoted his poetry to him, without prompting.

"A lot of it is juvenile and toxically masculine, and leaning too heavily on the appeal of despicable anti-heroes, but some parts are very good. Especially the parts where you stop trying to show how smart you are. You just let it flow."

"Hey, thanks. You're right. The best of it was the stuff that wasn't forced. But how do you even know about it?"

"I retired early from teaching and went back into the family business. Not long after that, an extremely pushy woman came into my bookstore and rammed your book down my throat."

"Lydette."

"Your agent?"

"Was, during the good times. She bailed on me years ago. Now she's my ex-sister-in-law."

"I was a decent-looking fella, back then, if I do say so myself, but she made all these ridiculous, almost vaudevillian sexual overtures that made me feel sorry for her. As if she'd gladly give herself to me in exchange for shelf space for your book."

"Definitely Lydette." Huntley tries to push away all the bad memories and remain in the moment. "I'm sure she was there with good intentions, despite being a nasty flirt."

"She didn't need to do any extra selling. I liked the book well enough and stocked it."

"What bookshop was that?"

"Henrikson's. In Freo. Don't use the past tense. It's still there. Not every bookshop has disappeared. I still work there, a couple of mornings a week. To keep an eye on things."

"Holy shit. You're Henrikson?"

"Son of. I took over the store when my father died."

"I love that store. How's business? Please tell me it's good. I'm always worried the whole world will stop reading."

"Flourishing. Plenty of readers out there. Reading a book remains the number one thing to do at the beach. Plus, books are still the go-to present for birthdays and Christmas, when people can't think of anything else."

"That's good to hear. In my family, we still give each other books at Christmas."

"The same with mine. Now we've established who we both are, you can tell me how you're tied up in all this. You're too old to be Ekaterina's boyfriend, and not quite in her league anyway, and I seriously doubt you're family."

"I don't know her. That's the truth. A pair of detectives visited me at my uni office this morning. Said they found my book in her apartment. In her violin case."

"Strange. Why your book?"

"That's what I've been asking myself. The detectives thought there was something in it. Especially the guy, Booth. He's convinced I did it."

"Watch out what you say to him. Powerful family. Trust me on that."

"Noted. Weird they took my book, but left the case where it is."

"Maybe they didn't think it was important."

"Yeah. Maybe."

Henrikson gives Huntley a long look, then says, "I believe you."

"You do? Thanks."

"But I don't believe you're here to prove your own innocence. The police can do that."

"What then?"

"You're actually not interested in her, are you? You want the story for yourself. Your first book was a true crime retelling, which happened, if I remember rightly, when you were there and writing it. That's why it felt so visceral and present. Are you trying to replicate that process?"

"No. Maybe. I don't know." Huntley leans back in the sofa, making himself comfortable. "It's just all so shocking."

"It is."

"The nature of her death, this fountain pen stabbing in the neck, I can't think about anything else. I need to know what happened."

"Because it will make a good story?"

"Yeah. Fine. You got me, Henrikson. I want the story. I can't lie about that, and I'm not ashamed to say it, as selfish as it sounds."

"Understandable. You never did write a second book."

"The feeling, it's there. Like it was the first time. God, that was incredible. I just think that if I can get more information, I can flip the switch and it will all pour out."

"Such as who did it and why."

"Of course. But also who the girl was. It's her story that matters. I've got this sense the who and why will be easy to get if I solve the puzzle that is the PSO's third violinist."

"Important," Henrikson says, "is the how. The pen. A fountain pen, no less. Why not a knife? Or even a gun?"

"Right. Why use something so unconventional? What point is the killer trying to make?"

"It would be interesting to see the toxicology report."

"Poison? I hadn't even thought of that."

"A fountain pen is kind of like a crude syringe."

"You're right. Booth showed me a gruesome photo. Her neck was all green. The detectives said it was ink from the pen."

"The report will have it." Henrikson turns to his laptop. "I want to know who did this just as much as you do. I'll see if I can get it."

"Do you know someone in the police?"

"I'll hack into the system."

Huntley laughs. "No. Come on. How?"

"Don't let appearances and secure undergarments fool you. Technology has always fascinated me. I've become a bit of a computer nerd in my old age. You should always try to gain something for everything you lose. That's a very important part of ageing."

"You're full of surprises, mate. You must be the oldest hacker on the planet."

"I'll take that as a compliment. But here's another surprise." From a drawer, Henrikson pulls out a set of keys and throws it to Huntley, who catches it. "The smallest one opens the balcony door. Keep your hands in your pockets, so you don't touch anything. But you probably already know about stuff like that."

"Uh, thanks?"

"You really didn't think I'd call the cops, did you?"

"I hadn't thought that far ahead, to be honest."

"Whatever happens from here on out, keep doing that with me. Being honest."

Huntley, still finding it hard to believe he's just been given the keys to the apartment, stands up.

"Don't take anything," Henrikson says. "Just in case they come back. They probably itemised everything in there."

Huntley nods, then goes out onto the balcony. Once he's through the bamboo partition's ever-larger hole, he lingers at the balcony door, keys in hand, wondering if it's all some kind of elaborate trap. Why is this former teacher and current bookstore owner, landlord and computer hacker bothering to help him?

He uses his shirt sleeve to slide the door open and edges inside. It smells a bit rank, so he leaves the door fully open. The breeze gently rattles the blinds.

The layout is identical to Henrikson's place. There's a large combined living room and kitchen, a bathroom near the front door, and a bedroom leading off from the small dining area. But while Henrikson's place has a sleek Scandinavian style, the Ukrainian's apartment feels like a sad hotel room. Bland furniture, inoffensive colours, no private touches, and no lived-in atmosphere. Huntley doesn't get the sense he's invading anyone's personal space. He thinks it feels transient, as a place that has already housed many different renters. It could be that Henrikson rents this one as a holiday flat, or as a short-term let for people recently arrived and looking to settle.

The only standout thing is the violin in its case, placed on a coffee table near a music stand void of sheet music. Close by, the stain on the carpet shows where the murder happened. Huntley stands near the spot and looks at the music stand. He gets into a violin-playing position.

Stabbed while playing, he thinks. Playing for herself, or playing for someone else?

He decides it has to be the latter, and that the girl let that person in. Because the door has three locks on it, and it would take a seriously dexterous and quiet killer to get through that door and ram a fountain pen into the girl's neck, all without being noticed.

"Prior knowledge," he says.

Just by standing there, the stories start to appear. A romantic connection. The girl playing to impress and possibly woo someone. Or a professional connection, an audition of sorts with someone important. But what audition ends in murder?

Two potential encounters: love or music. He's tempted to put them together, love and music, or the love of music, but that's a little too neat. This was murder, and while he knows killing is inevitably messy and complicated, the motivations for it are usually few. Love, hate, jealousy, cruelty. Or a person is simply standing in the way of something or someone. And if that was the case with the violinist, the big question is who or what was she impeding?

He goes into the bedroom, fascinated to see that the bed is crisply made, the sheets tightly tucked and the pillows in a puffed-up shape. It makes him like the violinist, though he knows almost nothing about her; he likes that she understood how important structure is. And order. Those things matter, in music and art and life. Huntley believes things should go in their rightful places, perfectly lined up and positioned with care. Because every aspect of life has the potential to be poetic, if such care is taken. Poetry is the ideal delivery of structure and order, with words in the right places, never wasted.

Now, Huntley is sensing a kindred spirit, in this bland apartment, gone from the earth, but still lingering here. Someone like him. Someone who would want fucking Miguel to get his half of the container in order. Someone so determined to be good at something and to get everything in the right place, they question themselves daily whether they are measuring up. Ekaterina Valoskiya channelled all of that into music, only to become third violin in a far-off orchestra. He wonders if she even deserved that. Maybe there was someone more determined, who missed out on being third, because of her.

That story quickly unfolds in his mind. The competitive orchestra. The limited places. Leiland Taverton lording over it all. The foreigner, out of nowhere, taking what should have been a local's place. Somewhere, the person who missed out wants to get what they feel is rightfully theirs. The Ukrainian girl was standing in the way.

In his mind, words start forming on a page: *May the intense want for something, that someone else envisions, as theirs ...*

He needs pen and paper, but can't touch anything in here. He dashes out of the apartment, leaving the balcony door wide open and just about barrelling through the hole in the bamboo partition.

Henrikson looks up.

Huntley, breathing heavily, says, "I need something to write with. And on. I need to get this down."

Henrikson takes some paper from the printer's tray and holds this up for Huntley, who jogs to the desk and drops the keys on the glass.

"I left the door open. Sorry."

"Probably good, to give it an airing."

Huntley takes the pen and paper from Henrikson, then goes to the sofa. He sits down and drags the coffee table towards him. "Try not to do anything distracting."

He savours the moment, pen in hand, as the magic builds. It's there. He can feel it. The intensity of it. The electricity. The last time he felt like this is so long ago, he's forgotten how incredible it feels. Every synapse firing. It's otherworldly, like being possessed by everything that's good in the universe.

The longer he holds the pen, the more it builds. His hand shakes a little. It's all in him, he knows it. All those years of doubt can vanish. He just has to let go and allow the pen to move across the page, and not second-guess any of it.

The doubt demon lingers.

"No, no. You, fucker. Stay away."

With the pen, he parries away the demon and gets to work. The pen hits the paper with such force, it tears a hole with the first word. He pushes on and the pen starts flying. Letters form words. Words form phrases. Phrases form stanzas. Commas are exquisitely positioned. Complex rhymes come without effort. All of it like it was always meant to be there, and was there all this time. A seam of gold that just needed locating and tapping.

He can't quite believe this is happening; can't quite accept that he deserves it. But the pen doesn't stop. It moves and moves and knows exactly what to do.

When his hand finally stops and the poem is done, for now, his eyes are moist. He wants to cry. Not with happiness. But with relief.

Because he still has the magic.

He stares straight ahead, at a painting on the wall of the Cottesloe groyne. All those rocks, seemingly placed randomly, but actually placed perfectly to form a sea wall.

Henrikson's voice sounds like it comes from far away: "My wife painted that. It's beautiful, isn't it?"

"Yes. It is."

Huntley's afraid to look down and read through what poured out of him. It's safer to keep staring at the painting. What if it's terrible? What if the magic is actually poison? What if his first book is the best and only thing he'll ever do? What if the whole idea of him being a poet is delusional? What if he's a fraud and has been all along?

"Would you like to share what you wrote?" Henrikson asks.

"Uh."

Huntley closes his eyes, then opens them and looks down at the page. He reads.

It's good. Not great, but good, and easily the best thing he's done since *Ragged Claws*.

"You got something, so it seems. Getting into the apartment made a difference."

"It did. Thanks."

"You almost started levitating, while you were writing. Like you were going to float away."

"It felt a bit like that. Kind of, out-of-body."

"Spiritual?"

"I think I owe you. Big time."

"For not calling the police?"

"For letting me in there." Huntley folds up the paper with care and puts it in his front pants pocket, with the Landy's keys. "It's been a long time since I felt that ... inspired."

He goes to hand the pen back to Henrikson.

"I think you should keep it. I know writers can be superstitious. This might be a lucky pen. It seems to have served you well today."

Huntley sees that the pen has HENRIKSON'S BOOKS on the side. "Thanks, Mr Henrikson."

"Oh, no. Drop that title. That makes me feel like a teacher again."

"So, just Henrikson then?"

"Yes. I like that. It gives me some seniority over you, and makes me sound somehow wise."

"Well, wise hacker, how did you go with the report?"

"Did you solve the crime with the poem?"

"Not yet. But it's a step in the right direction. There's a motivation behind this murder, and a single blow with a pen is not enough to kill anyone. That green stuff wasn't just ink."

"I haven't found it yet. That doesn't make me an unskilled hacker. It just means the cops are taking their time. It hasn't been shared with anyone or put in the system. If you leave your number, I'll let you know when I get it."

"Why are you doing this for me?"

"Not just for you, Quintus. Ekaterina deserves justice."

Huntley checks his pockets. "I left my phone, uh, at home. I don't know the number."

"Find me at the store tomorrow. I'm doing the morning shift."

"You're on. Thanks, Henrikson."

Huntley goes to the front door.

"Hey, pirate?"

Huntley stops and turns.

"Maybe bring some rum, as payment for services rendered."

"You got it."

<>

Detective Everest sits on a bench, under the shade of one of Russell Square's colossal Moreton Bay fig trees, and vapes. Around her, people hustle out of offices and fall into cars, eager to escape the central business district now that the work day is done. That so many people finish work at 5pm on the dot around here makes her think there should be some kind of loud hooter to signal the day's end.

As her own day is just about finished, she can allow herself the luxury of vaping a mild cannabis-nicotine mix, without guilt, to take the edge off the day while hoping it will also dull the pain in her wrists.

It's really good to have this quiet moment.

She blows vapourish smoke in the direction of the office building across Aberdeen Street, where inside is some independent lab that forensics have outsourced their work to this week. In that cloud of smoke, she tries to envision what was on that very spot two decades ago, and go back there in time, to the red-brick warehouse with the sinking roof that housed Farley's nightclub. It was in that derelict joint that Salty Lemonade played their first gig, in their school uniforms, which was the explicit requirement from creepazoid Farley himself. But fuck him if they didn't rise above that and make the uniform part of the band's identity, in the process attracting legions of schoolgirl fans and graduating to bigger clubs and better-paying gigs where club management treated them with far more respect, and they became the punk-queens of Northbridge.

Everest takes another deep inhale and lets her mind drift back to those times. It's vague, but she remembers once sleeping under this tree.

Northbridge was a fenceless zoo back then, when it seemed everyone going out at night was buzzing on ketamine and speed, and looking for an outlet for their pent-up energy. With the local club scene conquered and their debut album recorded, Salty Lemonade headed east, to wear out the coastal and country roads between Sydney, Brisbane and Melbourne. Fans followed them from one concert to another, and the band was often blamed for thousands of kids wagging school; they often tapped into this by playing matinee shows at outside venues, drawing kids from all over. Then they crossed the ditch to New Zealand for more touring, and went back to Perth for a bunch of outdoor festivals, including three consecutive nights filling the Showgrounds. It all happened fast; none of them even had the chance to finish year 12 at Perth College, but being dropouts, still in school uniforms, added to their mystique. Venues in Europe were lining up to host them. How could they possibly say no to that? Those six months spent in hotels, clubs and buses, crisscrossing Europe, were the best in Everest's life, despite that being the time when the constant trommel pounding took its toll on her thin wrists. She got some special braces and medicine to ease the pain in Germany, and powered on. Everything was on a huge upward swing; she wasn't going to let a bit of pain stop Salty Lemonade from conquering the world, or stop them from having so much goddamn fun. The States beckoned. Everything was booked, including two-dozen stops in Canada. But out of nowhere, Charlene got the total yips: couldn't play her bass anymore, couldn't write songs, and couldn't even sing, something she did even more naturally than talking. They did their best to cover for her, until that night in Amsterdam when Charlene smashed her bass against a stack of amps and walked off the stage. She got into a taxi outside the club and went straight to Schiphol. The rest of the band had no choice but to do the same. When they were all back in Perth, numerous attempts were made to help Charlene re-find the rockstar within. Therapy, acupuncture, diets, yoga, exercise, and even hypnosis, which worked for about a week and gave them a glimmer of hope, but then wore off and left Charlene worse than before. Almost catatonic. It was a scary time, not only because the band went on hiatus and they feared they were done. Ellie was scared she would lose her best friend, and it was only a matter of time and organisation. She spent every minute she could with Charlene, fully suspecting self-harm was likely if given a moment alone. But even round-the-clock surveillance didn't help in the end, as Charlene managed to quietly hang herself from the handle of the bathroom door with a low E bass string. Shattered, Ellie blamed herself and tried to make sense of it all, to pinpoint where things had gone so wrong. But she had no explanation, which made everything harder to bear. Julz, SL's manager, said it was the kind of gruesome death that could massively damage the reputation of the band and thus couldn't be made public. So, after two full days with a focus group discretely organised by the PR company run by Julz's sister, and in consultation with Charlene's suddenly present, low-rent parents, who would now benefit from her share of royalties, it was decided that OD'ing on drugs was a rock'n'roll death fit for public consumption, one that might even enhance the band's status, and that was what went into the final press release, announcing Charlene's tragic passing. An appropriate mourning period completed, ideas were thrown around for a replacement singer and auditions were held. But Ellie was having none of it. For her, Salty Lemonade was done. Any attempt to keep going with someone else brandishing Charlene's bass and belting out her lyrics was wrong, and it would only act as a constant reminder that they'd lost her and she was never coming back.

The cannabis is helping to take the edge off the day. Everest thinks that having a supplier at the office is one of the best perks of her job. Perhaps the only perk.

Charlene dying and the band breaking up was more than 20 years ago. Guitarist Kiana became a successful session musician for the worst kind of bubblegum-autotune pop, while Maxine, keyboards, pivoted to pedagogy, and last Everest heard had managed to go full circle, by taking a prestigious position in the music department of Perth College, where they'd all met as skinny and awkward scholarshipped twelve-year-olds. Except, Charlene was never awkward. She exuded the kind of excessive confidence that inspired as much envy as admiration. Until she lost all of it and couldn't handle living anymore. Ellie herself struggled in the post-Lemonade years, drifting from one thing to the next, not knowing what to do with her life while also having so many people around her suggesting directions to take. Julz wanted her to go solo, but Ellie knew she didn't have the magic mojo that Charlene had, and had lost. Instead, she drank too much, worked all night as a DJ and experimented with drugs, as if alcohol, noise and chemicals could take away all the pain she felt. At one point, she tried writing a tell-all book, one that included Charlene's actual cause of death and everything that led up to it, but Julz and her legal team swooped down with NDAs signed in triplicate and put a stop to that.

But the royalty cheques continued to flow in, funding the lavish-bogan lifestyle of Charlene's despicable family, and also supplying Ellie with a steady income, as all the songwriting credits were shared between her and Charlene, whose sudden, tragic death greatly boosted the band's popularity. Ellie used the money to go to Europe, but was haunted by too many memories of that incredible last tour across the continent. She fled over the Atlantic to Toronto, where Kiana had established a foothold in a number of Canadian studios, helping talentless waifs churn out vile pop songs. After two days of non-stop partying, a series of misunderstandings and a case of mistaken identity resulted in Ellie being arrested for a con scheme she had nothing to do with. During the course of several lengthy interrogations, which included a lie-detector test and the police watching hours of CCTV footage, she not only proved her innocence, she offered to help the police solve the crime by helping to lure the con artist into a trap; it turned out Ellie was a dead ringer for the wanted girl, who was posing as a Swedish princess. The whole sting operation provided Ellie with such a kick and sense of satisfaction that, once given the all-clear from the Toronto cops – several of whom she had befriended – and allowed to leave the country, she flew back to Perth and signed up with the WA Police. She quietly went through the academy and did her tour of duty in the speed camera and random breath-testing trenches, before setting her sights on becoming a detective.

As she vapes, under the fig tree's shade and with a gentle enough breeze still blowing to scatter all her smoke, she flexes her wrists and does some joint rotations. Bones click; there's a bit of pain, the sensation acting like a time machine, transporting her back to the sweaty clubs of Europe, pounding the drums while trying not to stare at Charlene's beautiful arse so snug in cut-off jeans-shorts.

She wants to cry.

The pain in her wrists barely compares to the hurt she feels in her soul whenever she thinks of Charlene. It is a hurt so deep and firmly lodged, she knows it will be with her until she dies.

Booth crosses Aberdeen, a baton of papers coiled in his right hand. Everest is glad for the distraction. She pulls herself together and executes a mimed drum roll.

"And the winner is," she says, once Booth is standing over her.

"She wasn't pregnant, if that's what you're thinking."

"How could you forget all those condoms she had with her? You're way off. I wasn't thinking that at all. But there was something in her system."

Booth sits on the bench. "What makes you say that?"

"I don't believe she bled out." Everest offers her vape pen to Booth. "You want a hit?"

"No. Yes."

Everest feels a warm glow from the dope, and reminds herself to be nicer to Booth.

"You get this from downstairs?" Booth has a hit and blows the smoke out of his nose.

"Don't tell your dad."

"He knows. Trust me, he's glad it's this we're using. Back when he was young, there was much harder stuff available on site. So he says."

"I can believe it. Once upon a time in this hood, you could buy ketamine like it was candy. People called it Special K."

"The breakfast of champions."

They both laugh.

Booth inhales again. "Ah, that's good stuff."

"Stop keeping me in suspense. What was in the fountain pen?"

"It just so happens that you're right. Happy?" Booth hands back the vape and unfurls the papers. "The secret ingredient was arum maculatum."

"Bloody scientists. This is Latin for what?"

"More commonly known as," Booth says, turning a page over, "wild arum. Found mostly in Europe."

"Never heard of it. Poisonous?"

"I asked the same thing in the lab. I have to say, those guys were really rude. Using all that science jargon, as if everything fancy they know is common knowledge. They're just showing off."

"I bet."

"Hey, when it comes to poisonous plants found in Europe and their deathly uses, I'm the first to say I'm a complete idiot. But they could at least talk in a way that's understandable."

"A plant?"

"Or a weed. Definitely not something I want to smoke."

Everest vapes some more. "A toxic plant. Interesting."

"According to the report, there was an extremely high concentration in the victim's bloodstream and around the wound. It caused her to asphyxiate."

"A European plant made her to choke to death?"

Booth nods.

"You can't make this stuff up," Everest says, handing the vape back to Booth. "Here. You can finish this. I've reached just the right balance."

Booth takes a long drag and they both silently stare up at the tree. The haze of vapour wafts up towards the broad overhanging branches. A couple of figs plop to the ground. The only other noise is the intermittent drone of cars coming from Aberdeen Street.

"Don't you just love this time of day? Especially when the wind drops like this." Booth weaves his hand through the smoke vapour he exhales. "The temperature goes down and it feels like the whole city is just starting to relax. Right now, people all over the city are kicking their shoes off and having a cold brew."

"Or getting high."

"That too. It's turning into a beautiful evening."

"You sound like you want to be down the beach."

"Actually, I have a strong desire to climb this tree."

"Where's that coming from?"

"The house I grew up in had a tree like this in the front yard. Not this big, but big enough. I used to climb all over it. My own personal playground."

"You're a tree hugger? I did not see that coming."

"Tree climber," Booth says, giving Everest that surfer-boy grin of his. "It was a platonic relationship."

"Where was that?"

"Bunbury, before Dad got promoted to Cockburn and we moved up. Still plenty of family down there."

"My memories of that place are thin," Everest says, "but I do remember it being pretty run-down and hairy."

"It's not like that anymore. Cleaned up. Modernised. A big arts community. You'd like it. Good live music scene too."

"Maybe I should visit."

"Get this band of yours back together and go on tour. I can't believe you were a drummer. Why didn't you say something?"

"It's a lifetime ago." Everest is keen to move the conversation away from her rock past. "But going to Bunbury could include a swing down south to Ravensthorpe, to find out what inspired that weirdo Huntley to write that book of his."

"Long drive. Still, that is the countryside, where someone could secretly cultivate a crop of this wild arum stuff."

"Do you think it was him?"

"You don't? He's all we've got, right now."

Everest shrugs. "It doesn't really fit. Why would he leave his own book there?"

"Like a calling card?"

"I doubt it. What was he like as a professor?"

"He's not a professor. He's an assistant lecturer. Part-time. I checked. His position is the same as when I was there."

Everest feels the vague disappointment that results from a dope high slowly wearing off. "Did he publish anything else?"

Booth shakes his head. "Nothing. You know, back when I was a student, I thought he was really clever. He was so entertaining. And funny. Riffing on anything and everything. If there was something he didn't like, he could absolutely destroy it. I expected him to write a bunch of books and become famous. What a waste."

Everest tries not to think of all the songs she and Charlene could have written together. She sniffs loudly.

"Did I say something wrong?" Booth asks.

"No, no. Just allergies, I think."

Booth rolls up the toxicology report and looks through it like a spyglass, up at the tree. "So? What now? Shall we keep an eye on Huntley?"

"He knows we're interested in him. Let's leave it and call it a day. Go down the beach, Justin. You're right. This is a beautiful time of day. Best enjoy it."

"I'm too stoned to move."

"After a couple of vapes?"

"It's powerful stuff. I don't have the built-up tolerance of a former rockstar."

"Trust me. When you're on the road and playing gigs every night, drugs are the last thing you need. We ended every gig with cups of chamomile tea."

"Served by groupies?"

"Not at all. But tomorrow, we do need to find a drug expert. Specifically, an expert on poisonous plants."

"We should keep an eye on Aphra Massey too. She built a wall in that kitchen today. She's withholding something."

"She is. Well observed, Justin." Everest stands up. "We'll split the work. You go to Massey. She seems keen to get you alone. I'll follow the plants lead."

"And Huntley?"

"I'll look into his past. Maybe there's something there. And I'll do some reading tonight. Find out what these ragged claws are all about."

"If you do, let me know."

"You did his course but never read his book?"

Booth stands up as well. "You wouldn't believe the reading lists I had at uni. Course readers like fucking telephone books. You needed a trolley to cart them home at the start of every semester."

This makes Everest smile. She finds it reassuring that her time working speed cameras and random breath testing was perhaps better spent than it might have been at university.

"We'll trade notes at lunch tomorrow," she says, starting to walk away. "You're buying."

"Why me?"

"You owe me for the weed."

Everest's car is parked at the corner of Aberdeen and Shenton. Once inside, she lowers all the windows to let the heat out. She takes a moment to ponder her next move. Waiting for her at home in Doubleview is a cat that doesn't need feeding and does quite well without her. A microwave dinner. An evening of awful reality TV or unfunny talk shows. A couple of drinks too many, to keep the hurt at bay, but eventually only ever amplifying it. She thinks it's all best avoided, with work being the most viable distraction at hand.

She wonders: who was Ekaterina Valoskiya?

Earlier today, the interview with Leiland Taverton had been an awful 17 minutes. The head of the PSO was combative and rude, and he expertly dodged questions like a veteran politician, deflecting and dismissing everything Everest threw at him, all while he looked only at Booth. Taverton did make one disclosure; the PSO rehearses at Scotch College. So, in order to avoid the walls closing in on her at home, Everest starts the car and joins the last wave of the workday's exodus from central Perth. The windows go up and the air-con comes on. Some bullying is required to get on the freeway, which then moves at a crawl. It takes half an hour to cover the two kilometres to the Mounts Bay Road exit, and once on that, bumper-to-bumper at 30 km/h feels like she's flying all the way to Claremont. On the journey, the sky gloriously turns from yellow to orange to pink to purple. The last of the colour is just fading as she pulls into the parking lot at Scotch.

She pops some very minty gum in her mouth and gets pointed in the direction of the rehearsal theatre by a harried late-leaving teacher. Once she finds the way inside, she sees the orchestra building to the finish of something dramatic. The conductor, a short man, not Taverton, wields his baton like a child with a sparkler. His shock of grey hair flounces and flops, as if it's conducting an orchestra of its own.

It's incredibly loud, a big orchestra in this small rehearsal theatre. Everest's insides vibrate wonderfully every time the drum is pounded, and it awakens something dormant in her soul. She notices three violinists in the string section.

All the seats are vacant, except for a man slouched in a row, halfway down. He's asleep, his head far back and his mouth wide open, enough for the light to catch the gold fillings in his molars.

It's Huntley.

She falls into the seat next to him, bumping his arm in the process and waking him. He sits up slowly.

"Detective E's."

"What are you doing here?"

Their seats are in the acoustic sweet spot of the theatre, enabling them to hear each other without shouting.

Huntley blinks a few times. "What can I say? I'm a supporter of the local arts scene. A music lover."

"Surely reggae, not classical. You smell like something that washed up on a Jamaican beach."

"I admit I've been celebrating, for most of the afternoon."

"The same way you did this morning?"

"That was different."

"Celebrating what?"

Huntley, more awake, looks closely at Everest. "Are you all right? Your eyes are all red."

Everest looks towards the stage. "Hay fever."

"Yeah. Let's go with that. To save you from getting all, hah, high and mighty about me toasting some small smidgen of success."

"You found the orchestra. So what?"

"I've done more than that today. This has been the best day in a very long time."

"Nice. A girl dies a horrible death, and you're a person of interest in the case, and you celebrate."

Huntley laughs, a little too loudly, causing the conductor to wave the baton in his direction as a signal to lower the volume.

"Yeah, you're right," he says. "I should probably tone it down a bit."

"Especially since you're still a suspect."

"Bollocks. But that makes me think you followed me here. Are you following me?"

"No."

"You should be."

"Is that right?"

"Because I'm a step ahead. The story is expanding. It brought me here."

"To do what? Cover your tracks?"

"I keep telling you it wasn't me. But my research did bring me to the scene of the crime."

"This isn't it. She was killed in her apartment."

"It's not her apartment," Huntley says, waggling a finger briefly. "She was only there temporarily."

"How do you know that?"

"That's where she died, but this is where the crime took place." He points at the young man in the third violin chair. "You need to talk to him."

"He barely looks old enough to drive."

"Oh no, you misunderstood me. It wasn't him. He's no killer. Someone did it for him. The Ukrainian girl, may she rest in peace, was standing in his way, and someone cleared the path. There he is, already having replaced her. He was just waiting in the wings."

"You figured this all out, then celebrated your cleverness?"

"If only you could be as keen as I am to prove my innocence. I just assumed that because you're here, you're at the same point in this investigation as me."

"Why don't you tell me how you got to this point, and I'll let you know what I think."

Huntley moves in the seat, to face Everest. He puts an arm over the back of her seat, smiles and says, "Well, it's all a story. Right? With characters and conflicts. The victim. The killer. The motive. The beneficiary. It's all so obvious that it's almost a tale told by an idiot. You know, signifying nothing. Except the girl was killed for a reason and that's not nothing. Plus, there's a poison pen involved, which I think is brilliantly poetic."

"You know about the poison?"

"Is it true, then?"

Everest doesn't reply, but Huntley doesn't need her to.

"It is true," he says, trying to keep himself from laughing. "What kind of poison? How many green poisons are there? Snake venom, is that green? Or hemlock?"

Everest is about to reply, but the orchestra goes up a gear, building towards a thundering finish. The conductor is up on his toes, both hands high in the air and shaking. Then, he drops them and the final crescendo sounds, its last collective note reverberating around the theatre.

Huntley claps. "Bravo!"

Again, the conductor waves his baton in Huntley's direction, to silence him, then taps the music stand with it.

"I do not have the words to describe how utterly awful, amateurish and antagonising that was," the conductor says, speaking almost in a whisper and carefully enunciating each word. "Don't any of you ever bring that kind of fifth-rate performance into my theatre ever again. Ever. Or I will break your precious instruments and the hands that play them."

The musicians start packing their instruments away, no one seemingly paying much attention to the conductor.

"Damn," Huntley says. "Harsh."

The conductor uses his baton to wave the orchestra members away. They start exiting, stage right. The new third violinist lingers, taking his time putting his instrument in its case and carefully adjusting the bow. The conductor has a word with him, standing on his tiptoes to whisper something in his ear, then patting him gently on the back. It appears far more encouraging than the diatribe delivered to the orchestra as a whole.

Once the conductor walks off the stage, through a gap in the curtains that seems reserved only for him, Everest stands up and goes down the stairs, heading straight for the young violinist. Huntley scrambles to his feet and follows.

Everest stops at the stage and turns to Huntley. "What do you think you're doing? You can't be part of this."

"I'll just stand quietly in the background and listen in. Like a bodyguard."

"Stay out of it."

"Don't forget that I'm the one who said you should talk with this kid."

Everest is about to reply when Huntley gestures for her to look at the stage, where two women, both toting skinny flute cases, are taunting the young violinist. They take turns banging his legs with their instrument cases.

"What did you do to get this?" asks one of the women.

"Leave me alone."

"This is the Perth Symphony," says the other. "Not preschool."

Everest gets onto the stage and positions herself in front of the violinist. "That's enough," she says, holding up her ID. "Go on home. The rehearsal is over."

"Are you here to arrest him?"

"Has he done something wrong?"

"It's a crime he's even in the orchestra."

The two women laugh and walk away.

"What a nasty pair," Huntley says, standing next to Everest.

"Why are you still here?"

"You looked like you needed some backup."

Everest shakes her head, then turns to the violinist. "Are you all right?"

"I'm fine. I don't need your help. Whoever you are."

Huntley steps forward and thrusts out his hand. "Quintus Huntley. Pleasure to meet you. I thought you played superbly. Well done."

The violinist, who has the plumpness of privilege, as if he has spent most of his teens overindulging, gives Huntley a dead-fish handshake, which Huntley pumps exuberantly anyway.

"Your parents must be so proud. So very proud. To have made it this far at such a young age. Who else would be proud of you?"

"What do you mean by that?"

Huntley opens his mouth to answer, but Everest cuts in. "I'm sure you know what happened to the violinist who sat in that chair before you."

He shrugs. "I heard. So?"

"She was murdered, kid," Huntley says. "Did you hear about that part? Murdered for you."

"Huntley, please. Stop talking." Everest steps closer to the violinist, who gives her a snide smile. "May I ask how you ended up getting this spot? Is there some kind of substitutes' bench?"

"I was invited. I got the call this morning."

"You took that chair pretty quickly," Huntley says. "Like you were ready and waiting to. You knew it would be vacant. Today."

"That's enough," Everest says. "One more word from you and I'll have you arrested for obstruction of justice."

Huntley holds up his hands and backs off a little.

"I thought you were both from the police," the violinist says.

"I am. He isn't."

"What's he doing here then?"

"He's ... helping. In a way. The investigation. We're a bit understaffed, at the moment."

His snide smile is replaced by a look of derision. "You outsource police work? That makes me feel so safe."

"Look, just tell me how you ended up here," Everest says, starting to lose her temper.

"I drove up from Mandurah after school. For this rehearsal."

"School?" Huntley asks.

"I'm in year 12."

"You seem pretty close with the conductor," Everest says.

"He was my teacher. When I was younger."

"He's not the regular conductor?"

"Only for rehearsals. He teaches here at Scotch, now. When Leiland's too busy, he takes over."

Huntley laughs.

"Why is that funny?" the violinist asks.

"What? Apart from this second-string conductor getting off on cutting down musicians far better than himself?"

"He was right. The orchestra was way off tonight."

"And you know that? The year 12 third violinist who bolted in from down south because he knows the backup conductor?"

"Huntley," Everest says, "you're not helping."

"Sorry." Huntley walks over to the grand piano and sits down at it.

"What's your name?" Everest asks.

"Marcus Ford-Brackman."

"Oh, God," Huntley says. "You're one of them. That's just perfect. All the pieces fit now. The Mayors of Mandurah. They own everything down there. You know that, Ellie? Have done for decades. Going way back to when Mandurah was a ramshackle holiday town with dirt roads and outside dunnies."

"I know who they are."

"Leave my family out of this," Marcus says.

"They probably ponied up their dirty money to pay that weaselly conductor to give young Marcus here lessons when he was just starting out."

"So what if they did?" Having established his family name, Marcus grows in confidence, drawing on all the petulance and entitlement that comes with old money. "I was a prodigy."

"I bet you were," Huntley says. "Nothing says prodigious quite like suitcases full of cash."

"Can you account for your whereabouts today?" Everest asks.

"I was at school," Marcus says. "All day. It's intense. Then I drove up here when Calveshawn called me."

Huntley laughs. "Calveshawn? That's beautiful." He plays a few bars of *Galveston* on the piano and sings, "Calveshawn, oh Calveshawn."

Everest suppresses the urge to laugh. "Is that your conductor friend?"

"Sounds more country than classical," Huntley says. "Cal needs to put down his stick and pick up a guitar. Sing about trucks and horses and broken hearts."

Marcus gives Huntley a nasty look.

"Please, please," Huntley continues, "tell me that name is a mononym."

"A what?"

Everest tries to stay composed. "What about last night?" she asks. "Where were you?"

"I don't like this line of questioning," Marcus says, folding his chunky forearms.

"Nothing is being implied. I'm just trying to establish where everyone was."

"Forget it, Ellie," Huntley says. "The family will protect him."

"I was at home."

"Ah, yes, the Ford-Brackman estate," Huntley says to Everest. "Massive place. Down at The Cut. They all live there, behind walls and under armed guard."

"It's not all it's cracked up to be," Marcus says. "I feel like a prisoner."

"Wealth and luxury suck, don't they?"

Marcus picks up his case and turns to leave.

"Yeah, you're free to go," Everest says.

"Oh, I am?" he asks, with a generous lashing of sarcasm as he trudges off the stage. "Well, thank you."

"Hey, Marcus," Huntley calls out, making the young violinist stop. "Tell those two blowers you're a Ford-Brackman. They won't go near you after that."

The stage door slams shut.

"What do you think that bullying was all about?" Everest asks.

Huntley shrugs. "Probably some weird hazing thing. It won't last, once the connection is made."

"The family." Everest folds her arms and lets out an exasperated sigh.

"Yep," Huntley says. "I think you know exactly how things work in this big country town. So, what now?"

"You need to stay out of this."

"I thought we made a good team. I'd say we should drive down to The Cut, but my Landy's still at the uni, probably being liberally decorated with parking tickets by one of your mean colleagues."

"You are in no condition to drive."

"And you are? Or is Booth listening to the radio in the parking lot? I hope you left the windows down for him."

Everest lets out a short laugh, then composes herself and says, "The family must be involved. Given their history."

"They're actually quite tame. Business people, trying hard to go straight. Grandma Ford-Brackman remains an absolutely vile piece of work. Stabbing someone with a pen isn't within her physical capabilities, though I wouldn't put it past her to pay someone to do it."

"I need to talk to them."

"Don't waste your time. They'll lawyer up. Close ranks. You won't even get past the gate. And trust me. They never get their hands dirty, unless they're breaking ground on some new subdivision."

"Maybe it was a hit then. They hired somebody."

"I bloody well hope not."

"Why?"

"Because that would make things decidedly more boring. It's imperative the story stays interesting. I need something powerful to continue with. That's why I came here. To get inspired. I won't be able to sleep until I get all the right words in the right places."

"That sounds obsessive. You're writing about this? Isn't that a bit callous?"

Huntley flexes his fingers, getting ready to play. "Art usually is. Callous. Obsessive. Selfish. Egocentric. You can't go at art half-arsed. Hah. How good does that sound? You gotta be all in. But you know what I mean."

"All in enough to kill people?"

"No way. I'm a poet, Ellie. That's all." Huntley tinkles a few high keys, thinking about something Henrikson said. "It's all about the pen."

"Yeah. What hired gun kills someone with a fountain pen?"

"Filled with poison, no less. You haven't said yet what it was."

"I'm not going to."

"How unfair. After everything I've contributed so far. You wouldn't have known about Marcus Ford-Brackman if not for me." Huntley punctuates this with a resounding daan-daan-daah chord progression on the piano, then adds, "The poet's doing all your work."

"You look like you're enjoying it."

"It's grim, I'll admit, and not the circumstances I like. But I'm finding there are more than a few fascinating correlations between storytelling and detective work."

Huntley starts playing *Galveston* again on the piano, and hums along.

Everest looks around, her eyes falling on the theatre's drum kit. She thinks it's weird to be in this empty theatre with Huntley, which not so long ago was filled with orchestral music that he was sleeping soundly through. She considers leaving, but the cat-microwave-TV-alcohol-grief-combo waiting for her at home isn't exactly appealing. She goes to the drums and picks up the sticks that are on top of the snare. She twirls one of the sticks in the fingers of her right hand and pulls the band out of her ponytail with her left hand, shaking her hair loose in the process.

It's all completely wrong, but she can't resist. She runs through a punkish riff.

Huntley stops playing. "Oh, yeah. What took you so long?"

<>

Upon entering the Mangy Mongrel, Aphra Massey immediately picks up on the distinct kith and kin vibe. Open mic nights are often like this, she knows, and what might look like a collective show of support for the local poetry scene is actually a combination of various get-togethers of friends and family asked along to hear someone read. Many of them have the flat faces and bored stares of people forced to attend out of obligation. They nurse drinks, clap politely and wait patiently for whoever they are there to support, yet spend most of their time thinking of all the things they would rather be doing. Like a church sermon or school assembly, they are all forced to sit through it to the very end.

Aphra goes to the bar and orders a gin and tonic with a twist of lime. As she waits, she looks around, not seeing anyone she knows, but also finding it interesting that everyone seems somehow familiar. A crowd of interchangeable people. Quintus Huntley isn't among them, and this is disappointing. After she didn't find him at the university earlier, she came here; a long shot she thought worth taking, as this is the only event happening in Perth tonight remotely connected to literature, and Huntley is the kind of once-famous poet who might attempt to milk his fleeting fame by showing up at otherwise insignificant poetry readings.

The drink arrives and she sips, annoyed the G&T is about 50 per cent tonic, 47 per cent ice, two per cent gin and one per cent lime. Though it's a blessing, perhaps, given she still needs to get home on her Vespa.

As an elderly man on stage reads his disjointed battlefield poetry, Aphra tells herself that she doesn't sit in the same fleeting-fame boat as Huntley, and she certainly doesn't need the adoration of this vague assemblage. He's not here. She can finish her watery drink and escape before anyone recognises her.

Not that she doesn't admire those reading. She claps as the elderly man finishes his piece and a middle-aged woman takes the stage, papers in hand. Getting up in this setting to read something original is an act of bravery that many people don't appreciate; to share stuff created from nothing, that's usually personal, and which will leave some of the friends and family present wondering if it's about them, and which will probably never appear anywhere in print, unless it's self-published, requires a very special kind of courage. Aphra likens it to standing on the stage naked, because writing always reveals something private about the writer, and those listening, looking and judging often fail to see past its imperfections. Meaning, it's a piece of self-expression reserved for here and now, providing a small window into the writer's soul. And maybe, just maybe, out of the entire evening, there might be one line that lands. One metaphor that resonates with those present. One moment where everyone present gets what the writer's trying to say and admires them for how they say it.

Right now, the middle-aged woman is reading clumsy verse that reimagines herself as a 1950s housewife. Aphra thinks it's an interesting hook, but the poetry has the rawness and inconsistencies of a first draft. Her own collection went through so many drafts, she lost count, but it got marginally better each time.

It was here, in the Mangy Mongrel, which was far more mangy back then – a run-down, junkie-infested, hole-in-the-wall bar on Henry Street in Freo, before an arts grant aided the renovations that also doubled the price of drinks and halved the alcohol content – that Aphra first read her poetry to an audience. She was 17, petrified and alone, as she read out a poem that went into explicit detail about all the ways to kill the guy who had date-raped the main character. The poem was delivered in the first-person singular and composed from first-hand experience. In reality, she never actually killed "Jye Parsons", as happens in the story. But she did make it her lifelong hobby to ensure her "Jye" had a totally miserable existence, deploying a combination of sabotage and networking to prevent him from getting anywhere in life. He was currently doing another stint in Casuarina Prison, for stealing the spare wheels from the boots of cars, which he had tried to sell to wreckers to fund his crystal meth addiction. He was sharing a cell, thanks to a member of Blair Blake-Stendahl's legal team with connections to the prison authorities, with a very large man in prison for grievous bodily harm, who was hopefully inflicting various grievous punishments on "Jye" every night when the lights went out. Her early poems evolved into the collection *How to Kill Jye Parsons*, published several years later by an east-coast publisher, as no one local had the guts to touch it. The book won a couple of big poetry awards and a TV adaptation was talked up, but it never eventuated, again because no one local was brave enough to try it. But short-term fame did bring Aphra into contact with powerful women, including BBS, who was then running as an independent for the seat of Nedlands and needed speechwriting support, to help craft her "local narrative".

Aphra smiles into her drink, feeling no remorse for all the suffering she's inflicted on "Jye" over the years.

She sips some more, wanting to finish and sneak away. The tonic is cold, the lime slightly refreshing, the gin almost non-existent. Any thoughts of Katie get pushed to the deepest reaches of her mind.

"That's a beautiful dress," a man says.

"Thanks."

"Can I buy you a drink?" he asks.

She turns to see a young man, strangely good-looking, though his nose and mouth don't seem to sit quite in the centre of his face; he looks like a rat trying to sniff at something off to his right. He's dressed chic bohemian, in the kind of clothes found on the expensive racks in second-hand shops. As he's standing too close for her liking, she takes a small step backwards.

"I've got one, thanks."

"Finish it and I'll buy you another."

It's the kind of pushiness she despises; the pretence of overt friendliness that masks a nasty type of desperation. She knows turning this kind of guy down requires tact, as he will likely take rejection badly.

"I'm driving," she says. "And unfortunately, I'm not able to stay."

"You should. I'm on next. You got here just in time." He reaches out his hand. "Purvis Irving."

Aphra doesn't shake it. She takes another step away from him and says, "You're that protester. At the wetlands. You chained yourself to a tree, or something like that."

"They were platforms," Purvis says proudly. "I led the protest where we all took up residence in the trees."

"Beeliar Regional Park?"

"Yep. You're right to be impressed by that. 19 days up there. We stopped the developments and preserved all that beautiful nature."

"You and your supporters camping in trees for weeks must've been great for the local ecosystem."

"Nothing was built. We won."

"You think that was you?"

"Sure it was. We saved the wetlands. I did."

Aphra would like to put this pushy hipster in his place; tell him that the only thing that stopped the project before was money, which has since been quietly obtained, and that she's seen blueprints for everything that's planned for the wetlands, and that the bulldozers will be knocking over trees well before any further protest camps, or platforms, can be set up, and that the project's kick-off meeting tomorrow morning is the first appointment in BBS's very busy Tuesday. But Aphra signed an NDA and can't tell him any of that, and she doesn't want to waste more time talking to him anyway.

"Of course you did," she says. "Well done."

The crowd claps half-heartedly as the time-travelling housewife, whose face has turned beet-red, bows to the audience and leaves the stage.

"My turn," Purvis says, a crooked grin on his crooked face. "Please stay."

As he moves between the tables, shaking hands on the way with people he knows, Aphra finishes her drink, pays for it and heads for the door. Exiting the Mongrel, she accidentally bumps into a woman coming in.

"Excuse me," Aphra says, continuing down the street.

"Stop right there, Aphra Massey. Don't you walk away from me."

Aphra turns and looks at the woman, trying to place her. She's middle-aged, but not quite coping well with it, and her daring attempt at appearing professional and sexy in a tight skirt with a leather jacket just seems sad; the very-end-of-cocktail-hour-at-the-yacht-club sad. But still somehow posh and privileged, her heels planted on the Henry Street footpath like she owns the whole of Fremantle. It's the possessive stance that helps Aphra remember.

"Lydette Gifford."

"You say that like there's a question mark at the end." Lydette comes in close for a double air-kiss. "I championed your book from the very start."

"It was published in Sydney."

"Yes, I know people over there. You really should be more grateful for the strings I pulled."

Aphra nods.

"I tried to become your agent, but you ridiculously said you didn't want one."

"That's not correct. I didn't think I needed one, as I had no plans to write a follow-up."

"Shame about that. Just when you were building an audience."

Aphra would like to say that she's written a lot of stuff over the years that reached a bigger audience than her poetry ever would, but instead asks, "How are you?"

"I'm fabulous." Lydette leans back to look through the Mongrel's glass door. "It's brilliant to see you. I love your dress. What kind of flowers are those?"

"Yellow ones."

"Did you do a reading?"

"No, I was looking for someone."

"And now you're leaving."

"He's not here."

"Whoever he is, forget him. I've got someone far better for you. My young eco-warrior star, who's just about to take the stage."

"Purvis Irving? He's already on."

"He's the real thing. The latest thoroughbred I've added to my stable of writers."

"Is he a warrior or a racehorse?"

"He's everything. He's going places."

Aphra smiles. "Right to the top of the poetry tree."

"Ah, you're familiar with his work. Of course you are. He's tapping magnificently into the zeitgeist. He's fully and utterly of the moment."

"He's definitely full of something."

"Talent. In copious amounts. His stuff is wild. Feral. It takes you to places you never imagined you'd go. He's like LSD."

"Mind scrambling?"

"Trippy, darling. There's lots of emotion involved. It's all daringly modern and courageously vital."

Aphra feels the warm comfort of tough decisions made long ago which continue to pay dividends. Her exchange with Lydette is a pleasant reminder of why she decided not to write another collection and instead escape the publishing world, which is lorded over by people like Lydette and worse versions of her. By comparison, politics was simple to navigate.

"Will there be a book?" she asks.

"It still needs a publisher, but I'm all over that. It'll be out in time for Christmas. Purvis is here tonight to keep building his following."

"Great to see them all here."

"He's huge on social media. That's online, darling."

"Ah, so that's how social media works. Who knew?"

"He's incredibly prolific. He also writes lyrics for a rapper in Brisbane."

"Sounds exciting."

"That could've been you. If you'd had me as your agent. Normally, I'd say something encouraging, like, there's still time, or your best is yet to come. But you had your chance. Your time passed."

"Wow. Don't hold back, Lydette."

"The truth can be harsh."

"No, it's fine. Your honesty is so refreshing."

"I tell you what, I'll send you an invite for the book launch. It's VIP. I'm already getting the list together. I'm sure I can make room for you."

"Thanks. I'm honoured." Aphra is hit by inspiration. "What about Quintus Huntley? Will you invite him? He's family, isn't he?"

"Barely. Ex-family." Lydette says this with distaste, while also managing to smile. "I won't be inviting him. He's an embarrassment to himself and the Perth arts community."

"That bad? But his book was very well received."

"And what has he done since? Nothing."

"Weren't you his agent?"

"I dumped him decades ago. He has some menial position at UWA, which he only got thanks to me. He's lucky to have that. He's practically living on the street."

"Really?"

"You wouldn't believe it. He's in some camper near the red dingo, last I heard. That's how far he's fallen. A family member let him park there, so my niece says. Not from my side of the family."

"Interesting."

"Stay away from him," Lydette warns, smiling again. "He's a disaster. The kind of poison that infects everyone around him."

"Noted. Look, I have to go." Aphra ramps up the perkiness of her tone to add, "It's been just wonderful to see you, darling."

"A brilliant surprise," Lydette says, matching Aphra's tone, and sounding similarly disingenuous. "Take care now."

Lydette pivots on a heel and enters the Mangy Mongrel.

Aphra feels like she needs a shower. Or at least another G&T, far heavier on the G.

At her Vespa, she dons her flag of Italy helmet, then rides out of Fremantle and over the Railway Bridge. When she reaches the Dingo Flour Mill, she does a U-turn at Craig Street and rides on the footpath to the base of the red dingo mural. In the darkness, she makes out the silhouette of a caravan parked between the trees, one light on inside.

The door is opened. "Who's there?" Huntley asks, coming out.

Aphra takes off her helmet and gives her hair a shake. "Hey. Hi, Mr Huntley. I'm sorry to just show up like this. I tried to find you at the uni."

"Bit late for that." Huntley tilts his head a little. "You're Aphra Massey."

"Yes, I am. How do you know that?"

"Your book was sublime. I still use it, when I'm teaching."

Aphra is flattered. "You do?"

"Yeah. It's good stuff. Well done on that."

"Thanks."

"What are you doing here?"

"Please don't get the wrong idea," Aphra says, getting off the Vespa, "but can we talk inside?"

"No, we can't. No visitors allowed. That's part of the deal."

"Does that explain why the caravan has trees painted on the side, as camouflage?"

"Not effective enough. You found it."

"I saw the light."

"I only just arrived and turned it on. Who told you I was here?"

"Lydette Gifford."

"Hah. That vixen."

"She didn't exactly say it. It's more she let it slip."

"I doubt that very much. She doesn't waste a word. Everything has meaning and purpose for her. If she said it, she wanted you to know."

"Maybe."

Huntley takes a few steps away from the caravan. "So, why are you here?"

"I need to talk to you about a friend of mine. Ekaterina Valoskiya."

"She was your friend? I'm so sorry about what happened."

Aphra nods. "You sound like you know her."

"The police questioned me. I didn't do it. I swear on my father's ashes. I never met her in real life."

"She had your book in her violin case. Do you have any idea why?"

"That's why the police came to me." Huntley goes into the caravan, turns off the light and comes back out. "You're very direct. I like it. Listen, we can't talk here. Let's walk to the beach."

Aphra places her helmet on the Vespa's seat.

"Nice ride," Huntley says. "I saw your headlight, but it's weird I didn't hear the scooter. Those things normally make a racket."

"Mine's electric."

"That's good."

None of the vehicles passing by on Stirling Highway are electric, making it a bit too noisy to talk as they walk towards the North Fremantle train station. While waiting at the lights to cross the road, there's a momentary lull in the traffic.

"Ms Massey. Again, I'm really sorry. About your friend."

Aphra's face is expressionless. "Thanks."

Waiting for the light to turn green, there's a strong sense they're circling each other, like boxers waiting for the other to throw the first punch.

"I came to find you because I want to know why your book was in Katie's violin case."

"I didn't put it there," Huntley says, "if that's what you're insinuating. Like I said, I never met her. I'm starting to think the killer put it there, as some kind of message to me."

"A message? As if, to frame you?"

"The detectives, one of them …"

"Booth?"

"You met him too? He thinks I did it. But I think it's an attempt at communication. The killer, reaching out to me. Why else would she even have a book in her case? Is that something she actually did?"

The light finally turns green and they cross the road.

"Did you tell the detectives that?"

"Not yet," Huntley says. "I've got them looking in another direction. What about you? What do you think happened?"

"I don't know. I just can't believe she's gone."

Once across Stirling and the railroad tracks, where the train's platform is scarily empty, they go down Freeman Loop, towards the beach. The evening is very still, the wind having dropped when the sun went down. Every streetlight has a collection of insects, flitting in and out of the light's immediate glow.

"I can give you my version of the story," Huntley says. "If you'd like to hear it."

"I would."

"It's straightforward. She was killed to free up the third violin chair in the PSO."

"That doesn't sound like something to murder someone for."

"It's the strongest story that's presenting itself. The strongest motivation."

"I don't think it's enough."

"Well, the chair's already been filled, by one Marcus Ford-Brackman, and that, in my opinion, greatly increases the chance of foul play in this game of musical chairs."

"Ford-Brackman?"

"You heard of them? The landed gentry down in Mandurah. Very powerful in that small enclave of our fair state."

"I'm aware of that. I also know they've got ambitions that extend beyond Mandurah."

"Is that right? In which direction?"

"North. Everywhere south of the river, for starters."

"How do you know that? I don't think even Detective Everest knows that."

"They're supporters," Aphra says.

"Of what?"

"The WA Republic Party."

"Hah. The WAR Party. What do you have to do with them?"

At the end of Freeman Loop, they reach a circular picnic area. A dozen men, with a dozen eskies, are gathered around the public barbecue facility, where dozens of sausages are sizzling. Aphra sits on the bench furthest away from them and looks towards the inky ocean.

"I will take your silence as an admission you work for them," Huntley says, sitting down as well. "Something writerly, I assume. Social media manager perhaps? Or speechwriter? Because I haven't seen a book from you since that first one, and that's a while ago now."

"I can say the same about you, an even longer while."

"At least I didn't cross over to the dark side."

"Well, at least I'm not living in a caravan."

"That's a choice. I can control a small space much better than a large one."

"Such as that massive place your ex-wife inhabits? You must've been lost in there."

"I was. Sounds like Giorgie's still tight with Blair."

"She is. Didn't you get anything in the divorce?"

Huntley smiles thinly, finding Aphra a little too aggressive and snarky. "I think I got to keep the pen I signed the papers with. An unlucky pen, that one."

"Excuse me?"

"Ah, forget it. But no money or titles or deeds, if that's what you're thinking. I wouldn't have taken them anyway. All of that stuff is tainted and cursed. Poor Verity will get it, one day."

"Who's Verity?"

"My daughter. She's 13. A vicious, precious angel."

"You still should've fought for something, to get somewhere decent to live."

"There was nothing to fight for. Giorgie's dad made me sign a prenup. Don't misread that. Harland Gifford, despite everything, is a pretty decent bloke. It was his father and grandfather who were the fuckers. Harland's thinking at the time was that the prenup would inspire me to become a big-time best-selling writer. He genuinely wanted that for me. When I signed it and Giorgie and I got married, that was still on the cards."

"What happened? Did you get blocked?"

Huntley clears his throat. "No. Not blocked. Just ... bereft. Of an idea I believed in. I know that now. I thought the words had dried up, but what was really missing all along was a decent idea."

"You shouldn't have signed that prenup. Someone should've explained to Harland the economics of publishing. It's not quite the same as farming land you got for nothing 150 years ago."

"I had no problem with the prenup. I absolutely married Giorgie for love."

"Proven by the fact you came out of the marriage with nothing."

"I like to think I still have my dignity."

"And the university appointment."

"Such as it is. A container office and derelict students, at just above minimum wage. I should've been clever like you and started writing for cashed-up villains."

"The people I write for are way smarter than me," Aphra says. "They exist beyond any levels of categorisations. But you definitely could've put your skills to more profitable use."

"Maybe I'll start by coming up with a better name for the WAR Party."

"I had nothing to do with that. Blair says it shows her fighting qualities. The acronym's a disaster."

"Don't discount it just yet. The Australian government isn't going to let go of its cash cow without a fight. WA becoming its own country may require a war, of some sort. Maybe a war of words, which will mean Blair will need you at the front line."

Aphra doesn't reply and the two of them lapse into silence. The men with their tinnies and snags are loud enough to drown out the soothing sounds of waves crashing. Still, they both stare at the water, which intermittently glistens with the silver of whitewash.

On the grass area, there's now a man throwing a tennis ball for a dog to retrieve, getting advice from all twelve onlookers how best to do it. The man, annoyed, throws the ball as far as he can to the beach. The dog follows the ball and the man follows the dog, leaving those around the barbecue needing to find another focus for their joviality.

Aphra, looking in that direction, thinks it's only a matter of time before one or all of those men saunter over to this bench. Her thoughts go to Katie, who always had men sauntering over to her.

"What do you think will happen?" she asks.

"With the case?"

"The Ford-Brackmans are untouchable."

"They are, and even if they are involved, there'll be no way of getting anything incriminating on them. They'll be clean. I think it was an ordered hit to free up the chair. Ellie's not so sure."

"Ellie?"

"Detective Everest."

"First name basis already." Aphra rubs her arms, feeling cold. "So, Katie was possibly killed by a pro. For money."

"Technically, for a chair. Plus, the killer knows how to kill a person with a pen, and knows a thing or two about poisons. And local poetry. That should narrow it down quite a bit. Very specialised. Ellie, Detective Everest, I mean, said she's going to look through the old files, for similar cases."

"Poison?"

"I know. So Shakespearean. Am I right? So theatrical."

"What kind of poison?"

"Everest knows, but she wouldn't tell me. Which I think is selfish of her, given all the deduction I did."

"What deduction? You just identified who had the most to gain from Katie's death, and made it all up from there."

"I did a bit more than that."

"Nothing that I couldn't have done myself. It could all turn out to be wrong. You have no evidence. All you have is a story."

"Yeah? Well, tomorrow I'll know what the poison is and then I'll find the person who did it. I don't need you telling me the things I do have no value."

Huntley stands up and starts walking back to Freeman Loop.

"Hey, wait." Aphra follows him.

"Oi, darling," a drunk man calls out. "If your date's not going well, you're welcome to join us."

"Hard pass," she says.

"We've got plenty of thick snaggers here. We're happy to share."

Their laughter is loud enough to startle the seagulls lurking near the barbecue.

As Aphra hurries to catch up with Huntley, she hears one of the men say, "If she's gonna dress like that, she's fucking asking for it."

"Dickheads," she says to herself.

"Don't ask me to protect you from those idiots," Huntley says, walking quickly.

"I don't need your protection." Aphra matches his pace. "Look, I didn't mean to offend you. I just like to deal with facts."

"Really? But you work in politics? You're a spin queen."

"Even so, just because something's obvious to me, doesn't mean it's obvious to everyone. Your story has value."

"Great save. You make it sound like I'm really clever for a stupid person. The one-eyed elder in the blind tribe. Maybe you should hire me to write messages for the WAR Party's lowest common denominator."

"I didn't expect you to be this sensitive. You wouldn't get anywhere in politics. Are you one of those writers who can't take any feedback at all?"

"Wrong. Everyone's free to have an opinion."

"But do you ever listen to it? Or give it credence?"

"I'm an open book."

Aphra wonders where her desire to get under his skin is coming from. "That's good, because it's not like you write any."

Huntley stops. "Just you wait," he says, then continues walking.

"If it helps at all," Aphra says, hustling after him, "you can insult me all you want. I don't care. A decade in politics has made me immune to criticism."

"And what an impressive body of work you have produced during that time. Are you the one responsible for turning Blair Blakè-Stendahl, who's really not the sharpest hook in the tacklebox, into such a great public speaker? The spokesperson of our generation?"

"You have no idea how much training she's had. I just write the speeches. Your wife is pretty impressed with her."

"Ex-wife."

"What could've been alimony cheques to you is actually money that goes into Blair's coffers."

"That's not politics. That's a trade. Giorgie wouldn't donate anything to Blair without wanting something in return. But you're wrong. Harland's the one who pays off the pollies. He has plenty to gain if his farming profits stay here. Giorgie's too busy with her galleries and charities. She doesn't care about sheep, cattle and grain. And Lydette only cares about Lydette."

They cross the railroad tracks. Aphra's glad she doesn't have to wait on the dark, vacant platform for a train.

"What about you?" she asks, hoping to make up any ground she may have lost. "What do you care about?"

At the traffic light, Huntley whacks the pedestrian button and looks towards the giant red dingo mural on the side of the flour mill, which in this light and from this angle appears dark brown. He considers Aphra's question, annoyed with how forthright she is, although he concedes that anyone trying to get ahead working in politics would need to have a personality that was at least 50 per cent bulldozer. An answer forms in his mind, but he doubts its usefulness. He wants to be honest; to say he cares about structure and order and putting the right things in the right places. But he knows from experience that this can be easily misinterpreted.

He hits the signal a few more times, trying to get the lights to change. They stay defiantly green, giving the traffic priority, even at night.

"Mr Huntley?"

"That was my father. I don't like being called that."

"What should I call you then?"

"He'd know what to say to you. He cared about sharing. A total socialist, he was. If you can be anything, he said, be generous. Give far more than you take. That's probably completely lost on a muckraker like you."

"Muckraker? Excuse me?"

"Mudslinger then. A counterpuncher. A finger pointer. A blame attributer. That's what politics in this country is all about. Blaming others and getting ahead by calling the other person out. All these debates, these question times, are just little kids throwing honky nuts at each other."

Aphra folds her arms. "Okay. I've had enough. I expected so much more of you. Your worldview is as limited and pathetic as your living space."

"Don't you insult my caravan."

"I'm insulting you."

Aphra starts walking up Stirling Highway, leaving Huntley at the traffic light. When there's a break in the traffic, she slips across the road, dress billowing around her. Someone in a white van honks at her.

Huntley, seething, watches her go to her Vespa, put on her helmet and zip away. The pedestrian walking light remains red.

The Hallucinating Nightswimmer

How far out is far enough?
Is it dawn and he's swimming towards the sun?
So much regret, a life too rough
Be not him, of weak heart, taken too soon

What's this alien-being within?
Causing this startling awakeness, this horrid dream?
Let it stop, begone foreign thing
Yet this floating, beneath stars, so pleasant, it seems

On a sunny morning, before the breeze comes in, the Indian Ocean lapping against the Perth coastline is a startlingly beautiful blue; the kind of blue that can be stared at for hours. But it's also a cunning blue, very cold, very salty, and ruinous to a dead body. The face gets all bloated and any exposed skin is nibbled on, sometimes with great chunks ripped off, revealing flesh made pale by the salt, giving it the look of cured ham. With enough time, the salt and sea-life will eat away at the whole corpse. But a relatively intact body that washes up on the beach, regardless of how many days it has been at sea, is not something anyone wants to happen upon when trying to start the day right with an early morning swim or surf.

For the unsupervised six-year-old girl poking in the shallows of the small stretch of North Trigg Beach, the body trapped on a submerged rock holds endless fascination. She uses her small plastic shovel to poke at the body, which is face-side down; poking in that initially gentle then increasingly forceful way used to rise someone who refuses to wake.

The girl's father, up on the headland, in mirror shades and a floppy hat, drinks coffee and watches the surfers bobbing around the break curling off Trigg Point. He tilts the coffee cup at his mouth almost vertically, to get the dregs, then calls, without looking in her direction, for "Emmy" to come to him. But Emmy stays where she is, now down on her haunches in the shallow water and trying to lever the body off the rock with her little shovel.

"Emmy!"

The girl briefly turns her head to look towards the headland, but as her father isn't beckoning her in any way, or even looking in her direction, she stays where she is.

Annoyed, the father, still with eyes on the surfers and smiling each time one of them wipes out, throws his coffee cup at the bin, and misses, then heads down the short laneway usually reserved for vehicles that back boat trailers down to the water. Barefoot, he keeps his eyes on the sand as he goes from the trailer path to the water's edge.

"Emmy, get out of the water. There could be stonefish in there."

It's only when he reaches her that he sees the body.

"Ugh, fuck me."

He scoops the girl up so fast she drops the shovel, which lands, and gets stuck shovel-end down, in the dead man's exposed bumcrack, making it look, from a distance, like a highly unusual murder weapon.

Even though no one had been watching the girl or had noticed the body in the small bay, the ruckus made by the father – who runs like a lifeguard, knees up high, stonefish be damned, as he carries his daughter out of the water and up the trailer path – gets everyone nearby looking. They edge towards the water and point at the body. Emmy's father wants nothing to do with it. In the car park, he drops his daughter into the passenger seat of a twin-cab utility, fires up the diesel engine and drives off.

About 200 metres away, on the grass area between the dune and the cycle path, Justin Booth peers around the side of his canvas, perched on an easel, and looks towards North Trigg. He's wearing a cap and sunglasses, but still raises a hand to shelter his eyes from the sun.

"Something's up down there," he says, recognising the curious-bystander collective that often gathers around the scene of an incident.

Booth's father, seated on a low fold-out stool, giving him the hunched pose of a man struggling on a toilet, doesn't look up from the charcoal sketch he's working on. "What's going on?"

"I don't know. But there's a crowd."

"You want to call it in?"

"Let me check it out first."

Booth's father applies some heavy strokes to his beach sketch, which is far darker than the blue-dominated watercolour idyll Justin is working on, and asks, "What are your instincts telling you?"

"Maybe a disagreement? Surfer fight? You know how territorial they are."

"I'm calling it in." Booth's father puts the sketch down, then dips his fingers in a small container of water, the way diners do when eating prawns with their hands, to wash away the charcoal.

"Okay. But call Everest first. Get her here."

"You're learning. Always respect the hierarchy. That never goes unnoticed."

"She lives nearby anyway."

Booth jogs towards North Trigg. When he gets there, the crowd has swelled, including half a dozen guys with wetsuits pulled down to their waists and boards under their arms. He pushes his way through. Two scrawny men, both in singlets and heavily tattooed, walk purposefully through the shallow water with pilfering intent.

When Booth sees it's a body that has everyone's attention, he yells, "Get out of the water. Now! Everyone stay back."

"Who the fuck are you?" one of the scrawny men asks.

"Detective Justin Booth."

"Detective? You look like a preschool teacher."

"Nah, mate," says the second man. "He looks like one of them fancy hairdressers. Gender-whatever, or something."

Booth slips out of his shoes and goes into the water, but without his ID, he keeps his distance from the two scrawny men, who seem able to handle themselves.

"You can't touch that body," he says. "Move away from it. Please. Do the right thing."

"Why should we?"

"You wouldn't want to touch that body and leave anything that might tie either of you to the crime."

"He's in the water, mate."

"Leave him there. Otherwise, I'll have to arrest you both for tampering with a crime scene."

The two men don't move. They share a look of disbelief, and laugh a little.

"Exit the water immediately," comes a crackling voice from the beach.

Booth turns to see a brawny lifeguard in a tucked-in white polo shirt holding a bullhorn authoritatively. With him are two young lifeguards in yellow long-sleeve shirts, untucked, who are using witches' hats and red-white tape to cordon off the beach, shepherding all the onlookers behind it.

"Everyone off the beach," the lifeguard says through the bullhorn. "Please clear the area. This is not a drill."

The two toughs wade out of the water, bumping shoulders with Booth on either side as they pass him.

"Young man. You, in the hat. Move away from the body and exit the water."

Booth turns. "It's okay," he shouts to the lifeguard. "I'm police."

"Show me your ID."

As Booth walks back to the beach, he sees most of the onlookers dispersing, the lifeguards exerting the kind of authority he himself couldn't.

"I'm Detective Justin Booth," he says. "I don't have my ID with me, sorry."

"I see." The lifeguard lowers the bullhorn. "More of you on the way?"

"Yeah. It's been called in already. Thanks for securing the area."

"You got pretty close. What's with the kiddie spade in his bum?"

"No idea. Looks like it got stuck there, somewhere along the way. I don't think it killed him."

The lifeguard's weathered face falls flat. "The kiddie spade to his bum didn't kill him. You must be one of Perth's best detectives."

"No need for sarcasm, mate. There's a dead body out there."

"Just offering some levity. It's probably a suicide. Like the last one here. A couple of years back."

"What happened?"

"Fella who I guess was done with life swam out with a jacket full of rocks."

"Even with that, he got washed back in?"

"He didn't get past the breakers."

Booth leans close to the lifeguard. "This happen a lot? I've never seen this before and I've been coming to Trigg for years."

"I know. You paint up on the hill with your old man."

"Do you know who he is?"

"Never spoken to him. But I like the charcoal stuff he does. Really brings out the danger of the water."

Booth is about to explain the exalted position his father holds in the WA Police, but the lifeguard cuts him off.

"It usually happens at night. Suicides, that is. People swim out when there's no one here to stop them. They don't always get washed up on shore, unless they're dumb enough to fill a jacket with rocks."

"You think this was a suicide as well?"

"Reckon it's your job, detective, to find out what happened."

Booth is really starting to dislike the lifeguard.

"Unless you're going to stick with the kiddie spade theory," the lifeguard adds.

"Yeah. Right."

"Listen, we're in completely the wrong part of town for anything remotely like a murder or a body dump. This is a family beach. People around here behave responsibly."

"What about sharks?"

The lifeguard gives Booth an annoyed look, then trudges away.

"A legitimate question," Booth says to himself, once he's alone.

A pair of jet skis passing close to the beach creates enough wash to move the body off the submerged rock, so it's floating, though the little shovel stays stubbornly in place. Booth realises he needs to get the body to the sand, to prevent it from possibly being drawn back out by the current. He goes out and gingerly uses his feet to move the body back to shore, a process made all the more difficult as he can't bring himself to look at the mangled and chewed flesh. When the body is on the damp sand and staying there, face-down, the remaining onlookers let out groans of disgust and turn their heads away.

Glancing down, Booth sees the dead man is wearing blue dress shorts and a yellow collar shirt, the kind of golf attire worn on private courses. He bends down to inspect the shorts, which are riding below a well-toned arse. From the back pocket he extracts a soggy scorecard: Lake Karrinyup Country Club. He places this on a flat section of sand to dry.

"Looks like you're on top of things," Everest says.

"Morning."

"A busy one, by the looks of it. Who's this?"

"I haven't identified the body yet. It was hard enough securing the area."

"The lifeguards told me they did that." Everest points at the shovel. "Can you explain that?"

Booth shakes his head. "But I did find that scorecard. I guess he was playing golf. Who knows when? Should we roll him over?"

"Is this your first floater?"

"I can handle it."

Unconvinced, Everest asks, "Have you had breakfast?"

"Just a coffee."

"You should be able to keep that down. Let's turn him. Pick an end."

Booth looks at the man's savaged legs and screws up his face. He goes to the torso end, but takes a few moments to psych himself up.

Everest is fine with the legs, because she knows the top half is the hardest part to stomach, especially the face. While waiting for Booth to work himself into a state of readiness, she puts on plastic gloves and removes the little shovel, placing it next to the golf scorecard. Then, together, they try to roll the body up from the water, but they only get halfway, as Booth steps back and turns away on seeing the man's bloated, chewed-on face. There's just enough momentum for Everest to finish the job, and the body flops onto the sand with a sickening sloshing sound.

"Oh, yuck," Booth says, pacing a few metres from the body, unable to look. "What was that?"

"Water. The human body becomes a massive sponge in situations like this. Water gets into every possible orifice."

"That's disgusting." Booth sneaks a look, seeing that the man's eyes have been just about pushed out of his skull. "It's like he's been pumped up with it."

"That's an accurate assessment." Everest bends down to inspect the body. "If you need a minute, take it."

"I'm good, I'm good," Booth says, stomach convulsing a little. "How can we identify him when he looks like this?"

Everest taps at the man's pockets, glad the shorts haven't ridden so far down on this side as to expose his manhood. "Hopefully, he'll help us. Saving that, dental records."

"Anything on him?" Booth decides to concentrate on the golf scorecard, keeping his back to the corpse. "There's no name on this. I guess the ink washed away."

"No wallet." Everest extracts a set of keys from the front shorts pocket. On it is a black key fob. "But there's a car nearby."

"Nearby? It could be anywhere. It looks like he's been in the water for weeks."

"No. He's fresh."

"He could've floated up here from any point along the coast. Or he was dumped from a boat."

"He's only been out there for a few hours," Everest says. "If you think this is bad, you don't want to know what a body looks like when it's been out there for days or weeks."

"Have you seen a body like that?"

Everest, holding the keys, stands up and stares at the man. "What's this guy's story?"

"The lifeguard, who I have to say is a pretty unpleasant fella, thinks it was suicide."

"Surely his golf day wasn't that bad. Usually, it's the clubs that get chucked in the water."

"How are we going to find the car?"

Everest holds up the key fob, looks at Booth and presses the UNLOCK button. Something beeps up on the hill in the carpark. "Well, what do you know? The car's nearby."

"I can't believe it." Booth is only too happy to turn away from the body and look towards the carpark. "How did you know that? It's almost too easy."

"Stay here and keep an eye on him while I check out the car."

"I think I should help you with it."

"It's better you look at him some more. Get desensitised to it. There'll be plenty more floaters down the road."

Everest goes up the path to the carpark. She stands in the middle and beeps the fob again. The lights on an upmarket white SUV flash. It's carelessly parked, diagonally, taking up three spaces. There are several notes under the windscreen wipers. Everest has a quick read. In colourful language, they describe what the locals think of the driver's parking skills. All the notes get shoved into her pants pocket. She opens the driver-side door and looks in the car. There's no wallet or phone, which makes her wonder if the man was robbed, outside the vehicle, perhaps at the beach's public toilets; held up by a junkie who panicked, did something stupid and tried to get rid of the body the quickest way possible, by hauling it out into the water. The problem with that theory being that the body appeared to have no fatal-looking wounds. An enterprising junkie could have drowned the man, but it seems unlikely.

Everest takes a moment to think of Huntley and his concept that detective work is a form of storytelling. She's standing here, looking in the dead man's vehicle, but no stories are jumping out at her.

She climbs in and sits in the driver's seat. The glove box is empty, as are the other compartments, which she finds strange. It makes her wonder if the car is a rental, or recently bought, because a vehicle is normally an extension of the owner's life; personal detritus gets into all the various nooks and storage spaces. On the back seat is a briefcase, which looks as new as the car. She turns and leans between the front seats. Inside the briefcase is a pile of brochures for some development called the "Southern Everglades". On the front cover is a digital rendering of an idyllic new sub-division, with modern houses, green lawns and happy residents. On the back is a photo of the project lead, smiling and handsome, with the same sandy-coloured hair and physical dimensions as the man on the beach. On the bottom is the man's name and contact details: for Lance Ford-Brackman.

<>

Following a restless night during which he dreamed of all the different people who could have killed the Ukrainian violinist and conjured up various backstories of traumatic childhoods and high school bullying, Huntley is up early. He needs something to do, to divert his creative thoughts while also giving him a chance to put other thoughts in order. So, with his car still at the uni, he starts walking to Fremantle, weaving between the vehicles on Stirling Highway, and taking the back way down to Pearse Street. Once known as Pong Alley, for its decrepitude and smell, Pearse these days is gentrified and affluent, lined with residences that are heritage listed, every second one sublimely renovated and housing some kind of artist's studio or trendy workspace. The verandas are lush with plant life, hanging and potted, while trees on both sides of the street supply ample shade. Though he doesn't see any people, he gets the sense of a tight-knit and cliquey local community, breaking into which would be nigh on impossible.

Pearse Street is where Quintus Huntley has always wanted to live, tracking back to when he was a 19-year-old upstart from the country, cycling this way every day to UWA from his shared flat in East Fremantle. Later, he pushed Giorgie, when she was pregnant with Verity, to escape the Gifford estate and move to Pearse, but she wanted none of it. Now, he sees no For Sale signs, and every house looks deeply occupied, by residents who have been here for decades and who will likely die here. It doesn't matter; there's no way he could afford a place in this enclave, and it makes him wonder how the artists here do.

Inherited, he thinks to himself. Old money.

He pictures his Landy and caravan parked at the corner of Jackson and Pearse, close to the train line, but concedes setting up his mobile home so close to a playground would give the locals the wrong idea about him.

He finds it interesting that Pearse Street now feels exclusive and pretentious. With so much murder on his mind, and with an overwhelming determination to solve the case, aspiring towards living in an overpriced colonial three-and-one to be neighbours with a bunch of failed artists subsidised by old money seems like a very low goal indeed.

He quickens his pace.

Crossing Tydeman Road, busy with trucks carrying shipping containers down to the port, he starts to sweat a little. The sun is already high and hot. There's no cover as he ambles down the bicycle path to the Railway Bridge. The handful of cyclists who come from the opposite direction, pedalling into the morning easterly, look like they're not enjoying themselves at all.

On the bridge, his brain works through the blurry transcript of last night's conversation with Aphra Massey. He can't remember a lot of what was said, but she was unpleasant to him, and he was unpleasant back, and in the warm light of morning, he regrets it. Because Aphra was surely dealing with her friend's death, her murder, and took her feelings out on him. He chastises himself for not having been more empathetic. Yet one comment he does remember, about his "limited worldview", is really eating at his insides, and he can't dismiss it as a mere tit-for-tat insult. He'd like another chance to talk with her, to prove that he thinks in much broader strokes.

Also rankling is that thing she said about him putting his skills to better use, and how he'd failed to do so. While he harbours zero ambition to work in politics or business, he certainly believes he's wasting away at the university, dying a slow death in that miserable container Miguel values so much. He wonders now if detective work was the right creative outlet all along. It only took a little bit of snooping yesterday to break him gloriously out of his writing funk and ignite the spark for a narrative ode to Ekaterina, which in turn provided several investigative leads for Everest to pursue. So, he shoves the conversation with Aphra aside and focuses on what next to look into regarding this murder.

"The poison," he says.

There's a spring in his step as he passes over the glistening Swan River. He spots a dolphin circling one of the pylons of the train bridge, hunting for breakfast. The Perth-bound three-wagon train rumbles over, completely empty.

On the Fremantle side, the giant black octopus painted on the old Naval Store Building looks him in the eye and gets him thinking of inks. And poisons. Creatures squirting in defence or attack? He hopes Henrikson has the toxicology report, which will enable him to follow a trail of poisonous breadcrumbs potentially to the next poem.

He feels ridiculously alive this morning.

The last time he approached a new day with such drive and hunger was during that incredible time in Ravensthorpe, when delving deep into the Gurney-Edwards feud surfaced so many ghosts; using his nights to write poetry while the whole commune slept and he could hear the dingoes howling. What was then primary writing research for the *Ragged Claws* he now repositions as his first foray into detective work.

As he passes a bus stop, the woman waiting there, wearing a floral-print dress, returns his thoughts to Aphra. He's not sure what to make of her. Sellout or smart-arse? Confident or compensating? Talented in many ways, no doubt about that, but her character and personality were not what he expected. He blames himself, again, for lacking the required empathy in the moment. Still, he didn't think the capitalist, elitist and quietly racist WA Republic Party was something she should hitch her wagon to, unless her politics leaned that way, and he doubted that was the case. Which would mean she's in it for the money, and so she should be, as earning 20 cents a book will never keep the power on or fill the fridge on a week-to-week basis. And that makes him decide he should admire her, for how she elevated herself above a traumatic teenage experience, then rejected the poetry and publishing scene in order to carve out a career writing the kind of communications that people actually pay attention to.

A blue car comes soundlessly to a halt next to him. The passenger window is lowered.

"Quintus?"

Huntley bends down to look through the window. "Henrikson? What are you doing still driving?"

"Careful. I won't give you a lift with that attitude."

"Sorry. I take it all back. I'm cooking out here."

"Hop in."

Huntley does so, sighing with relief. It's very cool in the car. The passenger window slides back up.

"I assume you're on the way to the store, though I don't see you carrying any rum."

"Ah. I decided against it. I'm trying to stop the day drinking."

"Probably a good idea." Henrikson checks the mirrors, then pulls onto the road. "You're a fool to walk on a morning like this. You don't even have a hat on."

"I wasn't really thinking straight. Slept badly. I just started walking, to get my thoughts in order."

The car makes almost no noise as it moves along, making it seem like it's levitating.

"Nice wheels, mate. An electric?"

"Everyone should be driving one," Henrikson says.

"I can actually hear the cars around us, but not this one."

"And I can hear you, without having to crank my hearing aids up full blast. You put me in a louder car and I've got no chance. But in here, I can talk to my grandkids when I drop them at school."

"Come on, mate. Admit it. You're a tech head, from what I've gathered so far. You like having that latest whiz-bang thing. This is your little spaceship."

Henrikson smiles.

Closer to the centre of Fremantle, the traffic slows to a crawl.

"Any joy with the report?" Huntley asks.

"It was easy. Disappointingly easy. I was hoping to have a tough nut to crack."

"How on earth is hacking into police records easy? That should be the hardest thing to do."

"Not even close. It's best to think of the WA Police as a company, not a service. Like any company, it's very much focused on bottom lines."

"Really? But it's the police."

"It's the basic earn more, spend less approach. They try to earn revenue through fines, and try to save money by outsourcing work to independent contractors. This cuts internal costs by not having those overheads. In this case, the lab work was done by a student research group in Northbridge.

They store everything in a cloud, and that cloud isn't very secure. Once the report was there, it was ripe for the taking."

"Henrikson, you are the most impressive person I've met in a long time."

"Thank you, Quin. That makes me think I'm getting better with age."

"Hope so. Because that means I've met you at just the right time."

Henrikson laughs a little. "I confess I wasn't the nicest man when I was teaching. It's a demanding job."

"I bet. And? What did the report reveal? What poison was it?"

"You sound sure that it was poison."

"Detective Everest confirmed it, last night. Right before we had an almighty jam in a rehearsal theatre at Scotch, then got kicked out by security."

"Busy evening. What does she play?"

"The drums. Like a freaking rock star. She was in a band, Salty Lemonade, a couple of decades back."

"I remember them. Some kids used to wear the t-shirts to school, on non-uniform days."

"She wouldn't reveal the name of the poison," Huntley says. "That really bothered me. After all the help I gave her."

"Did you write any more poetry? I have to say, it was fascinating yesterday, watching you work."

"The river has momentarily run dry. The poison will get things flowing again. I'm sure of it."

"Slow down. You're not getting that for free."

Henrikson parks in front of the bookstore, in a space reserved for electric vehicles.

"What do you want in exchange?"

"I like to keep things balanced. It's something I've learned in my old age. I had the bad habit when I was younger of doing lots of things for people, and then they just took advantage of me."

"Fair enough. You've given me a lift this morning. So, I owe you for two things."

"Three, because I didn't turn you in yesterday."

"Bloody hell. All right. Hit me."

Henrikson presses the "Power" button, switching the car off. "I revisited your book last night."

"Yeah?"

"It reads differently, now that I've met you."

"How so?"

"I don't have any criticisms, if that's what you're expecting. I'm more interested in the way it all came together, based on how you're now writing about Ekaterina. Because if I give you this report, which I obtained illegally, that puts us in cahoots. I need to be able to trust you."

"You can trust me, Henrikson. All you're doing is giving me the name of a poison. You just have to say its name."

"I will. But there's something I need to know. In your book, the narrator is a witness to all the violence, but there are also plenty of hints that the narrator is complicit in what happens. He's not just a bystander. He's involved, encouraging the violence to continue, working both families to ensure it escalates."

"So?"

"I read interviews where you said the book was narrative non-fiction, written as poetry. The narrator-as-witness was a structural device you used to bring the reader deeper inside the story."

"Not exactly groundbreaking, but pretty good for a kid who had no idea what he was doing."

"On further investigation, I learned those families have been fighting for over a hundred years, on and off. Killing each other's sheep, poisoning crops, and other stuff. But there was a long gap when nothing happened. There was peace. That changed with your book."

"What are you getting at, Henrikson?"

"I think the narrator restarted the feud."

"That's a big leap."

"Am I right?"

Huntley stares straight ahead, unprepared for this line of questioning, having thought his morning would involve a poison hunt and nothing else. Next to the bookstore, a café is opening for the day. Outdoor tables are being set up, and three women pushing prams, looking like they've come from an early yoga class, are waiting to take the best table. As they sit down, the prams get positioned at arm's length and cut off the footpath.

One mother opens an umbrella that's attached to the pram, slanting it for added baby shade, rendering the footpath unpassable.

When Huntley doesn't reply, Henrikson adds, "The narrator is you."

"This is a bit like asking a magician to reveal his tricks."

"I'm doing this to establish trust. And trust is the nucleus of friendship."

Huntley grunts with annoyance. "Sounds like you're in the insurance business. You want something to hold over me. Did you do this when you were a teacher? To keep the kids in line?"

"To understand that you get nothing for free is a lesson everyone should learn, I'd say. I wish I'd learned it sooner. You have no idea how often children, and adults for that matter, expect to get something for nothing."

"Oh, I do. My daughter is the crown princess of manipulation. I'm pretty sure her first word was 'gimme'. But maybe that was because she heard it so much from the people around her."

"You're dodging the question, Quin. Are you ashamed of what you did?"

"I was just there when it happened. Look, I'll be honest with you."

"I expect no less."

"Right. You need to know there's some stuff here that's going with me to my grave." Huntley takes a deep breath and lets it out. "My father, I guess you could say, inadvertently, got the feud going again. It wasn't his intention. You see, I grew up on a commune outside of Ravensthorpe. It was a patch of land that once upon a time was Gurney land. Dad won it in a boxing match against Nodge Gurney. Bare-knuckled, last man standing, really primitive stuff. This was back in the 70s, when Dad was all into free love and free agency, but he could definitely handle himself. He wasn't some wimpish hippy. This land, the Gurneys didn't want it, as it had salinised years before, as part of the feud, though none of the Edwards clan had ever admitted as much."

"I love this, Quin. Family histories are so fascinating."

"It gets better. Dad knew people from the CSIRO, from his time working in Antarctica. He brought some of those scientists down from Perth to test the soil. Sure enough, they helped revitalise the land. It took a few years, but soon that land was fertile again and growing crops. The commune became just about self-sufficient, which brought more people to it. The years went by and the commune did well. As you can imagine, this really pissed off Nodge, who by then was already on the way to becoming a senile old geezer with one foot in a whole other reality, probably from one too many bare-knuckled knockouts. He tried to get the land back, but the mayor then was Mart Edwards and he'd hang himself from a tree before he'd cut the Gurneys a break on anything. This slowly fuelled a disagreement between Nodge and Mart, and the rest of them, and Dad saw an opportunity."

"What did he do?"

"In great Aussie tradition, he stole a sheep. But not just any sheep. He stole a ram lamb from the Edwards farm. He did this because, so the legend goes, that's how the feud started, way back when. The early settler Gurneys needed a ram and couldn't afford one, so they took a ram lamb from the Edwards clan."

Henrikson smiles broadly. "That's brilliant. Your father did this to get Nodge off his back about the land he'd won fair and square. But he actually set the families against each other again."

"It took a while to get going. Small stuff, at the beginning. A lot of name-calling. A few fights in the pub. Then vandalism, knives in tyres and animal shit thrown at front doors. Mart's beloved sheepdog was fed poison. Then old Nodge was found dead out in Hatter Hill, which is miles from town. It was never made clear if it was murder, because he was alone out there and not really with it in the head, plus way up there in age. But the Gurneys were convinced some Edwards family member did it. Things really picked up from there. I just happened to be visiting, at the time."

"The narrator is your father then?"

"Yes and no. It's a device. A composite. That's all I'm saying, Henrikson."

"Well, thank you. For telling me all of that. Sounds like you could write a family history of your own."

"Mate, I got nothing to do with those families. I want to stay far away from them."

"Because you immortalised them in print. They must hate you for that."

"Fortunately, not many of them read poetry. But those that did read the book said I should've changed the names and all that. Protected the innocent, but none of them are innocent. I felt like a reporter, documenting this news as poetry rather than in articles. There was no embellishing or misuse of facts. There's nothing that can truly be denied. It all happened. Which is why they could be angry about it, but they couldn't dispute it. The only thing they don't know is my father's role in it all. He took it to the grave. I will too. And, Henrikson, you'll now do the same."

"Not any time soon. I'm planning to live as long as I can. Man nappies and all."

"Good."

"Your secret's safe with me."

"Also good." Huntley lets out a long sigh. "I've never told anyone that before. It feels nice to shed it. I haven't even thought about it in years. Yesterday's events really woke me up."

"What happened to the ram lamb?"

"Funny you should ask that. We couldn't keep it. This living evidence. Dad sold it to some farmer up north and used the money to buy a new caravan."

"Out of all that, your family came out on top."

"A rare victory for hippies. I'm glad I told you this. I'm also glad I knocked on your door yesterday."

"So am I." Henrikson takes out one of his phones. "So. Here we go. Wild arum."

"What?"

"That's the poison. Arum maculatum, commonly known as wild arum. High concentration, injected in the bloodstream via the fountain pen, causing asphyxiation."

"Oh my fucking God. That's tremendous. Wild arum? Please tell me there's an amazing story behind this stuff. Like, it's something witches used to use. Or someone killed a pope with it 2,000 years ago."

"It's a plant," Henrikson says, looking at his phone. "I haven't checked its nefarious historical uses. But I do know it's not common in this part of the world. Which means whoever used it most likely grows it for themselves. That should narrow things down considerably."

"A green thumb assassin. I love it. Where do I start?"

"I did some research already. There's a naturopath in Vic Park who's using wild arum to treat haemorrhoids."

"Fighting fire with fire, so to speak."

"Yes, indeed. Here's the address."

Huntley takes the small piece of paper Henrikson hands him. "Sensational. You're a legend. I'll go there right now. Can I borrow your car?"

"Absolutely not."

"I left mine at uni yesterday."

"You better go get it. Imagine what you'd need to divulge in order for me to let you use this car. It would have to be huge. Bigger than what you just offered."

Huntley laughs. "Don't you start a feud with me, Henrikson."

"Never." Henrikson, smiling, thumbs behind him. "There's a bus stop at the end of the street. Good luck. Let me know how you get on."

Huntley opens the door and climbs out of the car, the heat hitting him like a slap in the face.

<>

The taxi gets stuck on the two-lane bridge leading up to the Stirling Highway-Canning Highway intersection. Sitting in the back seat, Aphra Massey looks out the window; every face she sees has the knitted eyebrows of annoyance. That's not interesting, though. What is interesting is that the drivers appear surprised, as if they hadn't planned for this jam and it's come out of nowhere. Which is ridiculous, because traffic often bottlenecks here. It reminds her that she needs to raise the issue of infrastructure to Blair, when there is a free moment, because Perth's road network desperately needs improving. The highways, arteries and routes people use, such as this antiquated intersection that links the main roads of the southwest and southeast sides of the river, were all built for a population a quarter of the size of what Perth is now. The only modernisation in recent years has involved the freeways, which everyone uses and which make the city look, Aphra thinks, way too much like Los Angeles.

She turns her focus back to her laptop screen, using this lull in movement to work some more on Blair's morning speech and avoid any small talk with the driver, who keeps eying her in the rearview mirror. Blair's heavily amended document, sent just after midnight, requires patience to go through. This is, without doubt, the hardest and most frustrating part of her job: trying to balance what needs to be said and the best way of saying it with Blair's penchant for woefully bad rewrites and inane comments. At times, trying to decipher a "tracked changes" document from Blair, which has also been shared with members of her close circle who supply their own woefully bad rewrites and inane comments, is like trying to translate it from some made-up dialect – of crossing outs, highlights, boxes and coloured fonts – back into proper English. She learned early on that Blair's changes take precedence over all others, but has also earned enough respect and trust over the years to have the scope to improve those changes.

This delicate operation is not made easier with a deadline, meaning Aphra's glad the traffic jam is buying her some extra time.

"Sorry about the hold-up, love," the driver says.

The syrupy way he inflects "love" makes her want to get out of the taxi right there, but they're still on Stirling Bridge, hemmed in on all sides.

Eyes on the screen, and typing, she says, "I wouldn't expect anything less here at this time of day. Love."

Saying that last word, separately and with distaste, seems to have the desired effect of putting the man in his place. But whether he understands how stupid and disrespectful he sounded when he used it himself is hard to tell. Aphra raises her eyes enough to see him shift in the seat, perhaps running through in his head the various complaints he'd like to make about "bloody feminists" and "not being able to say something nice" which he wisely keeps to himself. The traffic suddenly starts moving, and he pushes hard for the green light at Canning Highway only to get there on orange and trigger the red-light camera as he goes across.

"Fuck," he says in a way that suggests Aphra's to blame.

Over Canning, the next bottleneck is Leach Highway. Aphra starts to worry she won't get to Beeliar on time for the 9am meeting. But even if arriving late, she still needs to get this speech done and send it to Blair before the meeting starts.

It's difficult. One sentence has "beneficial" inserted three times, coupled with a comment, from Blair, to avoid repetitions. The bingo sheets from yesterday help, to ensure all the right phrasings and compound nouns are included. She sifts through the added fluff, removing the worst of it, then hammers home the central "localisation" theme: creating homes for hard-working local families, work for local companies and jobs for local people, which is the kind of repetition she knows Blair likes.

Once it's done and sent, she looks up, but has lost track of where they are.

"Are we almost there?"

"About another five," the driver says, his voice trailing off a little, as if he was about to add "love" or "sweetheart", and thought better of it.

"Would you be kind enough to hurry up, please? I'm running late."

The driver nods, then says under his breath, "Typical. She's nice when she wants something."

Her response forms quickly, and it's spicy, something she's delivered a few times before to men of similar ilk. But she holds it back. Normally, this is the kind of educational exchange she throws herself into, because she enjoys the challenge of trying to change a person, especially a man stuck in his ways. She wants to change the driver, during the few minutes they have left together, so he won't use "love" anymore, and he might evolve to be more respectful of women, and stop leering at them through the rearview mirror, and stop thinking them bitchy just because they stand up for themselves.

But she's not in the mood today. She's grieving, quietly, and this guy just isn't worth it. Something in her bones tells her that Katie's murder might have had a gender roles subplot. Did she rub some insecure guy the wrong way?

When the taxi turns onto Beeliar Drive, Aphra asks, "Do you know that women in this state, on average, live five years longer than men?"

"Uh, no. That right?"

"It's a lot. Five years. Don't you think?"

He doesn't reply, but shifts again in the seat. He has one of those beaded covers on his seat, hooked over the headrest, and the beads make a bone-cracking sound when he moves.

"I wonder why that is," Aphra adds, hoping to provoke a response.

"Well, you know," he says, eyes darting to the rearview mirror, then back to the road, "men, they, kind of, work pretty hard. It takes a toll. Over the years."

"It does. But women work equally hard, often doing a job and taking care of the house and raising children."

"True. My mum raised three kids on her own. And she worked."

"How old is she, may I ask?"

"Going strong at 71. Still working too. Part-time. And volunteering." The driver points at the turn-off. "Down here?"

"Yes. The Grange. Then left down at Leseur Pass."

"It's all forest down there. Isn't it? What brings you out here? It doesn't look safe, for a pretty thing like you."

Aphra blinks, amazed this idiot just can't help himself.

"Work," she says, gathering her things together. "You can drop me here. I'll walk the rest of the way."

"Settle, petal. We're almost there."

But when the taxi turns down Leseur Pass, it can't go any further, as there are black vehicles parked down both sides of the road.

"The Premier doing something here?" the driver asks.

Aphra pays. "Can I have a receipt, please?"

The driver complies, handing the slip of paper backwards without turning in the seat.

"Thank you." Aphra opens the door. "Live long and treat all women like you would treat your mother."

Once she's out, the taxi does a U-turn and is gone. Aphra shoulders her bag and weaves between the parked cars to the forest side of the street. She follows a dirt road to a clearing, which looks freshly created, to where a small container office has been set up. There's no one outside, but she can hear the hum of conversation coming from inside. She opens the door to find it very crowded with people chatting animatedly, and blessedly air-conditioned. No one notices her arrival. She grabs a bottle of water from the catering trolley and drinks from it liberally, trying to wash away the distaste of the taxi ride, though hoping her last comment to the driver will give him pause for thought.

More composed, she starts nodding at the various members of the WA Republic Party who have now spotted her. Blair, exhibiting the fidgety movements of someone just holding it together, makes a beeline for Aphra, who readies herself for a biting critique of the speech sent barely 15 minutes ago.

"Thanks for the revisions, A. Last minute, but a great job."

Aphra, relieved, says, "I'm glad you like it, Blair."

"I'd definitely prefer to take another run at it myself, but there isn't the time."

"Everything you need to say is in there. Trust it."

"Which means you're saying I should trust you, but this is a tough room."

"There's plenty of support for you in here."

Blair shakes hands with two plump middle-aged men who pass between them. "Did you just arrive?"

"Stuck in traffic."

"I know. A nightmare this morning."

"Every morning. We need to talk about that."

"What?"

"Perth's infrastructure. This is an important topic. It could be a big win for you and the party, if you have the solution."

"Oh, I agree. Roads matter. Let's workshop it back at HQ. Did you see Lance outside?"

"Isn't he here?"

"No one's seen him. He's not answering his phone. This all hinges on him being here. This is his baby. We can't start without him."

"He'll be here. Try to stay focused on what you're here to do."

"Yes. You're right. I need to focus on me."

The container door is opened. Aphra and Blair turn, both hoping to see Lance. Everest steps purposefully inside, followed by Booth.

"Okay," Everest says, surveying the room, as everyone falls silent and looks at her. "This I didn't expect."

"Who are you?" Blair asks.

"We met yesterday," Booth says enthusiastically. "I'm Detective Booth. This is Detective Everest."

Blair leans towards Aphra, but keeps her eyes on the detectives. "Are these the two people who interrupted me when I was in full flow?"

"Yes." Aphra tries to sound sincere as she adds, "When you were smacking aces."

Blair asks the detectives, "Do you know how many people I see each day? I can't possibly be expected to remember them all, even when they expect to be remembered."

Sensing Blair's tongue is a little too loose this morning, a sign she didn't sleep enough, Aphra decides to take control. "Let me handle this, Blair."

"We're not here to talk to you, Ms Massey," Everest says. "We didn't know this gathering was taking place."

"Why are you here?"

Everest looks around the office. "Is there anyone here from the Ford-Brackman family?"

"There should be," Blair says. "Lance. But he's late."

"I don't think he's coming." Booth helps himself to a coffee from the catering trolley. "No point waiting for him."

"Why the hell not? I blocked my whole morning for this."

"Blair," Aphra says calmly, "let's not lose perspective. Something must've happened. Something major enough to warrant the presence of these detectives."

After a deep breath, Blair nods. "You're right. Thanks, A. I'm so glad you're on my side. If only you weren't an apple-islander. You'd be my second-in-command otherwise. Could you take these two outside and find out what's going on? I need to make some contingency plans if Lance isn't going to show."

Aphra grabs her bag and gestures for the detectives to follow her. Booth lingers, sipping coffee while standing next to Blair, and smiling at her. Everest makes a slight beckoning move with her hand, to get him moving.

"Excuse me," he says to Blair, trying to give her a charming grin.

Outside, Aphra walks to the shade of a tree, where she's joined by the two detectives.

"Forgive our esteemed party leader," she says, "and her less than politically correct language. She's a little cranky today."

"Don't apologise for her," Everest says. "Not with that Tasmania comment she made. She was just about to call you inbred."

"It's playful banter. She's flustered, and she's definitely said worse things than that. When she's like this, all pent up and stressed, she just unloads it on whoever's nearest. We're trying to work on that. To improve her filter."

"There's no need for name-calling and insults in the workplace."

"There isn't. But this is politics, and it's not a normal workplace. Politicians wouldn't have much to say if they couldn't vent their spleens or hurl insults."

Everest looks towards the vacant billboard, positioned next to the office. It's a blank canvas waiting for a pictorial announcement of the coming sub-division, likely with the same imagery from the brochure.

"This looks to me more like real estate than politics," she says.

"In Perth, those two go hand in hand."

"They do. What's Lance Ford-Brackman's involvement in this Southern Everglades project?"

This takes Aphra by surprise. "How do you even know about it? This is highly confidential. Everyone in that office has signed an NDA."

"NDA?" Booth asks.

"Non-disclosure agreement," Everest explains.

Aphra laughs a little.

Booth is about to reply, but Everest holds up a hand to stop him. "I found a brochure in his vehicle," she says. "For this project."

"That must be hot off the press. For investors only."

"So it seems."

"What were you doing in his car?"

"We believe Lance Ford-Brackman washed up at North Trigg this morning," Booth says, trying to reassert himself. "Though I'm still waiting for confirmation on the body."

"Are you not sure it's a body?" Aphra asks.

"Well, it was seriously messed up. That came out wrong. We're waiting for a relative to ID the body as Lance Ford-Brackman."

"He's dead? That's awful."

"We're here doing background on him," Everest says. "This was the address on the brochure."

"How did he die?"

"He drowned," Booth says.

Everest wants to clip Booth over the head. "That's the initial conclusion, but we're investigating all angles. How are you involved in this project?"

"I'm not. Blair is, to assist with government approval. I wrote Blair's speech for today's meeting."

"On?"

"I can't tell you that. None of this is for public consumption, just yet."

Everest looks around. "You can't build here. This is protected land."

"Like that ever stopped anyone in this state. The whole metropolitan area is built on protected land."

"Perth does have a serious housing shortage," Booth says.

Everest shakes her head. "No, it doesn't. People just want big houses and big backyards. Anyway, these wetlands are off-limits. There's a court order in place."

"For now," Aphra says. "Why do you think Blair's here? That order's nothing that can't be removed, with a bit of leverage. Of course, a change of government would fully pave the way for the development."

"And wipe out all these trees in the process. How can you support this?"

"At what point have I given you my opinion?"

"You're the one writing the speeches."

"I'm a freelancer, doing the jobs I'm tasked with. Anyway, whether I agree with this or not won't stop it from happening. You just need to look at history. Like I said, Perth has been built on stolen land, and this development, and others like it, is merely a continuation of that tradition."

"Oh, not that old line," Booth says. "I can't hear that anymore. How can you be in the WA Republic Party, yet believe the country was invaded?"

"I'm not giving you opinions or beliefs. I'm giving you facts. And I'm not a member of the party."

"Why not?"

"I prefer to stay objective. I look at history with the same objectivity. People came here in boats and took over from those already here. That's an invasion. How else do you want to explain it?"

"They were settlers. They built this city when there was nothing."

Everest steps between Booth and Aphra. "This is getting us nowhere."

"I agree," Aphra says. "It seems your partner is a detective who isn't interested in facts. Now, what happened to Lance? We've danced around this long enough. It can't be a coincidence that twice in as many days a murder has some connection to the Ford-Brackmans."

"Twice?" Booth asks. "What was the first one?"

Aphra rolls her eyes. "My friend Katie, who has already been replaced in the PSO by Marcus Ford-Brackman."

Booth points at Aphra. "How do you know that?" Then, he points at Everest. "Do you know that?"

Everest, ignoring him, gives Aphra a curious glance. "Did you speak with Leiland Taverton?"

"No."

"So, how do you know?"

"Quintus Huntley told me."

Everest shakes her head a little. "That meddling idiot. You said yesterday you didn't know him. Sounds like you're actually quite close."

"We're not. I met him for the first time last night."

"How?"

"I went looking for him. Because of the book."

"He's a suspect," Booth says. "That was a really risky thing to do."

"I'm glad I did it. Seems to me that Huntley's made more progress with the case than you two." Aphra gestures at Booth. "You didn't even know about the Ford-Brackman connection."

"I only found out last night," Everest says. "How did you know Huntley was doing investigating of his own?"

"I didn't. But it wasn't a huge surprise. His book, the one you found in the violin case, is essentially investigative journalism, done as poetry. With Katie, he's clearly got the whiff of another story, one he hopes might spark a literary comeback, and help prove his innocence."

Everest smiles thinly. "That's good, but it's not it. You had other reasons."

Aphra and Everest stare at each other.

"Well, aren't you clever? Much more clever than your rookie partner who's learning it all on the job."

Booth puts his hands on his hips, a movement that lifts his shirt to show his sidearm. "Hey, wait just a minute."

"In this line of work," Everest says, "you get lied to a lot. After a while, you start to see that people are pretty similar. They do certain things when they're withholding the truth."

"What do you think I'm withholding?"

"The only connection between you, your friend and Huntley is the book. A book which you said Ms Valoskiya put there to keep her violin from bumping around. That's not true, is it?"

"It isn't?" Booth asks.

Aphra is impressed with Detective Everest. "No, it isn't true."

"It's just a book?" Booth's cheeks turn pink with annoyance and embarrassment. "Why lie about that?"

"It made me think Huntley was involved. If I could confront him about it, then maybe I could figure out his role in Katie's murder."

"What did he say?" Everest asks.

"He thinks his book was put there on purpose."

"To frame him?"

"We're way off course here," Booth says. "It's Lance Ford-Brackman we're concerned with right now."

"You said he drowned." Aphra would like to finish this conversation and get back inside the cool container.

"The lifeguards think it was suicide."

"What do you think? You turned really pale just then. Is the body in a bad condition? Is that why you can't identify him?"

"I found the body," Booth says, sounding both disgusted and proud of himself. "I was down the beach this morning."

"Painting," Everest adds.

When Aphra raises her eyebrows, Booth says, "It's something I do with my dad. As bonding, and for mindfulness. To get our minds off police work. We meet at Trigg in the mornings, when it's not too windy."

"Our? Oh, right. Booth. It all makes so much sense now."

"It's not what you think."

"I'm not thinking anything, except that I'm surprised the penny didn't drop on this sooner."

Everest wants to move the topic away from Booth. "You don't seem to believe it was suicide, Ms Massey."

"No."

"Explain."

"You know about the project now, so I can refer to it. Why would someone on the verge of making a huge amount of money with this development suddenly decide that life wasn't worth living? The profit predictions are off the charts. Not to mention Lance coming from a very rich and powerful family. And Lance being the kind of guy, as far as I could tell, who loves money and all the great things it buys, which I fully respect. Topping himself seems very unlikely."

"Perhaps." Everest can't decide if she likes Aphra Massey or not. She wonders what Huntley's take on her is. "What's the start date for the development?"

"Well, you didn't need much convincing. The start's confidential, and pending some backroom deals to get the necessary approvals. If you're thinking the Southern Everglades project could be a motive, you're way wrong. All the people who know about it have vested interests in it. So, whatever foul play is involved, it's coming from somewhere else. God. Foul play. Sounds so old-fashioned. I guess it fits, given Katie was poisoned."

"Ah, Huntley again?"

"A tongue looser than Booth junior here."

"There's no need to be nasty," Booth says.

"Nasty? This is me being nice. You don't want to see me nasty. You'll certainly want to hide behind your daddy then."

"Now, just a …"

"Booth," Everest says. "Take a breath."

"This is my case. I found the body."

"Which you couldn't even look at."

All three of them turn towards the office as the door is opened and the attendees, tired of waiting and with other appointments to keep, pour out, making beelines for their black cars, where drivers get out to open the rear doors.

"What's going on?" Booth asks.

"I think word reached someone in there that Lance is dead," Aphra says, "and that someone told everyone else. Blair most probably."

"Do you think the project will die with him?"

"That's poetically put. Do you spend the windy mornings inside, writing poetry with your esteemed father? Even if Lance isn't here to make this money, you can be absolutely sure someone else will step in to take his place. Probably another Ford-Brackman."

When Blair exits the container, Aphra hustles to catch up with her. "That's my ride. If you need us, we'll be at the office."

"I think someone got up on the wrong side of the bed this morning," Booth says to Everest. "Can you believe her? So rude."

"Yeah, shame on her for being smart and speaking her mind."

"Sharing an opinion is not the same as being insulting."

"Maybe you should invite her to Trigg for some therapy painting sessions."

"It's dealing with people like her that makes me need those sessions. To get me centred again."

"She throw you off balance?"

"Please. It'll take more than that." Booth looks at the bushland. "Can you believe they're going to build here?"

"Why not? She's right. All that it requires is the right people wanting to do it."

"Might be worth investing in. I should ask Dad about it."

Everest, shaking her head, walks out of the shade and joins the others trudging towards the road.

<>

Two bus rides and a long walk later, he reaches the crowded university carpark, sweating, and goes towards the Landy. Sitting on the bonnet is Verity, the heels of her bulky black school-issue shoes clacking rhythmically against the grille. He's happy to see her, though she presents an unexpected problem to solve, which is annoying. Even more annoying are the two parking tickets lodged under the driver's side windscreen wiper.

"Where have you been, Dad?" she asks. "I called you, like, a hundred times."

"Hello to you too. How are you?"

"Bored. I've been waiting here for hours."

"Why aren't you at school?"

"Why don't you answer your phone?"

Huntley taps his pockets. "I left it at home."

"What home? You live in a glorified dog house on wheels."

"Hey, that's my caravan. I love it. It was my father's."

"You can do so much better than that."

"Come on, you used to love hitting the road with the caravan. Going down south and up north."

"I was too young to know better."

"And now as a worldly teenager, you know everything better."

"Enough to know caravans are awful."

"A lot of history in mine."

Huntley pockets the tickets, then leans against the bonnet next to his daughter, amazed she looks more mature every time he sees her. He reminds himself that 13 is a tough age, as is 14, and 15, and all the teen years. He decides empathy, which he failed to show Aphra last night, is the best way forward.

"I enjoyed those trips. Caravans are what I know best. I've got great memories of you and me, on adventures around the state."

"I probably just liked hanging with you, and being away from the number one fun killer."

"How is your mum?"

Verity shrugs, her shoulder-length blonde hair bouncing a little. "You know. Doing her thing. Because that's the only thing that matters."

"Your thing is wagging school. Am I right?"

"No. There's a swim carnival today. I get a free pass for crap like that. Everyone's over at Perry Lakes."

Huntley smiles, loving his daughter's unusual penchant for using old place names. "Yet you're still dressed for school. In your Methodist Ladies' militia outfit."

"I forgot the carnival was on."

"Liar."

"For real. I got to school, on time, and no one was there. It was really scary, all those empty classrooms and hallways. One of the cleaners told me to go home."

Huntley chuckles. "You get those storytelling abilities from me."

"What?"

"Come on, Vee. I'm seeing right through this. None of the back story matches the present plot machinations."

"Why not?"

"Well, you don't have your school bag, for starters."

Verity pouts and back-heels the grille some more. "Fine. I had to get out of the house. I can't stand it there."

"You could've gone to the carnival."

"Ugh, and breathe chlorine all day? No way."

"Fair enough."

They watch the students arriving for late morning classes and tutorials; everyone's in a hurry. With their books, folders and papers, the students seem strangely analogue for the digital era.

"I'm sorry things are bad at home," Huntley says. "Is Harland still being forceful about you one day taking over the family business?"

"Looks like he'll get a grandson for that. To take under his wing."

"Lydette's pregnant? That I can't believe. I thought she hated kids, like some evil witch in a German fairytale."

"Not her."

Huntley swallows. "Since when is your mum seeing anybody?"

"Long enough for her to get, you know, knocked up. She and her latest squeeze are filling every corner of the house with their relationship."

"That's quite a feat, given the size of that place."

"Pretty easy when you're Mum and wanting to always be the centre of attention."

"Come on. She's not like that. Don't judge her so harshly. And you're entirely too young and from the wrong generation to be using a word like squeeze. Unless you're putting lemon in your bubble tea."

This makes Verity laugh, a sound so sweet and packed with memories it makes Huntley sad for all the times he's missed out on hearing it.

Verity watches some of the students. "Uni looks stressful. I thought this is when everyone parties. Mum always talks about it being the best time of her life."

"She's lying. You being born was the best part. It certainly was for me."

Verity smiles and looks down at her heels kicking the grille.

"But preggo?" he asks. "Really?"

"She hasn't said anything."

"So how do you know?"

"I found a test in the bin. One of those weird white pen-type things."

"What do you think? About having a little brother? Or sister?"

Another shrug. "Who cares what I think?"

"I do. Maybe it's a good thing. It'll get Harland off your back and you can take your life in the direction you want, without all that pressure."

Verity looks at him, appearing to like this idea, and it inspires him to find more positives in Giorgie having a baby.

"I love my hodge-podge family," he adds, "and all my step-brothers and step-sisters. They mean a lot to me."

"We should visit them."

"Oh really? And spend the weekend in a glorified dog house on wheels?"

"I didn't mean that."

"I know. The reunion's coming up. Why don't you join me for it? Get out of that ten-bedroom love-nest."

"School is just so all-consuming at the moment. Even in the holidays we get given stacks to do."

"You seem to have plenty of time to sit on my car."

"Ha-ha. The carnival. Remember?"

Huntley sings: "Life is a carnival, it's in the book."

"What's that?"

"The Band. My dad loved them. Listened to them all the time."

"There was a band called The Band?"

"Yep. There's probably a story behind it, but it escapes me right now. Dad would've known it."

"Bizarre."

Huntley clears his throat. "This squeeze, let me guess. An artist?"

"A sculptor. Does strange stuff with old metal. I don't really get it."

"Famous?"

"Doubt it."

"Name?"

"Daley." Verity says this with distaste. When Huntley gives her a questioning look, she adds, "I think that's it. One of these artists with one name. As if that makes him special and unique."

"Maybe it's a family thing. He has a sister named Hourly. One guess what her job would be."

"Ha. Spawned from parents named Monthly and Yearly."

They smile at each other, then look away, both watching the harried students arriving.

"Can I spend the day with you?" Verity asks.

"No. I'm taking you home."

"We can hang out there. Watch a movie. Or something."

"Harland banned me. Remember? From the house."

"Then I'll sit in your classes. I'll be quiet. I promise."

"You're almost getting to the point where you could pass as a student. You just need to get out of that uniform and look more like you're one failed exam from a nervous breakdown."

"I can do that."

Huntley shakes his head. "Sorry, Vee. I'm not teaching today. I've got something very important to do instead."

"What?"

"I need to see someone in Vic Park. A naturopath who treats haemorrhoids with wild arum."

"Okay. That's too much information. I don't want to hear about those kinds of problems."

"It's not for me. I'm investigating." Huntley leans close to his daughter. "A murder."

"Since when? What does it have to do with you?"

"It's a long story, and getting longer and more complex with every passing hour. It all centres on my book, which was found at a crime scene, in a violin case."

"No way."

"I think the killer put it there, my book, to send some kind of message."

"You would think that. Your book is such a relic, finding it anywhere must be a big clue for something."

"Harsh, Vee. No need to be cruel about it."

"Sorry."

"No worries. The whole investigation thing, this fascinating murder, it's got me writing again. The verse I wrote yesterday is the best I've done in ages."

"Can I read it?"

"Not yet. I need to get all the pieces together first."

Verity nods slowly. "By solving the murder."

"Right."

"What do haemorrhoids have to do with it?"

"Not that. Wild arum. The victim was poisoned with that stuff. I need to know about it, which is why I'm going to see this expert in Vic Park."

"Let me help."

"No."

"I can be useful."

"You're 13. You can continue enjoying your childhood."

"I'll be your assistant. Your tech support and researcher. You need this, because you never have your phone."

Huntley likes the idea, but fights against it. "Your mum would kill me if she found out you're helping me solve a murder."

"It'll be our secret. Our thing. Something we can do together."

Huntley likes this even more, and relenting is easy. "Get in."

Verity jumps down from the bonnet and runs around to the Landy's passenger side.

"It's going to be weird," Huntley says, unlocking the driver's door and opening it, "with the school uniform and all. Like it's take your daughter to work day."

"This isn't your job." Verity climbs in. "We can stop at home and I'll change."

"Bad idea. Harland's probably patrolling the garden with a shotgun." Huntley starts the car and is shocked by how loud it is compared to Henrikson's electric, but liking that the Landy feels more alive, the rumbling engine its beating heart. "Anyway, there's no time to waste. We'll go straight to Vic Park. On the way, my young assistant, you can research wild arum and bring me up to speed."

"Yes, sir."

Verity takes out her phone and gets to work. Huntley backs the car out, narrowly missing a student flying past on an e-scooter.

"Watch it, Dad," Verity says. "We're trying to solve a murder, not commit one."

"Sorry. I'm suddenly so energised."

"It's a bit hot in here. Can you make it cooler?"

"Sorry again. Air-con died ages ago. That's why I always park in the shade, further away from my office. Better put the window down."

"You need a new car." Verity lowers her window. "This is borderline embarrassing."

Huntley works the gearstick and drives out of the carpark. "You're welcome to get out and make your own way to Perry Lakes."

"No, thank you."

"Good. I love this car. I bought it with my first royalty cheque."

"How much was that? 50 dollars?"

"Cruel, Vee. Just cruel. Once your aunt got her talons on that first cheque and took her share, there wasn't much left. Just enough for the Landy."

Huntley, patting the dashboard with one hand, turns onto Mounts Bay Road, centre-bound. It's mid-morning and the traffic moves steadily. A speed camera is set up just past the Blue Boathouse. The attending cop is sitting in a fold-out chair, facing the river, like he's fishing.

Verity, with her head over her phone and hair framing her face, says, "Aunt Lyd's been bragging lately she's found some other star."

"Don't tell me she's still an agent. There's no way she'd survive without Harland helping her out. Who is it?"

"I can't remember his name. Pervert something."

"His name is Pervert?"

"Sounds like that. Perv or Merv, I don't know. She calls him the voice of my generation. Climate change and eco-warriors and all that."

"How old is he?"

"How should I know? What does it matter anyway?"

"The voice of your generation should at least be a member of your generation. Who wants some old fart telling youngsters how to live?"

"Yeah. That's right. I think Aunt Lyd's in love with him. He must be closer to her, age-wise. Which, yuck."

"Age differences never stopped her before. So? What about wild arum?"

"Checking. Okay. It's called lords-and-ladies. Whatever that means. Also known as cuckoo pint. Likes the shade."

"Don't we all."

Verity reads off her phone: "Self-seeding." She looks at Huntley. "What does that mean?"

"It spreads its own seeds. Like invasive weeds do, to take over areas."

"Sounds like Daley. He's doing all the seed-spreading. He even looks like a weed."

"Hah. What about its use as a poison?"

"Hang on. I'm getting to that."

Huntley merges the Landy with the traffic flowing over the Narrows Bridge. He needs to be forceful doing so, as no one lets him and each vehicle is barely a metre from the one in front.

"Specifically," he says, "when injected in the neck, causing asphyxiation."

"What's that?"

"Choking to death."

"That fits. It says here it can cause the throat to close."

"Bingo." Huntley points at the side of his neck. "She was stabbed with a fountain pen, right here, and there was wild arum inside."

"What a bizarre way to kill someone."

"I know, right?"

"Wait. She? It was a girl?"

"It was. Young. In her 20s."

"Who was she?"

"A violinist, from Ukraine, by the fabulous name of Ekaterina Valoskiya."

"How do you know all this?"

"Like I said, I'm investigating."

Huntley proceeds to tell Verity everything he's learned about the case so far, leaving out the part about the detectives accusing him of being the killer. By the time he's finished, they've reached Victoria Park.

"Do you think it was the new violinist's family?" Verity asks.

"They're involved," he says, thinking again about what Aphra said last night, about a "chair" not being motive enough. "Somehow. They'll do anything to get what they want."

"Why kill a girl just to free up a spot in the orchestra?"

"Good question. Maybe there's more to it. What's the back story?"

"What if this Marcus guy was supposed to get the chair? Then they brought in the girl from Ukraine and he missed out."

Huntley considers this. "That's clever thinking. She wasn't standing in his way. She took what was promised to him."

He parks on the street, in front of the naturopath's house, an unobtrusive, low-roofed suburban dwelling with a burnt lawn out the front, in the middle of which is a sign with "Nolene's Naturopathy" on it. It looks like no one's home. He feels the trepidation he often gets in suburban Perth, where otherwise non-descript houses hold so many secrets.

"I think you better stay in the car," he says.

Verity gets out and starts marching towards the front door. Huntley hustles after her.

"Why don't you ever listen to me?" he asks.

"I listen." Verity presses the rust-tinged bell. "I just don't agree with you."

The doorbell makes the sound of a gong, heard faintly from the outside.

"Hear that? What kind of weirdo has a bell like that? You never know what's going on behind the walls of these houses. You need to be more careful."

"Hey, you're the one who invited me along on this escapade."

"Because you wouldn't take no for an answer."

Verity bites her lower lip. "What's our story? What are you going to say?"

Huntley has no time to reply, as the door is opened. Behind the flyscreen is a woman of indeterminate age, anywhere from 50 to 70, the dusty, cobwebbed screen making it harder to tell. Her grey hair is a thicket, tangled together with bits of string and a few colourful bows, flowing down to what looks like a 1970s floral curtain repurposed into a full-length dress. Huntley thinks it's the kind of hair that requires a hedge trimmer for maintenance. Imagining birds and rats fleeing her hair as the trimmer cuts into it makes him laugh a little, which he tries to cover up by coughing.

"What do you want?" the woman asks.

Huntley is bereft of ideas. He looks at Verity, then at the woman, and at Verity again.

"Uh," he says.

Verity takes a short step forward. "Hi. Are you Nolene?"

"Yes."

"We're looking for a nature-something."

"Naturopath," Huntley manages to say, following through with more laughter-concealing coughing.

"Sounds like you need help," Nolene says. "Chest infection?"

"Is wild arum good for that kind of thing?"

"That's an obscure yet ridiculously precise question."

"Yes, it's ..."

Verity jumps in: "It's for a school project. About using natural remedies, in place of usual medicine."

"That explains the uniform and why you're not in school." The woman looks at Huntley. "Are you her teacher?"

"I'm trying to teach her lots of things, but she never listens."

"He's my dad," Verity says. "I needed someone to drive me out here."

"I see no resemblance." Nolene's smile is almost sardonic. "Perhaps that's a good thing."

Huntley, trying not to sound offended, asks, "Can we come in? I feel like we're visiting you in a prison."

"Pardon?"

"This heavy screen door."

"I just want to ask some questions," Verity adds. "About your very important work."

"Right." Huntley nods. "And wild arum."

"Arum maculatum," Nolene says, in a know-it-all sounding voice. "Use the correct name."

"Sorry. My daughter's missing her Latin class as we speak."

The flyscreen is unlocked with a heavy click and swings open.

"Shoes off."

Inside, Huntley expects it to be cooler, with the air-con running, but it's actually warmer, and more humid, due to the abundant plant life in the house, which fills every corner and lines every wall and window. There's so much greenery, and so many smells, that it feels like an interior garden the woman somehow manages to live in.

"This is quite the jungle," Huntley says, removing his shoes. "Do you grow everything you use for your naturopathy yourself?"

"I try, but not everything takes. Some species have very specific environmental and care needs."

"What about wild arum?" When Nolene shoots him a glance, he adds, "Arum maculatum, I mean."

"It's through here."

They go down a hallway that almost needs a machete to get through. Huntley weaves between and bobs around the various leaves and branches, unwilling to make contact with anything. On the back veranda, which has been converted into an enclosed greenhouse, the heat and humidity are even more intense. Huntley stands there, perfectly still, and feels his face bead with sweat.

"It is without doubt," Nolene says, bending at the waist to pick up a pot, "an absolutely beautiful creature."

She shows them a green-leafed plant centred with an oval-shaped scoop. There's a dark prong coming vertically out of the base of the scoop.

"Is that it?" Huntley asks. "No wonder they call it lords-and-ladies."

"What does that mean?" Verity, pink-cheeked from the heat, gets closer to the plant, but Huntley gently pushes her back.

"He's referring to the undeniable sexual appearance of arum maculatum. That it depicts the female and male genitalia in the act of copulation."

"Hey, tone it down," Huntley says. "She's 13."

Verity points. "So this is the penis and this is the vagina?"

"Yes, dear." Nolene is even holding the pot in a vaguely sexual manner, like it's there for the taking. "You wouldn't believe the folklore about this little plant. It has so many names, many of them disgusting."

"I don't think we need to hear them," Huntley says. "Let's stick to its uses. Poisonous, right?"

Nolene is about to answer when the gong sounds from inside the house. She hands the pot to Huntley, who takes it at full arm's length, like she's passed him a bomb. He stands there, sweating, unable to move.

"Don't touch it," he whispers to Verity, who's inspecting it closely. "Don't even breathe it in."

"It looks harmless. How did this little flower kill that girl?"

"Maybe it's like snakes and spiders. The smaller they are, the more potent the poison."

"Or there's a special way to prepare it."

"You mean like boil it in a cauldron and add wing of bat and eye of newt?"

"What?"

"Macbeth? Shakespeare? What the hell are they teaching you at that exclusive school?"

Verity looks around, then asks, "Do you think it was her?"

"I'm not seeing the story. She doesn't look like she ever leaves the house. Can't imagine she would do that to kill a violinist on the other side of town."

"Money? From that family?"

"Vee, that woman is weird, but she's not an assassin."

"Maybe this is the best cover. No one would ever suspect her."

"Okay, now you're reaching. She's a character in a narrative entirely of her own. She's got roots here. Do you recognise that? And she's a healer, not a killer."

"You're holding the weapon."

"Doesn't mean she used it."

The naturopath returns. "Well, this is unusual. Someone else is interested in the willy lily."

Detective Everest steps onto the veranda. "Huntley? What on earth are you doing here?"

"And you all know each other." Nolene gives Huntley a fierce look that nearly makes him drop the pot. "Using your daughter like that. Shame on you. Taking her out of school for your own heinous means."

"Heinous?" he echoes.

"You're clearly here with ulterior motives. You have liar written all over you. I can see it in your aura. There's nothing genuine in the colours around you. They are like warning lights." Then, to Verity, she adds, "You'd best stay away from him. Even if he is your father, he will take you down bad paths."

"Now, hang on just a minute," Huntley says.

"Look at how he sweats. All that bad energy seeping out through every pore."

"It's bloody hot in here. You're in no position to be telling me my energy's bad. You look like you haven't had a wash since the last century."

The woman puts her hands on Verity's shoulders. "You see? An aura of negativity. You've been warned. It will continue to pollute your being."

"Okay, everyone just calm down a little." Everest moves towards Huntley. "You have no business being here."

"This is it, Ellie. Wild arum."

"How did you even find out that's the poison?"

"What poison?" the naturopath asks.

"I know it might look a tad incriminating," Huntley says to Everest.

"It does."

"But this is my first time seeing it." Huntley would like to put the pot down, but is stuck with it. "The fact you're here too means there aren't many people in Perth who specialise in wild arum."

"Arum maculatum," Nolene says, annoyed.

"There are a few. We're checking out the others." Everest thumbs towards the naturopath. "I came here first because she's got a record. For growing plants of an illegal variety."

"It was medicinal. I was cleared. I demand you explain what this is all about."

Everest's phone rings. She moves away to answer it. "Yeah? What? No, leave it with me. I think I can find out about it."

"What's happened?" Huntley asks.

Everest ignores him and addresses the naturopath. "Do you have something called jimsonweed?"

"Datura stramonium? Absolutely not. The devil's trumpet is not to be messed with."

"Why not? What does it do?"

"It's from the nightshade family. Horrid stuff. It can take you to another planet."

"A hallucinogen?"

"Worse. It will make you crazy, lose all touch with reality."

"Has there been another murder?" Huntley asks. "With this jimmy stuff?"

"Thank you for your time," Everest says to the naturopath, turning to leave. "I'm sorry we've all disturbed you."

"Holy shit. There's been another murder." Huntley hands the pot to Nolene. "Verity, come on. Follow that detective."

On her way, Verity is stopped by the naturopath. "Beware," she says intently, holding the pot.

"Uh, yeah. Okay."

When the three of them are outside, Huntley stops Everest just before she reaches for her car door handle.

"You need to tell me everything," he says.

"No, I don't. You need to stay the hell out of this."

"What's jimsonweed? Who's dead? Someone else from the orchestra?"

"What are you doing getting your daughter involved in this? Are you crazy?"

"I had no choice. There's no school today. Some swim carnival. I couldn't leave her unsupervised."

Everest smiles at Verity. "Is that what you told him? Swim carnival?"

Verity shrugs.

"She has a heart condition," Huntley says. "She's exempt from school sports."

"That might be true. The carnival bit isn't. She just said that to skip school."

"How do you know that?"

"I went to Perth College. All the swim carnivals happen in February and March for the private schools. Including Methodist Ladies."

Huntley turns to Verity. "Vee? What the hell?"

Another shrug, followed by her strolling around the Landy and getting in the passenger side. She shuts the door and sits with her head angled over her phone.

"I like her," Everest says. "But if you're going to play PI, you need to leave her out of it. Anyone could've been inside that house."

"Such as the killer? Yeah, yeah, I'm a terrible parent."

"I didn't say that. She just manipulated you. When I was her age, I was an expert at that. I bet you had that going on as well."

"Seems to me it's a teenage girl thing."

"No way. Boys are just as bad. Look at what a conniving adult you are. You're lucky I don't throw you in jail for the night."

Huntley nods. "Yeah. You're right. Sorry. The heat in there, and that woman, it was all getting to me. Jonty, my brother, was like a conman when he was Verity's age."

"You need to stand up to her. Otherwise, she'll just walk all over you."

"I would. If I got to spend more time with her." Huntley wipes his forehead with his shirt sleeve. "I think I lost a kilo in there."

"How did you end up here? Who told you about wild arum?"

"I can't tell you that. Are you going to tell me who died? You might as well. It'll be all over the media anyway, given how much this town loves a horrible death. It'll take a few days, but it'll still get out. They're probably writing about Ekaterina right now."

Everest opens her car door and leans on it. "I'll tell you if you agree to stay the fuck out of it."

Huntley nods again. "Sure."

"I'm going to hold you to that. It was Lance Ford-Brackman."

"Holy shit. Older brother of Marcus, right?"

"Booth is down there now, with the family. Probably taking an hour just to deliver the news."

"This jimbo thing? Did that kill him?"

"Not directly. We found a water bottle in his car, which had traces of jimsonweed in it. I'm guessing it made him high and he decided that trying to swim to Africa at night was a really good idea."

"I'll follow you," Huntley says, walking towards his car. "To Mandurah."

"No, you won't."

"But ..."

"This has nothing to do with you. Remember?"

"Yeah. Booth's down there anyway. Waste of a trip. Where are you going?"

"To take care of the body ID. You should take care of your daughter. Get her back to school."

"Yeah. I should. Can we meet up afterwards? Swap notes? Another jam maybe?"

Everest shakes her head, severe ponytail swishing, then gets in her car. Huntley watches as she sits in the driver's seat, folds her arms and pouts, in very teenage-girl fashion. Then, she starts the car and drives off.

"Jimsonweed," Huntley says to himself. "For the hallucinating nightswimmer."

<>

Another hour goes by and it's wasted time. She tries to work, on something about improving Perth's infrastructure, but she's not feeling comfortable, alone in the container office like this. Plus, as the time passes, she becomes more annoyed at being stuck here. Because that's what she hates the most: waiting. Being at the mercy of someone else's schedule, and that certain someone was supposed to be here over two hours ago.

Not to mention that it feels like a punishment, to "take care of the Lance situation", as Blair had put it, and break the news to his business partner. Except that Nathaniel Winslow hasn't shown yet, and his appearance becomes less likely with every passing minute.

Sure, Blair was angry and Aphra bore the brunt of it. She knows this and lets it go. It's Winslow she's annoyed with.

The air-conditioning switching off kicks her into action. It was set on a power-saving timer, for the duration of the planned meeting, which Lance's death ended before it even started. She'll be damned if she keeps on sitting in here while the container slowly starts to bake. She's tempted to get a taxi all the way to the city and bill Blair for it, but there's still the partner to take care of. A quick search on her phone reveals that Winslow Properties is located in Cockburn, on the other side of Beeliar Regional Park, which she finds even more annoying, as Winslow is essentially walking distance away and still hasn't bothered to show up. She takes a bottle of water from the catering trolley and fishes around in the closet for a hat, extracting a merchandise cap for FB Lobsters which she dons and tucks her hair under.

He's bound to have excuses, she thinks, opening the container door to the heat, and it'll be best to let them all slide, given Winslow's place in Blair's coterie and what's happened today.

Outside, the sea breeze is in early, thankfully, swirling up the dirt into little eddies that spin away down the tracks. There's still a heated weight to the air, which the breeze will gradually blow away over the course of the day. She's glad she found the cap, even though it most likely last sat on Lance's head.

Following her phone's map, she sets off northeast down the sandy track. Hot grains come over the sides of her sandals and hit her feet like the sting of small embers from a fire. It quickens her pace, aided by the release of endorphins that comes with the sense of taking control. The trees are dirty green and provide just enough shade on the right side of the path, where the sand is also a tad firmer. Despite being called wetlands, the overwhelming dryness makes her feel the moisture is being sucked from her skin.

She worries about snakes.

After ten minutes of walking, she's deep in the park, out of sight of any houses or buildings. The park suddenly feels huge and the venture she's undertaking misguided.

She walks faster.

Her bag, weighed down by the laptop inside, pulls at her right shoulder.

When she arrives at the lake, she's shocked to see how low the water level is. It's more scummy pond than lush expanse. What water there is has a thick layer of brown sludge on top, which is only stirred by the ducks wading through it. Those ducks move cautiously, as if they too are surprised how low the water is. The whole area is teeming with insects, mosquitoes mostly, unusual at this time of day. She pulls a leafy twig off a tree and uses this to swish the mozzies and flies away. If she's got her geography right, the development plans involve building an Olympic-sized pool right where this lake is. While it's hard to envision right now, even with the 3D renderings that lurk in her memory, she can't help thinking such a pool would be a vast improvement on this so-called lake.

She follows the track north, swishing the branch around her.

The lack of people and life in the park adds to its eeriness. There aren't even any birds in the trees. So, when a small, tan-coloured dog of mixed breeding, not unlike her own, comes running towards her, tongue out and tail wagging, she's glad to crouch down in the shade and give the dog a serious ear scratch. The dog sits, panting with enjoyment.

"Looks like someone found a friend."

Aphra looks up to see the poet from last night coming towards her. He's smiling, his mouth pulling away to one side of his face, looking as eager for attention as his dog. She feels something stir in the pit of her stomach.

"Hey, it's you," he says brightly. "From the Mongrel's open mic. That's amazing."

"Hi."

"What a coincidence. I almost didn't recognise you with that cap on. It's just off the chart random that we'd meet like this. Out here."

Aphra, wondering how best to deal with this, slowly stands up. "Yes. Very random," she says, with a slight smile, deciding to play it friendly. "What are you doing here?"

"These are my woods. Remember? I saved them."

"Right. You did."

"What brings you out here? You have the tan and beauty of a western suburbs girl."

"I guess you could say I'm experiencing the wetlands, before they're gone. Though I think drylands is more accurate."

"Yeah, 37 days without rain. But who's counting?"

"You are, it seems."

He steps closer. "I never got your name. You left too soon last night."

"It's Aphra. I confess I've forgotten yours."

"Purvis. I wish you'd stayed for my performance."

"I had somewhere else to be." Aphra continues to pat the dog, keeping it between her and Purvis. "You have a nice dog."

"Thanks. He likes you. Dogs are always the best judge of character."

Aphra feels slightly vulnerable standing still, so starts walking. The dog follows her immediately, as does Purvis.

"Are you going this way?" she asks.

"I can go any way I want." He points to the east. "I live in Success. On the other side of the lake."

"It's not much of a lake."

"We really need some rain."

They walk side by side, the dog between them. Aphra racks her brain for a way of politely getting Purvis to go away.

"So," she begins, thinking she might talk him away and make him lose interest, "let me see if I got this right. You're a protester who is against any development of this park, yet you live in Success, a subdivision built on what was once bushland like this. And probably protected land at that."

He holds up his hands and laughs a little. "That's not my fault. We don't choose where we're born. My mum had an old cottage there, in the bush. She was bought out by the developers. Part of the deal was getting one of the new houses at a really low price, on a double block of land. Mum couldn't resist a big garden."

"Sounds like she made a good deal."

"She sure did. The house is now worth three times as much, at least."

"You're still living with her?" Aphra immediately regrets asking this.

He bristles. "What's wrong with that?"

"Nothing. There are plenty of boomerang kids moving back home. I know it's hard being a writer. Hard to make any money."

"I'm not struggling. Quite the opposite."

"Ah, you're an environmentalist and a capitalist. Maybe you'll find a way to turn a profit from Beeliar as well."

"I'm fully against any developments here. This area is staying exactly how it is."

"Yes. Dry as a bone."

"The rain will come. It always does. Then, this place thrives."

Aphra wants to tell Purvis, who doesn't really scare her anymore, all about the Southern Everglades; about how the sandy path they're now walking on will one day be a boulevard lined with McMansions, curving around a leisure facility with an Olympic-sized pool. But she decides baiting him is more fun.

"Maybe you should chain yourself to a tree. How about that one? Or that one?"

Purvis smiles. "Mock me all you want, but what I'm doing is for the greater good."

"This is prime real estate in a city that seriously values prime real estate. You can't ignore that. The freeway's nearby. Plenty of schools. Plus, if you're looking far enough ahead and the climate predictions are right, it'll be pretty close to the beach, eventually."

"With all your western suburbs washed away by then."

"Maybe."

Aphra makes a mental note to consider selling her North Cott condo; to make a profit on it now and move a little further inland. Because, even though Blair Blake-Stendahl and the WA

Republic Party aren't putting great stock in the impact of melting glaciers or other climate disasters, they've definitely been privy to the latest reports and calculations, as Aphra has. They just sweep all of it under the carpet, as it's something the electorate doesn't want to hear.

After walking for a while in silence, as Aphra ponders the planet's future and how this impacts her real estate options, Purvis says, "That's an unusual name. Aphra."

"So is Purvis."

"We could get together and ship it, as Aphris."

"Definitely better than Purphra."

They both laugh.

"I've never met anyone with your name," Purvis says.

"Maybe you should read more poetry."

"I actually try not to read poetry. It ruins my voice and style. I find myself subconsciously imitating others."

"A poet who doesn't read and an eco-protester who likes profit. How does your dog judge your character? Or better yet, your integrity?"

"He likes me just fine. There's nothing wrong with my integrity."

"Of course. Sorry, I'm just a bit flustered by this heat."

"What's the origin of your name?"

"My parents both work in the mining industry. They wanted something connected with that. I guess they thought I would follow in their footsteps. Aphra is an old Hebrew name. It means dust."

"Yeah? I like that. Dust. What happened? With your mining career? You don't look like a girl who gets her hands dirty."

"I patted your dog. He's pretty dirty."

"He likes rolling in the sand. And digging around in it. But you don't obviously."

"I never wanted that. The mining life. Fly in, fly out. I also think there's something wrong about it, pilfering the land like that."

"Oh, I agree. Totally."

"After a while, my parents didn't want it for me either. It's a hard life. Getting harder."

"Are they still working?"

"They've got a number they want to hit, financially, before retiring."

"What is it?"

"That's not really any of your business."

"A million? Probably not enough." Purvis picks up a stick and throws it for the dog to retrieve. The dog stays next to Aphra's side. She tries not to laugh.

"The money isn't the problem. They already have enough, to retire, buy a caravan and start noodling around the country. It's more that they don't want to stop. This life, it's what they do. That's hard to let go of."

"Why? It's just menial work, and bad for the environment."

"They don't see it like that. They're worried their lives will cease to have meaning if they stop doing the singular thing that defines their existence."

"Woah. That's deep. But doesn't everyone have that problem when they stop working? They need to find a new meaning. A new definition. They have to change."

"Says the guy who's against new subdivisions, but who lives with his mum in a subdivision."

Purvis gives Aphra a wounded look. "You're oversimplifying it."

"Hmm, seems I hit a nerve. One minute I'm deep, the next minute I'm simple."

"I didn't mean it like that. Stop twisting my words."

Aphra finds Purvis's crooked smile somehow endearing, as if she should feel sorry for him.

"You're like some devilish word-spinner," he adds.

"Deep, simple and the devil, all in one." Aphra senses her opening. "You'd be wise to turn around and walk in the other direction, far away from me."

"Look, I'm sorry. You're definitely clever. You're pretty too. Why don't you have dinner with me? I could cook for you."

Aphra's disappointed that getting rid of Purvis won't be that easy. "What about your mum?"

"Or lunch? I could whip us up something. It's ten minutes from here."

Like he was last night, he's too pushy. The kind of guy who thinks it's charming to never take no for an answer; who thinks women will be turned on by his confidence and persistence. Tact is needed, she thinks, to let him down easy now and prevent any further proposals in the future.

"I'll stop you right there," she says gently. "It's best we avoid any attempts at seeing where this might go. Sure, I'm flattered, and don't take this the wrong way, but with this land, this area, I fear we have conflicting interests. We shouldn't allow ourselves to get tangled up in something that might reflect badly on both of us."

Purvis stops walking. "I feel like I've just been very politely rejected by a politician."

"I'll take that as a compliment."

"You never said what you do for work. Are you a politician?"

"No comment."

"Bloody hell. Who are you?"

"If you were better read, you might know."

"I don't know how to respond to this. I'm lost for words. Very rare for me."

They walk a little further, reaching a fork in the path. Aphra checks her phone.

"Hey," Purvis says. "You still didn't tell me what you do."

"My work is taking me to a meeting in Cockburn." She points to the path on the left. "Which is that way. My map tells me your suburb is straight ahead."

"I don't need a map to tell me that."

"Probably not. You're on the path to Success, so to speak. That's a good path to be on." She starts walking away from Purvis. When the dog follows, she adds, "No, you go back to your master. There's a good boy."

"Can I have your phone number?" Purvis calls out.

"No. That's not a very good idea."

Aphra shoos the dog, to send him back to Purvis. The dog sits in the middle of the path and watches her. Purvis whistles, but the dog doesn't move.

Yes, Aphra thinks to herself, you really do know his character.

She focuses on her phone, clearing the messages and emails she received while walking with Purvis. When she looks back again, she's already around a bend in the path. Purvis and the dog are out of view, but still she walks quickly, just in case he's following.

Even though she didn't give him her phone number, she thinks he could easily find her, if he wanted to. There would only be a handful of Aphras in Perth, if that. There's also the problem of their mutual acquaintance, Lydette Gifford, should Purvis make that connection.

Out of the bushland and across Beeliar Drive, she puts the cap in her bag and takes out the water bottle. It's tempting to rinse her mouth and spit the water out, as that's how the exchange with Purvis made her feel. But she drinks it down, emptying the bottle by the time she reaches the office of Winslow Properties. It's a standard building, nothing flash, except for the gleaming white luxury SUV parked right out the front which has the personalised license plate of NATE WINS.

Inside, the receptionist is on the phone, gesturing with a long-nailed finger for Aphra to wait. Shandorah has the glossy refinement and deep tan of someone who might double as a flight attendant on weekends, when she's not roasting herself at the beach. Aphra wonders why she's wearing a name tag.

The reception area is less a showcase of real estate and development projects, and more a place of less than subtle bragging. The walls are adorned with blown-up, framed photos, under glass, of charity events and sponsorships, where Winslow Properties has been a generous benefactor: sports clubs, a children's hospital, cancer fundraising, arts and culture events. Among them is a photo of the Perth Symphony Orchestra, performing at the Perth Concert Hall, Leiland Taverton conducting. Aphra looks at the violin section, all male in this photo. A wave of sadness for her dead friend rips through her, and she pushes those feelings deep down inside her.

She thinks of Purvis, and how she might actually find a way to like him if he wasn't so aggressive in his pursuit. Her most recent tryst, with Maruzio in Bologna a few months back, had also involved an aggressive pursuit, but she had enjoyed that then, deeming it part of the Italian courting experience. While Maruzio was persistently romantic, Purvis comes across as persistently creepy.

"Can I help you?" Shandorah finally asks, sounding disinterested.

"I'm here to see Nathaniel Winslow."

"And you are?"

"Aphra Massey. I work with Blair Blake-Stendahl."

This makes the receptionist brighten. "You do? That must be amazing. She's got her finger right on the city's pulse. Really smart woman."

"She is."

"I don't see you in Nate's calendar."

"He was supposed to be at the Beeliar site this morning."

"That was hours ago. He had something important to attend to."

"Has he been here all that time?"

"Uh, I believe he has, yes."

Aphra wonders if Winslow is sleeping with the receptionist. It seems too obvious, and too much of a cliché, but she can't help thinking Shandorah looks like an upmarket groupie.

"And now?"

"I believe he's at a lunch meeting. Would you like to wait?"

Aphra thumbs behind her. "His car's out front. That is his car, right? With the Nate wins plate?"

"Ah, oh, yes, it is. I guess it was cancelled."

"Tell him someone from the WA Republic Party is here."

"I know who Blair Blake-Stendahl represents. What's it concerning?"

"Mr Winslow's dead business partner."

"My God. Who died?"

"You don't know?"

"I know," says the man standing in the doorway that leads to the offices. He steps forward and extends a hand to Aphra. "Nice to see you again, uh, Ms ...?"

"Massey. Aphra Massey." She shakes his hand, which is dry and chalky, as if he powders his hands after using the bathroom.

"Nathaniel Winslow."

"We met very briefly when the first renderings for the Southern Everglades were presented."

"Yes, sorry, we did."

"My condolences for Lance."

Shandorah is shocked. "Lance is dead?"

"Unfortunately, yes," Winslow says. He gives the receptionist's shoulder a squeeze as she stifles her sobs with a tissue. Shandorah grabs that hand, pressing it a few times in a way that presupposes intimacy, or the desire for it.

"You should've said something," Shandorah says.

"You're right. I'm sorry. I guess I'm still in shock." He takes his hand from the receptionist's shoulder and looks at Aphra. "It's why I didn't get to the meeting this morning. I've been in damage control mode the last few hours, trying to keep the project afloat. I was just about to call Blair and give her an update."

"You can fill me in instead."

"Sure. Sorry. I still can't believe what's happened. Please come through to my office."

As Aphra follows him down the hallway, she pegs Winslow as the kind of upper-middle-class go-getter who apologises a lot, but never really means it; who cultivates an aura of self-made success when he actually got most things very easily, via friendships and connections with the right people. He's tall and solidly built, filled out now in his late 40s, but may have been an athlete when he was younger. Aphra goes with rugby, with Winslow playing in the first XV of whatever private school he attended, and still friends with all of them. Now, she thinks he's a golfer, and possibly a sailor, as both would supply access to private clubs and vital business networks. His hair is styled to hide its loss, while his slight paunch shows he likes a beer with the lads and cracking a bottle of wine with dinner. Crow's feet at the corners of his eyes, made worse when smiling, which he does a lot, even when apologising, and a wind-tanned face that further suggests a liking for nautical weekends. And still just good-looking enough for glossy receptionists and part-time flight attendants who like that sort of thing.

They pass small offices where younger versions, male and female, of the Winslow type work, whether at computers or on the phone. Plenty of them look young enough to be on the intern payroll, working for peanuts in exchange for gaining the kind of connections that might help them get ahead in Perth.

"Have you made any kind of announcement yet?" Winslow asks, looking back over his shoulder.

"I was about to ask you that very question."

"Do you think I should? To the media?"

"Is there anything to say? Maybe it's best to leave it to Lance's family."

"The project's very hush-hush right now. I'm sorry. I'd rather keep myself out of it."

"What was all that time spent on damage control then?"

Winslow stops and turns to Aphra. Working for Blair Blake-Stendahl has brought her into contact with hundreds of men and women like Winslow. They're the people who get things done in Perth, who all seem to know each other, as members of a vast mover-shaker network. Sandgropers to the core, who think that going to Sydney or Melbourne is a laborious chore, though Brisbane and the Gold Coast are good for holidays. People who have strong ties to the WA Republic Party because they want to see their assets and profits remain within the state.

Winslow, hands on hips in a take-charge manner, clears his throat. "Sorry. I needed to find someone to take the lead. Now that, Lance, he's, well, the project needs a face. A leader."

"And? Successful?"

A disarming smile. "Yes. I think so."

Winslow gets moving again. In his office, he steps over a practice putting green and sits at a desk overflowing with brochures and papers. Prompted, Aphra takes the chair opposite him.

The phone rings. Winslow picks it up. "Yeah? I'll call you back."

Aphra watches him slam the phone back in its cradle, then take it off again, to prevent further calls.

"Sorry about that," he says. "I'll be honest with you. When I found out, I couldn't face going over to Lance's set-up. All those people."

"You weren't even there at the start of the meeting. You must've got the news early."

"Yeah. I did." Winslow starts looking through the papers on his desk. "I was on the way, then I got a call."

"The Ford-Brackmans?"

"I had to pull over. I was ... stunned."

"A pair of detectives came to the container office. Have you spoken with them?"

Winslow shakes his head. "Detectives? No. Why? I was told Lance drowned. Are you saying there's more to it?"

"Is there?"

"We're doing this project together," Winslow says, in a pointedly measured voice. "We were. That's it. How am I supposed to know what he does in his free time? I'm sorry, Anna. We weren't friends, or anything."

"It's Aphra."

"Right. Sorry. How's Blair doing? Is she okay?"

"What makes you think she wouldn't be?"

"That's why you're here, isn't it? She's got her panties in a twist because she thinks the project won't continue without Lance."

"I'd rather you didn't talk about the state's future premier in that fashion."

Winslow smiles and waves Aphra off. "Relax. I know a lot more about the future premier than you do. Blair doesn't mind that kind of talk."

"Well, I mind."

"Makes me think it's not Blair who has her panties in a twist."

Winslow gives Aphra the same kind of smarmy look as the taxi driver on her ride over to the container. She wants to slap it right off his face.

"What's the status of the project?" she asks. "No doubt you're aware how important the support from the southern suburbs will be in the next election cycle."

"Leave Blair to me. She deserves an update and to hear it from me. Speaking of support, she must be getting close in the government to pushing for no-confidence, to force an early election. That would be really helpful."

"We're still building towards that. She needs more help from certain people on the floor and to increase her approval ranking with the right voters."

"Such as the well-heeled southerners? I know, I know. I'm well aware of what's at stake. Don't worry. The project is still on."

"Another Ford-Brackman?" Aphra asks, both impressed and revolted by Winslow's easy charm.

"I can't say much, but I have reached out to them. You need to remember Lance was a bit of an outcast. He really wanted to do his own thing, away from the family. You know, live his own life, according to his own terms."

Winslow clears his throat again and looks sad. Aphra isn't sure if he's putting it on or not.

"I didn't know that," she offers, to keep him talking.

"He's a bit different. Was. Then it occurred to me I might need someone like that. You know, without the really strong family ties."

"Someone cleaner?"

"What are you implying?"

"Nothing."

"I reached out to Niranda Stone. Do you know her?"

"Formerly Niranda Ford-Brackman."

"She married Carrington Stone. He died a few years ago, but she kept his name. She's in real estate, like Carry was, and she's looking to expand her business interests. She'll come on board, after a certain mourning period. It wouldn't look right if she stepped immediately into her nephew's shoes."

"No, it wouldn't," Aphra says, aware Niranda has political aspirations of her own.

"All going well, and if we get the approvals, we'll break ground on schedule."

"Blair will be happy to hear that. I won't take up any more of your time." Aphra stands up. "One last thing, though. If it turns out you or anyone you know were involved in Lance's death, Blair will be forced to cut ties with you immediately. Regardless of how much history you have."

Winslow is angry. "How dare you say that? You've got serious nerve to walk in here and accuse me of ... of ... being involved in Lance's death."

"I'm not accusing you of anything. I'm simply informing you of the potential repercussions. Nothing can come back to Blair."

"You're out of line, young lady. I'm the last person who wanted Lance dead. He ... this project has mega profit written all over it. He was a lovely bloke. I ... it doesn't seem real that he's gone."

"Do you know if he had any enemies?"

"He's a Ford-Brackman. The list would be very long. But he was also caught up in some shady stuff. I warned him about it, but he wouldn't listen."

"What stuff?"

"Sorry. I'm not going there. Not my place to say."

Aphra goes to the door, then stops. "Out the front, in the reception area, you have a photo of the PSO. What's your involvement with that?"

"We're one of the sponsors. It's a tax dump, to be honest. You know how that goes."

"Why the PSO? You could tax dump anywhere."

"Me and Leiland went to Aquinas together."

With that one statement, Aphra thinks she could write Nathaniel Winslow's entire life story.

"Shame about that violinist," he says.

"Yes, a shame."

Aphra leaves, walking quickly down the hallway. She can't get out of there fast enough.

<>

At North Trigg beach, the sea breeze is in full blow. The lifeguard flags are ramrod straight and fluttering noisily. As the Canteen didn't have rum, Huntley had to settle for a hot toddy without the boost of positivity, just black tea, which is probably good given his resolution to give up day drinking. The tea is in an environmentally friendly paper cup that's biodegrading as he drinks from it, losing shape and becoming increasingly harder to hold. Over in the carpark, a lone police officer is pacing around the back of a badly parked white luxury SUV, using the vehicle as a windbreak. Huntley bins the remains of the paper cup and goes towards him.

He has no idea what he's going to say, but tries to walk with confidence and purpose.

When the police officer sees Huntley coming towards him, he says, "Finally. I've been waiting here for hours."

"Yeah, sorry, mate," Huntley says, deciding to play along. "Family business."

"I was told someone from the Ford-Brackmans would be here an hour ago. What took you so long?"

"Uh, traffic? It's a long trip from Mandurah."

"Do you really think I've got the time to stand around, waiting under the beating sun for you, and in this bloody wind?"

"Again, I apologise. This death, you know, it's come as a shock to all of us."

"Well, okay. Right. I'm sorry for your loss. Anyway, you're here now."

Huntley takes the key fob the police officer hands to him. The officer nods, then walks to the nearby police motorcycle. He puts on his helmet and rides off, looking both annoyed and cool when doing so.

Huntley presses the key fob. The lights flash on the white SUV. He gets in, blessedly out of the wind, and is very tempted to start the vehicle and drive away; go directly to Ravensthorpe where the ever-enterprising Jonty would know what to do with it. Change the engine serial numbers, repaint it, put on different plates and so on, then sell it somewhere out of state. It's not like the Ford-Brackmans, rich beyond measure, would be much bothered by losing one vehicle from the family fleet. But as he gets comfortable in the driver's seat, fleshing out Lance's story takes priority over repurposing his vehicle.

Huntley wonders: what brought Lance here? Was he alone? Was it just the jimsonweed that compelled him to go out in the water?

He looks at the passenger seat, searching for any sign that someone might have sat there. It appears the police have picked clean anything that might have been left behind. The seat is spotless.

The vehicle still has a faint new-car smell.

The wind rocks the car ever so slightly. Grains of sand get whipped up and ping against the windscreen.

He considers the narrative, of Lance alone in this car: arriving at the beach, parking the car across three spaces. Had he already drunk from the laced water bottle? And then? High, feeling euphoric and indestructible. Feeling like he could do anything. The world his playground, taking the shape of whatever his addled mind envisioned.

Huntley looks at the water. "Maybe the drug cooked him, made him feel hot," he says to himself.

Huntley turns in the seat and looks at the open briefcase, wondering why the police left it behind. He fingers through the brochures, seeing that there's nothing else in the briefcase, and takes one.

"Another development. Is nothing sacred in this town?"

He's surprised to see how young Lance looks in the brochure.

The glossy digital renderings of the Southern Everglades aren't accompanied by any prices, for land or houses, which he finds strange.

Through the windscreen, he looks at the water, which is so choppy and churned by the wind to be almost white. No one's surfing off the point, and no one's swimming. He feels sorry for the lifeguards huddled in the raised lookout not far from the water's edge. The whole scene looks massively unappealing, ruined because the sea breeze came in.

Huntley's never been a beach guy. It wasn't part of his Ravensthorpe upbringing, but he's often wondered if his coastal disinterest might be genetic; that a portion of his DNA prefers to be landlocked rather than waterside. Smart, he thinks, would be to visit Switzerland and see if that land talks to him. He wonders, not for the first time, what relatives he has over there and what they're like. It's a challenging puzzle to solve: how to find a Swiss family when all he has to go on is the name of Soleil, most likely made up.

But that's a problem for another day, because right now, it's the car that's talking to him, and if he could just turn off all those other thoughts, he might get a better handle on Lance's story. This hallucinating nightswimmer.

"How far out is far enough?"

Slowly, it comes to him.

The story.

The verse.

It's all forming of its own accord.

He fishes around in the glovebox, but doesn't find a pen. Then he remembers: he still has Henrikson's magic pen from yesterday in his pocket. The inside page of the brochure's back cover is blank. He folds it over, balancing the brochure on his thigh. It's an awkward position, but nothing's going to stop him. He pictures Lance, running from the car and heaving himself into the water, fully clothed. It feels good, the cold water. A relief. Purifying. Strengthening. But also confusing. This drug. This jimsonweed. Out and out and out. But thinking at some point he was swimming back in?

Is it dawn and he's swimming towards the sun?

Like yesterday at Henrikson's, the words appear on the page without effort. He's out there, in the water, with Lance, who crazily swims out, loses his bearings and is unable to return to safety. What remains is the question of who put the jimsonweed in the water bottle; the poem hasn't provided any answers.

The knock on the window startles him. He's stunned to see the chubby face of Marcus Ford-Brackman staring at him through the window and motioning for Huntley to lower it.

The wind rifles into the car once the window is open.

"Hi, Marcus."

"What are you doing in my brother's car?"

"Uh, keeping watch. The police officer left, and gave me the key."

"Get out."

"Why are you here?"

"To pick up the car and drive it back. Why else?"

"A long way from Mandurah on public transport, isn't it?"

"I came up with my aunt."

Huntley would really like to raise the window, block out the wind, and read through his poem again. "Where is she?"

"She's gone to Northbridge. To identify Lance."

"I'm really sorry about what happened."

Marcus reaches through the open window and grabs the door lever. "Get the fuck out of the car."

"All right, all right." Huntley rolls up the brochure and climbs out. The wind ruffles his clothes and feels like it's trying to lift him up. "I was just minding it. Like the cop asked me to."

Marcus gets in and closes the door, which really slams with the wind assistance. "This isn't your property. You had no right to sit in this car. You look like you were about to drive off with it."

"The thought of that never crossed my mind. I got in for some protection while waiting. From the wind."

"You could've waited in the café."

"Yeah, maybe. Hey, your aunt, who brought you here? Was that Niranda?"

"What's it to you?"

"She's a good friend of my wife, Giorgie. Ex-wife."

"Her? She was at the house last night for dinner."

"Really? What was it all about?"

"Why would it be about something? They're friends, right?"

"Giorgie doesn't consume a single morsel without a purpose. She considers every dining table a negotiation table. If I recall rightly, Niranda's the same."

Marcus fastens the seatbelt, which pinches around his soft middle. "I heard them talking about some new gallery. I don't know. I got there late. And I had to practice anyway."

"Right. You need to hold on to that third chair, now it's yours."

"I'm not the incumbent yet. But I will be, once the trial period is done."

Huntley leans on the open window. "Look, for what it's worth, I'm sorry about your brother."

"You don't look it."

"You're having a bad run of it," Huntley says, curious to see how far he can push Marcus. "The second death in two days."

"It's the first. I had nothing to do with that girl."

"Except that you so quickly took her place. Any gardeners in the family?"

"What kind of question is that?"

"What about a botanist? A plant-lover?"

"You're seriously fucking weird."

Marcus raises the window, forcing Huntley to remove his hands from the frame and step back. Marcus reverses in the blasé fashion of someone used to others getting out of his way.

Huntley watches the car leave, then wanders back to the Landy, parked near the Canteen, shoulders bent into the gritty, salt-tinged wind. Once in the driver's seat, he sits there, considering his next move.

"I need to find Lance's place," he says, turning the key and roaring the Landy to life.

<>

The spidery, long-armed attendant pulls the sheet back from Lance Ford-Brackman's bulbous face. Niranda Stone's heels click on the tiled floor as she steps towards the stainless steel bench.

"Dear God. What have you done to him?"

"That was the water," Everest says. "It inflates the body."

"He looks hideous."

"It could've been far worse, given a few more days."

"Is that supposed to be comforting?"

"No. I ... Are you sure it's him?"

Niranda nods at Everest, then looks stoically at her nephew. "That overbite of his, from his crossed-over teeth. He never liked the dentist."

"Who does?"

"When he was a teenager, he refused to wear braces."

"Thank you for making the long drive up."

"When can we bury him?"

Everest isn't enjoying the cursory way Niranda Stone speaks, as if each sentence is barely worth saying and she's wasting precious time making this conversation. But Everest is amazed by the woman's strong stomach. She wonders what else Niranda has blandly grimaced her way through.

"The investigation isn't at the point yet where we can release the body, I'm afraid."

"He killed himself. What's the hold-up?"

"Maybe you should take this outside," the attendant says, delicately sliding the sheet back over Lance's face. "You should not speak about the dead, around the dead."

"Do you think he'll hear us?" Niranda asks.

"It's about respect." The attendant snaps the plastic gloves off his long fingers and lobs them into the bin. "De mortuis nil nisi bonum."

"Am I supposed to know what that means?"

"It's Latin. Do not speak ill of the dead."

"I'm not speaking ill of him. I want to bury him. With respect, and without delay."

"I understand that," Everest says. "We can discuss this further outside."

"I'm not leaving without him."

"Please, Mrs Stone. Follow me."

Niranda, a woman who clearly likes to be ahead of everything and everyone, pushes past Everest and really muscles the door to the side. Her heels echo as she strides down the long hallway, phone in her left hand and a large handbag looped over the wrist of her right. While Everest thinks the blue dress-suit is very corporate, with a dash of politics, she can't help but admire the confident figure Niranda Stone cuts as she walks with such purpose, owning this dank basement hallway the way she owns hallways everywhere. Still, she wonders whether it is the confidence gained through hard work and diligence, or simply passed on through money and privilege.

"Hurry up," Niranda says. "I don't have all day."

Everest decides not to concede anything to this woman.

Outside, Niranda checks her phone and says, "Have your underling prepare Lance for transportation."

"We're not ready to do that. Besides, he won't fit in your car."

"The delivery is your responsibility. Get it done today. Move him to FB Funeral Directors in Mandurah."

"Your family owns a funeral home?"

"They own lots of businesses."

Everest thinks such a business would be an effective way to get rid of unwanted bodies. "He stays here until my superiors release him. It's not my call."

"Your superiors? You don't have that power? What kind of detective are you?"

Everest grits her teeth.

Niranda extracts a pair of large sunglasses from her handbag and puts them on. "If only your superiors can release him, then why am I bothering to talk to you?"

"You'll get the same answer."

"You're so sure of that? I know a lot of people in this city. I'm pretty certain I know your superiors."

"Go for it." Everest folds her arms, then decides to take a different approach. "What can you tell me about Lance? We're having some trouble with this part of the case."

"There is no case."

"I want to know his background, and no one in the family has been forthcoming with any information."

"I'm part of that family. What makes you think I would do anything differently?"

"I got the impression you've distanced yourself from Mandurah. You're taking a straighter road towards success. Your company is in Port Kennedy, to start with. You married out and changed your name."

"Are you suggesting I'm going clean? All my family does is run businesses, and I do the same."

Everest smiles, glad to have landed a punch. "Lance was doing something similar, right? This Southern Everglades project."

"That is top secret. There can be no mention of it in the press."

"Why not?"

Niranda lets out an exasperated sigh. "Because trying to develop land in Perth requires more than a few sideline deals. Which necessitates, naturally, having a steady flow of cash to line the pockets of particular people. Don't look so shocked. This is just how things get done in Perth. You always shake the hand that has money in it. That's the way it's been ever since the colony was founded, and it's what everyone understands."

"You're saying Lance needed cash to pay off people just to get the Southern Everglades underway?"

"Among other things, which I'm not at liberty to talk about. Even if I was, I wouldn't talk about them with you, someone so powerless she can't even sign a body out of a morgue."

"At this stage, until we know more, your nephew is staying on that cold table for as long as I want him to."

"We'll see about that." Niranda pivots in her heels and moves quickly across the car park, phone already at her ear.

"What a piece of work," Everest says to herself.

It's mid-afternoon, and a little too early, but she feels like she's earned a hit. She takes the vape from her pocket and has a long, enjoyable inhale of the cannabis-tobacco mix. She blows a cloud in the direction of Niranda's departing Porsche and wonders what Lance was doing to generate extra cash. It also opens the door as to who Lance was bribing.

Everest inhales again, trying to cleanse herself of that exchange with Niranda. There must be people, she thinks, in a position to green-light or kill the Southern Everglades project.

Booth, in his bright orange, urbanised off-roader, pulls into the car park and stops next to Everest, hip-hop blaring on the car stereo. He lowers the window, and also lowers the volume.

"Found you. You're not answering your phone?"

"I was busy. The body ID."

"How'd that go?"

"There were issues. How was it down south?"

"Painful. Massive jam at Thomas Road, going there and coming back. Whatever happened to the Freeway being a free way?"

"I meant with the family. What did they have to say about Lance?"

Booth reaches his right arm out of the vehicle, for the vape. "Can I? My stress level is through the roof."

Everest gives it to him. "The family?"

Booth shakes his head as he inhales and exhales, blowing a huge cloud of vapour out the window. "Not a thing. They didn't answer a single question. I got the sense they'd already disowned him. He doesn't even live down there."

"I know. He has a place in Mosman Park. Near the golf course."

"Have you checked it out?"

"Not yet. I suppose we should."

"Can we do that?"

"The window of opportunity ... it's closing fast."

Booth hands the vape back. "How many of these have you had? You sound way gone."

"Are you gonna tell on me? Fine. I had a few tokes with Kendrick downstairs, to fortify myself. You'd do the same."

"Totally understandable. The morgue is awful. I don't understand vaping with Kendrick, though. He totally gives me the creeps."

"Then I spoke with Niranda Stone, and that was almost as bad as being in the morgue. She's convinced it was suicide."

"Yeah, the rest of the family said that too. The lifeguard was right, after all."

"It wasn't suicide, Justin. The water bottle."

"Right. That jiminy-shit." Booth laughs a little. "The weed made him do it."

Everest laughs despite herself, feeling pleasantly high. "Jimsonweed is powerful stuff. And someone put it there."

"Maybe he did. It was his own little habit. I got the feeling in Mandurah that there's some secret around Lance, but none of them would say it."

"His place might hold the answer. Let's go there." Everest moves around the orange off-roader to the passenger side and climbs in. "Take me to Mosman Park."

"Come on. I've done enough driving for one day."

"Stop whining. Just crank those beats back up and we'll vape all the way."

Booth obliges. On the journey, they pass the stick between them until it's empty, rocking all the way down Stirling Highway. Traffic is light, as they get in that mid-afternoon window when all the school runs are done and work hasn't yet finished.

Booth turns at Wellington Street and gets around the golf course onto Colonial Gardens. He stops at the Mosman Waters complex, turning off the engine and cutting the music.

"You've got to be fucking kidding me," Everest says.

"What?"

"That's Huntley's car."

"Quintus Huntley? What's he doing here?"

"Making more trouble."

"Let's arrest him. Get him in an interrogation room, see what he says under pressure." Booth's phone rings. He looks at the screen. "It's my dad."

"I guess Niranda knows someone important after all."

"What does that mean?"

"Ask your father."

Booth answers the phone. "Hey. Yeah. Okay. You're sure about this? All right. I'll be there in half an hour."

"Back to the morgue?"

Booth's shoulders slump. "More driving." He checks his watch. "Rush hour now, to make things worse."

"Let me guess. You have to sign the body out."

"Yep."

"As you said, it's your case."

Booth nods slowly. "Can you handle him alone?"

"Huntley? He's harmless."

"He's still our main suspect."

"Maybe he'll confess to me." Everest opens the door. "If you speak to Niranda Stone, give her my very best regards."

"Careful. She's not an enemy you want to have."

Once Everest is out of the car, Booth drives off, stereo blaring again.

Mosman Waters is a complex of grey-toned condos, all in a row, extending slightly up a hill. It's all so modern it looks like the cement hasn't fully set and the paint would still smear a finger if touched. Everest pushes open the not-quite-closed gate and goes to condo B, weighing her options on how to deal with Huntley. Up to now, the more she's pushed him to stay out of it, the more involved he's become. She decides enlisting his help could be more fruitful than trying to keep him on the sidelines. Plus, shoved in the far recesses of her mind is the trauma of having tried to push Charlene back onto the stage, which had a devastating result.

She'd really like to have a cry about it, and beat herself up a bit, but now isn't the time. She buries the pain.

There's a section of very clean glass between condo B's front door and its wall. She looks through, hands cupped around her eyes, and sees Huntley standing next to the dining table. He's not moving, and could almost be asleep standing up. She knocks on the glass and Huntley just about jumps. He comes to the door and opens it.

"Detective E," he says. "You scared one of my nine lives out of me."

"What are you doing here?"

Huntley lets her in, then closes the door. "Okay. I know I said I'd stay out of it, but I thought I'd try to help. I've actually been waiting for you. I assumed you'd get here eventually. I haven't touched anything."

They go down the short hallway and into the open-plan kitchen-dining-living area.

Everest reminds herself to get Huntley on her side. "What then?"

"I ... you know ... I was just taking it all in and trying to decipher what it says to me."

"And?"

"A couple of things, but it's mostly conjecture."

"How did you even get in?"

"The landlord." Huntley points next door. "He lives there. He saw me coming, like he was waiting."

"Did he know that Lance is dead?"

"Nuh. I told him. Said I was here investigating."

"You can't do that. It's a serious crime to pose as a police officer."

Huntley smiles. "I never said I was police. To be honest, though, he let me in way too easily. Not your typical landlord. So trusting."

"So, that confirms Lance was a tenant, not the owner."

"Yeah. Why would he rent? The family's loaded and then some."

Everest walks through the living room. It's neat, but clearly lived in. There's a large workspace set up near the door leading to the small garden. She goes to the desk, which has piles of papers, plus a stack of the same brochures that were in Lance's briefcase. A laptop cable snakes across the desk's middle.

"They'd have enough money to buy this whole block," she says. "But it fits."

"How so?"

"It's becoming clear Lance was the black sheep of the family."

"Sounds like they didn't approve of his lifestyle."

"What lifestyle? Do you mean living in Mosman Park and not in Mandurah?"

Huntley looks at Everest, confused. "You don't know he was gay?"

"How do you know that?"

"The landlord told me. He even used the term 'gentleman callers', which makes me think Lance liked older men."

Everest tries not to show she's surprised to hear this. "Are the Ford-Brackmans really so old-fashioned?"

"They probably never cared about his orientation," Huntley says, joining Everest at the desk, "but you can bet they care what everyone else thinks about it."

"How is this even still an issue? For anyone?"

"Don't underestimate the power of public opinion, especially in circles where reputation matters, like sports, business, crime, economics, politics and the arts. Wow, they feel like the six sides of a cube. Roll the dice and see what comes up."

Everest puts on plastic gloves and starts looking through the papers on the desk.

"We're talking about the heir to a vast and, let's face it, highly criminal empire," Huntley continues. "Pardon my language, but that family doesn't want someone of Lance's persuasion to run that show. They'd lose all credibility and power."

"That's ridiculous."

"Agreed. But let me ask you this. Is it any different in the police?"

Everest would like to say she gets propositioned at least once every couple of weeks by someone, when on the job, and has managed to decline all offers so far while keeping it under wraps that she herself is bisexual.

"Your silence is saying a lot."

"You can be gay. It's just suggested you keep it to yourself."

"I'll have you know the university is exactly the same. 'Be discreet' is the unofficial line, if I recall rightly. Though I fall asleep during a lot of those compulsory, so-called 'diversity' training sessions."

"So much for free thinking."

"But how about progress? About letting people be how they are? Have you found anything?"

Huntley reaches his hands towards the desk, but Everest stops him. "Look, but don't touch," she says. "Otherwise, you'll be arrested for breaking and entering."

"Yes, ma'am. I could always say I'm a gentleman caller. I guess that's more entering than breaking. Although who knows what Lance was into."

Everest can't help herself; she lets out a short laugh.

"What are you looking for?" Huntley asks.

After clearing her throat and composing herself, Everest says, "Lance's aunt hinted he was involved in something dodgy."

"Oh, that Niranda. An untameable shrew."

"You know her?"

"I know that she would know all about dodgy deals."

"Like what?"

"She may have acquired a cleaner surname, but that doesn't make her hands any less dirty."

"I'm starting to get the impression you know everyone in this town."

"Only by association. I married into notoriety, then I was really happy to get divorced from it. But, yeah, back when I was Giorgie's plus-one, I went to so many dinners and events, which were like society trade fairs. Because that was where all the big business was being done. Forget the boardrooms and offices, and even Parliament House. The deals get cut in the evenings in Perth, in some huge house or at an exclusive club. My father-in-law once bought a farm during the races at Ascot. On a Saturday night."

"We've placed Lance at Lake Karrinyup Country Club, in the hours leading up to his death."

"No surprise. Plenty of meetings happen on golf courses. Guys like very much mixing business with pleasure. A golf course is a great place to have candid conversations without the threat of being overheard, while also keeping the pretence of everything being laid back and casual. I'm quoting Harland Gifford, an avid golfer, almost verbatim here."

"Perth certainly has a lot of golf courses. Public and private."

"Like schools, right? The private school boys doing private business deals on private golf clubs. Think of them as places for remote working."

Everest manages to stifle her laughter this time.

"Pubs and bars used to be good places for that kind of stuff," Huntley adds. "But there are too many cameras in there these days. Inside and out. So much that's traceable."

"You know what's weird?" Everest puts her hands on her hips. "There's no computer. It wasn't in the car either."

"Can it be he didn't have one?"

"All the cables are here. Can't do business without it."

"I don't have one."

"I'm not surprised. What business are you in exactly?"

"Hurtful, Detective E. I'm old school. A pen and paper guy, and proud of it. Maybe the killer took it."

"From his car or from this desk?"

"Either or."

"If it was here, it could have been taken any time since last night. When did you get here?"

"Literally five minutes before you. I was just getting my bearings."

"Yes," Everest says with a smile. "I saw you standing frozen to the spot. What did you come here looking for?"

"All the back-story. All the clues. Same as with the violinist."

Everest shoots a look at Huntley. "Did you get into her place as well?"

"Ah, I might have."

"This is all just poetry for you? Two people have been murdered, and all you care about is your work?"

"Hey, I'm coming off a really long dry spell. And when you think about it, we both want the same thing. To solve these two crimes. Think of me as a consultant."

"You're still a suspect."

"Stop saying that. I'm delving into the psychology and motives, to give you an idea of how things happened. I'm offering narrative assistance. For free, I might add."

"Okay. Fine. You think you're so useful. Let's run with that. What happened to Lance?"

"Easy. Superman syndrome."

"What?"

"Come on, Ellie. You were a rockstar. You must've done some serious drugs, back in the day. Harder than the whacky-baccy you're on now."

"Are you implying the jimsonweed made Lance feel like Superman?"

"Yep. And it cooked him. That happens with mind-alterers. Though you probably know that. He went for a swim to cool off. Maybe he got it in his head he could swim all the way to Rottnest. Maybe he just lost his bearings."

"Or he passed out. But your story has no boat involved. And no one else involved. You think he wasn't somehow coaxed into the water?"

"Any evidence someone was in the car with him?"

"No. The car was clean."

Huntley mutters, "It was. Very clean."

"What did you say?"

"Oh, nothing. What do you know about the tainted water bottle? Anything on that?"

"Like, fingerprints?"

"Yeah, for example."

Everest shakes her head.

Huntley walks away from the desk, towards the kitchen. "Strange methodology, to try to kill a person by drugging them and then hoping they harm themselves."

"There was plenty left in the water bottle. Maybe the full dose would've been deadly."

Huntley fills the kettle and puts it on. He starts hunting around the kitchen, finding the fridge well-stocked. "Seems a shame to let all this go to waste."

"Stop touching things."

"Too late for that." Above the fridge, Huntley finds a storage area for alcohol bottles. He extracts the rum. "Hello, my friend. Right. Dry week starts next week, because we're definitely not letting you go to waste."

"Huntley, please."

"You want a drink? Hot toddies all round, I say. Lance even has cinnamon and lemons, bless him."

"Is that a drink or the name of a male stripper troupe?"

"You'll love it." Huntley gets to work making the drinks.

"I think my grandma used to have that. Is it hot tea with alcohol?"

"It is. Rum, to be exact."

"She used to say it took the edge off after a hot day."

"Oh, it does. Incredibly."

"Or it takes the edge off when you're in a hot container."

"Same."

Everest, having resigned herself to Huntley taking over in the kitchen, sits on one of the stools at the counter. She removes the plastic gloves and flattens a piece of paper on the counter.

"You found something?" Huntley asks.

"Maybe. It's an agenda, for a local council meeting. The City of Cockburn. A couple of weeks ago."

"Beeliar is in that area. This Southern Everglades thing."

"You know that too? This secret project isn't proving very secret."

Huntley slides a steaming hot toddy towards Everest. "Okay. I confess. I found a brochure in his car."

"Pardon? What were you doing in his car?"

"Minding it. Cheers." Huntley has a sip. "Oh, that's good. The police officer who was supposed to be watching it decided to leave. I was a victim of good timing. And guess who shows up to drive the vehicle back home? The PSO's replacement third violinist."

"Marcus Ford-Brackman." Everest blows on her drink, then sips, and sips again. "I've got to admit that's good, if not a bit over-generous with the rum."

"Aye." Huntley holds up the bottle. "It's talking to me. It wants to be drunk. That's the ending for this bottle. Emptiness."

Everest, after another sip, says, "We might as well clean out the kitchen. Before some Ford-Brackman comes to take it all away."

"I like the way you think, Detective E."

"So? What's for dinner? I'm suddenly so hungry."

"I think I can put together something good."

"Don't ask me to help. I'm completely lost in a kitchen, unless something needs heating up."

Huntley goes to the fridge. "I got it. My commune upbringing involved a lot of food growing and food preparing."

"Good. You can make dinner while I work through this list of attendees, to see if there's anyone interesting." Everest looks at her empty glass. "That went down like velvet. I think I need another male stripper."

"Coming up. Hah."

<>

She rings the bell of apartment 9.

After a long and difficult day, which started at dawn with skipping the beach in order to fix a speech for Blair that wasn't needed in the end, and finished with Blair shooting down her infrastructure proposal with the blithe comment that it would be too expensive to redesign Perth's major arteries and that taxpayers would never support it, Aphra had to force herself to detour to Peppermint Grove on her way home, to do this one last, very sad task.

The locks click and the door is opened.

"Yes?"

"Mr Henrikson? I'm Aphra Massey. A friend of Katie's. We spoke on the phone."

"Did you get the all clear?"

"Yes. The police said I can collect her things from the apartment."

"It's a bit late, isn't it?"

"I couldn't get here earlier. I only just finished work."

"Well, it won't take you long," Henrikson says. "The poor lass only arrived with a suitcase and a violin."

"I know. I met her at the airport. Now, I'm taking care of everything."

"You have my sympathies. For what it's worth, I enjoyed your book."

"Uh, thanks."

"You sound surprised."

"I just wasn't expecting that. I don't come across many readers these days."

"That's a shame. We still have copies in the store, but I think it's been a while since we moved one. Doesn't mean it isn't good."

"Who reads poetry anymore? Right?"

"I do." Henrikson turns and goes back into the apartment. "I'll get the keys."

Waiting, Aphra nods at a middle-aged woman in a grey work uniform who comes slowly up the stairs, several full shopping bags pulling at her arms. Now that it's evening, the wind has finally dropped, but the slight hum of traffic still carries over the buildings and trees from Stirling Highway.

The old man hands her the keys.

"Henrikson," she says. "The bookstore in Freo."

"That's the one."

"It's an honour to meet you."

"The honour is all mine, Ms Massey. Your book is outstanding. So honest and daring, going where no one would be brave enough to go. Was it too much to follow?"

"Because I didn't publish anything else?"

"I assume a collection like that takes a lot out of the writer. It must be difficult to keep that going."

"Not difficult. Just not exactly lucrative."

"What do you do instead?"

"I write poetry of the profitable kind."

"Putting good words in the mouths of others? Or selling stuff?"

"A nice balance of both."

"I have no doubt there's a living to be made from those trades."

"There is."

Henrikson nods. "We've had plenty of events in the store over the years, for readings and signings, that barely got a handful of people."

"That's for successful writers. There are thousands of writers out there who can't even get their work published."

"Would you like to come in?" Henrikson asks. "Have a cup of tea? Help me solve the mysteries of publishing and economics?"

"There's nothing to solve. Anyway, if you don't mind, I'd like to get this over with, late as it is."

"Understandable. Perhaps you'll visit the store one day. Sign your books."

"Sure." Aphra holds up the keys. "I'll bring these back. I won't be long."

"Take all the time you need. I'm not one of these seniors having dinner at three and in bed by seven. I'll be working late into the night."

"On what?"

"Family history."

"That's good. That's something of value."

"It's a passion project, and it keeps me busy."

This makes Aphra smile as she walks to apartment 10. She unlocks the door and enters, focusing on the smart choices she made, while also feeling proud of the book she wrote. Because it was writing out her trauma as poetry that led to her realising she had a talent with words. Without it, she would never have found her current calling. She also never would have met Katie, which would have saved her this heartbreaking task of packing up her friend's entire life for disposal.

This is her first time in the apartment. She edges in, unsure of the state she'll find it in. Though gregarious in person, Katie was intensely private about her living space. It was like that in Kyiv, when Katie had been so keen to show Aphra the city, yet never invited her home.

Now, Aphra feels like she's intruding.

In the living room, the stain that remains on the carpet, plus the chalked body outline, is too much to bear, so she goes into the bedroom. The black suitcase is on the top shelf of the closet, white airline tags still looped around the handle. She gets this down and open, and starts stuffing it with clothes, not bothering to pack neatly. Not even the expensive performance gowns get folded. There's a lot of black clothing. It's only when she finds the yellow dress Katie wore at the embassy event in Kyiv that she stops, takes a moment to understand exactly what's happened and starts crying. Katie's gone. Murdered.

What hurts the most is the loneliness of her grief. She is the only person on the planet feeling this loss. There's no family. No friends. No one in the orchestra cares, and a replacement violinist is already in the third chair. The PSO has turned the page and is playing on. She doubts any of them will even bother to attend Katie's funeral. Soon, the stain will be cleaned from the carpet, the chalk vacuumed away, and someone will move in, to fill these closets with their own clothes and erase Katie's energy from the apartment forever.

She uses the yellow dress to wipe away her tears.

"Enough."

She throws the yellow dress into the suitcase, then starts pulling out the drawers and emptying them on the bed. Katie's underwear, socks and shirts get scooped up and shoved into the suitcase, which has to be sat upon to get its latches closed. Once done, she decides to leave the bathroom stuff and food for whoever cleans the apartment. All that remains is the violin. She doesn't know what to do with it, but grabs it anyway.

Outside, she wheels the suitcase to apartment 9 and rings the bell.

"The keys," she says, handing them to Henrikson.

"You were quick. I think I managed one paragraph in that time."

"I left a lot of stuff. Food and whatnot. I hope that's all right."

"It'll probably get thrown out."

"I just wanted to be out of there."

"It can be very difficult living with the remnants of people. Every little thing sparks some kind of memory. What will you do with it?"

"Donate it, I guess." She holds up the violin case. "I have no clue what to do with this."

"Maybe you use one of the strings to strangle the killer."

This takes Aphra completely by surprise. "Pardon?"

"An eye for an eye. Just like in your book. Revenge is therapeutic, isn't it?"

"That was fiction."

"Was it? I apologise. It struck me as something experienced firsthand. The details. The sensations. The rollercoaster of emotions and second-guessing. It's very difficult to make that stuff up."

"Well, I did."

"All through history, the greatest writers lived what they wrote about. It's necessary, to get the authenticity. To capture the moment, and be able to transport the reader to that moment."

"Are you saying I killed Jye Parsons?"

Henrikson smiles warmly, and is rather handsome when doing so. "I'm sure the name was changed. I'd say to protect the innocent, but he certainly wasn't that."

"Okay. Look. I've had a hellish day. I'm standing here with all the personal effects of one of my closest friends, and it's my responsibility to bury her as well. Please respect I'm not in the right frame of mind to discuss stuff I wrote years ago. I just want to go home."

"I respect that. Fully. I meant no offence." Henrikson smiles again, then closes the door.

Aphra stands there, staring at the number 9.

<>

Huntley sits in Lance's swivel chair and watches Everest sleep. Rather than curling up on the sofa, cat-like, she sleeps flat on her back, fingers interlocked over her stomach, which gently goes up and down with each breath. It's as if she fell asleep during a session with a therapist. Sometimes, her head moves to one side, pulling the ponytail's band and making her hair looser each time, but her body keeps the same position. He wonders if that's how she slept on all the tour buses, tucked into one of the narrow bunks. It makes him think she would sleep very soundly in a caravan.

The rum is just about finished. He's drinking the last of it straight from the bottle, which feels reckless and outlaw-ish, and also a little sad. If not for the detective's presence, he would consider the situation he now finds himself in rather pathetic. But because of Ellie, and having made her dinner and hot toddies, and talked through the case, and now watching over her as she sleeps in this dead man's condo, it all matters a bit more. Quite a lot, actually. Two people are dead, and it's on him and Ellie to find out who did it.

One killer, he thinks, getting the strong feeling that the cases are connected.

Everest snores a little, like a child, in short snorts.

He wonders how many tour buses she slept on during her drumming days, and how many couches she surfed. While that touring life was no doubt hard, he envies her for having had the experience, and also admires her for casting it aside in order to become a detective and fight crime. There's more to that story, he knows, specifically to do with the singer's death. Because there's always more story, if enough digging is done.

He has another swig and thinks: keep on digging until all the secrets are unearthed and your claws are ragged.

The rum feels really good. Now he's at the end of the bottle, he thinks it's a shame there isn't more of it. He puts the bottle on the desk, aims a thumb and index finger shaped like a pistol at it, and shoots it.

There's a lot of story in here too, he thinks. They could be on the run, hiding out, in the almost darkness. Only the kitchen light is on, shining on the ridiculous mess they made, and will likely leave behind. Though Everest did fill the dishwasher, like a crazed juggler, tossing plates and glasses in at all angles, then slamming the door shut, turning it on, and hoping for the best. It's still rumbling, over in the kitchen, and every now and then there's a thunk or a clank as something moves inside, possibly breaking.

On the run. Huntley likes this, and his mind easily constructs that alternative world, where he's a renowned poet and she's the drummer for a famous band. What they both achieved in early adulthood didn't disappear; it got better. He published more books to extensive acclaim and she recorded more albums that rocked. They both reached the kind of glorious fame that brings silly money and makes it impossible for them to walk down the street without being mobbed. So, they take to hiding out in other people's houses and apartments; eat their food, drink their booze, sleep on their couches and pretend to have regular lives while the outside world screams for more poetry and songs from them.

As things become hazy around him and his mind flits from one creative thought to another, the only thing he's acutely aware of is that he is very drunk; too inebriated to be able to tune into this place and mine it for the right words. He wants to get up and put a blanket over Everest, but even that's unmanageable. Every time he tries to stand, the chair swivels to the left or right.

Oh yeah, he thinks. Rum is heavy.

Though drunk, he doesn't feel any attraction towards Everest, which he finds curious. She's pretty, even with that severe ponytail, and without question, whole legions of men would salivate when seeing her flail at the drums with her hair flicking all over the place, like she did last night in the Scotch College rehearsal theatre, but he himself feels protective towards her. Brotherly almost, as if he wants to adopt her into his patchwork family of children born from sunlight. She's only a few years younger than him, and she's certainly accomplished more, but still she seems far younger.

Or, it's the case that he is far older. Born into independence and self-sufficiency. A quasi-parent to abandoned children when he was a child himself. Raised on a commune where he learned how to work and cook and clean and grow things. Where he understood very early on the importance of seasons, weather and wind directions, and where his father taught him to notice the subtle changes in things. That included taking notice of people; how to read them and empathise with them, and work out how they got here, why they do what they do and where they're going. Every single person was a mystery to be solved. Which was why he arrived in Perth not as a country hick with no clue about the wider world, but as a fully formed adult way ahead of the coddled, sheltered kids he went to uni with who couldn't make toast. Those kids saw him as a freak anyway, as a young old man. It was at uni that he met Lydette, and she tried to make him her project; to citify the country boy. But he was never interested. Her older sister, though, already graduated and running her first gallery, was another story, one he tried to write himself into.

Watching Everest sleep, feeling no desire towards her, and having the rum amplify all the regret inside him, he knows that Giorgie still owns him. She has his heart, secured away in a vault in some gallery in the western suburbs. That she's been impregnated by a sculptor with one name fills him with sadness, making him wonder again how he let their relationship go so wrong. People drift apart, fall out of love, yes, that happens. But his main regret is that he didn't work hard enough. And when he was ready to work harder, it was too late.

It's both disappointing and good that all the rum is finished. He knows that trying to drown this regret will just inflate it and make it float to the top, bigger and more dominant than ever.

He's grateful, to be here, in this dead man's condo, with Everest.

After all that's happened in the last two days, events which have woken him from what felt like a couple of decades of sleepwalking through life, it's the visit to the naturopath that stands out. That vile woman with the thicket of hair who called him evil. That house full of natural poisons. Wild arum and jimsonweed and whatever else deadly that grows all by itself. The human race has spent thousands of years perfecting weaponry and warfare, yet all that time the planet grew plenty of weapons of its own.

What's this alien being within?
Causing this startling awakeness, this horrid dream?

He taps the pocket of his pants, feeling the torn-off back page of the brochure, folded in there.

That's two decent ones, he thinks, in two days.

It's more than he's done in two decades.

He closes his eyes and wonders what plant he could use to kill Daley.

Sleep's coming, wafting towards him like a friendly spectre. He wants to move to the floor; lie flat on a hard surface, on his back like Everest, rather than pass out all bent and twisted in this swivel chair. But it's too weighty, this boozy haze. He's stuck. His head starts to tilt back, straining his neck, stretching ligaments and tendons to their extremes.

Then, a noise from outside snaps him awake. It makes him straighten in the chair, to listen for it again. A key in a door. The scratch of metal on metal. A lock clunking out of its slot. A hinge whining. The hall light switching on. The door closing. A man silhouetted in the hallway, the light behind him.

"Who the fuck are you?" the man asks, loud enough to make Everest bolt upright on the sofa.

"I can explain," Huntley somehow manages to say.

Everest, ponytail half loose, fumbles around her, then gets her gun out, almost dropping it in the process, and points it at the man. "Don't move."

"Hey. Just calm down." The man holds up his hands. "There's nothing of value in this place. No drugs. No cash."

"We're not thieves," Huntley says, sobered slightly by the commotion. "Or junkies."

"You both look pretty wasted." The man turns to the kitchen. "Looks like you're cleaning the place out."

"There's nothing worse than waste."

"I'm Detective Elenore Everest." She keeps the gun steady. "Who are you? How did you get in?"

The man holds up a key. "How did you get in?"

"We're investigating the death of Lance Ford-Brackman," Huntley says. "We have every right to be here."

"Say your name, please," Everest orders.

"Nathaniel Winslow."

Everest lowers the gun slightly. "You're on the list."

"What list?"

"The City of Cockburn council meeting. I found an agenda on the desk. Your name's on it."

"So? I'm a property developer. My office is in Cockburn."

"The Southern Everglades," Huntley says. "Are you involved in that? Are you and Lance partners?"

Winslow pauses, then says, "Yeah. Business partners."

"Ellie, put the gun down."

"Why?" Everest asks.

"There's no danger." To Winslow, Huntley says, "Why don't you come in and tell us about your relationship with Lance. And maybe why you waited until midnight to come here and retrieve your things."

"Sorry, but you got it way wrong, mate." Winslow steps forward and falls into one of the dining room chairs. "We weren't a couple."

Huntley rubs his eyes, then turns on a desk lamp. "There's a fair age difference, not that it matters, but some people think it does. I'm guessing that's not the issue. No. All this, coming here, being with Lance in secret, it's a whole other part of your life. You're probably married with kids."

Winslow's mouth hangs open a little. "Sorry. Who are you?"

Everest holsters her gun. "Why are you here, Mr Winslow?" she asks, resetting her ponytail with practised precision.

"You need to tell me why you're here. The case is closed. Niranda told me it was suicide."

Huntley laughs, a little too loudly. "Don't believe a word that comes out of her mouth. Lance was poisoned."

"What?"

"Huntley, please, keep it in check." Everest stands up and goes to the dining table, where she stays standing, to exert power. "There are circumstances leading to Lance's death that need explaining."

"He drowned. What's this about poison?"

"Jimsonweed," Huntley blurts out, the rum dissolving every filter. "Ever heard of it?"

"Is that what you've been smoking? What are you even doing here? Eating Lance's food and drinking his booze, then sleeping here like you own the place. How is that part of any investigation?"

"Good question." Huntley swivels in the chair a little. "A very pertinent, on the money question."

"Why don't you stop fucking around and answer it."

"Ah, tough guy. You get things done in this town, right? Well, you see, tough guy, I have a bit of a skill that the police, with Detective Everest here, are taking advantage of."

"What skill?"

"I can fill in the gaps, so to speak, just by being present in a certain place."

"You're a seriously shabby-looking clairvoyant."

"Easy. No need for insults. I can't see the future. But I'm definitely good at constructing the past, which then helps me get an idea of what might be coming. Because it's all one big story, and it reveals itself to me."

"That sounds like the biggest pile of bullshit I ever heard. Lance and I worked together. That's it."

"Maybe I'm not explaining it properly. It's been a long day."

"From the looks of it, I'd say you've seen better ones. Does that make me clairvoyant too?"

Huntley shrugs. "Am I wrong about your alternative lifestyle?"

"Yes."

"Did you decide to take on this project specifically so you could be closer to Lance and spend more time with him?"

Winslow scoffs at this. "No."

"That's a lie."

"It's about the money."

"That's a truth."

"Can I get my stuff?"

"What stuff? If you weren't together, what have you left here?"

"Business-related stuff."

Everest holds up a hand. "Wait. This project. Was anyone against it? Did Lance have any enemies?"

"Apart from his family?"

"The Ford-Brackmans? Do you really think they'd hurt one of their own?"

"As far as I know from Lance, they didn't consider him one of their own. They're getting close to tossing young Marcus onto the street."

"Playing violin could be a fabulous cover for a criminal honcho," Huntley says.

"Are you seeing more stories there, Mr Clairvoyant?" Winslow asks. "You're pathetic, mate."

"No need to make it personal."

"You did that, by breaking in here."

"While you did the entering."

Winslow stands up. "Now, you listen to me. You should be ashamed of yourselves. Fucking police are useless in this town. You're gonna clean up that mess and then we're all leaving together."

Everest motions for Huntley to follow her to the kitchen.

"Come on," she says. "He's right. We can't leave it like this."

"Can't we just call the kitchen a crime scene and be done with it?"

"I'm not doing this alone."

"Yeah," Winslow says. "Come on. Get to work."

Huntley manages to get to his feet and shuffle to the kitchen. The dishwasher makes another loud clunk.

"You had the right idea," he says. "Putting everything in there and letting it all be destroyed."

"I'll wash." Everest tosses Huntley a tea towel. "You can dry and put away."

"I don't know where anything goes in here."

"You found everything when you were cooking."

"Hunger is motivating."

"Put it anywhere," Winslow shouts out, at the desk now. "I don't think Lance is going to care."

They get to work. Everest washes the pots and pans with serious intent.

"You have really strong hands," Huntley says, leaning against the counter.

"They were once a lot stronger. I smoke medicinal marijuana for the pain in my wrists."

"The downside of drumming. I'm sorry."

"It's all right." Everest lowers her voice and adds, "Try to be nicer to Winslow."

Huntley matches her whisper: "Why? Because he's grieving?"

"Because he could report you. Have you arrested. He could report both of us."

Huntley thumbs towards the desk, fumbling with a glass lid in the process. "He's not going to report anything. Because if he does, it will place him here, at this time, and it will make all his lies unravel."

"Do you really think he and Lance were lovers? He keeps denying it."

"It was all in the pause. Plus, the body language. The fact he came here so late. His type, which are a dime a dozen in Perth, living one way and wanting another, whatever that other is. These men of quiet desperation. It was obvious."

"Yeah, maybe."

"Every person is a walking, talking piece of evidence of their own story."

Everest stops scrubbing a pan and asks, "What's mine?"

Huntley matches the pots with the lids. "No. I'm doing that. I like you too much. You know it anyway. Everyone knows their own story, even if it involves lying to themselves."

"Are you saying a lot of people are living lies?"

"Absolutely. He is. What's his name again?"

"Nathaniel Winslow."

"Right. I didn't catch it before. There was a lot going on in the living room. Like you pulling out a gun."

"He took me by surprise." Everest finishes the last wooden spoon and pulls out the plug. The water drains noisily. The dishwasher thunks again.

"I've heard that name," Huntley says softly, watching Winslow. "Or seen it somewhere. But, if you ask me, this is the story he wants. His wife and kids and whatnot, they're lies he's telling himself. Maybe they're even a kind of cover story. He couldn't do business without them. But this is where he wants to be. This is who he really is. I bet he's hurting right now."

Winslow comes into the kitchen carrying a small bag. "Are you done?"

"Is he allowed to take anything, Ellie?" Huntley asks. "The investigation's still open, right?"

"There's no case," Winslow says. "I'll take whatever I want."

"Your wetlands project is a massive mistake. It'll never happen."

"Sorry, mate. You can't be more wrong about that. Half of it's already been sold."

"Do you have the approval to clear the land and build?" Everest asks.

"Lance was sorting that. But I've got someone else to take that over now. It's just a matter of time."

Huntley is about to speak, but Everest jumps in: "Who's standing in the way?"

"The usual idiots. Local councils without any vision, drunk on what little power they have. While they lack vision, they love incentives."

"Ah, you're gonna bribe them," Huntley says. "Who are they?"

Winslow shrugs. "As I said, Lance was handling that."

"Mr Winslow," Everest says, "I'm very sorry for your loss. I'm also sorry you found us here in this way."

"I just want to go home. I think we can all agree, given the situation, that none of us were ever here."

Winslow ushers Huntley and Everest through the front door, then locks it. Without another word, he drops the keys in the post-box and walks to the gate. Huntley and Everest follow a few metres behind. He gets into a white SUV.

"God, look at that," Huntley says. "Nate wins."

"I swear that's exactly the same car that Lance had."

"Minus the egocentric license plate. A his-and-his purchase, you think? Matching cars?"

"Or just the fleet for the project. Speaking of cars. Are you in any condition to pilot this old tank of yours?"

"No. You seem far more coherent than me. Plus, if we get pulled over and tested, you'll be able to flash your badge and talk your way out of it."

Everest doesn't want to go home and have Charlene keep her up all night. "Where's your place?"

"It's not far. You're welcome to crash there."

"All right. But that's all I'm doing. Crashing. Because I'm finished with today."

Huntley tosses Everest the keys. "Relax, detective. My interest in you is purely professional. I want my endings. For both murders."

Once they are in the car, Everest moves the seat way forward. "I've been reading some of your work," she says. "Heavy stuff."

"Thanks. Good word that. Heavy. There was a lot of weight involved in writing that book. It was heavy carrying all those stories around. I couldn't sleep. A bit like now. These murders are weighing on me."

Everest starts the car and drives forward. "I used to write poems. In high school. Then I met someone who turned that teenage angst poetry into lyrics and we rocked the fucking world with it."

"The singer?"

"Yeah."

"What a shame you stopped."

"Indeed. A shame." Everest gets onto McCabe Street. "Where am I going?"

"Go straight. To Stirling. My caravan's under the red dingo."

"Caravan?"

Councilwoman in Coma

Be vanilla never plain
Lush salad enough as main
"I'm watching closely what I'm eating"
Diets inducing mental strain
Sweet flower tastes so strange
"I think I'm blind, no exaggerating"
Money clip of size insane
Don't ask, don't tell, don't explain
"Everything around me is dissipating"

The small café has an informal pop-up feel, nestled in the middle of the B Shed of Fremantle's Victoria Quay, in a converted workshop. No sign out front; just a chalkboard menu offering seafood fusion brunch and lunch at exorbitant prices. Every table is covered with too many glasses. Wine on portable racks. A lot of wood and metal fittings. The bar is an old workbench and has a massive vice on the end of it. The waiting staff all look like they've come straight from university and haven't changed clothes. It's packed, with everyone looking around and checking out the other diners, wondering how they also know about this place with no name.

At a half-moon table in an alcove, just off from the bustling dining area and cramped enough for it to possibly have been a toilet cubicle back during the venue's workshop days, Niranda Stone and Giorgina Gifford are having brunch with Chandice Cowdrey. The very rectangular Chandice, whose idea it had been to dine here, sits in the middle and is really holding court, acting like she owns the place. It's the kind of excessive flaunting that Niranda and Giorgie see right through and would normally baulk at, but they are humouring Chandice today, because of what's at stake. The alcove affords the three women some privacy and a certain exclusivity, away from the rabble huddled around the tables in the middle, banging elbows with each other as they consume their tiny portions. In the centre of the table, leaning against a skinny perfume bottle that has a single pink rose in it, is a crisp white envelope. Lacking bulk, the envelope appears to hold a letter or card.

While they're all around the same vintage, Chandice looks and behaves like someone several decades older.

They forgo appetisers and anything breakfast-y, as Chandice is trying to lose weight, and start instead with Aperol spritzes, at Chandice's insistence, that come in massive, long-stemmed, balloonish glasses and have half an orange in them, peel on. Niranda uses two spoons to haul that half-orange out of her glass, considerably reducing the volume of its contents.

"I prefer alcohol garnished with fruit," she says. "The other way round is breakfast, especially with this orange."

Giorgie laughs, but stops when Chandice doesn't join in.

"It's not an orange," Chandice says sharply. "It's a tangerine."

"Whatever it is, it doesn't belong in my drink."

The excess fruit gets dropped on a bread plate, where it oozes Aperol.

"To Lance." Chandice raises her glass with two chubby hands. The wedding band on her left hand is really strangling the finger it's on, turning it far pinker than the rest. "Such a terrible tragedy."

They clink glasses, the half-tangerines bobbing around in Chandice and Giorgie's glasses like dissected testicles preserved in embalming fluid.

"So young." Chandice sips delicately, fingers encircling the glass, as if taking communion. "A real shame."

Niranda drinks with the gusto of someone trying to finish her drink in a hurry so she can order something she actually wants. Giorgie puts her glass down when Chandice isn't looking, and drinks water.

"You must be just devastated, Niranda," Chandice says.

"We're all shocked, but I'm no stranger to losing people."

"Of course. Your Carrington."

Niranda has another long drink, then says, "I learned the best thing to do is move forward. Keep going. Keep living. Keep building. That's what Carry wanted for me, and I'm certain it's what Lance wants for us."

Chandice glances at the envelope. "I'm very happy to hear that. I was worried things may have stopped with Lance."

"He would want us to get it done. As you know, Giorgie also has big plans."

"Yes, this studio and exhibition space. It sounds brilliant. Do you already have an artist in mind, Giorgie dear?"

"I do. Daley. The metal sculpturer. He did the installation in the garden of Parliament House."

"That rust pile?" Chandice, whose very round, plump face looks like an artist's hasty sketch, shaping them out by drawing a circle inside a square, on top of a rectangular body, screws up this face in an ugly fashion. "I don't recall being invited to that unveiling."

"It was a very small affair," Giorgie says. "Invitations were at the Premier's discretion. I'm sure many important members of community councils were overlooked."

As Chandice's expression doesn't change, Niranda adds, "Daley's doing incredible things with used metal right now. He's turned upcycling into an art, which means the new studio in Beeliar will have the added benefit of sustainability. I'm certain many members of the City of Cockburn care about that very much."

"It's always high on the agenda. A real catchword." Chandice takes a large mouthful of her drink, and the other two women wait politely, as she clearly has more to say. "But I'm not supportive of all this greenwashing. You need to be careful of that. It has to be seen to be making a tangerine difference. Oho. Excuse me. A tangible difference. What a brilliant slip of the tongue. I think I need another drink."

"You're welcome to have mine," Giorgie says, sliding her glass towards Chandice, slaloming it between all the other glasses.

"Why aren't you partaking? You don't like what I ordered for you?"

"It's not that." Giorgie looks at Niranda, who gives her a slight nod. "It's just, I'm pregnant."

Chandice brightens. "That's wonderful. You're positively glowing. I'm so happy for you, especially at your age. I'm sure it will all work out well."

Giorgie manages a smile. "Thank you."

"Then let me do the celebrating for you." Candice takes the half-tangerine out of her near-empty glass and plonks it in Giorgie's drink, causing the Aperol spritz to brim to the glass's rim. Now, it really looks like testicles on display. As Chandice sips, the two half-tangerines bob close to her mouth.

Niranda and Giorgie watch with the polite expressions of women deeply experienced at smiling through all levels of disgustingness in order to get what they want.

"Please tell me the father isn't that lousy poet husband of yours," Chandice says, already sounding half-drunk.

"Quin? No, no. He was sent from the stable years ago."

"Straight to the glue factory, I hope." Chandice follows through with a domineering cackle that makes people look in her direction.

"I'm not ready to say who the father is," Giorgie says. "No one knows about it yet. So, please, keep it at this table."

"Your secrets are always safe with me."

A sombre waitress, who looks two years into an arts degree she'll never use, places their meals on the table, removing a few glasses to create space. Chandice has the octopus royale salad, Niranda the baked barracuda risotto and Giorgie the snapper soufflé linguine. All three meals are served on huge plates and seem very small. No one says thank you. The waitress mopes away, a stack of superfluous glasses in her hands.

Chandice tucks in with the ravenousness of someone who has gone all morning, and possibly most of yesterday evening, without eating.

"How is it?" Niranda asks, eyeing the salad like it's something foul that washed up on the beach.

Chandice slurps up a tentacle. "Delicious. I'm getting wonderful hints of sweetness, and it's contrasting delightfully with just a tang of bitterness."

"Well, enjoy."

"I will indeed. This is the only meal I'm allowing myself today."

Niranda has a small mouthful of risotto and doesn't appear to like it. "Listen, Chandice. I know you were working closely with Lance on certain approvals. Where are you with that? I trust your diligent work will continue, even with Lance out of the equation."

"So tragic. Such a nice young man. Though he certainly liked fruit with his alcohol, if you know what I mean."

Niranda, just keeping it together and having lost all appetite, says, "A lot of people are relying on you. Without the right approvals, the project can't go ahead. We need to get moving, before the rains come and winter makes clearing the land difficult."

Chandice's round face turns stony, though her cheeks remain pink. "I'm well aware of that. I'm putting in the hours, I assure you. I don't need any reminding. But I will remind you that overtime should be properly compensated. That envelope looks very thin."

"I took the liberty of setting up a safety deposit box for you." Niranda gestures at the envelope. "The key and the details are inside."

"Wrong. That's traceable. Lance promised cash. That's the money that talks. You can't question cash. We don't need this box thing."

"It's completely secure."

Chandice chews and shakes her head. "There'll be cameras in there, wherever it is. I want cash handovers. No cash, no overtime."

"Be reasonable. This is far easier. No one will know."

"Niranda, you're not listening. I'm telling you it's not what I want." Chandice puts her fork down and coughs a little, then wipes her mouth with her napkin. "I need the cash as something to pass on. I have my own wheels to grease."

"What does that mean?" Giorgie asks Niranda. "You said this was the only deal we needed to make."

"I can't do anything without a majority in the council," Chandice says, coughing some more. "I'll buy it, if I have to. You can count on me. But I need cash to do that."

Niranda and Giorgie both look at Chandice, who appears to be struggling to breathe.

"Are you all right?" Niranda asks. "You've gone very pale."

"I ... so ... hungry."

Chandice's round face goes straight into what's left of her salad, sending tentacles, leaves and sprouts flying.

"Chandice?" Niranda pokes her in the shoulder with a fork. "Hey?"

"Is she dead?" Giorgie asks, in barely a whisper.

"God, I hope so," Niranda whispers back.

"We need her."

"Do we?" Niranda puts two fingers on Chandice's wrist. "I guess we do. She's got a pulse."

Giorgie turns to the dining area. "Someone call an ambulance. Now!"

As the two of them stand up from the table, to make room for the staff to help, Niranda picks up the envelope and slides it into her handbag.

<>

With no desire or need to go to the office today, Aphra and Fozzie reach Swanbourne Beach at mid-morning. It's warm, but this will be as hot as it gets today; the first hints of breeze are already wafting in from the southwest. Given that it's a workday, there's no one at the beach, except for her mother, who is sitting on a bench near the empty playground, sipping coffee from a disposable cup.

"You're early," Aphra says.

"Hey, Aph. I thought I'd go for a jog or something, but then I got here and couldn't be bothered."

"Well, I'm here now. What important thing do you need to tell me? You know, I really hate getting messages like that, right before I go to sleep."

"Sorry. It's not massive. No one's dying, if that's what you're thinking."

"Just tell me, please."

"Let's have a swim first." She stands up and drops the cup in the bin. Then, with a big smile, she bends down to rub Fozzie's ears. "Look at you. You love the beach, don't you? Get this leash off, Aph."

"Not here. I've been told off for that too many times to count. We need to walk a bit."

"Lead the way."

From the Swanbourne Surf Lifesaving Club, they trek north in the soft sand, getting far enough away from the main beach to allow Aphra to let Fozzie loose, at which point the dog goes on a massive tear, running at full speed towards the water and chasing after seagulls.

Aphra and her mother meander through a checklist of small talk that covers work, health and family. This talk continues as they swim, with Aphra in the nude and her mother in a white one-piece that emphasises her stunning tan lines earned through several decades of outdoor work in 40+ temperatures wearing shorts and t-shirts. They both compliment each other on how good their figures look, though her mother is shy about taking such praise.

It's only when they're wrapped in towels and sitting on the sand, as Fozzie continues to dart around with boundless energy, that her mother finally shares her news.

"We're being laid off."

"What? Both of you?"

"Half the workforce, just about. It hasn't been made explicitly known yet, but those who are going all know. Anyone over 50 is being given the boot."

"They can't do that," Aphra says. "They are labour laws. Contracts. Job security, especially for older workers."

"Those contracts are full of loopholes, to allow the companies to get rid of employees. It's why the pay's so high, because there is no job security. There's not even any guarantee a mine will keep operating from one day to the next. It's always been like that."

"You never said anything about this. The whole time, you and Dad have been basically temp working?"

"Yes, essentially. You need to get out of the city more, Aph. It's the wild west up there. It has its own laws. Fifos are the first to go, when the culling begins."

"So much for loyalty. You guys have been doing this for years."

"Not just us. This is a snatch-and-grab business. The only loyalty is to profit. You know that."

Aphra looks at the water. With the wind starting to pick up, the white caps are moving closer to the beach.

"We did really well to make it this far," her mother adds, resignation in her voice.

"We can fight it. I know people who can help."

"I don't want any help from your party."

"It's not my party. I just write for them. There are others. Some lawyers I know."

Her mother shakes her head. "There's no fighting this. We signed NDAs too. They made everyone do that. I'm not legally allowed even to be telling you all this."

"How's Dad taking it?"

"Bad. He's happy that we can retire early, but he's really sorry for all his mates who'll be out of work."

"But there's a payout, right?"

"Yes, and it's generous, all things considered. They could've just given us knock-off gold watches and shoved us on the next flight out. But everyone will get the chance to make money from this."

"They're buying your silence."

"They may be greedy, but they're not stupid."

"Cash?"

"We were given a choice. A small redundancy package or an investment opportunity."

"What did you choose?"

"The investment. It's a way better deal. Everyone's taken it."

Fozzie, completely worn out, sits on the sand in front of them and pants.

"I hope it's legit," Aphra says.

"Why wouldn't it be? Working in politics has made you so cynical, Aph. Don't worry. It all checks out. I'm not allowed to tell you, but I'm going to anyway, just to prove to you that it's safe. We were offered an early buy-in on a new subdivision in the south of Perth. Getting the land at a bargain price."

"Where exactly?"

"Beeliar. The land's so cheap for us, we bought more. When the development begins, we can sell the land back and triple our money, at least."

"You used your own money?"

"On top, yes. It was too good to pass up. Relax, Aph. It's totally secure."

About 50 metres from where the waves are gently breaking on the sand, Aphra sees a dolphin's dorsal fin slice up through the water.

"You're saying a lot by saying nothing, Aph."

"I know all about this development. But I wasn't aware of any land sales. There are still a few things standing in the way of it. They can't already be selling the land."

"You should be happy for us. We can retire early, and we'll be rich."

"I don't know, Mum. One thing I've learned about working in this city is that if something sounds too good to be true, it often is."

"I can show you the land titles. It's all correct and proper."

"Who sold you the land? Was it a guy called Lance Ford-Brackman?"

"HR took care of everything for us." Her mother's leathery hand pats Aphra's knee. "Stop worrying. These mining companies have ludicrous amounts of money. Why shouldn't the workers they lay off get some of it?"

"I fully agree with that. But this is an indirect payout, through this investment. A little extra incentive to keep everyone quiet."

"It's an industry where everyone's paid off. The companies don't even own the land they mine. They lease it. In order to do that, they line the pockets of whoever they need to so they can dig the holes they dig. Pocket money for the locals at the bottom of the ladder. Dividends for the elites at the top. Everyone's getting a piece of it. Now, we can too."

"I hope that's true. But that's the finance side of things. What about adapting to life without working? Without the one-week or two-week rhythms?"

"I won't miss the flying, that's for sure. Those white-knuckle rides."

"Understandable."

"But that does bring me to the actual news."

"Getting laid off isn't it?"

"No. We're going back to Tassie."

"What? For good?"

"It was your dad's idea, and I think it's a good one. Don't get me wrong. We love it here. Always have. But he's not happy with the direction the state is going in. He wants to get out, while we can. I think he's a bit extreme, but I'm supporting him on this."

"Why do I think that Blair's to blame for this?"

"If not her, it will be someone else. Plenty of people want WA to become its own country. It's just a matter of time. You should hear the way they talk up north. But your dad thinks it's the worst thing that could happen. It's un-Australian, he says."

"Which explains why he's not here. He can't face me."

"He was dog-tired when we got in last night."

"Don't make excuses for him. Is he going to avoid me now?"

"He loves you."

"But not my politics. Writing for the party is just a gig, you know. A really well-paid gig. I'm not a member, or a believer."

"You're just the one brilliantly shaping their narrative, in a way that everyone understands."

"Thank you," Aphra says with a smile. "Best review I've had in ages."

"You should be focusing on the work you actually care about."

"Great solution. Write poetry and starve."

"We could help you. In a few months, we'll be millionaires. You could come with us. Back home."

"This is my home."

"You grew up here, but you weren't born here. That makes a difference, don't you think?"

"Sometimes. Our research shows that the majority of people who weren't born here support WA separating from Australia."

"That doesn't surprise me. A key part of succeeding here, and being accepted, is fully buying into it. Something your dad and I never really did."

"Separation's a long way off," Aphra says, "in my opinion. Blair calls it independence. The problem is her approval rating is still too low. There's something about her that people don't like. She isn't a person of the people."

"No, she isn't."

"In this business, you can take a male politician, get him to roll up his shirt sleeves and stick a shovel in his hand, and suddenly he's a man of the people. Instantly working class and relatable. You can't really pull off the same kind of photo op with a woman. And Blair just has privilege written all over her."

"She does. But she's just the figurehead. The real power is in the economy. Just look at the mining industry. All the companies up north are sick of seeing their money go to Canberra."

"Ah, yes. That story. WA keeping the rest of Australia's economy afloat."

"I hear it a lot, Aph."

"It's partly true. The idea is to use local money to make this state better."

"Self-sufficiency for Sandgropers. Keep it local. Invest in hospitals and schools. These are all your lines, right?"

"Blair's doing the talking."

"With words you give her."

"That she pays a lot for."

Aphra's mother laughs a little. "I guess you got into mining after all. A kind of story mining. Digging up the words that others profit from."

They sit for a while in silence, both staring at the water, before Aphra stands up.

"I'm starting to burn," she says.

"Shall we head back?"

Aphra nods. Once they're both dressed, they start walking back to the lifesaving club, keeping to the area where the waves are washing up, as the dry sand is too hot for bare feet.

"I'll definitely miss the ocean," Aphra's mother says.

"Why did we live by the river then?"

"It's too windy on the coast. That's what everyone said when we first arrived. What they didn't say is how nice the mornings are. I envy you, living out here."

A shirtless runner, his upper body sculptured, comes from the other direction. He has the wide-legged running style of someone who normally jogs with a heavy backpack, making Aphra think he's a soldier from nearby Campbell Barracks.

"Are you seeing anyone?"

Aphra thumbs behind her. "Do you mean some meathead adonis like him?"

"Or whoever takes your fancy."

"I'm happy with how things are, right now. I don't have the headspace for someone else, with work so demanding and now everything with Katie."

"That was so sad. Sorry, Aph."

"There is a guy on my radar, and he's definitely interested. But he keeps sending up red flags. Another guy has caught my eye, a little older, but I'm worried he doesn't have enough between the ears."

"You always were so picky."

"I'm patient and cautious. I think those are good things to be. My time also matters to me. I'd rather be single than spend my time with someone I was just settling for."

"Careful. I know what you're implying there."

"I'm not implying anything." Aphra whistles for her dog, which has followed the runner. Fozzie turns and trots back, tongue out. "But you know my history. I'm cautious and I'm going to stay that way."

"Okay. Good."

"What are your plans for Tasmania? When you're retired. What do people do over there when they have all the time in the world?"

"I don't know about your dad, but I'm going to study."

Aphra smiles. "Oh, I hate the way you do that."

"Do what?"

"Tell me all this stuff, these announcements you sit on, like a mother hen and her eggs. Then you finish with something like that."

"Are you saying I shouldn't go to uni?"

"The absolute opposite. I think it's a great idea. What field?"

"Promise you won't make fun of me?"

"Depends."

"I've applied at the University of Tasmania. Political Science."

Aphra laughs, then puts an arm around her mother. "That's brilliant. Just think of all the debates we'll have when I come to visit. Oh, Mum. I'm so proud of you."

<>

A phone's incessant buzzing slowly draws Huntley out of his sleep. When it stops, he gives in and is just about to fall back to sleep, when the buzzing starts again.

"Oh, come on."

Having given Everest the bed in the caravan's shallow loft, Huntley managed to shape his body into a U and positioned himself around the half-circle bench under where she's sleeping, comfortable enough to pass out, one arm balanced on the table to keep himself from slipping off. It's on this table that the phone is buzzing, sounding angrier and more insistent with each buzz. Eyes barely open, he moves his arm to grab at that phone, loses balance and tumbles to the floor. There, he lifts his head too quickly, banging it against the underside of the table with enough force to make the phone bounce to the floor, where it continues buzzing.

"You evil thing."

Rubbing his head, he sees it's Everest's phone, Booth the caller. He crawls out, phone in hand, and gets to his feet. He slaps the loft's mattress a few times.

"Detective E. Your better half's calling."

Somewhere, under the blankets, Everest groans.

"Yeah. I hear you up there." Huntley tosses the phone into the loft. "This must be important."

"Ugh. That male stripper nightcap was a bad idea."

"Don't blame me. You wanted it."

The buzzing stops. "Justin. Yes, good morning. Give me a minute. I'll call you back."

"It's now officially a dry week," Huntley says. "From this morning on. Wednesday to Wednesday."

Everest appears in the loft, socked feet hanging over the edge, her hair a delightfully tousled mess. "I'm never drinking rum ever again."

"If you ask me," Huntley says, leaning forward to flick the door open, letting in harsh light, "it was the vaping. That's some strong dope in there. I had one toke and the cosmos opened up."

"It's medicinal."

"So you keep saying. Very strong medicine." Huntley squints at the light. The cars driving on Stirling Highway sound incredibly loud, even from here.

Everest struggles with her ponytail. Trying to move the elastic band from her wrist to her hair, she inadvertently shoots it at Huntley. It hits him in the eye.

"Hey," he says, bending down to pick it up.

"Sorry. Friendly fire. I swear."

He hands it back to her and she gets the ponytail set. She puts the phone to her ear.

"Justin? What is so urgent?"

"You want some coffee?" Huntley asks.

Everest nods. "What's that got to do with us?"

Huntley puts the kettle on the small two-burner stove, then stands in the doorway, facing the sun, eyes squinted.

"You're right," Everest says into the phone. "That's a connection. Send me the name of the hospital. I'll meet you there."

Everest ends the call, then looks at her phone's screen, momentarily stunned.

"Yes," Huntley says, turning to her. "That really is the time. Your medicine is a definite sedative."

"I have to say, even though I'm really hungover, that's the best I've slept in ages. It's like a cocoon up here."

"I like the way you sleep on your back, like you're on display at a funeral."

"Tour bus habits are hard to break."

"I thought as much," Huntley says, raising his voice above the rising crescendo of the kettle. "I want to hear all about those adventures, one day."

"What happens on the road, stays on the road." Everest puts a hand to her forehead. "There's too much noise in here."

The kettle boils. Huntley pours the water into two cups and stirs the coffee. The aroma draws them both back to reality.

"Milk?" he asks.

"If you have it and it's not off."

"Why would it be off?"

"I don't know. We're in a caravan."

"Which you slept very soundly in."

"Is there any electricity? Is there a fridge?"

"It's got everything. Think of it as a really small tour bus, plugged in for all the necessities. There's running water and power. A shower rigged at the back."

Everest gets herself down from the loft, stumbling a little on landing. "What are you doing living in this thing?"

"What are you doing smoking dope on the job?"

Huntley hands Everest a cup. They both sip, savouring the caffeine.

"Instant coffee with off-milk never tasted so good," Everest says, smiling. "It's for my wrists. I told you that, didn't I?"

"I think you did."

"I got tendinitis from the drumming. And carpal tunnel. It still flares up. The doctor says I'm old enough now to consider it arthritis."

"That's awful. The doc prescribed you dope to vape?"

"My choice, because the alternative was daily painkillers and monthly cortisone injections. I wasn't doing that."

"Wise, I guess. Big pharma and all. The weed is probably cheaper than prescribed pills, and less addictive." Huntley blows on his cup, sips, then asks, "Where do you get it?"

Everest raises her eyebrows. "As in, who's my dealer?"

"It's got to come from somewhere. Ask me nicely and I could get it delivered from Ravensthorpe."

"The commune?"

"Very fertile land. But you're a cop. You didn't hear that from me. You wouldn't want to be caught doing something illegal."

"You can put just about anything in a vaping stick. No one will know what's in there."

"Interesting. That might explain why I see a lot of teenagers with those things."

"Plenty of adults too."

"Everyone getting high, in plain sight." Huntley finishes his coffee. "The question remains, where is it all coming from?"

"Not my area."

"Yeah, you wouldn't want to put your supply in jeopardy."

"If I told you where I get it, you wouldn't believe me."

"Well, if it dries up, a steady stream from Ravensthorpe could be all yours. Organic too. Anyway, what did Booth want?"

"Something's happened."

Huntley smiles brightly. "Another murder?"

"Don't look so pleased. A coma." Everest checks her phone. "At Fremantle Hospital. Fancy a drive?"

"If you tell me what's going on."

"Justin thinks there's a connection to Lance Ford-Brackman. Sounds tenuous, but we have to explore all the angles, and I can't be seen shooting down all his ideas."

"What about the one where he thinks I'm a suspect?"

"I'll put a temporary hiatus on that long enough for you to take me to Freo."

"Hah. Let's go."

"You're just driving. There's no way you're coming in."

"I have other business in Freo as it turns out. Someone I need to see."

This makes Everest curious.

"I'll tell you about it later," Huntley adds. "We can trade information."

"No, we won't."

Once they're outside, Huntley locks the caravan door. They walk to the Landy.

"But, thanks," Everest adds, "for letting me crash. And for being a gentleman about it."

"You're very welcome."

"But that doesn't make us partners or anything."

"Heaven forbid."

They both get in. Huntley muscles the car onto Stirling Highway, southbound. Everest works her phone the whole way, catching up on missed calls and supplying creative truths to explain why she wasn't at certain morning meetings. Huntley is glad to tune her out and focus on driving, while collating and ordering his own thoughts. Namely, that before Everest arrived last night, he found a box of vapes in Lance's closet, and took one, because having a full box suggested far more than Lance partaking of a casual habit. This appeared to be a commodity, and if the vapes prove to have something hard inside, such as dope or hash, it could make Lance a drug dealer. There have been rumours for years that the Ford-Brackmans run ketamine labs in small towns across the southwest, but he's never heard anything about them running a dope trade. The first step is to find out what's in the vape; he's certain that Henrikson can help.

As he turns down Alma Street to the hospital, he wonders if he should tell Everest about the box, because she didn't search the apartment beyond inspecting the desk.

"Sounds like everyone's wondering where you are," he says, when Everest finally gets off the phone.

"They don't need me. They're just keeping tabs."

"Will you, uh, you know, search Lance's place?"

"If it doesn't get declared a crime scene, we'll have to stay out of there. The family already has the body. The Ford-Brackmans even run a funeral home. Can you believe that?"

"If it's in Mandurah, they own it."

"The case might be closed quickly, even with the jimsonweed. It'll be recorded as a suicide. Justin will likely sign off on that, and it seems to be what Niranda Stone wants."

Huntley joins the line of cars edging into the hospital parking area. "She's used to getting what she wants. Watch out for her. She's greedy. So, you won't go back to Mosman Park? To look for clues?"

"I didn't find anything last night. Did you?"

"Who, me? No. No. Nothing. But you have that list. The council meeting."

"That's why I'm here. I sent it to Justin last night. One of the people on the list is in here, in the hospital."

"The coma? Who is it? Not Winslow, surely."

Everest takes a piece of paper from her pocket and unfolds it. "Chandice Cowdrey. Ring a bell?"

Huntley shakes his head. "What happened?"

"Food poisoning, apparently."

"Someone slip jimsonweed or wild arum into her cereal?"

"This isn't funny, Huntley."

"Do you hear me laughing?" Huntley moves the car slightly forward. Some idiot honks from behind. "But two deaths and two plants. Maybe there's something plant-related here, too."

"I know you want this to be your big story, but you're confusing connection with coincidence. I think it's just chance that the violinist who replaced the Ukrainian girl is Lance's brother. Perth's a big small town, after all."

Huntley disagrees. "Also a coincidence that our paths continue to cross?"

"Because you keep sticking your nose into things."

"That's very ungrateful."

Another horn sounds from behind. Huntley wants to get out and find the driver responsible.

"Wrong. I appreciate what you've contributed. Last night, that was a great meal."

"You can go it alone, if you want. Detective."

"You say that, but I'm not convinced you'll stay out of it."

"Nuh. I've got other fish to fry today."

Everest looks towards the hospital, then at the cars in front. "We're going nowhere. I can walk from here. Thanks for the ride."

"Sure."

"Will you keep me in the loop?" Everest asks, opening the door.

"Will you?"

Everest frowns and nods reluctantly, then gets out and shuts the door. Huntley watches her walk between the cars to the hospital entrance. As she goes in, Giorgie comes out and heads for the busy carpark.

"What are you up to, Giorgie girl?" he asks himself.

He feels a pang of desire and tastes the bitterness of rejection, and wonders again how he could have done things differently to give that story the happy ending it deserved.

She climbs into a huge SUV, while two cars get ready to jostle for the parking space she will free up. Giorgie's vehicle is black, brand new and horribly boxy, looking like its exterior is made entirely of biodegradable plastic. As she backs out, both the waiting cars try to go into the free space at the same time. They get stuck and the drivers get out to vehemently remonstrate with each other.

Just as Giorgie drives past, her eyes straight ahead, Huntley manages to turn his Landy around and squeeze out through the carpark exit, flattening a few plants on the curb in the process. At Alma Street, the plastic tank turns left, away from Fremantle. He's torn, keen to follow Giorgie while also wanting to tap the resourceful Henrikson and find out what's in the vape. He chooses the latter, because he needs to let her go. She's with someone else now, and pregnant, which was probably why she was at the hospital. Part of him hopes everything is all right.

On the drive to the bookstore, crawling through Freo's streets, he tries to pinpoint when the relationship went sour. It was his fault, he knows, but having written solid verse in the past two days, he realises now that Lydette has a lot to answer for. Because she was the one who sowed the early seeds of doubt, when he was trying to write a follow-up and she was scathing with her feedback. Seeds that grew into poisonous plants in his mind and soul, had him questioning every line, word and idea, the frustration from which he took out on Giorgie, who rightly wasn't going to stand for it. Questioning his work on a daily basis meant he started questioning everything else, including whether he was worthy of Giorgie's love and worthy of living on the Gifford estate. That was when he spent most of his time in his caravan, parked off to the side of the property's circular driveway, trying so hard to write something that Lydette would like, losing all sense of himself in the process and becoming consumed by doubt.

As he circles the block, looking for somewhere to park, he wonders if Lydette deliberately set out to sabotage his writing and his marriage, as some form of revenge for rejecting her when they were at university.

Once parked, the next problem is that he doesn't have any coins, or a credit card, for the ticket machine. He doesn't see any parking inspectors around, so decides to chance it.

Henrikson, behind the counter, is happy to see him when he enters the store. "Quin. What a nice surprise."

"How's business, mate?"

The bookstore is empty.

"Slow, this morning. What can I do for you?"

Huntley runs his fingers along the books on the centre display. None of the minimalist covers appear worth cracking.

"How did it go with the naturopath?"

"Yeah. Good. Good."

"Did you find out more about wild arum?"

"Mate, I held it, in a pot. It's like a flower sticking its tongue out at you. Or giving you the finger."

"Yes, I've seen pictures."

"Meanwhile, there was another plant-related crime, with jimsonweed. But it was too weird at the naturopath, and I couldn't stay there to learn more about that."

"What is it, this jimsonweed?"

"A hallucinogen. Caused a young fella to go out swimming at night. He drowned."

"I'm sorry to hear that. Do you think there's a connection?"

"Don't know. Maybe. I kind of lost my mojo, on the drive here."

"Ah. Tea?"

"Yeah. Thanks. Tea's good."

Henrikson goes into the office behind the counter. Huntley stays where he is, respecting the owner's domain. He takes a copy of Aphra's book from the stack near the register; the inside title page has been signed.

"Was she here?"

"She popped in early this morning. To sign her books, which was very good of her."

"Yeah?"

"Do you know each other?"

"We're acquainted."

"Nice lass. She was friends with Ekaterina."

Huntley nods. "I could sign mine too, if you like."

"I don't think we have any in stock. I could order it. Is it still in print?"

"No idea."

"If it's been digitalised, it should be printable. As a print-on-demand book."

"That would require someone demanding it be printed. It's been years since I saw a royalty cheque."

"You're on the way to writing something new," Henrikson offers. "How's that going?"

"All right. But I hit a bit of a wall. Maybe you can help me with it." Huntley takes the vape from his pocket. "I need to find out everything about this."

"Is it a plastic pipe?"

"A vape. A modern way of smoking. I think there are drugs inside. Marijuana, most likely. But it could be something else."

Henrikson takes the vape and inspects it with a magnifying glass.

"That is so old school," Huntley says.

"There's a small snake on the side. Maybe that's a brand of some kind."

"Viper. Vape. I get it. Can you help?"

"I'll contact Bernie. He was a science teacher at my school. Loves a puzzle, does Bernie."

"Thanks, Henrikson." Huntley turns to leave. "That's much appreciated."

"You're not staying for the cuppa?"

"Maybe next time, mate. Sorry." At the door, Huntley stops. "Hey, uh, Chandice Cowdrey? That name mean anything to you by chance?"

"Is she dead?"

"She's in hospital."

"Let me know when she's dead. Vile woman."

"What did she ever do to you?"

"Not me," Henrikson says. "My wife. She clashed with Chandice many times. Whenever she tried to do something good for the community, Chandice would make it her mission to stop it. She's crooked too, taking money from everyone. Worst of all, everyone knows and everyone hates her, and still she sits on several councils and committees."

"Crooked? Like, bribeable?"

"She is more prostitute than public servant. And always on a diet. My wife called her, not at all politely, I might add, the Hangry Hippo."

"Hah. Nice one. Can you find out what she's up to now? What councils she's on? Hack into civil records, or something."

"With pleasure. But it will have to wait until later. The network here isn't secure."

"Okay. Thanks. You're superb, mate."

Huntley goes out of the store and jogs down Henry Street to his car. There's a piece of paper under one of the wipers. He scrunches it up and shoves it in his pocket.

"That was barely five minutes." He gets in the car. "I swear these pricks are hiding out and watching, just waiting to come out and write a ticket."

Back at the hospital, he leaves the Landy on Alma Street, as there's still a long line of vehicles waiting to get into the carpark, and walks to the entrance.

Inside, at reception, he asks which room Chandice Cowdrey is in, claiming that he's a member of the family.

"Since when?"

Huntley turns to the woman behind him and feels his whole body groan.

"Niranda."

"Quintus."

"Are you here to find a small child to consume?"

A passing nurse gives him a fierce look.

"I'm kidding," Huntley says to the nurse.

"Always with the drama," Niranda says, calmly. "And the lies. You're not in any way connected to Chandice."

"I was simply trying to expedite the process. Everyone looks busy here. Plenty of people waiting. You should see the carpark outside. Chockers."

Niranda takes a few steps away from the crowded reception area, to give them a semblance of conversational privacy. Huntley is compelled to follow.

"You look," Niranda says, looking Huntley up and down, "ragged."

"I was up all night saving the world."

"And now you're here to save Chandice."

"I don't know. How is she? Awake?"

"She's in a coma."

Huntley takes a moment to admire Niranda, who remains really well put together. Bizarrely, he still finds her vicious streak attractive. He should absolutely regret having sex with her during Carrington's wake, in his den, of all places, but he doesn't. If she asked him now to slip into a supply closet with her, he'd have a very tough time saying no.

"That's awful," he says. "I will say there's a friend of mine really hoping she doesn't pull through."

"Still keeping the best company, I see." Niranda folds her arms. "Why don't you tell me the real reason you're here."

"If we find somewhere private, you could ... beat it out of me."

"Surely we're not back at that point, Quin. Not that I don't appreciate that you were there for me during a difficult time. But you lost your appeal long ago."

"When I was no longer Giorgie's possession, to be nabbed and rebranded."

"The people we keep closest are the ones who reflect the best on us," Niranda says. "Or worst. Giorgie divorcing you said a lot."

"Wow. You can take a girl out of Mandurah, but you can't take Mandurah out of the girl. How's that going, by the way? Your hostile takeover of your family?"

"I don't know what you're on about. I'm focusing my energy on other, more profitable areas."

Even though he's not firing on all cylinders this morning, Huntley's rum and dope mangled brain somehow manages to connect the narrative dots. "You're not taking over the family businesses. You're taking over from Lance. This project in Beeliar."

Niranda, momentarily flustered, lowers her voice: "How on earth do you know anything about that? Did Giorgie tell you?"

"Nope. I'm just quietly helping to find Lance's killer."

"There is no killer. It was suicide."

"That's a really convenient outcome, isn't it?"

"I don't like what you're suggesting. Someone has to take Lance's place. I'm certain he would've wanted to keep it in the family."

"What a shame he's not here to speak for himself."

"No one is sadder about that than me."

That Niranda says this with a very slight smile makes Huntley wonder if Lance was standing in the way of her ambitions. But then, if Niranda had wanted Lance dead, he thinks, she would've been much more complete about it. She wouldn't have poisoned a water bottle with some unknown weed in the hope he harmed himself fatally. No. Niranda's an opportunist, seizing this moment in a similar way she did with him, to have a mourning wrestle on her husband's still-warm armchair in his den.

"It's tragic," he says. "Is that the right word? Is that what you're all using? A shame. A tragedy. And so on."

"The project can go ahead as a way of honouring Lance."

"Seriously? Lance didn't want the same things as you. Your family practically threw him to the street. He was following the rainbow to his own pot of gold, and now you're going to take it from him."

"That's not correct. One thing we both definitely want is to see Marcus fulfil his potential."

This slaps Huntley to attention. "As what? A violinist? Certainly not as the heir to a dubious empire."

"The PSO is just a stepping stone for him. He's bound for New York or London or Paris. Nothing would make me, or Lance, bless his soul, prouder than to see that happen."

"Good thing that third chair became available when it did."

"Sometimes tragedy can open the door to opportunity," Niranda says, oozing voluptuousness and viciousness in equal measure, just about making a disc move out of place in Huntley's lower back. "What matters is how hard you grab it with both hands."

"Oh, bring it."

Niranda, smiling, looks past Huntley, making him turn. Everest and Booth come down the hallway, heading for the exit. But when Everest sees Huntley, she walks towards him.

"I thought you had other business in Freo," she says to Huntley. "What are you doing here?"

"I asked him the same question. Careful. He'll most likely lie to you." Niranda pushes past Everest. "If you'll excuse me, I have a friend to visit."

All three of them watch her walk down the hall, heels clicking, striding like the hospital has her name on it, and making even harried hospital staff step out of the way.

"That woman." Huntley looks at Everest. "She's in bed with Chandice Cowdrey."

"We know," Everest says.

"This coma is no accident. Niranda's involved, somehow."

"We know that too. Niranda was having brunch with Chandice, when she passed out."

"What's the story? Did she have a stroke? I can't believe food poisoning would induce a coma."

"We're waiting for the results," Booth says. "The doctor thinks it had something to do with her very low blood sugar level. And," he checks his notes, "her anaemia. What's that again?"

"Low iron," Everest says. "Not uncommon for a woman of her age."

"Right. Plus other underlying health issues. High cholesterol, apparently. The woman's a wreck."

"There's more to it than that," Huntley says, and he tries to show Everest with his eyes he has more to say, but he doesn't want Booth to hear it.

Everest gets the hint. "Justin, can you get a copy of Cowdrey's file from the receptionist?"

"Why? The doctor can update me over the phone."

"I want a hard copy. Get the file, please."

Booth slumps towards the reception desk.

"He's getting a bit hard to work with," Everest says. "You have no idea the pressure I'm under with him. Fucking nepo baby."

"Forget him." Huntley steps closer to Everest. "Niranda's taking over the project from Lance. Chandice is the one she's trying to bribe, to get whatever approvals are needed to kickstart this project."

"Interesting. How did you get to that ... plot point?"

"I found out that Chandice has a history of taking money for stuff. She's crooked."

"Even if that's true, getting local approval won't be enough. It's a first step, but it won't mean they can start clearing trees. It'll have to go higher than that."

"Maybe Chandice holds the key. She knows the right people. Can influence the right votes, on up the chain."

"Except," Everest says, "she's in a coma and not able to vote on anything or influence anyone."

"Which excludes Niranda from the list of suspects. She needs Chandice, awake and voting."

They look at each other. Everest sees that Booth is already coming back, a yellow folder in his hands.

"What's the verdict?" Huntley asks. "When will she wake up?"

Everest shrugs. "Maybe today. Maybe tomorrow. Maybe never. It's a coma."

"Then Niranda will need to get someone else in her pocket."

"Yes." With Booth now next to her, Everest adds, "We're due for a meeting in the city. Meanwhile, stay out of the way."

Everest walks for the exit. Booth follows, then stops.

"By the way, I think you should know your ex-wife," and he checks his notes again, "Giorgina Gifford, was at that brunch as well. Interesting, isn't it?"

"She's free to eat with whoever she wants," Huntley says, keeping his expression as steady as he can.

Booth has a spring in his step as he walks to the exit.

Huntley wonders: what are you doing, Giorgie?

<>

After Blair's assistant calls asking where she is, Aphra explains she's taking a personal day, to sort things for Katie's funeral. But rather than actually do that, she gets on her Vespa and rides it all the way to John Tonkin College in Mandurah. Because finding out who killed Katie is right now more pressing than burying her, and focusing her attention on the one person who had the most to gain seems pertinent.

In the admin building, her glossy WA Republic Party business card gets the receptionist's attention.

Aphra spent the journey workshopping, in the lull between the cars and trucks trying to knock her from the road, what she could say to get Marcus Ford-Brackman out of class, without raising any alarms.

"How can I help you?" the receptionist asks brightly.

"We're looking for students to join our internship program," Aphra says, trying to match the receptionist's brightness. "Marcus Ford-Brackman is on the shortlist. I wonder if I could have a quick word with him."

"That's wonderful to hear. I'll try to locate him."

While the receptionist gets bounced around on the phone, Aphra wonders if she is the mother of one or two students at the school, because she has a motherly look and she was way too quick to believe Aphra's story. Being a mother would make her privy to local and school gossip.

"I've found him. In one of the greenhouses. He's on his way."

"That's great."

"Would you like some coffee while you wait?"

Aphra, who finds long rides on the Vespa hard on her kidneys, and a full bladder only adds to the discomfort, says, "No, thank you. I'm fine."

"This internship, can anyone apply? I'd like to let my daughter know about it. She admires Blair Blake-Stendahl a lot."

"Uh, I'd have to check. We might be taking applicants again next year."

"I've got your card now, so I can contact you."

"That's right. You can."

"It's really good for Marcus. He needs a win."

Aphra decides to play dumb, to garner the local version of events. "Why do you say that?"

The receptionist drops her bright tone: "He lost his brother yesterday."

"Oh, that's awful. What happened?"

"He drowned. Suicide. Perth just continues to chew people up and destroy lives."

"Do you think he killed himself because city life was too hard?"

"He had work issues, so I heard. He was struggling on several fronts."

"Perhaps he should've stayed here, out of the city."

"Absolutely. The community would have taken better care of him. That's for sure."

Aphra nods slowly, disliking the receptionist and her supposed community.

"Best not to ask Marcus about any of that," the receptionist advises. "He's a very sensitive young man."

"I'll focus on the internship. But why is he even at school today? Shouldn't he be at home with his family?"

"Not my place to say. Life has to go on. The year twelves have very full schedules."

"And he's a musician. According to his application."

"Yes. Now in the Perth Orchestra. The youngest ever. We're so proud of him."

"Well, let's hope the city doesn't ruin him."

"Too true. Here he is." The receptionist gestures to her right. "You can use the meeting room."

"We'll talk outside. It's all very informal, at this stage. I just want to introduce myself and get to know him."

As Marcus enters the admin building, Aphra goes up to him. She holds her hand out, but he doesn't shake it.

"Sorry," he says, holding up dirty hands. "I didn't get the chance to wash. You pulled me from the middle of gardening."

"Marcus, I'm Aphra Massey, from the WA Republic Party."

"Do you work with Blair?"

"Uh, yes. That's correct. I work very closely with Blair. Sounds like you've met."

"She's been to the house a couple of times."

Aphra feels the receptionist's judging eyes. "Can we go outside?"

Marcus shrugs in blasé teenage fashion, then goes first through the admin door, letting it swing closed on Aphra. Rather than take one of the benches in front of admin, Marcus walks about 50 metres away from the school and stands under a tree. He starts vaping.

"We're not allowed to do it on school grounds," he says, once Aphra is under the tree as well.

"But students always find a way."

Marcus blows out a huge cloud of smoke. "What do you want?"

She's finding it rather disgusting to watch this chubby child of privilege vaping with dirty hands. But aware anything she says could get back to Blair, she chooses her words carefully. "I'd like to talk with you about a potential internship. At the party."

"What, like, answering phones and licking envelopes? No, thanks."

"I'm sure you could join the area that appeals to you the most. Like comms and PR, for example."

More smoke, blown from a sneering mouth. "Is that what you do?"

Aphra nods. "I help craft messages for the party. Speechwriting and socials."

"I hate English. If I hear someone say something about storytelling one more time, I swear I'll scream."

"But you're involved in music," Aphra says, trying to hide her annoyance with Marcus's faux malaise, not to mention the vaping, which is horrid to watch and makes it seem he's sucking on a dog whistle. "Music is composition, telling a story. Songwriting is similar to speechwriting. Do you write your own stuff?"

"There's no time for that. Anyway," massive exhale, "I play the violin. I'm in the PSO."

"That's impressive. And you got there while still in high school. Well done."

"I'm just getting started." Marcus sniffs and looks at the ground. "Lance was really looking forward to my first performance."

"I'm very sorry about your brother."

"All he wanted was for me to pursue my dreams, and not let others dictate to me what my dreams should be. Which is what you're doing right now. I have no interest in politics."

Aphra can feel him slipping away. "Truth be told, neither do I."

The vape is empty. Marcus looks at it, disappointed. "Which means you're trying to sell me something you don't even want. You pulled me out of gardening class for this?"

"What kind of class is gardening?"

"It's part of the mental health and well-being programme. I like it, getting my hands dirty and helping things grow. I need to be careful, though, with my fingers."

"Your family must be very proud of you. How did you get into the PSO? Did you apply, last year or something like that? Did you audition?"

"What's that got to do with anything? I thought you were here to get me to answer phones for Blair. Which I would never do. Aunt Niranda tried to get me into her group as well. But she's leaving me alone now, so I can focus on the orchestra."

Aphra is surprised to see Marcus toss the used vape behind the tree.

"You wasted your time," he says, "and mine."

As he trudges back to the admin building, Aphra wants to pick up the vape and shove it down his throat. "Entitled little shit."

At her Vespa, she puts on her helmet and takes a few moments to compose herself, wondering if Marcus has it in him to kill. Without a definitive answer, she starts the long journey back to Perth.

<>

He stops the Landy, lowers the window and looks through the gate's vertical bars at the house which played such a meaningful role in his 20s, feeling now far removed from this place and the person he was when in it; as if that Quintus Huntley is a fictional character, this house part of his back story. The whole estate is so huge and prestigious, so out of reach, it seems unreal even to him, and he lived there. A creation of the imagination.

He tries to focus on this moment; the task of finding out why Giorgie had brunch with Niranda and Chandice. If Lance and Chandice have both been targeted because of their involvement in the Southern Everglades, he wouldn't want Giorgie to be next. But he doubts the headstrong Giorgie will listen to him.

It's fitting that Lydette is the one who comes out of the house and heads for the gate, with that unusual, short-stepped penguin walk she has. She was the one who first invited him here, for an end-of-semester party attended by well-off students who all lived in the area, at various levels of prestige, making him, the country hick, a novelty they could pass between each other for their own amusement. Except that even then he had a finely-tuned dickhead radar, and he just smiled at those who tried to make fun of him, and felt sorry for them. His father had taught him to be sceptical and dismissive of wealth, and also to feel empathetic towards those who inherit it, because wealth is always tainted and it taints those who have it. He took the various attempts of party guests to make a fool of him in good humour, refusing to take the bait, which meant they soon lost interest in him and he was free to explore the house on his own.

He found Giorgie in the library, where she was quietly reading poetry while sipping a hot toddy.

The large gate has a door-sized section which Lydette opens and slips through. She totters towards Huntley's car.

Unlike her sister, who from the glimpse he got this morning continues to age sublimely, as if instead of sleeping she is cryogenically frozen for eight hours each night, Lydette is maturing badly. He concludes it's the result of both trying too hard, with expensive clothes, excessive make-up and shocking dye jobs, and not trying hard enough, with poor eating, too much alcohol and too little exercise. As she bends towards the open window, he sees many late nights in the crow's feet at the corners of her eyes and the creases on her forehead, while decades of fake smiling have carved a set of parallel crevices into her face, running from the corners of her lipsticked mouth halfway up the side of her nose.

She slides her sunglasses up into her hair, revealing the grey at the roots, and casually leans an elbow on the open window.

"Lydette."

"This is not a good idea, Quintus."

"Nice to see you too. How do you even know why I'm here?"

"You're still driving this rust-bucket. It must be money. Right? Of course I'm right. You've always been so transparent."

"I don't want your money. I'm here to speak to Giorgie."

"She's resting."

"It's the middle of the day."

"That's your fault. She naps every day after lunch. You're the one who convinced her that sleep is the secret to longevity."

"Clearly I didn't convince you of that."

Lydette pulls her fake smile and laughs this off. "I sleep just fine, thank you."

"It was my father who always said that about sleep and longevity," he says. "He lived to be 99."

"Well, my father will be out here with a rifle very soon, unless you move on."

"The old fella loves a grudge, doesn't he? But surely he's more of a pitchfork guy. Or a whip. Didn't your forebears excel at whipping people?"

"After what you pulled yesterday with Verity, abetting her truancy, you're lucky you haven't lost visiting rights permanently. Giorgie doesn't want to see you, I'm certain of that."

"Verity wagged school all on her own. What version of events did that little rascal give you?"

"What an awful thing to say about your daughter. You may be an expert liar, and she may lie to you, but she never lies to us."

Huntley laughs. "She has got you wrapped around her finger. I'm proud she's waging her own little war against you lot. And winning it, by the looks."

"It's entirely your bad influence that's having an impact, which is all the more impressive given how little time you spend with her."

"That's beautiful. Let me guess. When she's horrible, she's a Huntley. When she's good, she's a Gifford."

Lydette nods. "You always had a way with words, even with tired clichés. Shame you let that go to waste."

"Word is you've hitched your broomstick to some up-and-comer."

"No, I found him." Lydette steps back from the car and folds her arms, her chin raised high. "I discovered him, and I'm in the process of shaping him."

"Lucky guy. What's his name?"

"Purvis Irving. Remember that. I'm going to make him massive."

"Let's hope he can handle your ... feedback. You wouldn't want him to start doubting his ability."

"He's tougher than that. Hardened by life, already."

"I'm happy for you. Someone else you can build up, suck dry and toss to the gutter when the words stop coming to him. He must be ecstatic to have you in his corner."

"Don't put your failures on me, Quintus." Lydette turns and goes to the gate's little door. "Now leave, before I call security."

"Always a pleasure, Lydette."

The door closes with the metallic clang of a prison cell.

Huntley starts the car and drives a few metres down the street, then takes a narrow laneway that follows the estate's east wall. He manoeuvres the car very close to the wall. From the open window, he climbs out, using the Landy's window frame for leverage, and clambers over the wall, landing on the soft grass of the tennis court. Its surface is in immaculate condition, the lines freshly marked, but the court hasn't seen any tennis in decades.

He sneaks across the court while scanning the garden, also immaculate, for Harland. He spots him crouched down among the roses near the house's main entrance, beekeeper's hat on.

Being back here, on this property, makes him feel a very particular kind of hate. Witnessing again, up close, this ridiculous wealth is a blatant reminder of how many people Harland, and Harland's father, and Harland's grandfather, and so on, must have wronged over the years in order to accumulate said wealth. All the lives they remorselessly destroyed and the people they stole from. He thinks guilt is etched into every block of sandstone the house is built from, the blood of innocents in the cement that holds it all together. And the Giffords live, day after day, in blissful arrogance, fully believing they deserve and have earned everything that they have.

Huntley, always a champion sleeper, suffered badly from insomnia when he first moved in. Each night, when everyone else was asleep, the house told him stories. Over 150 years of Gifford family history revealed itself to him. His imagination filled in the gaps. It started with him staring at the sepia photos on the walls, the family portraits and headshots, all of them so stoic and forthright. Every photo seemed to tell a story of villainy. Huntley couldn't turn it off, and he didn't want to; he wanted to dig up the truth. How did the Giffords acquire so much farming land? How was it fair for one family to have so much? Awake every night, surrounded by all the Gifford ghosts, he tried to write it down as poetry. But everything he composed was too nightmarish to even read through. Most troubling was the strong feeling that the truth was actually far worse than the poetry he wrote; that the early Giffords had serious amounts of indigenous and convict blood on their hands, which Giorgie had sometimes hinted at. It reached the point that he drove down to Ravensthorpe and brought back an old caravan. He positioned it off the main driveway and claimed it was his writing studio, but he snuck out there every night to sleep in it. Once Giorgie found out, she was convinced it was because he didn't want to sleep with her, nor take care of their baby. He didn't have the courage to tell her the truth, and things went bad from there.

He stays in the shadow of the treeline adjacent to the tennis court and gets to the house unseen. Giorgie could be anywhere, and he's careful as he looks in the windows, worried a member of the staff might spot him. When he locates her in the library, he thinks that's right. She's asleep on the sofa, stretched out seductively on her side, as if posing for a portrait, backdropped by a wall of bookshelves; it's the same sofa he first saw her on, all those years ago.

He taps the glass lightly. She stirs and rolls, but doesn't wake. He knocks harder on the glass, and she bolts upright and looks around.

Huntley waves once. Giorgie comes to the window and opens it.

"This is not a good idea, Quin," she says slowly.

"Your sister said the exact same thing."

"With good reason. You can't be here."

"You look fabulous."

"I wish I felt that way, and I wish I believed you."

Huntley holds up his hands apologetically. "I know I'm not supposed to show up like this."

"Show up? You've broken in. Did Dad see you?"

"No. I spotted him in the roses, wearing that hat with the netting around it."

"Why didn't you just call?"

"This is too important. I need to ask you something."

"If it's about money, I can arrange it for you."

"I don't want your money. Why is everything about money with you lot?" Huntley takes a breath, to ensure he keeps his voice down. "Look, I saw you this morning. Coming out of the hospital in Freo."

"Are you spying on me?"

"Absolutely not. I just happened to be there, dropping someone off."

"Who?"

"It doesn't matter. You were there to see Chandice Cowdrey, right?"

"Now I do think you're spying on me. How do you know that?"

"It's a long story, one I'd really like to finish. Can you help me?"

"How?"

"What happened to Chandice?"

"Food poisoning, as far as I know."

"What did she eat?"

"Octopus salad. It looked vile. No wonder she collapsed. Quin, what's this all about?"

"Salad? Did it have any weird ingredients?"

"That's a strange question." Giorgie pulls her hair back, but with nothing to tie it with, she just lets it fall to her shoulders. "It was a fusion restaurant. Who knows what they threw in."

Huntley would really like to run his hands through her hair. "What's it called? The restaurant."

"It didn't have a name. It's in the B Shed. It seemed new."

"What was the meeting for?"

"I can't tell you that."

"I know Niranda was there too."

"Ah, so it's her you're following. That fits."

"You're getting me all wrong. Look, this is going to sound cryptic, but if you're in any way involved in a new development south of the river, get out of it now."

"If you're talking about what I think you're talking about, you need to stop right there. That is massively confidential."

"It's dangerous, Giorgie. Stay away from it."

"Sounds like you think someone did something to Chandice on purpose."

"That's highly likely. I don't want you to be next."

Giorgie laughs a little. "I see. You're trying to protect me. What about Niranda? Are you protecting her? Protecting her brains out I bet."

"Careful. I know all about you and this Daley fella."

"From Verity?"

"Kids always know more than adults think they do."

"What does she know?" Giorgie asks.

"That you're ... you don't love him."

"I'm not responding to that. It doesn't matter to you anyway, and it's none of your business. What matters here, with us, is that I'm not in love with you and haven't been for a long time. You can't just show up like this."

Huntley swallows hard, and looks at the ground. "Still blunt, I see."

"You need to let me go. I let you go."

"You make it sound so easy. Like putting old shoes in the garbage."

"Goodbye, Quin."

Giorgie closes the window. Through it, Huntley sees her move quickly out of the library, possibly to the rose garden to alert Harland to his presence. He hustles across the tennis court, his shoes scuffing the grass a little. But the wall is too high to climb. A single attempt with a run-up leaves him sprawling on the grass. He drags a bench over to it, really digging up the grass, to gain some purchase. Once on the wall, he runs along it, arms flailing for balance, to his Landy. He slides through the open window and into the car. Visible in the rearview mirror, at the top of the laneway, is Harland Gifford, a large metal rake in his hands as he walks towards the car. Huntley fumbles with his keys, drops them, then retrieves them from the floor and fires up the Landy. He gets moving just as Harland is about to bring the rake down on his back window. Huntley roars down the laneway and around the first corner.

He lets out a long breath.

At the very least, he thinks, Giorgie has been warned. It's a seed planted.

The drive down Stirling Highway to the caravan doesn't register. He accelerates and brakes as required, going with the flow, but what's at the front of his brain is that first night in the library; trading playful barbs with Giorgie, savouring their instant chemistry, the two of them not so much clicking as recognising a worthy adversary. Their verbal sparring was fantastically flirtatious. Sitting on the floor in front of the fireplace, they debated into the night, about university, literature, politics, sports, history and even fashion, drinking one hot toddy after another. By dawn, they were lying on the carpet, holding hands and staring up at the ceiling, the fire still glowing with embers. After all the joshing and jibing, Giorgie said, very sweetly, that he had a gift for putting things poetically and should try his hand at writing. Huntley admitted he had never thought about it and wouldn't know where to start. Giorgie advised him to begin from a safe place, with something he knows well. That meant Ravensthorpe. And because they were young and feeling the dynamic sparks of fresh love, they left together right then, taking one of the cars from the Gifford garage and driving south with just the clothes they were wearing. They arrived just in time for Huntley to conspire with his father to steal a ram lamb from the Edwards farm.

With Giorgie beside him, so much suddenly felt possible for Huntley.

Then, those superb years, with his book getting published and the two of them fucking their way around the world, ostensibly to promote the book but burning through a generous outlay from the Gifford trust fund. The States, Canada, the UK, Europe, India, then back to Perth so he could start writing his second collection. But months went by and sleeping became impossible in the Gifford house, and Lydette was unhelpful to the point of being destructive. He was happily married, so in love with Giorgie, but wishing every day they would move out of the house. He kept dropping Pearse Street into the conversation, a chance for them to break away from tradition and do their own thing; to escape the legacy and the ghosts. But then Giorgie was pregnant and she wanted to utilise a house full of staff who could take on some, or most, of the responsibilities of child care. He took the part-time university job just to get out of that poisonous house. At the start, bereft of poetry of his own, he threw himself into teaching it to others, and was surprised to discover he had a knack for it. But his enthusiasm waned with every passing semester, while his marriage died a slow death at home. Huntley, always the outsider, was asked to hitch his caravan to his car and leave. He was both distraught and relieved. The Gifford ghosts would keep him awake no longer, and eating a meal wouldn't require swallowing down the accompanying guilt of how the food was paid for. Several years later, in a hot toddy haze when visiting on a boiling Christmas

Day, he trashed the library and smashed the old photos that hung on the walls, which resulted in Harland banning him from ever setting foot on the property again. His allocated time with Verity was also reduced, by court order, to fortnightly Saturdays.

Trolling through these recollections, while trying to process Giorgie's declaration that she hasn't loved him for years and has long moved on, means he arrives at the caravan in a morbid mood. He has afternoon classes to prepare for, which really seem to lack any importance, given two people are dead, one is in a coma, and he still needs endings.

Aphra Massey, sitting on the steps of his caravan with her back against the door, is the last person he wants to see right now. He takes his time to turn the car off, lift the handbrake and unbuckle his seatbelt, during which she stands up and starts walking towards him.

"You look like someone with an agenda," he says, getting out.

"Your help is at the top of that list."

This raises his spirits a little. "Really?"

"I can't sleep. I have to get closure."

"Your friend? Tell me about it. She left me with a poem that doesn't have an ending. Sorry, I didn't mean that to sound callous. I'm also sorry for everything I said the other night. It was insensitive of me, given the situation."

Aphra, surprised by this admission, nods. "Thank you."

As they stand there, Huntley tries to give Aphra a comforting smile.

"I think I know who killed her," she says.

"You do? That's probably information Detective Everest would love to have, yet you've come to me first, which I very much appreciate, as long as you don't think it was me."

"It was one of the Ford-Brackmans. Marcus or Lance. Or both."

"How did you get there?"

"It's all about Marcus's career. Right? Katie was killed so he could have her place."

Huntley takes a moment to consider this. He goes under the trees, out of the wind.

"It fits," Aphra says, following him. "That's the motive."

"A chair? A third chair at that."

"You know what that family's into. This is certainly not beyond them."

Huntley shakes his head. "I don't know. It's not really their style. They don't touch this sort of thing. Not directly, and not in that way."

"Then they hired someone."

"Maybe. I'm not sure a career in the PSO is a motive for murder though."

"People have been killed for a lot less." Aphra is thoughtful for a moment, her eyes boring into Huntley. "You know something. Do you have your own theory?"

"I'm not sure if it qualifies as a theory. It's more a sketchy plot outline."

"Let's hear it."

"Do you know Chandice Cowdrey?"

"I've had the unfortunate pleasure. She and Blair are distant cousins."

"Why is that not surprising? She sits on the City of Cockburn council, among other things. Currently, she's in Fremantle Hospital, in a coma induced by food poisoning."

"What has that got to do with Katie?"

"Come on. You're a storyteller. You see the connections before others do."

"What connection?"

Huntley uses his fingers to list things off. "Two people are dead. One is almost dead. It starts with your friend and this wild arum stuff."

"What's that?"

"Everest didn't tell you? Ekaterina was killed with wild arum," Huntley says, a little too flatly. He reminds himself of the importance of empathy. "I'm sorry you're hearing this from me. It's a plant. A poisonous plant. The killer put it in the pen that was jammed into her neck."

"Oh my God."

"Incredible, isn't it? The poison caused her to choke. Who knew plants could be so dangerous."

Aphra paces a little, then stops. "Wait. When I spoke to Marcus this morning at his school, he had come straight from gardening class. His hands were filthy."

"What kind of class is gardening?"

"I asked the same thing. It's something to do with mindfulness. I don't know. New age schooling. Anyway, he's really into it. He could've known about this wild arum stuff."

"That's interesting, but no. Marcus is no killer. And he would never kill his brother."

"Is that the connection you're trying to make? That Katie and Lance were killed by the same person?"

"Chandice too. Though she's hanging on." When Aphra looks at him quizzically, Huntley adds, "It's all about the plants."

"Lance was poisoned?"

"I'm probably not allowed to tell you this, but screw it. Yeah, he was poisoned. Someone put jimsonweed in his water bottle, and then he went swimming at night and drowned. Now, Chandice Cowdrey is almost a vegetable from food poisoning. She had octopus salad, and anything plant-like could've been thrown in there without her noticing."

"If it's the same person, how are these three people connected? I'm not seeing it. What on earth is jimsonweed?"

"It's like acid, as far as I know."

"You're pulling these things together so you can write about them. You want to profit from these people dying, including my friend."

Huntley is taken aback by this. "Hang on. I want justice, just like you. I want to find out who did this, and stop them."

"You're not convincing anyone. Come on. I do this kind of stuff for a living, trying to convince people of things. Your delivery lacks the required sincerity. You don't even believe your own words."

Huntley sits on the steps of the caravan. "I'm sorry if I sound selfish with all this. You of all people should understand what I'm going through. What I've been going through. I've got the magic again. I thought it was gone forever."

"Prove it. Show me something."

"It's not ready. I really don't want to be showing anyone a first draft."

"Then why should I believe this nonsense about magic?"

"Fine." Huntley pulls out the folded back page of the brochure and hands it to Aphra. "This one's about Lance."

Aphra takes it and unfolds it. "The Hallucinating Nightswimmer."

As she reads, Huntley watches her face, to gauge her reaction; it remains set, impossible to read.

"I like this bit about being awake in a horrid dream," she says, handing the paper back to Huntley. "But is awakeness even a word?"

"I allowed myself a little poetic license."

"It's nice imagery. Good work overall."

"You sound like a kindie teacher rating my finger painting."

"I didn't say it was bad," Aphra says. "I'm not sure how it solves a murder, though."

"Well, I still need the ending. I did this part while sitting in Lance's car. It all came in a rush. I know I can make it better."

"When it flows, it flows."

"That's right." Huntley claps his hands together. "Flow is a good word. The connection flows, from Katie and Marcus to Marcus and Lance to Lance and Chandice. Those last two are in cahoots on the Southern Everglades."

"You know about the development?"

Huntley holds up the back page of the brochure. "I found this in his car. A briefcase full of brochures."

"How did you even end up in his car?"

"I was following my instincts. Rightly, it turns out. What do you know about the project?"

"Plenty. Including that not many people know about it. Then, I found out this morning a lot of the land has already been sold."

"Can they do that? It's not approved yet. As far as I can tell, Lance was trying to bribe Chandice in order to get the permission to clear the land. They can't do anything if the land stays protected. Certainly not sell it."

"Chandice is too small for this kind of thing. She doesn't have any real influence."

"That land must be worth a fortune," Huntley says. "What's the matter?"

"I thought I was on track to find Katie's killer, but now I'm more confused than before."

"The pudgy violinist didn't kill anyone, believe me."

"Who was it then? If it's the same person, as you say, that person's had a busy week, and it's only Wednesday."

"Including getting to a restaurant to spike Chandice's salad."

"Where's the restaurant? We could go there, have a look around."

"You want to team up with me, after I called you a muckraker?"

"I guess what bothered me the most is that you're right. But I've always liked the challenge of it. Turning something mucky into something marvellous."

Huntley stands up. "I should admire you. You've made your work one long creative writing class. Speaking of which, I'm due at the university. Afternoon classes."

"No. We're going to this restaurant. We need to find out what happened there, because if you're right, it could help lead us back to Katie's killer."

"We?"

"It won't take long. You'll still make your classes, but I'm sure you'll agree this is more important. This is the horrid dream you want to wake up from."

"Let's go. It's in Freo. B Shed, at Victoria Quay."

"I'll follow you." Aphra dons her helmet and climbs on her Vespa.

Huntley, in his Landy, leads the way down Stirling Highway. Aphra is easy to spot in her Italian flag helmet, a few cars behind. Over the Railway Bridge, they veer down Beach Road. Huntley stops at the one place in the B Shed that has a menu board out the front. Aphra pulls up next to him.

"Do you think that's it?" she asks. "I don't see a name."

"It must be." Huntley parks his car and gets out. "How do we do this?"

Aphra takes off her helmet and shakes her hair loose. "Are you hungry?"

"Do you want to eat in a place that put someone in a coma?"

"Good point. Maybe a drink is safer."

They head inside. It's very full. Huntley scans the room for Everest and Booth, half-expecting them to be here doing interviews, but all the tables are taken by a late-lunch crowd. It doesn't appear the morning's events have impacted the restaurant's trade. As there are no free tables, they stand at the workbench bar. Huntley fiddles with the lever of the massive vice. It comes loose. The lever clatters to the floor, making everyone look at him. He's quick to reattach the nut holding the lever in place.

"Try not to bring too much attention to yourself."

"I'm a novice spy, I readily admit."

Aphra, eying the diners, says, "I feel underdressed."

Huntley looks at the chalkboard menu above the bar. "I feel underpaid. A little glass of wine costs more than a bottle."

A waiter sidles up next to them, phone in hand. "I'm sorry, we're full."

"We'll stand here, if that's all right," Huntley says.

"Sure."

"I'll have a water, please," Aphra says. "Sparkling."

Huntley thinks about his dry week, then says, "A hot toddy for me."

"What's that?" the waiter asks.

"Hot tea with rum and other goodies. Why don't you know that?"

"Probably because it's not on the menu."

"It should be. It's very easy to make."

The waiter holds up his phone. "I can't enter it if it's not in the system already."

"Let me behind the bar. I'll make it myself."

"I can't allow that. Anyway, it's wine only. There's no spirit."

"You got that right. Fine. An expensive sparkling water for me too."

"And your meals?"

"Do you expect us to eat standing at the bar?" Aphra asks. "What are we, horses?"

"We're not eating," Huntley says. "We're here on business. We need to speak to the owner."

"Carmello's at a produce screening."

"A what?"

"He's selecting ingredients for the dishes," the waiter says, as if this is self-explanatory and a common activity, and Huntley's an idiot for not knowing. "Everything in here is farm-to-table. And ocean-to-table. Carmello screens it all himself."

"Directly from suppliers?" Aphra asks.

"Last I heard, that's how farm-to-table works."

Huntley laughs. "How much extra are we paying for the attitude?"

The waiter narrows his eyes. "You get that for free, Mr Huntley."

When the waiter's gone, Aphra asks, "A student of yours?"

"Seems like it. Everyone expects to be remembered these days."

"If you ask me, it's more that everyone thinks they're memorable. We did some research on this, to gain insights into the likes and dislikes of young voters. Something they find important is a candidate who knows their name. This is a game-changer, because before it was all about getting the electorate to remember the candidate. Now, the candidate has to know everyone in the electorate."

"Just the names? Or what they want as well?"

"The more background, the better. Social media has been hugely helpful with this, to build profiles on people."

"How do you get Blair Blake-Stendahl to execute this? A Cyrano situation, with someone secretly feeding information into her ear?"

"We couldn't risk her being caught doing that. She'd lose all credibility. For the last few years, we've been training her for positive name recognition."

"What the hell is that?"

"Exactly as it sounds," Aphra says. "There are techniques that help commit names to memory. The obvious one is to use someone's name the first time you hear it. You say, 'Hi, I'm Quintus.' Then I say, 'Nice to meet you, Quintus.' That helps etch your name into my brain."

"Clever. It goes deeper the more times the name is used."

"It does, Quintus."

"I should use this with my students."

"Blair's become very good at it. You should see her work a room at an event. It's amazing to watch, all these exchanges that she makes so personal. You'd never know she's been training that skill for years now. But we also have a safety net."

"What's that?"

"She has Maritsa, an assistant, whose sole task is to maintain a database of every person that Blair meets, and to have that information available whenever Blair needs it."

"A little bit of Cyrano after all. I need a Maritsa. Does she have a twin?"

The waiter puts their drinks on the bar, spilling them, then holds out his phone.

"What are we supposed to do with that?" Huntley asks.

"Pay."

"What, with my fingerprint?"

Aphra takes out her phone and holds it over the waiter's.

"Everything is electronic in here," the waiter says. "We're proudly carbon neutral and paper-free."

"Not to mention spiritless, and farm-to-table," Huntley says. "You're absolutely nailing the sustainability angle. Send Carmello out here so I can congratulate him."

"I told you. He's not here."

"Ah, yes. He's meeting the meat. Auditioning the produce."

"Screening." The waiter puts one hand on his hip. "Don't disrespect him. Being sustainable isn't an angle. It's Carmello's lifestyle choice."

"Brilliant. I assume that extends to various receipts and invoices for the produce selected. It's electronic. Stored somewhere. In a cloud or such?"

"That's not new," Aphra says to Huntley. "It saves a huge amount of paper."

A diner calls for the waiter, who dives into the throng.

"I know it's not new," Huntley says. "But it does mean there's a chance we can get into their records. To find out who supplied the food here today."

"Which could lead us to someone involved in ... certain kinds of plants."

"Precisely." Huntley sips his water, then spits it back into the glass. "That is awful. You paid a small fortune for undrinkable water. That's trash-to-table. Toilet-to-table."

Aphra looks at her water, but doesn't drink. "What do you suggest we do next?"

"I have to get to class, Aphra. To learn my students' names, Aphra."

"Should we come back tonight to break in? How are we going to find out who was responsible for what went into Chandice's salad?"

"As it turns out, I know someone who can help. I think you know him too."

<>

Everest knocks on the varnished jarrah door frame of Mitchell Booth's office. He gestures for her to enter.

"You wanted to see me?"

"Come in, Elenore."

"Is Justin not joining us?"

"He's on something more pressing. Sit down."

Everest turns the chair around. That its back was facing Booth senior's desk makes her think Justin was the last one to sit in it, given his penchant for the backward chair thing.

"What's he working on?" Everest sits down. "Lance Ford-Brackman, I assume."

"I'm sure he'll update you when he's ready. Like good partners do."

"What did you want to see me about?"

"You missed the morning briefing."

"I was working a lead, on the violinist."

Booth leans back in his chair and nods his massive egg-shaped head. He's one of those middle-aged guys who started going bald not long out of his teens and decided to never have hair again. His fully shaved dome glistens in the light. It makes his head seem far bigger than it is, and somehow alien-like. He's the kind of bald man easily spotted from a mile away, yet is almost unrecognisable when wearing a hat.

"How's that going?" he asks.

"Some progress. We're trying to find people in Perth with access to wild arum. Nothing definite yet."

"What about that gardener in Vic Park? The one with the record. You seemed confident about her."

"She wasn't involved. But she did know about jimsonweed, even though it wasn't in her house. That was found in Lance's water bottle."

"Not your case. It's closed anyway. Suicide."

"Already? At least give us until the end of the week."

"Didn't you hear me? It's not your case. Did all that drumming ruin your ears?"

"My hearing's fine, boss."

Booth now leans forward and puts his hands on the desk, knitting them together into a fist. He has small hands, the nails neatly trimmed. "Let it go. Focus on the violinist."

"What if they turn out to be connected?"

"They're not. Stop reaching. Stay objective."

"I just think we're being ..."

"I got a call this morning from the Ukrainian Ambassador. At 7am. He wants to know if this has been a targeted attack on a Ukrainian national abroad. By Russia, or someone else."

"Russia?"

"This murder could be part of an international conflict. We need to take care of this."

"Are you suggesting Ekaterina Valoskiya is some kind of spy?"

"Why not? Seems like a decent cover, travelling the world as a concert musician. Getting invited to important events and gatherings. She was spotted at Parliament House, Justin told me."

"Representing the PSO. She certainly wasn't there to steal government secrets. This is Perth, not London or Washington."

"There's no need to raise your voice. Just look into this Russian angle and let me know, in case the ambassador calls me again at dawn."

"This was local, and I really think Lance Ford-Brackman is connected to it. I just need more time. If you close that case, I can't investigate him anymore."

"There's no if. It's closed. You'd be wise to stay away from the Ford-Brackmans altogether."

"What does that mean?"

"Elenore, I think you know exactly what that means."

"That's not right, boss. We can't be working cases with people who are untouchable."

"This is Perth, the big country town," Booth says, and it's hard for Everest to decide if this is said with affection or not. "It matters who you know, and who your family knows. Plenty of people in Perth are untouchable, you know that."

"No one should be exempt from the law."

"No one is. But relationships are important." Booth leans back again and puts his hands behind his big, shiny head. "Let me give you some advice, one detective to another. If you're going to investigate a murder, focus on the living, not the dead."

"You just ordered me to find out if the dead girl was a spy."

"By looking at which Russians, very much alive, benefit from her being dead. You've also got this Cowdrey woman in a coma. That looks like an accident, but maybe there's someone who benefits from that. Look at the living. I'm sure Justin could help, if he has the capacity."

"You said he was busy with other things."

"The pressure is on Elenore. We don't get many murders. But when we do, we better solve them quick smart, or the media and the public will crucify us. Like what happened with Claremont."

"But we caught the guy. Eventually."

"We did. My dad was part of it. But at the time, when those girls went missing, we couldn't walk down the street without being abused for not doing our jobs. You wouldn't believe how nasty people were. I got spat on a couple of times and I received some horrible letters. Just because I was helping my dad with the investigation. You wouldn't believe the hate mail he got."

"That was different. No one benefited, financially or politically, from those missing girls. It was just senseless violence. What if the violinist was a murder like that? What if we've got some crazy woman-hater roaming the streets again?"

Booth points at Everest. "Don't you dare let such an idea leave this building, Elenore. Or even this office. We are not going down that road again. Look for the Russians."

"But, boss ..."

"She wasn't touched. There were no signs of sexual assault. She was killed in her apartment, not abducted or taken to the bush somewhere. There are no similarities. Leave it. Focus on the living."

"Okay. Fine."

"Keep me updated, in case I get more calls from Canberra."

Everest nods, swallowing down everything she wants to say.

"Listen," Booth says, trying to sound fatherly, "take the afternoon off. Recalibrate. Forget about it all for a while, then hit it hard again tomorrow with a fresh perspective."

"Your hurry-up speech is actually a request I take some downtime?"

"It can be helpful. At the very least go home and clean yourself up."

"I'm working around the clock to solve this case."

"Obsessing isn't healthy. Trust me. It's why I took up sketching. To get some distance. You should get yourself a hobby."

"Like drumming?"

"If it helps, sure, get back into music. Or join one of these conga circles."

Everest stands up. "I have a cat. Does that count as a hobby?"

"Sometimes you need to put yourself first, however that means. You're dismissed."

Everest exits Booth's office, which was once his father's office and will likely one day be Justin's office. It's not just about knowing the right people, she thinks. Being born into the right family matters more.

Annoyed, she heads for her own office, with no plans to take the afternoon off to charcoal or join a drumming circle, though she would like to go home, have a shower and feed her cat. At the stairs, she stops, looks around, then heads down to the basement.

The evidence locker and archive are overseen by Deirdre Dennis, a heavily tattooed, sinewy ex-undercover cop in her late 50s who started working down there after testifying in several drug-related biker gang trials, which blew her cover. Everest goes there now hoping Deedee might know something about

Russians, because once upon a time she knew just about everyone in the Perth crime scene. When Everest opens the door and goes to the desk, she finds Deedee sitting back in her chair, sandaled feet up on the desk and reading *Playgirl*.

"Detective Everest," Deedee says, looking around the side of the magazine. "Back again."

"Anything good in there?"

"I just read it for the articles." She turns the magazine sideways. "Some of them are really, really long."

"You don't seem very busy down here."

"It's a slow afternoon. Wednesdays are normally quiet. I can do a little heavy reading."

"Can I get the usual?"

"Don't overdo it, sweetheart. You'd be wise not to make this a daily habit."

"It helps with my wrists. You know that. Anyway, all the kids are doing it these days. Vaping outside school, even in the toilets."

"Like we used to smoke."

"Right. Like that."

"They were cigarettes," Deedee says. "Not harmless, but not quite like what the kids are doing today. Back in the day, we smoked to look cool. Now, kids vape to get high."

Everest hands Deedee a 20-dollar note and gets a vaping stick in return. "Are you saying you can put harder stuff in this?"

"Sure. It's essentially a pipe. So, whatever you smoke with a pipe, you can put in there."

"Like meth?"

Deedee nods. "And crack and ketamine."

"Is that happening?" Everest asks, looking at the vape.

"Why wouldn't it? People can get happily high in public, whenever they want. Vaping doesn't seem to have the same stigma as cigarettes. Most people tolerate it, even when they don't know what's inside. That little gizmo has revolutionised the illicit drug trade."

"Where are you getting them from?"

"Ooh, I can't tell you that. As far as you know, I don't sell these things. Exposing me will just mean exposing everyone else. Let's leave it at that."

Everest brings the vape right up to her eyes. "Is that a snake?"

Deedee shrugs.

"Just give me a hint. I won't stop your business. I'm just curious."

"This is not a road you want to travel down, detective. Not unless you want to put your supply and that of our esteemed colleagues at risk."

Everest pockets the vape. "How about this? What do you know about Russians in Perth?"

"Is that a joke?"

"Nyet." When Deedee just stares at her, Everest adds, "That's Russian for no. You don't learn that in *Playgirl*?"

Deedee flips a page. "It's a different kind of education. But Russians here? Haven't got wind of that. I could ask around."

"Thanks."

Now that she has something to help her relax, Everest decides to do what Booth senior suggested and take the afternoon off. She goes to the door.

"Stay safe out there, detective," Deedee says.

Outside, walking to her car, she's tempted to start vaping, but thinks that's not the best look for the police carpark in the afternoon. Plenty of her colleagues could be spying on her from the windows above.

As school hasn't finished, traffic is light. The drive from East Perth to Doubleview is quick and easy. She's helped along by a succession of green lights, which are a welcoming treat at intersections that can sometimes take forever to turn from red to green.

After a hectic couple of days, with two corpses and a coma, it's good to have a moment of respite. She won't admit it out loud, but Booth senior is right; letting go is an essential part of investigative work. Overthinking leads to obsession, which results in frustration and sleepless nights. Distance makes a difference. She recalls how the same process helped with songwriting. When she tried too hard to write a song, when she forced it, the song was a pathetic mess. But once she let go and got her mind thinking about other things, at some point it came to her how the song should be. The song revealed itself, and from there it was easy.

She thinks: the really hard part about creativity is forgetting about it.

At her complex, situated on the hill of Stockdale Crescent, she parks in bay 16, and it's the only car in the parking area. While she doesn't know any of her neighbours personally, she's quietly glad they're all working professionals and functioning in the wider community. Once up the stairs and inside her apartment, she goes to the west-facing windows and looks towards the ocean. The jagged outline of Rottnest Island is on the horizon, plus half a dozen colourful container ships, spread out and seemingly not moving.

She breathes.

The ocean is deep blue from this distance It's tempting to wander down there and jump in, but the slithers of white amongst the blue give away how strongly the sea breeze is blowing. The same wind is rattling the windows in their frames, so inside she stays.

It seems like a long time since she last stood here and took in this view. So many months, and even years, have passed during which her goal was to get home late enough, to eat, shower and sleep, and avoid contemplating her past.

Her cat strolls over and does a figure eight of her legs, tail arched.

"Cookie, I've missed you too," she says, bending down to pick her up.

She feels her brain wanting to stay on the job. Ekaterina, Lance, Chandice, wild arum, jimsonweed, octopus salad. So many loose ends. So much to still figure out. And now this Russian espionage thing, at Mitch Booth's ludicrous behest.

She strokes the cat. "The loose ends must be driving Huntley crazy."

She wonders what he's doing right now. The scruffy poet. The charismatic jester. The gifted charmer. The cunning liar.

She smiles. Cookie jumps down.

One thing she can't deny is that he has a nose for the game. It's tempting to call him, to get him over and order some takeaway, and together they could forget about things for a while. Get close while getting distance. Because if she doesn't get some kind of distraction, her mind will eventually turn to Charlene.

She takes out her phone and dials his number.

"The mobile phone you are calling is switched off or not in a mobile network area."

She pockets the phone and goes to the sofa. Huntley's book is there. She picks it up, opens it to where she left off and reads a few lines. Now that she knows him, she can hear his voice in her head, reading to her. It's strangely comforting.

She flips to the cover, thinking back to when she first saw it in the violin case. Why this book? What has Huntley got to do with the violinist?

Cookie jumps up on the sofa and nestles in her lap.

"I'm getting the feeling you like me in the afternoon. You don't want to know me when I come home at night."

The cat purrs.

"Huntley said he didn't know the violinist. But what if he knows the killer? The book was put there to get Huntley's attention. So, Cookie, who would want to get noticed by Huntley?"

She tosses the book to the floor, where it lands, face down, its pages askew.

"Just let it go."

She closes her eyes and tries to think of nothing. But Charlene appears immediately, standing in a singlet and cut-off jeans shorts on the steps of the house they shared in Highgate, which was falling apart and has since been torn down, replaced by a cramped complex of studio apartments. She misses that run-down house, and that time. The afternoons they spent on the rickety back veranda, writing songs and trying to stamp their feet enough to make the whole veranda collapse. Charlene with her playful sneer, pale skin, freckles and bleach-blonde hair, so sexy and gorgeous, a rock'n'roll goddess even before she started singing. And once she did, she morphed from goddess to angry angel, and brought all the neighbours out of their houses and into their backyards to listen. That voice, at once sweet and pained, clear and cracking, sounded the absolute best exactly as it was, without amplification, technology or software, on the back veranda when Ellie felt Charlene was singing just for her. Everyone loved her, including Ellie, who channelled that unrequited love into her music, dropping hints in lyrics, but never acting on her feelings, while pounding the drums the way she wanted to slap Charlene's bare arse. It was that hurt, buried deep, which tore a noxious hole inside her when she found Charlene half on the floor of the Highgate house's spider-infested bathroom, neck suspended from the door handle, held there by a low E bass string that had pinched her neck, but hadn't broken the skin. She wanted to take that metal string and hook it around her own throat, to die beside Charlene's still-warm body. That hole has never healed, and Charlene never left. The hole has made it impossible for her to feel anything for anyone else. Even self-love has been challenging.

On the sofa, she feels tears coming. The pain is unchanged, through two decades. She misses Charlene as much today as when she lost her. But it's not bathroom Charlene she misses, nor stage Charlene. It's back veranda Charlene who she holds in her memory, from that glorious time when they dropped out of school, moved in together and were on their way to becoming famous. When they lived like a couple, sharing whatever money they had, and even sharing a bed, but never consummated their relationship.

Opening her eyes doesn't make the memories stop. But she is able to divert her attention, to Cookie. The cat is on the floor, clawing at Huntley's book, playing with it. Cookie manages to flip the book over and hold the back cover open with one paw. On the inside of the back cover, Everest sees a barcode sticker. She looks closer, getting down on the floor with her cat. Printed beneath the barcode is "Reid Library".

She grabs the book, gets to her feet and flies out the door.

<>

He likes it best being alone in the greenhouse. It's easier to concentrate; he can get intimate with his plants without distraction, cultivate the various relationships, and control the watering.

He adjusts the nozzle of the spray, for a finer mist, and squeezes delicately. Cannabis sativa needs exactly the right amount of water. The thriving of nature, he knows, is all about balance. Sunlight plus water plus nutrients plus air plus atmosphere plus companionship; all of that in harmony and within the defined parameters specific to the plant species. He considers plants to be like humans, perhaps even better than humans. More advanced, more evolved. Because only a human would be so stupid and cruel as to water a plant less or more than it needs. Only a human would leave a plant in the same soil for years on end. Brutal. Torturous. Plants need attention every day. Fresh soil, new pots, conversation, love. Atmospherics also matter, the right sound and mood, which he finds easier to achieve when alone in the greenhouse. He can bring the right energy in here. On days when he entered the greenhouse in a foul mood, he watched his plants droop in response.

This afternoon, he's feeling great, and the plants are responding to that energy, leaves reaching out towards him for affection.

Over time, and with plenty of missteps along the way, he has learned that cannabis sativa responds best to the news and current affairs. He puts this down to the plant being one that thrives on information; or it could be misinformation, as the news is so often biased, sensationalist, or just plain wrong. So, while doing his late afternoon moisturising round of the cannabis section, he has the television on, set to a news channel, the volume loud. When Blair Blake-Stendahl appears on the screen, he stops to watch. The caption is "WA Republic Party calls for state election."

He thinks that 20 years ago, Blair the shy and raw university student would've been infinitely fuckable, as long as she kept her mouth shut; even now she's exuding a certain middle-aged milf-ish appeal. The only problem is that everything she says is a total turn-off. Still, he accepts that cannabis sativa is responding well to her rabid talk of Perth no longer being safe and the government having lost the confidence and support of local people. The TV stays on.

"It's time for change," Blair says earnestly to the newswoman interviewing her. "A young woman was murdered in her apartment and the police and the incumbent state government have done nothing about it. How can local people feel safe in their homes? There are dangerous people out there on the streets, and those are the streets our children walk on the way to school. If the government can't guarantee our safety, the people should be given the opportunity to vote in a government that will. It's time for an election. For change."

He squeezes the spray and says, "As if any children these days actually walk to school."

"What can your party do that will be different?" the interviewer asks.

"It's very straightforward, Fiona. Once our prosperous, hard-working state is given the chance to take control of its own destiny, by becoming a separate, autonomous and powerful country, we could then ensure that the revenue from our growth industries stays within our borders. We could use it to bolster the police force and provide them with more resources and training to bring them into the modern era. Right now, as led by the current government, the sole interest of the police is to speed-trap local drivers and fleece them of their hard-earned incomes, which is money that should be going towards feeding and clothing children. Meanwhile, violent crimes occur and the police are ill-equipped, and let's face it, not interested in stopping them or solving them. As a result, all of these dangerous criminals continue to walk among us and make our streets unsafe."

With cannabis sativa nourished for now, he focuses on his special collection. These plants are all in pots, in a variety of sizes, with a fair bit of separation between them; he believes these noxious species, alpha plants all of them, need space and come into conflict with each other if they get too close.

"How else could WA independence be beneficial?"

"Beyond the clear economic advantages, it would enable us to better protect our borders. We will be able to decide who comes in and under what circumstances. This has nothing to do with race or gender or any kind of profiling. It's about having the right people join us on our collective journey towards becoming a strong and vibrant independent nation."

He realises that this so-called news report is actually veiled PR, as the interviewer is asking questions Blair appears prepped for. Plus, Blair's speaking in full, articulate sentences, as if reading from cards in front of her. But the plants don't seem bothered by the ruse.

"Are you ready for an election? Do you think your party will exceed its current approval rating?"

"We're ready. We're confident the people will make the choice that's right for everyone. Re-electing the current government, or worse, the opposition, will just result in more of the same. More murders. More ticketing. More pandering to Canberra. More times when WA will have to get down on its knees and cower to a federal government that couldn't give a stuff about us. With every economic crisis Australia has faced in the last 100 years, it has been the hard-working people of this state who have helped keep the rest of the country afloat. I'm tired of snobs in the eastern states who never get their hands dirty living large on the back of our industry and toil. It's not fair. WA is so economically vibrant. We deserve to be rewarded for that vibrancy. Local people deserve to reap the benefits of what they sow, and not see it shipped interstate."

"Can you deliver on this?"

"Without question. We've been preparing for this for years. I would go further and say the whole state has been preparing for years. This move is part of our destiny. From our side, we have several very exciting development projects in the pipeline that are ready to start, specifically in the southern areas of the city."

This gets his attention. He turns to the screen. "Oh, no you won't."

"The state government is selfishly holding these back right now," Blair continues. "These localisation projects have the potential to revitalise key areas of Perth, to create homes and jobs for local people and improve our quality of life. Where the government sees problems and despair, where they continue to stick their heads in the sand, we see opportunity and betterment. We want to make this state, this new nation, the greatest country on Earth."

"Strong words. Blair Blake-Stendahl, thank you for your time."

"No, thank you, Fiona."

He gives arum maculatum a smidgen of water, considering how to stop Blair. When he reaches the silky white umbrella-like flowers of hemlock, the plant all but nods at him.

<>

His classes done, Huntley drives to Leake Street in Peppermint Grove. When he arrives, Aphra is standing next to her Vespa, arms folded.

"You're late," she says, once he's out of the car.

"Sorry. Some students were a bit demanding after class. Good news, though. I used your little technique and now know their names. Most of them."

"Well done."

They head for the stairs.

"Why didn't you go up already?" he asks.

"This is your connection. I thought it best I go in with you."

"You don't need to be worried. Henrikson's an absolute gentleman. A diamond."

"How long have you known him?"

"Long enough to know that."

Up the stairs, Huntley knocks on the door. Henrikson opens it.

"You're just in time," he says, ushering them in.

"Have you found something?" Huntley asks.

Henrikson lowers himself into his desk chair. "First things first. That vape you gave me. Bernie wasted no time finding out what was in it."

"What vape?" Aphra asks.

"Must be great to be retired and have so much time," Huntley says.

"It's dope. Good quality, so he said. He smoked it. A soft high. Something to take the edge off without rendering you useless."

"That sounds about right."

"What vape?" Aphra asks again.

"Bernie was a total pothead all through his teaching career. Don't look so shocked. You have no idea what goes on in the teachers' room at schools."

"Probably no different to university," Huntley says. "Every second professor's hitting the hip flask before a lecture. And most of them during."

"There were a few days when I joined Bernie for a smoke. When things were particularly hard and I didn't have the time to take a walk. Every teacher has their own coping mechanism. Bernie's was grass, and I can assure you he wasn't alone."

"Fascinating." Huntley paces around a little. "Vaping as a way of surreptitiously taking drugs."

"Okay. Last time. What vape?"

"Quin? You never said where you got it from."

"No. I didn't." Huntley looks at Henrikson, then at Aphra. "This stays here. All right?"

They both nod.

"So. Last night. I went on a bit of an adventure, and a series of events, most of them fortunate, saw me end up in Lance Ford-Brackman's apartment, which is a pretty flash condo in Mossie Park. And in this condo I just happened to find a box full of vapes. I thought it was weird he had this big box, because that would mean a serious habit. Like, addiction level. But from what I've heard about Lance, he doesn't strike me as an addict."

"He was selling them," Aphra says.

"That's exactly what I thought. So I grabbed one and put it in my pocket, then gave it to Henrikson, who gave it to Bernie, who got high."

"He asked me for more," Henrikson says. "He's in a home. I don't think things are too good there."

"What were you doing in Lance's place?" Aphra asks.

"That's a great question." Huntley, tired from an afternoon spent on his feet trying to inspire lethargic students, sits on the sofa. "Everest asked me the same thing, when she showed up there."

"How about you give us a great answer? Instead of dodging the question. You really should go into politics."

Henrikson laughs.

"That's enough out of you, old man," Huntley says with a smile. "How about you put your skills to good use and tap into Carmello's system? Because if your drug buddy Bernie is right ..."

"He's right."

"It means Lance was engaged in some kind of drug trade. My guess is that he needed cash to line the pockets of whoever's brick-walling on the Everglades project. And because he's a Ford-Brackman, it's no surprise he turned to drugs. Though it makes me wonder why he didn't ask his family for the money. Anyway, I'd say one person he needed to pay off was ..."

"Chandice Cowdrey," Aphra says.

"Why do you both keep interrupting? Let the story flow."

Henrikson looks up from his computer. "You said she's in Fremantle Hospital. It might be easier to get the report on her than try to find out all of this Carmello guy's produce purchases."

"You said you liked a hacking challenge."

"I can't find anything from this restaurant. I'd say it's all bullshit. Everything's on paper."

"Naturally, it is. Even restaurants are in on the spin."

"Sustainability isn't his lifestyle choice after all," Aphra says.

"Meanwhile, the hospital is open for business." Henrikson turns his laptop screen to show them the hospital report. "Nerium indicum poisoning, so it says."

"Please tell me that's another plant," Huntley says, almost bouncing on the sofa.

Aphra takes out her phone and beats Henrikson to it. "Sweet oleander."

"That's a flower, isn't it? Is it poisonous?"

"Seems so," she says, scrolling. "Vanilla scent. Bitter taste."

"Yeah. Be vanilla never plain. Woah. Where the hell did that come from?"

"Maybe you should write it down," Henrikson says, tossing Huntley a pen. "I took the liberty of putting some paper on the coffee table."

Having caught the pen, Huntley takes a piece of blank paper. "Henrikson, I think this is the beginning of a beautiful friendship."

The pen immediately starts flying across the page. Huntley laughs a few times.

Aphra and Henrikson watch, amazed that the pen seems somehow ahead of Huntley's hand.

"Is that how it happens for you?" Henrikson asks her.

"Quiet in the peanut gallery," Huntley says.

Aphra leans close to Henrikson and whispers, "When it hits, you don't want it to stop. But I never tried to murder paper like that."

Huntley chuckles to himself. "Oh, yes."

"He's like a mad scientist," Aphra says. "Is he crazy?"

"I'm not sure yet. We only met a few days ago."

"Really? You two behave like old mates."

"We're kindred spirits," Huntley says, looking at the piece of paper. "Well, blow me fucking down. I like this."

"Let's hear it," Aphra says.

"Not yet." Huntley folds the paper carefully and puts it in his pocket. "But I can tell you these three crimes are definitely connected, in my opinion. Wild arum, jimsonweed, and now sweet oleander. Somewhere out there is a psychopath killing people with plants."

"Do you have any idea how strange that sounds?" Henrikson asks.

Aphra's phone starts buzzing. "Oh, no," she says, looking at the screen.

"What's happened?" Huntley asks.

"It appears Blair's gone rogue. Damn it. I take one day off and what does she do? She goes completely off-script."

Aphra heads for the door.

"Where are you going?"

"To fix this before some patriotic whacko makes a martyr of Blair."

"I'll be at the caravan if you need me," Huntley says.

When the door is closed, Henrikson says, "I like her."

"Yeah. Me too. She's got something. She's the right kind of tough."

"Are you interested in her? You pretty much invited her back to your place. Your, uh, caravan."

"I choose my living quarters carefully. I like my caravan very much." Huntley stands.

"I have no problem with it. Somehow it fits. For you."

"Thanks," Huntley says. "It's been a long day. I appreciate all your help, mate."

"Feel free to pop by anytime. Here or at the store. I'm enjoying these little challenges you give me. Though hacking the hospital was way too easy."

"Yeah? Maybe dig into Carmello's paper trail. He had students working there. Might be an employee worth looking at. In case it was an inside job."

Henrikson nods. "Be good."

Huntley leaves, goes down the stairs and gets into his Landy. He takes out his fresh poem and reads it, chuckling to himself again.

"Be in no way plain," he says, buzzing. "Be very good."

He gets on Stirling Highway with the last of the peak hour traffic.

The electrifying feeling fades on the journey, but he's still smiling when he pulls up at his caravan, where he spots an unfamiliar vehicle parked in the shadows.

He gets out slowly, staying behind the door for protection. Someone comes towards him.

"Where have you been?" Everest asks.

"Oh, Detective E's. It's you."

"Who were you expecting?"

"I don't know. I just had a sense of danger. And you look angry with me, so I guess I was right about the danger part."

"I tried to find you at the university. After I'd been at the library."

"Reid Library? What were you doing there?"

She holds up his book. "This copy is from it."

"Is that the one from the violin case?"

"It is."

"We probably should've noticed the library sticker earlier."

"Yeah. The book was put there, I believe, by one of your students. Or a former student."

"On purpose?"

"To get your attention."

"Thank fuck you finally stopped thinking I put it there." Huntley goes to the caravan and unlocks the door. "I need a drink."

"What about your dry week?"

"I think we need to make an exception. This is very troubling. Suddenly, I'm someone's target. Fancy a hot toddy?"

"No."

"I think I'm out of rum anyway."

He goes inside, and Everest follows. They sit at the round table, under the sleeping loft. It's cramped. Their knees touch.

"This feels a bit like an interrogation," Huntley says.

"Who's questioning who?" Everest smiles a little, then puts the book on the table between them.

"Did you read it?"

"Some."

"Any of the pages marked? You know, any clues inside?"

"No. I checked. And that's enough of you asking questions. Can you think of anyone who would target you?"

"Your partner maybe. He was a former student."

"Seriously?"

"Who would ever suspect him? The golden boy police officer."

"And the son of a high-ranking detective."

"Ah, nepotism. Don't you just love it? That must be hard. Having a partner below you who has, hah, relative power over you."

Everest looks around the caravan. "It could be worse. Much worse."

"Ouch."

"Caravans, containers, old cars. I'm not sure I want your life."

"You say that, yet you slept in my little alcove like someone who hadn't slept properly for years."

"I was sleeping off the rum."

Huntley smiles. "Caravans are really good for that."

On saying this, Huntley grabs an empty rum bottle from the shelf and puts it on the table. From his pockets, he takes three pieces of paper, the poems written so far, flattens them out and puts the rum bottle on top.

"Your first draft?" Everest asks.

"The beginnings of something. If you're looking to crash here again, you can have the bed."

"I'm not."

"You like roughing it. Don't you? Tour buses and vans. Being on the road. You're living the wrong life."

"Excuse me?"

"When I look at you, I don't see a detective or a cop. I see a whole other story."

"Oh, yeah? What do you see?"

"A burning desire for a comeback. A return to the one thing you're most passionate about. I saw it the other night at Scotch. Everything else is just time-wasting. Void-filling."

"I know what you're doing. You're trying to provoke me. I happen to like being a detective."

"That I believe. This is all coming from a good place, trust me on that. I think you funnelled your musical ability into police work, and there's nothing wrong with that. A poem, a song, a story, a case, they're all problems to be solved. Being a drummer and a songwriter has made you a good detective. At least, I think you're a good detective, even though two murders and a coma remain unsolved. And that's just in the first half of this week. Any progress?"

"You sound convinced the three are connected."

"You can bet your sweet oleander they are."

"What?"

"That put the councilwoman in a coma."

"How do you know that?"

"Not important. What is important is that we've got a green thumb killer on our hands. Still running loose out there."

"Any evidence to back that up?"

Huntley glances at the papers under the rum bottle. "It's all a bit circumstantial, at the moment. A work in progress."

"Did the hospital tell you about the sweet oleander?"

"Indirectly."

"You're proving to be very resourceful on your own."

"That's flattering to hear, but I'm getting some help."

"From who?"

"Not saying, detective."

Everest taps the book's cover with an index finger. "Did you take the same approach with this book? Got close to the real-life stuff, then turned it into poetry?"

236

"That was more happenstance than circumstance. Good timing, and being resourceful all on my own."

"What if someone from Ravensthorpe is trying to get some kind of revenge on you? Starting with trying to frame you for killing the violinist."

"I hadn't thought of it. That's not a very strong story. I'm not exactly in hiding. If someone wanted revenge, they could pretty easily blow up this caravan."

"Or the container."

"Precisely. And get the bounty on Miguel in the process. Why kill people who have nothing to do with me?"

Everest slowly massages her right wrist, looking out the caravan window at the darkness. "That's valid. Who's Miguel?"

Huntley ignores this. "I think your first point seems the most likely. Attention. That had occurred to me. That's a strong story."

"Can we get a list of your former students?"

"Probably. From admin. A job for tomorrow. If you go there, take a box of chocolates. They'll be more inclined to help you if you do. I'm proud to say I'm learning the names of my students this semester, if you want them."

"This feels older to me. Fountain pens and poisonous plants. That's not really a young person's game."

They stare at each other, then Huntley asks, "You don't like Booth, do you?"

"He's all right. It's Mitchell Booth who I don't like. He lives on the fame of his father, Wally Booth."

"I know that name."

"He investigated the Claremont murders, back in the 90s, and he was the one working behind the scenes when they finally caught the guy years later. Mitchell got promoted as a result, because Wally was already retired by then. Incredibly, once the guy was arrested, Wally died."

"I guess he was hanging on to see the job done. Pretty good really."

"Yeah. But Mitch walks around like he solved the case. Now, Justin carries a bit of that with him as well."

"Justin will probably get promoted before you."

"That's a very safe bet. But he's smarter than he looks, and acts."

"I got that impression too."

Everest reaches a hand out and slides the book towards Huntley. "Enough of this. How about you read to me?"

"Excuse me?"

"Read. Please."

"This is evidence, isn't it? I'm not reading this old stuff."

"Go with the new material then."

"You don't show first drafts to anyone, unless you trust them."

"You don't trust me?"

"I would if you help me get the endings."

Everest laughs. "Forget an interrogation. This feels like therapy."

"The good kind, right? Where we get everything off our chests."

"Do that. Get something big off your chest. Tell me what it's like getting stuck."

Huntley gives Everest a sideways glance. "What do you mean?"

"This book was all you wrote. What did it feel like, to be blocked for so long?"

"Now we are in therapy. That's a dark cave to explore."

"Be brave. You're on home turf. Help me understand it. Something like that, to have the one thing you're good at taken from you, it must be really hard to live with. Being constantly blocked."

Huntley and Everest stare at each other. Then, Huntley picks up his book and looks at it.

"You know, I never liked the cover. This slaughtered lamb. It was Lydette's idea. Supposed to be striking, and eye-catching. But it's just wrong. No lamb was killed. It was stolen."

"So?"

"Important difference."

As Huntley flips through the book, Everest stays silent, waiting for him to continue.

"To be clear, I'm not blocked and never was," he says. "I've written plenty, I just didn't believe it was good enough."

"How do you know that? Did you show it to people?"

"You don't share garbage."

"But that's your opinion. Maybe it was great and you just didn't have faith in yourself. It was all about confidence."

"And doubt. Always there, doubt. That ruinous fucker."

"How does that feel?" Everest asks.

"Great therapy question. It feels bloody awful. It's not like the devil on your shoulder, whispering sweet insults in your ear. It's a parasite. It takes over. And it eats confidence for breakfast."

Everest nods.

"Did that happen to you?" Huntley asks. "Back in your Lemonade days? Is that why you put the sticks down?"

Everest doesn't reply.

"Because I'm sensing empathy from you, which I certainly appreciate. Like you know what I'm talking about."

"Not me," she says, barely a whisper.

"The singer?"

Everest closes her eyes, wishing she'd never broached the topic; wishing she'd never come here.

"It's all about her," Huntley presses. "What was her name?"

Eyes still closed, knowing if she opens them she'll start crying, Everest manages to say, "Charlene."

"Yeah. Charlene. That wavy platinum bob. She was incredible. Did she lose confidence in herself? Is that what happened?"

Everest, eyes open and tears welling, starts to edge off the bench, but Huntley extends a leg, trapping her. "Let me out," she says.

"No." Huntley stares at her, seeing the whole story.

"Move your leg, or I'll shoot it."

"You need to free yourself of this."

"I do not. I'm not going to just let it out and then forget about her."

"Oh, my. Oh, my o my. You loved her. You still love her."

"That's not ..."

"Love is so cruel. I'm sorry you carried this the whole time."

"She ..."

Slowly, Huntley lowers his leg. "It's all right. You're not alone. Let go. She would want you to."

Everest puts her head in the cradle of her arms, on the table, and cries. Huntley places a hand gently on her left forearm.

"That's it. There is absolutely nothing wrong with being sad about the people we've lost. The people we let into our hearts, and maybe who even stomped on our hearts. We cry and we remember, and all of it is good. Because it's the experience that matters the most."

Everest's upper body heaves as she lets it all out, but she keeps her face hidden in her arms.

"Love," Huntley says, almost to himself. "So hard. You can see why people stay away from it. That they never give all of themselves, because of how much it can hurt."

"I should've told her," Everest says. "That's what I regret. Maybe that would've been the difference."

"Maybe. Who knows? But love not returned is really painful. That can make people do anything. Look at history. Rejection is a big motive for murders and violence." Huntley looks at the slaughtered lamb on his book's cover. "You know, this book is actually about love. Secret love. What if that's what we're looking at now? Maybe someone was in love with the violinist, and was rejected. That person couldn't take the rejection."

Everest, her face wet with tears and her ponytail coming loose, raises her head and looks at Huntley.

"If that's it," she says, wiping the tears from her face. "It could also mean it wasn't the first time."

<>

Waiting in the lobby for the elevator, Aphra tries calling Blair again. No answer.

Alone in the lobby, then alone in the elevator, she assumes everyone is still in the office, despite the late evening hour, helping to manage this crisis. On the ride to the 34th floor, she uses her phone to gauge the response so far. The online reception appears mixed, the level of support closely reflecting the 26% approval rating Blair started the week with. Most of the negative comments about Blair's afternoon tirade are zeroing in on closing the border and the racism angle. While there's no way to take any of it back, Aphra thinks there should be scope to issue a clarifying statement, or a press release, to limit the damage and prevent anything from being taken out of context by the media.

What bothers Aphra the most is that in one impromptu interview, Blair threw all of her media training out the window, along with a ridiculous amount of time spent carefully crafting her message. Aphra wants to know how this happened. Who decided they should go ahead without her storytelling and writing support? Who in the party thinks that Blair can face the public unfiltered?

When the elevator opens on the 34th floor, Aphra exits and finds the door to the WA Republic Party's offices locked. She knocks on it. Maritsa appears and lets her in.

"What are you doing here, Aphra?"

"I need to see Blair."

"She isn't here."

Aphra pushes past Maritsa and sees Blair in her office. "So, that couldn't possibly be her then."

"You shouldn't go in there."

"If you still want to have a job tomorrow, I definitely should."

Aphra knocks once on Blair's door.

"What?" Blair demands from inside.

On entering, Aphra is surprised to see Nathaniel Winslow, who gives her a disinterested look.

"You're on a well-being day," Blair says. "Why are you here?"

"We can turn this around." Aphra goes towards the small conference table Blair and Winslow are sitting at. "Just give me an hour. I can have a statement ready to beat the morning press. We can sort it all out."

"Sorry, we don't need that," Winslow says.

"What were you doing bothering Marcus Ford-Brackman at his school today?" Blair asks. "Niranda called me to say he was very upset. You basically accused him of killing that girl from the orchestra."

"I did no such thing. I ..."

"The family's going through enough as it is," Blair continues. "With Lance and everything. To go down there under the pretence of recruiting for my party, that's just wrong, on several fronts. Shame on you, Aphra."

"Shame on me? Blair, your news appearance ..."

"Was exactly the kind of risk I needed to take. I'm forcing the government's hand."

"It's so far from what we've been aiming at. You got on live TV and said WA should keep out whoever isn't wanted here. Which is one step from racial profiling and getting rid of those already here who don't fit the profile."

"So?"

Aphra, bewildered, says, "That's not the message you want to share."

"You're wrong, sweetheart," Winslow says.

Aphra bristles and glares at Winslow, who just smiles at her.

"It was Nate's idea," Blair says. "To get ahead of the game and speak from the heart. Everyone is sick of the wishy-washy language we use. It makes me sound too much like all the other politicians. I'm speaking plainly now, saying what I believe."

"Fiona Castle's a close friend," Winslow brags. "The award-winning journalist. She jumped at the chance for an exclusive with Blair."

"I know who Fiona is," Aphra says. "I don't recall her winning any awards."

"Settle down, darl." Winslow looks at Blair. "You need to get your girl here on a leash. She's all over the place. Needs more than a personal day. A muzzle, I'd say."

Aphra is about to let loose on Winslow, then decides not to let him provoke her. "Is this about the Everglades project? You've already started selling the land, so you need to get a new government in place to enable the project to start."

"It's about way more than that," Winslow says. "You think too small."

"Blair, he's just using you. Can't you see that? He doesn't care about our party or winning any election."

"Our party?" Blair scoffs. "Last time I checked, you weren't even a member of our party."

"I made this clear right from the start. It's important I stay objective."

"That's rubbish," Winslow says. "She's not on your side, Blair. Not committed. I'm on your side. Trust me, your appearance today on TV was brilliant. It'll go down as a key turning point in WA history. You don't need her."

"Thank you, Nate." Blair looks at Aphra. "I think it's best we part ways."

"You're ... you're firing me?"

"We're no longer on the same page. That's apparent to me now. My only regret is I didn't see it sooner."

"Smart move, Blair," Winslow says. "Let the excess baggage loose."

Aphra points at Winslow. "Stay out of this."

"Don't talk to me like that."

"I'll talk to you however I like. Blair, I can't believe you're letting this snake oil salesman manipulate you like this."

Winslow laughs. "Snake oil? What year is it?"

"This is exactly what we talked about," Aphra continues. "That people will try to take advantage of you. Of your platform and your profile. That's happening right now."

"Put a sock in it, sweetheart."

"Stop calling me that. My name is Aphra Massey. I'm not your sweetheart or your darl or any of that sexist crap."

"Sexist?" Winslow holds up his hands innocently. "Sorry. I'm just being nice."

"Then use my name and not something derogatory."

"Take it as a compliment."

"Saying I should be muzzled wasn't very complimentary."

"I was joking before, but now I mean it." To Blair, Winslow adds, "You know, yesterday, she had the nerve to say I had something to do with Lance's death. Where does she get off saying that?"

"That's not right. Blair, I wanted to be sure he wasn't involved, to protect your image."

"I don't need your help with that," Blair says. "Not anymore."

"No. I think it might be too late anyway. You've already tarnished your image beyond repair. The media will take these comments and run with them."

"Wrong," Winslow says. "She's actually enhanced her image. You were holding her back. Now's the time for Blair to be bold. The people are ready for a strong leader. The election will be held very soon and Blair will win."

"You don't win elections with a one-in-four approval rating."

"You're really out of touch. You might want to check that rating again."

"Okay, Nate, that's enough." Blair stands up. "HR will contact you, Aphra. Please clear out your office."

"I don't have one. You're the only person here with an office."

"Clear out your desk then."

"Wow, and you say I'm out of touch. I don't have that either. We hot-desk here. That was your idea. To build a stronger team."

Winslow sneers. "I can't say sweetheart. But you can say hot-desk. Talk about double standards."

"It means we share desks, you imbecile. We all sit somewhere different each day. For the benefit of the team."

"Well, you're certainly not part of this team. Never were, by the sounds of it. Maybe you were secretly sabotaging Blair all along."

"That's it," Aphra says. "I've had enough of this. Blair, you're making a huge mistake, but I wish you all the best."

"I wish the same for you," Blair says. "But don't think you can jump ship and work for one of the other parties. The NDA you signed stays in place for twelve months after you leave."

"How do you like that?" Winslow asks.

"Don't worry, sweetheart," Aphra says to him. "I'm done with politics. Look at the kinds of people you have to work with."

"What an attitude. How did you even get this far? Sorry. It looks like politics is done with you. Be a good lass and close the door on your way out."

Aphra wants to say more, but decides the best course of action is not to say anything. She might have no future in politics, but these two could surely pull some strings so she never works in this town again, in any industry. As she leaves, she consoles herself with the knowledge her parents stand to profit hugely from the Everglades project. So, calmly and with as much dignity as she can muster, she gives Blair a final nod, then closes the door gently. She hears Winslow say something, followed by both of them laughing, and hates them both. It's like high school all over again; the cruelty of nasty words spoken behind hands.

As an outsider brought in for her talents rather than her beliefs, there's no one to say goodbye to. The way Maritsa gives her a single wave from the hot-desk area at the far end makes Aphra conclude everyone already knows she's been let go.

The elevator takes a ridiculously long time to reach the 34th floor. She stands there, sensing that behind the WAR Party HQ door, those in there are talking about her. Laughing at her. Letting loose the criticisms and judgements they've held back for who knows how long. Saying all the things they'd never be brave enough to say to her face. It's another reminder of high school; the rumour mill that never stopped churning after Jay Palmer went around bragging that he'd slept with her. All those spotty, grinning boys who came up to her, thinking she was an easy lay. All the vicious girls who thought she would go after their boyfriends. No one in her corner.

The ride down is slow and solitary, and a little bit scary. Any man getting on from one of the high floors would have plenty of time to try something.

She follows the circular lights, counting down the floors, wanting to be out of the elevator and to never set foot in this building again.

What hurts most is the rejection, having put so much of herself into Blair's career and the success that has come with it. She's determined not to let them win, though, reasoning that the timing is right, as Blair is about to become a polarising figure. Getting distance from her is a good thing. Without the right filtering and guidance, Blair is bound to rub a lot of people the wrong way in the coming weeks and months.

Finally outside, breathing in the fresh evening air, she gets to her Vespa and finds the battery level low, having arrived here in a hurry and forgetting to plug it in to charge. She thinks she has enough to make it home to North Cottesloe, but decides instead to chance it and ride further south to Huntley's caravan.

<>

Something is hitting his foot. Something hard and metallic. It draws him from sleep.

"Dad. Wake up."

Huntley opens his eyes and sits up in the sleeping loft, careful not to bump his head. In the almost darkness, he makes out Verity, a pot in her hand.

"What are you doing here?"

"I'm happy to see you too."

"What time is it? Why aren't you at home?"

"I'm not wanted there."

"Bollocks." Huntley rubs his eyes. "I'm taking you back there right now."

"Please don't. It's all right. I told Mum I'm staying over at Janette's house."

"On a school night? How did she agree to that?"

"She's got other problems. Each one way more important than me."

Huntley gets down from the loft, turns on a light and pulls on his pants. "I'm glad to have you as my number one problem."

"Can I stay here?" Verity asks, dropping the pot in the narrow sink.

"Your little wagging scam got me in serious trouble. And now this? If your mum finds out I'm abetting another lying escapade, I might never get to see you again."

"I'll cover for you. I promise."

Huntley gives Verity a hug. "I'm happy to see you. I'm really glad you're you and you're my daughter."

Verity pulls out of the hug. "Where's this coming from?"

"Ah, yeah, it was an emotional evening." Huntley sits at the table. "A heavy day all round. What's up at home? You want to talk about it?"

"No." Verity slides behind the table, opposite Huntley. "I want my own place."

"Come on. That house is so big, you can go weeks without seeing other people in there. Get yourself a wing and cordon it off. Make it your own."

"I can't. Daley's all about quality time. Eating meals together and watching movies. He's the worst."

"Sounds like he cares about you. How awful."

Verity reaches for the papers under the rum bottle, but Huntley gives her hand a light slap.

"That's for my eyes only," he says.

"Did you find out who poisoned that girl?"

"There have been some interesting developments. Some weed-whacking, you could say."

"What?"

"A lot's happened in the last 24 hours. It looks like there's someone out there using plants to poison people. Two dead bodies already, plus a woman in a coma. Who knows what will happen next?"

"Your life is so much more exciting than mine."

"You're a teenager. All your good stuff is yet to come. Be glad about that. You don't want to peak early."

Verity looks around the caravan. "I'm already doing better than this."

"You'll do better than Gifford Manor too. Just promise me you'll escape that prison when you're old enough."

"I need to get out of school prison first."

"Hah. Speaking of school. I was on the bus on Monday and went past your place of incarceration. A lot of the kids out the front were vaping. What's up with that?"

"I'm not doing it," Verity says. "If that's what you mean."

"I never said you were. Is this a new thing?"

"I think so. Maybe since last year? The Christ Church guys started it. Passing them round after school. The older girls got into it. You know, to be social."

"Vaping and flirting. How times change. Do you know what's in it?"

"It's like a cigarette, isn't it?"

Huntley has a quick internal debate about whether he should tell his daughter about the viper vape, because it might tempt her to seek one out and try it. Then he thinks the little liar and schemer has probably had a hit from one already, possibly even today.

"Stop staring at me like that, Dad. You're freaking me out."

"Sorry. You're just looking a little bit red in the eyes there."

"Too much reading. All we do at school is read and do tests."

"A quality education, worth every cent of your grandfather's money." He can see his daughter retreating into her shell, so decides to change tact. "You've definitely got all the bases covered, with your friend's sleepover?"

She nods.

"You got your uniform for tomorrow, and everything school-related?"

Another nod.

"Toothbrush? Bathroom bag?"

Verity smiles and shakes her head.

"Okay. One night won't hurt. You can stay here."

"Yay."

"But you can't tell the wardens. That'll come back to me. Can I trust you?"

"Of course you can, Dad."

"All right then. You should probably go to sleep."

"Can you read something to me? You used to do that all the time."

"Bad memory," Huntley says. "I never read you anything. I made it up."

"Really? Like, improvising? I remember it always being so good."

"Hmm. I guess I had some magic back then too." He points at the papers. "I've been working on some new stuff. Do you want to hear it?"

"Yes. Please, yes."

"It's a bit graphic. I think you're old enough. I'm writing about these murders. They've lit a fire in me."

"Sweet. Let's hear it."

"Nothing here is in stone, okay? The cement's still setting, and there's more work to do." Huntley clears his throat, then reads his draft of *The Green Neck of the Violinist*.

"That's heavy," Verity says. "I'm not sure I get it."

"I need the ending. That will make things clearer. It might change the other parts too, because the ending sometimes affects the beginning. And the middle. We'll see. I want to take another run at it, when I've got all the pieces."

"I like it. Next."

He reads her *The Hallucinating Nightswimmer*.

"I think I get that one," Verity says. "Being awake and dreaming. Kind of stuck in between. Like my life."

"It's interesting you mention that."

"Why?"

"Oh, it's just that someone else picked up on that. I was thinking more about how we sleepwalk through life. Which is what I've been doing, if I'm honest with myself."

"You seem wide awake now."

"Because you woke me up. Banging that pot against my foot."

They laugh.

"I was also playing with two planes of existence," Huntley says. "Trying to. Being in one place, but not totally there. Maybe I need to try this jimsonweed, see what it does."

"Can you vape it?"

"Suddenly you're an expert on vaping, the red-eyed girl who's never tried it." Huntley recalls what Henrikson said. "You're on a soft high, right?"

"No."

"That's why you didn't go home, and created this whole sleepover sting. You didn't want them to see you stoned."

"I'm not stoned." Verity moves to stand up, but Huntley extends a leg to stop her, as he did with Everest.

"It's all right," he says. "It's completely normal to want to try something all the other kids are doing."

Verity sits back down and Huntley lowers his leg.

"I won't tell your mother. As far as I know, the dope in those vapes isn't particularly strong. Just enough for a bit of a buzz."

"A bit?" Verity giggles. "Yeah. Just a bit."

"No harm in trying, but it's not something you want to keep doing."

"Says the guy who's a borderline alcoholic."

"Hey. Not true. Don't judge a man by the empty bottle he uses as a paperweight. Anyway, your mother is more guilty of this than me. She likes a tipple, always has, though I'm sure she's laying off it now."

"Daley drinks some weird green stuff, in tiny amounts."

"Are you sure? Sounds like absinthe. That's poison. But, listen. Do you know where the kids are getting these weed vapes? This is an illegal drug."

"Most of the teachers do it too."

"They might not be doing the same stuff. That could be plain old nicotine."

Verity shrugs. "It looks the same. Definitely smells the same."

"Yeah. Right. What do the weed vapes look like up close? Does it have a snake on it? Like, a little brand?"

"You're so pushy."

"This is important. Any snakes?"

"The ones I've seen, yeah. That's Furina."

"Furina? That's a type of snake. I think. Surely it has some kind of street name, something clever. Furina sounds like a laxative for seniors."

"Yuck."

"Come on. What are the kids saying?"

"They call it Fuzz Buzz."

"Is that what you tried today?"

"Da-ad."

"Where did you get it from? Did one of your friends have it?"

"Stop asking me about this."

"It's okay. I know how it goes. Your friends are passing it around. There's a bit of pressure. You can't not do it."

"That might have been the way when you were young, but it's different now. I wasn't forced. I wanted to try it."

"Where did you get it from? Which friend? This Jannette?"

"I'm not telling you."

Huntley wants to keep pressing, but decides to ease up. Even if peer pressure is no longer a thing, the schoolyard is surely still a brutal place, where reputations are made and destroyed in one swift act. If at any point the vape supply were to be cut off and Verity was found to be responsible for that, the kids would make her life miserable.

"I'm sorry," he says. "There's a connection to these vapes from one of the murders."

Verity is about to reply when there's a loud knock on the door.

"Is that your mum?" Huntley asks in a whisper.

"She doesn't know I'm here," Verity whispers back.

"Maybe she's got a tracking device on you."

"What? Like I'm a lost dog?"

The knock comes again.

"Huntley? I know you're in there. The light's on."

"That's Aphra," Huntley says, standing up.

"Is she your girlfriend?"

"No. I don't know what she is. We just met. I don't think she likes me much."

"Why is she here then?"

"Let's find out." Huntley opens the door. "Hey. Bit late, isn't it?"

"Can I come in?"

"I have something of a full house already, but yeah, come on in."

Aphra enters. She and Verity eye each other curiously.

"Hi, there. I'm Aphra."

"This is my daughter. Verity." Huntley offers Aphra the spot at the table, which she takes, while he leans against the kitchen counter. "She's not here. You never saw her here."

"You have a really nice name," Aphra says.

"Thanks. So do you."

"You run away?" Aphra asks Verity.

"A temporary escape," Verity says.

"Are you okay? You look like you've been crying."

"Her eyes are red for other reasons," Huntley says. "What are you doing here?"

Aphra looks at the papers on the table, and picks up the poem about the violinist.

Huntley steps forward. "You shouldn't ..."

Aphra holds up a hand and continues reading. Huntley stays where he is.

"Interesting point of view," she says. "The language is a bit simplistic. You make it sound like Katie was killed for the chair. That was my theory, which you shot down."

"Did you know her?" Verity asks.

Aphra wipes a tear from her eye. "She was my friend."

Verity leans across the short table and hugs Aphra. "I'm so sorry."

Aphra's slow to react, but she puts her arms around Verity and the two sway a little from side to side.

"Thank you," Aphra says, once Verity releases her. "I needed that."

"We're going to find out who did this." Verity points at her father. "He can solve this. He's already getting close."

Aphra looks at Huntley. "Is that right? Have you got it all figured out?"

"My daughter speaks way too highly of me, but I'm getting there. How was it with Blair?"

"Who's Blair?" Verity asks.

Huntley smiles. "Blair Blake-Stendahl. General of the WAR Party."

"Oh, the politician? She spoke at my school earlier this year. She went there."

"You go to Methodist?" Aphra asks.

"Her speech was amazing. Really made me proud to be from Perth."

"There's a good chance she wrote it," Huntley says to Verity, gesturing towards Aphra.

Verity is impressed. "You work with her?"

"Not anymore. She fired me today."

"What for?" Huntley asks.

"My services are no longer required. She's going it alone, saying whatever she wants."

"That'll be disastrous. She won't last five minutes."

"It's not her fault. She's being manipulated and influenced."

"By who?"

"Nathaniel Winslow."

Huntley laughs. "Perfect."

"Do you know him?"

Verity's attention switches back and forth from Aphra to her father, like a rubber-necked tennis fan during an extended rally.

"I met him last night at Lance's place."

"What was he doing there?"

"Getting his stuff," Huntley says. "He claimed it was work, but he and Lance were more than just development partners. They were lovers."

"What? Is that a joke? He's married, with kids. And those kids have my deepest sympathies."

"Everest was there. She can confirm it."

"Well, if that's true, he's really fucking good at keeping secrets. I had no idea about this. He wasn't remotely sad about it when I saw him."

"I'd say he's well trained at keeping those feelings locked away. And watch your language, please. She's an impressionable young girl."

"She seems to have a good level of awareness to me," Aphra says. "Even though she looks high."

"I am," Verity says, seeming more willing to confide in Aphra. "High. Not impressionable. So what if this guy is secretly gay."

"He's living a lie," Huntley says.

Verity points at one of the poems. "No, he's like the guy in the poem. Living on two different planes of existence. One's a horrid dream and the other he's really awake."

"That's very perceptive," Aphra says. "Which is which?"

"Right." Verity nods. "Maybe they cross over. Or change. Like, alternate."

Aphra says to Huntley, "You got a smart girl here."

"Yeah. I think she's already leaving me behind."

"Smart enough to live in a proper house with walls and a roof," Verity says.

Huntley gestures towards the door. "You're welcome to go back there whenever you want."

"You can't send her home like this," Aphra says. "Her parents will ground her if they see she's high."

"I'm her parent. She has no problem being high in front of me."

"You know what I mean. You're the kind of cool parent."

Verity laughs, and it makes both Aphra and Huntley smile.

"That's the nicest thing anyone's said to me in a while."

"You're not that cool, Dad," Verity says.

"Cool enough." Huntley turns to Aphra and asks, "Why do you think Winslow's wheedling his way into Blair's party?"

"The Everglades project. Blair supports it. Getting her elected, or even as a coalition partner, will go a long way towards kicking that project off."

"Meaning he's motivated by money." Huntley paces as much as the tight caravan allows. "Then he won't need to bribe anyone on the Cockburn council. Which then means he won't need Niranda and he can go it alone, to maximise his own return."

"That's a neat story. Where do the bodies fit in?"

"The question is, where does the killer fit in? There's one person responsible for all this. I think the strongest connection, the one that really matters, is to Katie. Everest agrees."

"Because of the plants?" Verity asks.

Huntley nods. "Yes, clever girl, because of the plants, and for other reasons. There is no way this is random. I'm part of this plot line too. Because the killer knows me. Most likely, a former student."

"Your book in Katie's case," Aphra says. "You still think a student planted it there?"

"Someone who has access to Reid Library. Or had. Katie's murder is where all this started."

"Did it? Maybe this psycho's been operating like this for years. Using natural poisons to kill people, and pass them off as typical deaths."

"Or suicides, like with Lance."

"An assassin?" Verity asks.

"Could be." Huntley stops pacing and stands perfectly still. "The Ford-Brackman's killer for hire. Or, someone who simply likes killing people."

"Or both," Aphra says. "You should tell Everest to dig into old case files. For plant-based murders. God, that sounds so strange. Like I'm green-washing violent crimes."

"Sustainable murder," Verity says, and she and Aphra laugh together.

"It's not funny, you two," Huntley says. "This is serious. Everest is already way ahead of you. She's gone to the cop shop to look in the archives, to find any connections."

"Good." Aphra stands up. "What can we do?"

"It's a school night. My young charge needs to sleep. The cool parent's putting his foot down."

"I'm wide awake, Dad."

"In my horrid dream."

"That's rubbish," Aphra says. "You're loving this. You're the one who wants to solve these crimes. Come on. Let's do that."

"Okay. You got me. I'm all in. But there's only one person who can help us tonight."

"Who's that?"

Huntley looks at his daughter.

"What did I do?" she asks.

"Do you want to help?"

"Yes."

"Do you really want to help?"

"Yes, Dad. Anything."

"Right. I need to know where these vapes are coming from. This Fuzz Buzz." Huntley turns to Aphra. "This is the same one I got from Lance, which Henrikson's pal smoked. It's called Furina. We need to find the supplier."

"How will that help figure out who the killer is?"

"It's one more weed identified in a noxious garden."

Verity folds her arms. "I'm not taking you to see any of my friends. That's too embarrassing."

"Harsh, but I get it. Will you go with Aphra?"

When he sees the way Verity looks at Aphra, shy but clearly seeking her approval, Huntley knows he's hooked her.

"I'll stay in the car," he says. "I promise."

"Okay. What's the story?"

"She sounds just like you," Aphra says. "We can say I'm a cousin of yours, if that's not too much of a stretch. Say I'm off to a music festival down south and want some weed for it."

Verity stands up as well. "That'll work."

Smiling, Huntley opens the door to the caravan. Outside, the three of them hustle excitedly to the Landy.

<>

After stopping for a quick bite, she parks at HQ and heads downstairs.

Deedee looks up when Everest enters. "Back again, detective? Don't tell me you need more."

"I'm so glad you're still here."

"I was just about to leave. Is this about the Russians?"

Everest gestures towards the bulky computer on Deedee's desk. "Do you have access to the system on that old thing?"

"Why don't you use your computer?"

"I don't want to be seen upstairs."

"Say no more. Yes, this old thing's connected. Don't let the age of something fool you into thinking it doesn't function."

Deedee pats the top of the monitor. "This old girl is going strong."

"That's way too much insinuation. But I'm happy to hear it works. Can I use it?"

"No."

"Why not?"

"No one touches this computer but me."

"Then you need to stay and help me."

"With what?"

"Research."

"Why should I do that?"

"Because I'm asking you nicely. Please, Deedee. This could help me find the person who killed the violinist."

"I heard about that. Poisoned, right? I think that pen made it down here, at some point."

"A fountain pen."

"She's back in the news," Deedee says. "Blair with the big hair used the murder to make claims about Perth not being safe. I tell you, politicians are the real criminals in this world. They're dangerous the way they toy with people."

"This is why I need your help. The poison was natural, from a plant, called wild arum. I want to find out if this has happened before."

"It has. If you're willing to go way back."

"What are you referring to?"

"Back in colonial days, there were some seriously nasty white men, from a big farming family, who tried to wipe out the local indigenous people by leaving bottles of liquor around with poison in them. Not sure if those poisons were natural though."

"How do you know about this?"

"I read a lot. More than just *Playgirl*. I have to pass the time down here somehow." Deedee slides the keyboard towards her. "Where do we start?"

"I thought about this on the way here. We need to make a list of all poisonous plants, then search the database for them and see what comes up."

"Okay." Deedee starts typing. "The digital records only go back to the end of 1999. Anything older will require going through the filing cabinets by hand."

"Why?"

"Some clever fella, well before my time, thought the turn of the millennium would cause a massive computer glitch in the records. He was convinced everything would be lost. So he printed it all out and stored it in those cabinets. Then, get this, everything was deleted from the system. As a kind of pre-emptive strike."

Everest looks at the rows of filing cabinets. "I always wondered what was in there."

"Now you know. The evidence of idiocy."

"We'll be here all night."

"I got nowhere else to be. But you'll owe me a couple of books for this."

"Anything you want. Thanks, Deedee."

"I've already got a list of poisonous plants."

"Print it out."

Deedee taps the keyboard. They both look at the printer as it starts whirring.

"How about some music?" Deedee asks. "I've been digging into old Perth bands and have put together a playlist. There were some great bands, back in the day."

"Go for it."

As Everest takes the pages from the printer, through the speakers come the opening bars of *Skipping School*, Salty Lemonade's first hit.

The Politician's Death Sentence

False God, idle worshipper
The chosen one of fools
Let there be no second coming
Take this dreaded nightcap
This bitter elixir
No fountain of youth

Drink and wish
For a simpler time
Purer, without heresy
Or hearsay
So, here she stays
Frozen, dare I say

Hemmed in
Locked in
Slain astride porcelain

The secret to the successful marriage of Blair Stendahl and Clayton Blake has been limiting their time together. Theirs is a love that endures through absences. This involves living in separate houses, moving in different circles, and having the freedom to pursue their personal whims. Clayton, a wills and estates lawyer of limited ambition, throws much of his energy into amateur theatre productions while also indulging in twice-weekly court-themed bondage sessions. He has been a member of the Leederville Bowling Club since he was 19, going on to become the youngest ever, by a considerable margin, to receive life membership, at 36. The more ambitious Blair, a career politician focused solely on leading WA into a new, independent era, greatly enjoys all the trappings of local fame, pressing the flesh every evening at gatherings and parties across the broad spectrum of business, sports, entertainment and politics. While she has little interest in sex, Clayton is mindful enough to ensure her needs are met.

They are the same age, born 14 days apart, and the same height, making them photogenic when together, as a visual display of partnership and equality. A good team with an explicit understanding of what one can do for the other, they provide support as required – Blair at premiering amateur theatre shows and Clayton as Blair's arm at selected events – and make the absolute most of their hyphenated name, which has been beneficial to them both; adding a touch of class for the lawyer who rose from a low-income family in Bassendean, and snobbish, colonial gravitas for the leadership wannabe.

This arrangement has taken them through 13 years without a single major disagreement, as both get everything they want and never get on each other's nerves. The home-and-home sleepovers are Tuesdays at Clayton's condo in Leederville, where they never have sex, and Thursdays at Blair's house in Nedlands, where they have sex at Blair's discretion. Blair gives Clayton advanced notice when she would like to have sex on a Thursday; subsequently, that week he abstains from S&M in order to have the necessary drive, stamina and inclination.

While they certainly don't spend as much time together as other couples, and more than a few friends gossip behind their backs about the true nature of the relationship, they prefer things this way and are far happier than the majority of the couples they socialise with. They also both regularly take the time for small expressions of love, such as Clayton having flowers sent to Blair's office, or Blair, who knew all about Clayton's sexual habits before they wed, gifting him vouchers for his expensive bondage sessions at the Pleasure & Pain Palace in Northbridge.

So, when the small gift basket is delivered to Blair's house late on Wednesday evening, with the card that has "Thinking of you and I in Greece – C xoxo" written inside it, in bright red pen, Blair doesn't think twice about taking it into her kitchen. After another challenging day trying to change her small world for the better, she finds it nice to be reminded of her island-hopping honeymoon in the Aegean with her one true love.

The basket has a bottle of Assyrtiko wine, a jar of pitted black olives, a slim bottle of olive oil, a small bag of herbal tea, a large, firm eggplant and a yellow zucchini. The tea takes her immediate fancy, as the "Santorini Sunset" hand-written on the minimalist label has her assuming the herbal brew will calmly escort her into the evening.

She puts the kettle on. It's one of those fancy glass kettles, where she can watch the water slowly boil; providing 90 seconds of reflection on a day when she took control and saw her approval rating jump over 30% for the first time as a result. She feels the gleeful glow of popularity, which will only grow if she continues to speak from the heart. Getting rid of Aphra was good, she thinks. The kind of brave move that marks an important turning point, towards a more outspoken and honest era for the WA Republic Party.

She spoons tea leaves into a filter and places it in a pot, also glass. The water poured and the tea seeping, she leans over the pot to waft the aroma towards her nose, which was surgically corrected four years ago, on Clayton's suggestion, so that her face would look symmetrical when photographed from front on, for those all-important solidarity press shots. The tea smells fresh and sweet. Just like Santorini, she thinks. It has the colour of horse urine, but she decides to ignore this.

Pot and cup get carried to her home office, where she will need to spend a few hours crafting responses to the questions from journalists that flooded in all afternoon and into the evening. It's important to get this done tonight, to be part of tomorrow's news cycle. While this would've been something to delegate to Aphra, she attacks the work now with enthusiasm, happy she can finally say exactly what she wants.

The tea's initial dash of bitterness contrasts well with its strong caramel aftertaste. It goes down easily and quickly, and also subconsciously, because she gets so absorbed in her work. Every email sent means another refill of the cup, and the pot is soon empty.

She makes a second and types on. The deeper she gets into answering the questions, the more convinced she becomes that Aphra was wrong to focus on storytelling and narrative and messaging. This is too much for people on the street to get. Too cerebral. Too laborious to understand. Far more effective is plain talk. Short answers, easy explanations, simple metaphors, black-and-white statements. Free of Aphra's shackles, she writes in her own voice. With each query she addresses, her replies become more concise, the repetition of the work helping her condense her main messages into bite-sized form.

"Profit from our economy."

"Control our borders."

"Build a better future."

"Focus on community."

"Success starts with independence."

"Give West Australians the lives they deserve."

By midnight, the third pot of Santorini Sunset is half-finished and gone cold. All that tea drives her to the bathroom. She flexes her fingers and wrists as she pads through the house, sore from an amount of continuous typing she hasn't done since she typed out her thesis on "The Power of Community Government", bought from that girl up in Broome who had written it by hand.

She feels great. WA needs her, she's convinced of this, now more than ever. All these years, the state has been waiting for her to come along and lead it into a prosperous future; everything building towards this point.

But things start to get a little blurry in the hallway, and she has to steady herself momentarily against the table beneath the mirror. Using the wall for support, she manages to get to the bathroom and lower her leggings. On the toilet, the urine gushes out of her, like a faucet turned fully open. The room spins. She leans her head against the wall, to stop the spinning, and passes out, mid-stream.

<>

She swims further out than usual, then flips on her back and looks at the cloudless sky. It's a relief to be on her own clock this morning. There are no meetings to rush to. No events to oversee. No press conferences to marshal Blair through. No documents made indecipherable by idiotic changes to amend. No deadlines. No barracking of mandates and ideas she doesn't agree with. She can paddle around, at her leisure, carefree.

She thinks: there is no greater gift in the world than time. Important is not to worry about the job situation. There will be other offers.

If necessary, she can pivot towards marketing and advertising, to look for a permanent position or pitch for more freelance work. She decides to give Blair a week, in case she changes her mind, then ask her politely for a reference.

The morning sky is a hypnotic blue.

The memory of last night sits nicely in her brain. Teaming up with Huntley and Verity to track down whoever's selling weed vapes to schoolkids helped to block out the awful events at the office earlier in the evening. The pursuit yielded nothing, which was disappointing, but then the three of them went to Cottesloe and got a mess of fish and chips which they ate, picnic-style, straight from the paper, sitting on the grass next to the Surf Life Saving Club. It was late enough for them to have the whole area to themselves; even the seagulls had gone home for the evening.

Despite getting off on the wrong foot with him, Aphra is starting to like Quintus Huntley. There was no chance of anything romantic happening, with Verity present, and the dynamic resulted in Aphra feeling more like the big sister Verity has always wanted rather than announcing herself as a potential match for the girl's father. One thing that's clear this morning is the realisation that she can be herself around Huntley, though she would readily admit that has more to do with his knack for seeing through pretence than with any effort on her part to keep herself from putting on airs. This sits in stark contrast to her time with Blair and the WA Republic Party, which saw her very much playing a role, shaping her opinions and demeanour based on whatever room she found herself in.

Fozzie barking draws her attention to the beach. Down on one knee, giving her dog a serious pat where the water is lapping over the sand, is Purvis Irving. A shiver of trepidation runs down her spine, and suddenly the water feels cold. He's wearing jeans cut off at the knees, and his shirt is tucked in the back pocket. His torso is very white, making her wonder if he doesn't get to the beach often. It seems strange he has it off now. Bodies as white as his are a rare sight on Swanbourne Beach.

He's in shape, in a stringy kind of way, like he doesn't eat enough, or is on one of those extreme, restrictive diets.

Naked, she's tempted to stay in the water and wait until he's gone. But he stands up and looks directly at her. He smiles and waves.

"Hey," he calls out. "Aphra. It's me, Purvis."

Though she's far from the main beach, there are other people, walking dogs and swimming. One guy is slouched in a camping chair, next to a huge fishing rod in a plastic pipe buried in the sand. There's something threatening about Purvis, in the way he holds himself and the fact he's even here, but she's sure he won't try anything with people around. But what gets her out of the water and walking up the beach, without shame or embarrassment, is the thought that Jay Palmer is probably suffering horribly, in some way, this very minute in a prison cell because of her. If need be, she could, with a bit of research and application, set off a chain of events that would likely land Purvis in a cell adjacent to Jay; part of her would really like to try.

Purvis wolf-whistles as she approaches.

"Oi," says the man fishing. "No need for that. Be respectful."

Purvis ignores him. "Seriously hot," he says, ogling her up and down.

"What are you doing here?" Aphra asks.

"Learning how women get these beautiful all-over tans. Nude swimming. That's the secret. How's the water?"

She picks up her towel and wraps it around her. "Why don't you jump in and find out?"

"I'm not much of a swimmer. I prefer the bush to the beach."

"You're a long way from Success."

Purvis puts his hands up, feigning shock. "I had no idea you'd be here. Really."

"So, why are you here then?"

The man fishing takes his rod and casts the line anew. After sliding the rod in the pipe, he calls out, "That fella bothering you, miss?"

"I'm fine. Thanks. I was just leaving."

"You got me wrong," Purvis says, standing close. "This was pure chance."

"Like it was in Beeliar?" Aphra sees how hurt Purvis is and decides to ease off a little. "I sometimes forget what a small town Perth can be."

"I think it's great we keep running into each other."

Aphra gets her things together, keeping the towel tightly wrapped around her. "Fozzie!"

"Is that your dog's name? I like it."

Fozzie comes running over to them.

Purvis points toward the road. "I parked my van up there last night. I was drunk and needed a place to crash. I couldn't drive like that."

"Good. Then you can stay right where you are and continue enjoying the beach that you came to all for yourself." Aphra starts walking away, her dog following. "You can work on your tan."

Purvis moves with her. "I didn't know. I swear."

"Yet here you are, at my beach, right when I'm swimming with nothing on."

"That's destiny."

"Uh, it might be seen as strategy."

Aphra walks quickly, but Purvis keeps pace.

"Jeez, will you relax? You can't deny it. We just keep seeing each other, like the universe wants us to get together."

"Interesting," she says. "I spoke with the universe last night and it didn't tell me anything like that."

He laughs a little, trying to be charming. "Come on. I'm a nice guy. I'd like to get to know you better. I feel like you would, too."

Aphra realises the more she tries to push him away, the harder he comes at her. "Who told you this is my beach?"

"Nobody told me that."

"It's not good to start any kind of a relationship with lies."

"You are so perceptive. I like that. Okay. I confess. A little birdie told me you like bringing your dog down here in the mornings."

"A bird with long talons and a beak that never shuts up? Lydette Gifford, I bet."

"There's no need to build a wall. Perth's poetry circles are pretty small. We're bound to have people in common."

Aware she's in a bit of no man's land, between the nude swimming area and the main beach, where there's no one, Aphra quickens her pace. Up ahead, she can see lifeguards, in bright yellow shirts, setting up for the day, pitching a tent next to a quad bike with a trailer. She also moves away from the water, into the softer sand, trying to get some distance from Purvis, but he keeps matching her. He's exhibiting all the excessively pushy and needy behaviours she's seen too many times before, making her wonder again who is educating guys to be like this.

"We've got chemistry," Purvis says.

"I haven't noticed it."

"Why don't you just chill out and give me a chance?"

There it is, she thinks; it's my fault.

"One chance," he pushes. "That's all I'm asking."

"I'm not really looking for anything right now."

"That's not very fair. Why won't you even give me a chance?"

"Because you keep asking for one."

"We could have a lot of fun together."

This makes Aphra stop, because Jay Palmer, once upon a time, said the same thing, almost word for word. She's tempted to tell Purvis the whole story, as a way to warn him off forever and maybe even stop him from plying this trade with other women; because she's getting the sense that all of this behaviour is practised and these chance encounters will keep happening unless she does something final.

He puts a hand on her bare shoulder, like he's said something that's swayed her. "Just let down your barrier and get to know me."

"Take your hand off my shoulder."

When he doesn't, she shrugs it off and steps back. He reaches forward and grabs her elbow.

"Let go," she says firmly.

Purvis screws up his ratty face, confused. "What's wrong with you? I'm just being friendly."

"Yeah, that's right." Aphra shakes her arm loose from his grasp. "There's something wrong with me. Leave me alone."

He looks at her like she's not all there in the head.

"You need to lighten up, Aphra. You're so tense. I mean you no harm."

"Then don't grab my arm like that." Aphra turns, and continues walking towards the lifeguards.

"Look, if you need to relax, I've got something in my van that could help you. Make you more mellow."

Aphra stops and looks back. "What do you mean?"

"Something organic and light. A gentle high. Totally chills you out."

"How much?"

"Now, you're talking. You see? I'm a nice guy. For you, it's free. We can vape in my van."

"Vape?"

"Yeah. Really easy to consume. No rolling or filthy bongs or whatever. Best thing is, no one really knows you're doing it."

"Does this vape have a name?"

"Why does that matter?"

"You're right. Who cares about the name? I'll take one and I'll pay for it. I don't like getting things for free."

"Sure. Whatever you want. We can smoke this peace-pipe together."

Aphra starts walking again. "I'm going to take a quick shower. Meet me at the coffee shop in ten minutes. Bring the vape."

"Coffee's a great idea. We can think of it as our first date."

She goes into the changerooms. "You fucking dirtbag," she says to herself.

<>

Huntley comes back to the caravan after dropping Verity at school and is glad to see a familiar face waiting for him.

"Orville," he says, once out of the Landy. "Where have you been the last few days?"

"Compulsory training in the city. Really early starts. I told you about that."

"Right. I've been missing our mornings together."

"I've brought coffee." Huntley's stocky half-brother holds up a well-travelled thermos. "And bad news."

"If you're about to tell me I have to move, I'll pour that coffee over your head."

"Calm down, Quin. No one wants you to move. Looks like the caravan's growing roots."

"As am I. It's nice here. Best of all is being close to your office and you bringing coffee in the morning."

"You got any milk?" Orville asks.

"Sure."

"Is it still good?"

"Why does everyone ask that?"

Huntley goes into the caravan and grabs the milk from the fridge. He gives it a surreptitious sniff, then takes it outside, where Orville has set up two fold-out chairs.

"I just never see you go shopping," Orville says, his small, pudgy frame bundled up in the chair, the buttons of his Dingo Flour security shirt threatening to pop.

"I confess I stole this one from Miguel. He buys in bulk, and never seems to notice if a carton or two goes missing. Or if he does notice, he doesn't say anything. I think he secretly drinks my rum, when it's there, so it all balances out."

"How is work?"

Huntley ducks back into the caravan to grab two cups. "A pain. If you mean the university. I need to try harder. On the poetry side, I'm back, little brother."

"You're working on a new collection? That's great."

Huntley holds the cups as Orville pours. "I thought I was done. I'm a long way from having a book, but I'm just happy I have the magic again."

"Have you told the rest of the family? You know, we've been hoping for years you would write something else."

"I know. Let me get the first drafts finished. Maybe I'll have something to read at the reunion."

"I hope so. I always loved it when you read to us." Orville smells the milk, then adds it to his cup and Huntley's. "We were all so proud of you with the *Ragged Claws*."

"Thanks, Orv." Huntley can hear his phone buzzing in the caravan and happily ignores it. He lets out a loud, vinegary belch, the remnants of the late-night feed with Verity and Aphra. "Excuse me."

They both sip.

"What did you have for breakfast?" Orville asks.

"A highly stressful school run. The burn is from last night. I took Verity out for fish and chips. Down at Cott. Really nice."

"How is she?"

"Already turning into a young woman. Smart too. She's definitely getting that from our side of the family."

"Is she coming to the reunion?"

"I hope so. She's a bit anti-caravan, but she slept soundly here last night."

Orville shakes his head. "That's not allowed, Quin. You need to stick to the rules. You don't want to lose contact altogether."

"Spoken like a true Dudley Do-right security guard."

"Facility manager."

"Sorry. You need to get it embroidered on your shirt." Huntley has another sip. "But, yeah, you're totally right. I need to follow the plan. She just showed up. I couldn't turn her away."

"She's a sweet one. Hard to say no to her."

"So, what's the bad news?"

"I got a call from the police just now. In the office. For you."

"Those bloody parking tickets."

"She didn't say anything about that. She's just trying to get in contact with you. You're not answering your phone."

"She? Did you get her name?"

"No. Do I need to be worried?"

Huntley shakes his head. "I'm actually working with the police at the moment. On a couple of cases. Well, one case, that currently has three parts."

"Helping? I seem to recall you were always better at committing crimes than solving them."

"The worm has turned." Huntley smiles, then sips again. "This coffee's good."

"It should be. It's from our fields. The first crop of beans. Jonty sent them up yesterday, express delivery."

Huntley raises his cup. "Thank you, Nodge Gurney, for being glass-jawed enough for Dad to knock you out and win your land."

At the mention of Nodge's name, Orville goes quiet.

"Sorry, Orv."

"It's all right. Jonty says the land's never been more fertile."

"I bet he's using the best of that land for his dope crop."

They both laugh and follow through with sips of coffee.

"You better call this detective back," Orville says.

Huntley doesn't move. "Yeah, I should. My creativity depends on it."

"That's the new book? You're writing about these crimes, like you did back home?"

"I can't help it. The stories just present themselves. I come in contact with the crime, or the crime scene, and it all just flows. The pen hits the page and has a life of its own. The whole secret of it, for me, is not to think about what I write, no matter how strange it is. All I need are the endings."

"You mean, you need to solve the case?"

"Right."

"Do you think you can?"

Huntley is thoughtful for a moment, wondering, not for the first time, how hard it must be for a detective to live with an unsolved crime. Like Wally Booth and the Claremont murders. How did he sleep, all those years, with a story that had no resolution? Then he gets the guy and promptly drops off the perch.

"I bloody hope so," he says, draining the cup. "The whole key to it is the fountain pen."

"The what?"

Before Huntley can explain, a familiar SUV turns off Stirling Highway and drives towards the caravan.

"Looks like you've got another visitor," Orville says.

"The one and only Giorgina Gifford. If she asks, Verity was never here last night."

"You know I'm a terrible liar. I go all red in the face."

"Let's hope she doesn't ask."

The vehicle stops a fair distance from the caravan. Giorgie gets out. She walks slowly, orange summer dress hugging her slender hips, a faded denim jacket that's just retro enough to be cool over the top.

"God, she looks amazing," Orville observes.

"Stop it. You don't like that sort of thing."

"I know quality when I see it."

Orville hauls himself out of the fold-out chair to greet Giorgie. Huntley stays seated.

"Nice to see you, stranger," Giorgie says.

She and Orville kiss cheeks; Orville has to get up on his toes, as Giorgie doesn't bend down. Then, they walk arm-in-arm towards Huntley.

"You haven't changed at all," Orville says. "Still absolutely stunning."

"Stop that. I'm so hormonal right now."

Orville laughs. "Still absolutely blunt. I always loved that about you."

"You should've heard her yesterday," Huntley says. "Really blunt."

"What happened?" Orville asks.

"She booted me from the property. Was one step away from releasing the hounds."

"You shouldn't have been there," Giorgie says.

Huntley looks at Orville. "Her father chased me away with a rake. The sharpened, metal type."

"Sounds about right," Orville says. "But I would've thought a pitchfork was more his thing. Showing his farming roots."

"The only time he has ever set foot on a farm was when he was buying it out and evicting those living there."

"Maybe he should've had a scythe and a hood."

"Hah. Yeah. The kind you see the Grim Reaper travelling with."

Huntley and Orville laugh.

"That's not funny," Giorgie says, suppressing a smile. "You two. Always joking around. Like a comedy duo. You even look the part."

"There's an insult in there, Orv, and I think it's directed at you."

"I'm happy just the way I am. Great things, small packages." Orville steps forward and picks up his thermos. "I'll leave you both to it. Obviously, you have co-parenting matters to deal with."

"What does that mean?" Giorgie asks.

Orville's face turns red. "Oh, nothing. Not a single thing. I need to do my morning rounds. See you, Giorgie."

"Thanks for the brew, little brother." Huntley offers the fold-out chair to Giorgie. "Join me? You're not banned from this property."

Giorgie sits down and wraps her jeans jacket around her like she's cold, despite the warm morning. Her vanilla knees poke out enticingly from the hem of the orange dress. Up close, she even smells fabulous.

It's too much for Huntley. He looks away and mouth-breathes.

"I'm sorry about yesterday," Giorgie says. "I wasn't expecting you. I'm dealing with a lot at the moment."

"It's my fault. I just wanted to warn you. It was good intentions, poorly executed."

"Verity's been such a handful lately. She's having trouble at school, and she really didn't take it well that ..."

When Giorgie trails off, Huntley says, "That you're pregnant. She told me."

"Oh."

The way Giorgie exhales the word makes Huntley's heart just about stop. "Congratulations," he manages to say.

"Thank you."

"Don't worry about Verity. She'll get used to it. Kids are amazingly adaptable. I reckon she'll embrace it. You should use it as a chance to give her more responsibility. To help her mature. That helped me when I was her age."

"Maybe. All she does is create trouble at the moment."

"Give her space. I bet you were just as much trouble when you were a teenager."

Giorgie smiles. "I was worse. When I was her age, Dad made me take Lydette to the Royal Show, and I abandoned her in the wool shed so I could hook up with Greg Bensell behind Sideshow Alley. Just left her. That was so irresponsible of me."

"A bit like meeting a stranger in a house library and taking off to Ravensthorpe with him."

"Yeah. A bit. Back when I was reckless. Adventurous."

"I liked that version of you. It's a shame you were never adventurous enough to leave the house for good."

"Don't pin our failures on that."

Huntley wants to respond, but thinks better of it. In the silence that follows, he listens to the cars zipping past on Stirling Highway. It's Thursday morning, and he gets the sense everyone in Perth already has eyes on the weekend.

A pair of pink and grey galahs hop around on the grass in front of them, digging at the ground with their beaks in search of breakfast.

"You always see them in pairs," Huntley says, pointing at the galahs. "Did you ever notice that?"

"Listen. I've got something I want to run by you."

"If you want me to look after Verity more during your pregnancy, I'm totally up for it."

"That's nice, but it's not necessary. It's good the way things are. We need to keep the routines, for Verity's sake."

Huntley wonders if Giorgie wants to establish Daley as the main paternal figure in Verity's life. "Sure. Whatever you want."

"That's for Verity, not me."

"Right. So, what are you here for then?"

"I know you're not happy at the university, and you never really have been."

Huntley recognises the tone of voice Giorgie uses for something she's prepared in her head. "It's a living. I need to recommit to it. I've been getting lazy."

This doesn't seem to register. Giorgie continues her rehearsed pitch: "Would you be interested in doing something similar, teaching creative writing, and poetry, of course, on a community level? There are lots of people keen on this. Especially seniors. We could open a centre for it. A writing and community centre, for all ages."

"Perth has a couple of them already. In Swanbourne and up in the hills."

"They're cliquey and closed off. This would be more diverse and inclusive. Part of a bigger arts centre, with all sorts of artistic pursuits."

"Like metal sculpturing, perhaps?"

"Yes. That too. You'd like Daley. Trust me on that."

Huntley thinks there's no way he could like a one-named, absinthe-drinking sculpturer who knocked up the woman he's still in love with.

"You could have your own writing studio," Giorgie adds, "or make it available for writers-in-residence."

"Let me guess. All in a brand new building with easy access to the Freeway. Land at a bargain price for the right people."

"You're wrong about the Everglades, Quin. It's safe and secure. I'm giving you the chance to be part of it. In on the ground floor. This will be massive for Perth."

"You bought the land already?"

"I'm on my way there now to finalise the purchase."

"Not to visit Chandice Cowdrey in hospital? How is she?"

"Still in a coma. I might stop by later, if I have time."

"On a bright note, the project probably won't need her. If Blair Blake-Stendahl gets elected, she'll sign off on everything. You went to Methodist with her, didn't you?"

"Yes, but she was a few years behind me."

"Don't get me wrong. I appreciate you thinking of me and wanting to include me. But this project feels bad. If I put a foot wrong, I might wash up on Trigg Beach."

"Lance committed suicide."

"Yeah, that's the story being told. But it's not the real story." Huntley clears his throat. "Who are you seeing about the land, if I can ask?"

"The company handling it is Winslow Properties."

"Ah. Nathaniel Winslow."

"Why do you say his name like that?"

"Like what?"

"Like he's not to be trusted."

"I only met him once, and that was enough. I'm not fully certain about his story, but something's definitely off there."

"Is that still happening for you? Seeing stories everywhere?"

"Oh, yeah. It's in overdrive at the moment. Keeping me up at night, like it used to."

"You can't blame the house for that. You're sleeping where you always liked to sleep."

"You would be wise to get out of that house too."

"And go where?"

"I hear there's land available in Beeliar."

"That's business." Giorgie stands up. "Is that the story you're getting from me? That I just want to profit from the Everglades project."

"I stopped thinking of your story years ago. There was a plot twist I didn't agree with."

"The male protagonist manifested his own destiny."

"Hah. Yeah, let's go with that."

"Will you at least consider my proposal? You won't have to invest anything."

"I'll just end up working for you and Daley. And maybe even Niranda."

"That shouldn't be a problem for you." Giorgie starts walking away. "You always liked being under her."

As she gets in her SUV, Huntley decides right there to try to stop loving her.

<>

Everest is woken by someone shining a light in her eyes. She puts her hand up to it and squints her eyes open.

The light shifts upwards, lighting a man's face from below.

"Justin?"

"I didn't know how else to wake you," he whispers, "without waking her."

He flashes his phone's light towards the sleeping figure of Deedee, who has her bare feet up on the desk and is almost horizontal in her office chair.

"Are you scared of Deedee?"

"I'm not sure she likes me much. Dad told me to be careful of her."

Having slept on a pile of old blankets, Everest sits up slowly and stretches. "She's harmless. In fact, she's gold."

"What are you doing down here?" Booth asks. "I had to track your phone to find you here."

"That's good to know."

Booth edges around the sleeping Deedee. He shines the light on the papers on the desk.

"English yew?" he asks. "Dieffenbachia? What is this?"

"Known poisonous plants." Everest gets to her feet and resets her ponytail. "We were trying to match them to previous crimes."

"Why?"

"Because of the wild arum," Everest says, deciding to keep Lance Ford-Brackman and jimsonweed off the table.

"Oh, right. That thing. Maybe we should bring Huntley in for questioning."

"It wasn't him."

"You're so sure about that?" Booth seems unconvinced. "Any luck with this then?"

"Not really. I found something in the files, from the 90s, about some woman in the south of Perth who went on a cat-killing spree. Using aloe vera, of all things."

"We have bigger problems than some crazy cat-killer. Way bigger."

Deedee stirs in her chair.

"What's happened?" Everest asks.

"You haven't heard?"

Everest shakes her head. "You just woke me up."

"We need to go to Nedlands. Right now."

"Don't tell me there's another body."

"It's very important. Dad just told me about it."

"Has it been assigned to us? Don't we both have too much going on? I hear you're really busy."

"Dad wants us there to help out. Damage control, and to keep things quiet."

This sparks Everest awake. "Quiet? Who is it?"

Booth is borderline distraught. "It's Blair Blake-Stendahl."

"You've got to be kidding me."

Deedee sits upright, yawning. "Now that's the kind of news you want to wake up to."

"It's a tragedy," Booth says, moving towards the door. "Like killing Kennedy."

"Not even close, Master Booth." Deedee takes her feet off the table and turns on the desk lamp. She smiles when she sees that calling him that has given him a sour expression. "But it's unfortunate, nonetheless."

"Is it murder?" Everest asks.

"That's not clear yet," Booth says.

"I need to see the scene. Let's go." Everest turns to Deedee. "Thanks for all your help. I owe you a pile of books. Send me a wish list."

"You got it, Elenore."

Once they're heading up the stairs, Booth asks, "How did she help you?"

"Don't worry about that. Tell me what you know so far."

"The early assessment is she died of natural causes. But following her appearance on television yesterday, which I thought was really good, Dad says we should maybe consider some crazy person taking matters into their own hands. Just in case."

Outside, Everest is moving slowly, struggling to get going, her body stiff from sleeping on the floor. "Can you drive? I'm not fully awake yet."

Booth leads the way to his orange off-roader. Everest squints at the harsh morning light.

"You look like you're coming out of an all-night rave," Booth says.

"Wow. You certainly know how to flatter a woman."

"That's nicely meant. I like a good rave."

They both climb in. As they get moving, Everest lowers the sun visor and checks her appearance in the mirror. She looks dishevelled, and a bit tired, but that's pretty much a standard morning these days.

"What else do you know?"

Booth uses his knees to keep the steering wheel steady while flipping through his notebook. "She left the office just after seven, according to one of her assistants. I didn't get her name. Sounded like barista."

"Watch the road."

"Relax. I can multitask. Then she was at some dinner hosted by the Commonwealth Bank."

"How did she get invited to that? She wants out of the commonwealth."

"It's just a bank. It doesn't represent the old empire. Well, I don't think it does. Anyway, sources say she left the dinner before dessert was served and went home. Alone."

"Who found her?"

"Her husband. Uh," flips another page, "Clayton Blake-Stendahl. About half an hour ago. In the bathroom."

"The bathroom?"

"Specifically, on the toilet."

"You're joking."

"Shocking, isn't it? Like a rock star's death."

Everest wishes Booth hadn't made that reference, but then becomes acutely aware that Charlene isn't hurting her as much today.

"One step short of choking on her own vomit," Booth adds.

"What happened to this being a tragedy? You seemed pretty sad about it back in the basement. Now, it's all a joke for you?"

"Who got up on the wrong side of the floor this morning? I'm just trying to offer some levity in this difficult situation."

"Let's just stick to the job, shall we? If it was natural causes, it must've been a stroke or a heart attack, and no one was there to help her."

Booth puts his notebook away and focuses on driving. "She's too young for something like that. Isn't she? I mean, she's around your age."

"Careful how you say that. It seems highly unlikely to me she would just die like that."

"You think it was murder?"

"There has to be more chance of that than a heart attack. She pretty much said yesterday on live television that WA should become a country only for a certain type of Sandgroper and everyone else can get stuffed."

Booth not replying to this makes Everest wonder if he shares the sentiment.

"That surely pissed off some people," she adds. "It only takes one of them to do something crazy."

Booth continues to keep his mouth shut. They drive the rest of the way in silence.

Blair Blake-Stendahl's modest house on Birdwood Parade is opposite the Nedlands War Memorial. Two black SUVs are parked out the front, plus three squad cars, an unmarked car and a forensics van. Booth pulls up on the verge across the street, making both of them bounce in their seats.

"Is this the first time you've gone off-road in this thing?"

"You're not funny. Not at all."

Everest gestures towards the van. "Looks like I'm not the only one who thinks her death wasn't natural. Remind me to order a toxicology report from them."

"You're thinking poison. Like the others? Dad told me you were reaching on those other cases. Let it go."

Everest climbs down from the car. "Nobody's said anything about blood, which means she wasn't shot or stabbed."

"We're not going to know anything until we get inside."

In the driveway, they flash their IDs at the uniformed officers keeping guard. Another officer lifts the police tape at the front door step, and they duck under it.

"Weird that there's no media here," Everest says, as they go inside.

"Dad says we're keeping this off the books, for now."

"That won't last long. The neighbours will have seen all the cars out front. They surely know who lives here."

Everest spots a couple of night-shift detectives, whose names escape her, slouched in chairs at the kitchen table, drinking coffee from paper cups and looking tired. She keeps on walking, not wanting to engage in any debates about jurisdiction or go through the usual dick-swinging about whose case this is. If Mitchell Booth wants her and Justin to be here, they have every right to look around and investigate. This starts in the bathroom, where Blair's body is on the granite-tiled floor.

"Mr Blake-Stendahl?" Everest asks, finding it peculiar that he's been left in here alone.

He's sitting with his back against the wall near the door, head in his hands. He looks up, face glossy with tears. "Who are you?"

"I'm Detective Everest. This is …" Everest turns to see that Booth isn't with her, then adds, "I'm very sorry for your loss. Are you able to answer some questions?"

He nods.

"When did you find her?"

"When I got here. I wanted it to be a surprise, to have breakfast together. She was so good yesterday. Her approval rating is the highest it's ever been. I got champagne. The works. I was so proud of her."

"You didn't wonder where she was last night, when she didn't come to bed?"

"I don't live here."

"You don't?"

"Keep your judgements to yourself, detective. There's no need to look so shocked."

"I mean no disrespect. I just assumed, you being married."

"Well, you assumed wrong. We defined our marriage by our own terms, and we were both happy with it."

Everest looks at the body, finding it strange Blair's leggings are pulled up. "Did you move her?"

"She ... fell. I came in and Blair was sitting there." Clayton points at the toilet. "I thought maybe she was asleep. It wouldn't have been the first time she fell asleep in an unusual place. She works so hard."

"You moved her to the floor and redressed her?"

"I tried to wake her. You know, I poked her in the shoulder and tapped her lightly on her cheek. She slipped off and ended up on the floor. I couldn't do anything about that. She was a ... dead weight."

"What about the contents of the toilet?"

Clayton looks bemused. "Are you asking if I flushed?"

"Yes. Did you?"

"My wife is dead and all you care about is whether I flushed the toilet she died on?"

"I know this is difficult, but please answer the question."

"Yes. I flushed. Happy?"

Everest isn't, because it means she'll need to order an autopsy, which may get blocked by red tape if someone decides "natural causes" is sufficient for the report. A sample from the toilet would've possibly been the easiest route to discern if anything unusual was in her system. She turns to her left to see Booth standing next to her, notebook open, pen at the ready. She sees him write "husband flushed toilet contents" on a blank page.

"Justin," she says, "please help Mr Blake-Stendahl up and take him to the kitchen, in case our colleagues there have any further questions for him."

Booth steps forward and extends a hand.

"It's Clayton."

Booth helps him up from the floor. Clayton gives Blair one last look, then allows Booth to usher him out.

Everest, alone in the bathroom, bends down to inspect the body. Nothing strikes her as unusual. There are no signs of a struggle. No broken nails. No bruises. What takes her interest the most is the serene expression on Blair's face. She almost seems happy.

Everest thinks Blair looks drugged. She certainly doesn't look like she's had a heart attack or a stroke.

When one of the forensics guys enters, she says, "I need samples from her system. Blood, urine, whatever you can get."

"Sorry. We're not allowed to touch the body."

"What? Said who?"

"The fellas in the kitchen. I'm just here to help when the body box arrives. We're short-staffed this morning."

"Stay here. Let me sort this out. This is a crime scene."

Everest goes to the kitchen and is shocked to find it empty. Booth enters.

"Where is everyone?" she asks. "What's going on?"

"Detective Andrews said there was nothing to investigate."

"Is that right? From his chair in the kitchen, he decided she died on the toilet naturally?"

"There was a call as well."

"From who?"

Booth's blank face gives it away.

"Why does your father care about this?" she asks. "He's not even here."

"This is no time for a scandal. That's what he said. Our reputation has already taken a hit with Monday's murder. Now, there's this high-profile death. It's potentially a media nightmare. The press will jump on it, then jump all over us."

"It's a crime we need to solve, Justin. This isn't PR. Who gives a fuck about our reputation? We have to find out who did this."

"Can you lower your voice? The neighbours can hear you."

"You don't think they've seen all the cars?"

"The media will be here soon. Andrews is outside, ready to face them."

Everest, incredulous, paces around the kitchen. She just stops herself from picking up the gift basket and throwing it against the wall. "And say what? It's a tragedy? It's so sad? Thoughts and prayers to her family and supporters?"

"Yeah. Something like that. You know the script. Look around. There's no sign of forced entry. There were no wounds on the body. There's nothing to suggest she was attacked. You're pushing this poison angle too hard. You need to back off."

Everest wants to punch Booth. He seems to sense it and edges out of the kitchen.

"You need to know when to follow orders and when to leave things alone," he says.

Everest chastises herself for saying so much in front of Booth, who is bound to relay her insubordination and questioning to his father.

"Yes. Sorry."

"We're needed back at the office," Booth says.

After he's gone, she has a quick look around the kitchen. In the sink, there is a metal filter full of tea leaves. It's then she sees the open packet, near the kettle, with Santorini Sunset on it.

"That's the fakest-looking label I've ever seen," she says to herself, and she puts the packet in her pocket.

<>

He joins the flow on Stirling Highway, southbound. The road is busy in both directions, but he smiles through it all, refusing to let this journey – and Giorgie's devilish offer – define his morning.

Stopped on the Railway Bridge, he looks at the Swan River, where it expands towards the ocean and flows past all the giraffe-like cranes and busy docks. He thinks back over all the students he's had, trying to recall if any of them showed anything remotely like psychotic tendencies. Plenty had written macabre, and at times graphically violent, poetry in his class, and were only too eager to read it out or submit it for assessment, but he had always dismissed it as the apery of kids who had grown up watching slasher movies and playing brutal video games; who were so desensitised to violence, they presented it in verse as a form of humour. Not to mention those young fellas channelling the guns, hos and bling of hip-hop, some of which he found rather amusing.

One student, past or present, is trying to get his attention. A male student, who perhaps was also infatuated with and rejected by the Ukrainian violinist. Possible even is a poet who's frustrated he's not getting the recognition he feels he deserves.

He thinks: I should check out who's been reading at the Mangy Mongrel lately, see if any names ring a bell. And tell Everest to find out who last took out the *Ragged Claws* from Reid Library, though the book was likely stolen.

As Henry Street is full, he parks around the corner from it, a fair hike from the bookstore. Once again without any coins or a credit card to pay for parking, he jogs to Henrikson's, hoping the old man will help.

"Quin. Top of the morning."

"G'day, mate. Have you got some change? I need to feed the machine."

Henrikson takes a couple of two-dollar coins from the almost empty cash register.

"Thanks," Huntley says. "That's bare. Where's the money?"

"It's all electronic these days. No one carries cash, so why should we?"

"Good point." Huntley holds up his fist full of coins. "I owe you."

Outside, he jogs back to the Landy, where there's already a slip of paper under the windscreen wiper.

"Oh, what the fuck?"

He decides to let that ticket be his parking permit, because surely they won't ticket him twice. He marches back to the store, annoyed, and drops the coins on the counter.

"Machine broken?" Henrikson asks.

"The whole bloody system's broken." Huntley takes a breath. "Sorry, mate. How're you doing?"

"A bit flat, to be honest. Got my flu shot yesterday, and it kind of feels like I've got the flu today."

"Did you get a lead on anything from the B Shed restaurant?"

"As a matter of fact, I did." Henrikson lowers himself onto the stool behind the counter. "Can we talk about it?"

Huntley sees there are two people in the store, perusing like they're in a library, with little visible intent to buy. "Yeah. Why not? Everyone's in their own world anyway."

"I found that everything they buy is from a single wholesale market in Spearwood. At very low cost. Nothing from special suppliers."

"Superb. The whole place is a ruse."

"I got to see all of Carmello's records. I could even access his emails. The staff are very badly paid. He's making a killing with that place."

"You should see the price of stuff in there. Obscene. You need to take out a personal loan just to have a snack."

Henrikson taps his phone, then shows the screen to Huntley. "This is the staff list. Any names there look familiar to you?"

Huntley scrolls through and shrugs. "I don't know. Maybe. I've been bad with names, but I'm working on it. Can you print that out? It'll come in handy, for cross-checking with the class lists from the university, if Everest gets them."

"Of course." Henrikson taps his phone and the printer starts whirring.

"Your technical abilities are hugely impressive, Henrikson. I can't even remember to put my phone in my pocket, let alone charge the damn thing. Ask me to print something with it and I'd shut down half of Perth."

"You're a man living in the wrong time."

"I don't know about that. But maybe I should move back to Ravensthorpe. The simple country life."

"Do you think they'd let you? Those families might make your life a misery."

"It's ages ago now. Surely they're not still hanging on to all that. Anyway, I could hole up at the commune. Farm the land. Get a couple of muskets. Whittle. Learn to play the banjo. Live in peace."

"You'd waste away down there," Henrikson says. "You strike me as the type of bloke who needs inspiration, to be in the middle of things."

"True. The last few days, I've felt totally in tune with the world. I'm seeing stories everywhere."

"And it's coming out as poetry."

"It is, while also helping to figure out these crimes. It's been a fascinating process."

"A new career?"

"I don't know about that. I'm just grateful I can still write. I thought the muse was done with me. I just need all the endings."

"Stop obsessing over that. The end isn't everything. Readers are smart. They can create their own endings. All this thinking about how the stories resolve could be blocking you from seeing things that are right in front of you."

Huntley looks at the old man curiously. "Interesting thought. Care to elaborate?"

"Well, with all that's happened this week, what's the one thing you keep coming back to? I know that when I think about it, and it really is awful to think about, but I come back to one thing."

"The fountain pen."

Henrikson nods. "The pen. This is such an obscure and personal choice. Forget wild arum. Forget the ending. Focus on the pen, as a metaphorical object."

"The pen has its own story."

"Or it's the key to unlocking the whole story."

"That's clever. I teach that, using objects to tell stories. But I don't know where this pen is. There must be an evidence locker, or something, at the cop shop. I'll never get my hands on it."

"You don't need that pen. You need any fountain pen, and then you visualise it as the killer's."

"Yeah. Yeah. Do you have one?"

"I do." Henrikson slowly gets off the stool. "Follow me."

In the office, Huntley watches Henrikson rummage through his desk's drawers.

"It's in here somewhere," Henrikson says.

Huntley finds some paper and sits down at the edge of the desk, which, like Henrikson's apartment, has lots of framed family photos on it.

"Here." The old man hands Huntley a fountain pen. "I got this when I retired."

"All those teaching years and they gave you a measly pen?"

"That's now coming in handy. If I'd only known then they'd given me a murder weapon."

Huntley laughs. "You could've enacted some revenge."

"I know it's not the actual pen. But maybe just hold it and see what happens."

"You're fast becoming my guru."

"If you want to achieve enlightenment, that's on you. For me, I just admire your work and want to read more of it."

Huntley is really touched by this. "Thanks."

Henrikson smiles and closes the office door.

Huntley looks at the fountain pen. The black barrel is large and feels awkward to hold, as it's so much bigger than a regular biro or pencil. The silver nib is stained with tiny flecks of black ink. Instead of holding it for writing, he gets it in his fist, ready to jam it into someone's neck. Held like this, the nib takes on the appearance of the sharp end of a blade.

A small dagger that could pierce a jugular, he thinks. Would the nib bend or break on impact? The nib could be sharpened, if necessary, for violent purpose. Weaponised into a blade, loaded with poison.

"Poison pen," he says to himself, to get the words flowing. "Mightier than the sword. Ugh, so clichéd. Something phallic. Something intellectual. Something sexual. The neck an erogenous zone. This pen connecting two people."

He positions the fountain pen for writing and begins. Initially, he only creates splotches of ink on the paper, but then he gets the pen at the right angle and it moves smoothly.

He takes the point of view of the violinist:

Grab me, fill me, kill me
Toxic words spoken
During a poisonous flirtation
For this I ventured
From desolation war-torn
To paradisical worn shore
Leaving nothing behind
The same spirit prevails
Here, these dogged men
I wish only to play
Why don't you leave me alone?
Your ceaseless hounding

Yearning for attention
Be with you?
I'd rather die

He stops, realising he could be right about the motive of rejection. He also thinks the killer is likely a repeat offender. Ekaterina Valoskiya wasn't the first victim, and she won't be the last.

He reads through, not to judge his work, but to look for deeper meaning. For clues scoured from his subconscious. He's not seeing any, until he looks at the page itself; its splotches, scratches and smudges. He's seen this before. Poetry written with a fountain pen, submitted to him for assessment.

He stands up and throws the office door open. "Henrikson? She's right."

"Who is?" Aphra asks.

"Hey. What are you doing here? Don't answer that. You're just in time."

"After I wasted plenty of my time this morning trying to find you. At the university. At your caravan. Why don't you answer your phone?"

"I don't have it with me. Sorry. How did you know I'd be here?"

"She called ahead," Henrikson says.

"Why didn't you tell me she was here?"

Aphra looks confused. "I just got here."

"You spent an hour staring at the pen and mumbling to yourself," Henrikson says.

"Really? An hour?"

"I'm here now," Aphra says. "So, who's right and about what?"

"Ellie. Detective Everest. She thinks it was one of my students." He excitedly holds up the paper, like it's courtroom evidence. "This is it. Poetry in ink. I had a student who wrote with a fountain pen."

"What's his name?"

Huntley shuts his eyes and tries really hard, but it's not there.

"What does he look like?"

"I can't remember."

"Not even something this unique?"

"She has a point," Henrikson says. "To this day, I can still remember the names of students who had unusual quirks. They imprint themselves on your memory, whether you want it or not."

"I'm sorry," Huntley says. "There were many years when I wasn't paying enough attention. I'm alert now. But I know this, Aphra. Your friend was being pursued, by my former student. This is seduction gone very wrong. Maybe even stalker level."

"What makes you think that?" Aphra asks.

"Everest says there was no break-in. Whoever killed her, she let him in."

"Why would she do that, if he was stalking her?"

"Maybe she didn't think it had gone that far. Maybe she thought she could talk him down, reject him nicely."

"She never said anything about this. There was no mention she was being followed."

"She could've been embarrassed by it," Huntley says. "Or she thought she had it all under control. Anyway, I need to tell Everest about this."

He moves around the counter, intent on leaving, but Aphra stops him.

"Wait. I have something, too." Aphra takes out the vape she bought at the beach. "I think I've found Lance's supplier."

Huntley leans in close to get a better look. "Does that have a snake on it?"

She nods.

"Great work. I thought that lead was dead, after last night. Who did you get it from?"

"A guy named Purvis Irving. He's a sleazebag, but he seems harmless enough."

Huntley blinks a few times. "I heard that name, very recently."

"It's familiar to me as well." Henrikson takes the printout from the printer's tray and looks through the list of names. "He was on the staff at Carmello's, up until a few weeks ago."

"That might give him an opportunity to throw something extra into someone's salad," Huntley says.

"He's not working there anymore," Henrikson says.

"All the staff there looked like students, or like they had been once," Aphra says. "Maybe Purvis was your student, Quin."

"Maybe. I'm not sure. We can't point fingers until we know it's him."

"Is it worth confronting him?" Henrikson asks. "Even if he tries to deny it, he might give himself away."

"That sounds like a job for the police," Aphra says.

"They're too busy giving me parking tickets." Huntley turns to Aphra. "Do you happen to know where he lives?"

"In Success. I don't know the address, but I know someone who might. His agent."

Something on the computer gets Henrikson's attention.

"Why does he have an agent?" Huntley looks at the paper again. "Wait. He's a poet?"

"The next big thing, according to Lydette Gifford. I met him at the Mangy Mongrel."

"Yes. Of course. Lydette. The agent provocateur. This's her new guy."

"Hold on." Henrikson turns the monitor. "You both need to see this. Breaking news."

"The news is breaking in here, Henrikson," Huntley says.

"Oh, my God." Aphra stares at the screen. "Blair's dead."

"Say what? Did someone kill her?"

"There are no details," Henrikson says, reading quickly. "There's nothing in here about a crime. No cause of death either."

"After what she said yesterday," Aphra says, "I wouldn't be surprised if someone went after her. She has no security at home. Anyone could break in there."

"Where's that?" Huntley asks.

"Nedlands. Near the river."

"There are plenty of security guards in that swanky area, doing laps of the neighbourhood all night. The same in Peppermint Grove."

"This is awful. I can't believe it."

"It's not good. But let's focus on what we've got now." Huntley checks the ink is dry, then folds the paper and puts it in his pocket. "We need to find Purvis. Go to his place and see what he has to say for himself. Henrikson, can you get his address?"

"I can call Lydette," Aphra says.

"Don't do that. She might alert him, in some way. We can't let him get ahead of us."

"Are you for real? You and me, we get him? I want revenge for Katie, but I'm not sure we can do this."

"Why not? Henrikson's probably got a gun under the counter we can borrow."

"I have no such thing," Henrikson says. "This is Fremantle, not New York."

Aphra takes out her phone. "I'll call Detective Everest and tell her to meet us in Success."

"Yeah, that's a good idea," Huntley says. "She can get his address. But if you tell her what we know about Purvis, she'll order us to stay away. I want to be involved in this."

"But we should get the police in it as well, just to be safe."

"He could try to escape."

"Why would he do that? He doesn't know we're onto him."

"He'll definitely scarper if a bunch of police cars roll up at his street."

Aphra, still holding her phone, asks, "So, what do you suggest?"

"Call Everest," Huntley says. "But just get her to meet us in Success. No police cars."

"I know where we can meet."

"Say we've got something about the Everglades. Which reminds me. Where does that fit into all this?"

"Purvis led a protest last year to stop the development there."

"He's trying to stop it again? Lance and Chandice. Maybe he went after Blair as well."

"Katie had nothing to do with any of that."

"That's right. We need to talk to this guy. God, this is so exciting. I'm buzzing."

"Don't lose your head," Henrikson says.

"I'd feel better if you gave me a gun." Huntley goes back into the office and grabs the fountain pen. He holds it up and says, "I'm taking this weapon instead."

<>

They meet at the Surfing Lizard, at Coogee Beach. Niranda Stone is the first to arrive. She sits outside, under the awnings that are fluttering in the light breeze, and sips a flat white. When Winslow shows, she takes off her massive sunglasses, but doesn't stand up.

"Sorry I'm late," he says, sitting down. "Busy, busy morning."

"You heard?"

"Shocking news." He looks past Niranda, at the pancake-flat water. "I don't know if I can take much more of this. I'm still coming to grips with Lance being gone."

"What do you know, Nate?"

"About Blair? Probably no more than you. Just what I've seen reported online."

"Which is all very vague."

"It is. If the police know anything, they're not telling that to the media."

Niranda sips. "I could find out, if necessary."

"What difference will it make? She's gone, right when she was on the cusp of serious power. Everything she worked so hard for, over. It's so sad."

"I'm not convinced about that. Popularity can be fleeting. And misleading."

"Sorry, Niranda. Have you checked the polls? The party's rating is skyrocketing. It's higher this morning than it's ever been."

"Because she's front page news, for the wrong reasons. It'll pass. People will forget her."

Winslow looks Niranda in the eyes. "Unless someone takes her place."

"She was trying too hard," Niranda says, putting her sunglasses back on; they occupy half her face. "She always did that. And she was never sincere enough. In doing so, she greatly underestimated the ability of the people in this city to recognise a faker."

"Are you suggesting Blair didn't believe what she stood for?"

"She was pandering. Trying to carve out a niche, and she took it too far yesterday. Smart people see through that. All that popularity will disappear once she's buried. She won't even be a footnote in this state's history. It could mean the end of her party."

"Someone needs to step up. To prevent that."

Niranda smiles. "So, this is why you wanted to meet. It's not about the Everglades. It's politics."

"I think you'd be right for it. You'll have to start from scratch, but I think you're more than capable, and you have all the right connections. I'd say you're far more suited to this role than Blair ever was."

"That I agree with. Blair was too much of a bulldozer. She just churned through everything and everyone, with little forethought or understanding of the repercussions."

"Right. You'd be more tactful. More willing to negotiate and build alliances."

Niranda is quiet for a moment, then asks, "Why do you care who takes over from Blair? You have nothing to do with her party. You're in property, not politics."

"There are plenty of correlations. My main interest right now is to see the Everglades project get started. Too much has been invested to let it fail."

"If I move into a more public role, I won't be able to do the work behind the scenes to get the project approved."

"We won't need that. Because I'm certain you'll influence the right people, from your new position. You could also go on to become premier, which will open all the doors for this project and others."

"We both know it's not that simple."

"I'm sorry, Niranda. But only you have the skills, connections and character to do this. The party will fold without a leader like you."

"What you mean is that my family scares the right people."

Winslow smiles. "You can't deny how helpful that is."

Niranda looks around the café. Plenty of patrons have come straight from the beach, still in swimwear, trailing sand wherever they go.

"I'll agree to this on one condition," she says.

"Sure."

"We'll need to do some rebranding. I want to change the name of the party. Not only because the acronym is a disaster, but because the word republic scares people. It's too American as well."

"Agreed."

"The people in this state are slow to accept change. It's too much to have a party that puts WA first and also wants WA to be a separate country. It should be step by step. Build towards becoming independent. Make it something the locals want, rather than forcing it on them."

"See? You're already doing this better than Blair."

"We drop the word republic. WA Party says it all. It's simple and straightforward. That's the party I want to lead. That puts the state first. And that's the party that can win the next election. People have had their fill of Liberal and Labour. It's time for a new voice."

"Absolutely."

"It's important we get the timing right. I can't just jump in now. Only after a proper mourning period for Blair can we then make the move. It needs to look organic. Natural. A passing of the baton."

"But not the torch."

Niranda nods. "Now you're getting it."

"On this dark day, this is good news."

"Do you think the party will agree to this?"

"How could they refuse Niranda Stone? Sweetheart, you are the only one they could possibly want."

"Are you positioning yourself to facilitate the changeover?"

"Sorry," Winslow says. "This will be the end of my involvement. I don't want to be seen as a manipulator. You need to do this on your own."

"Understood. I actually prefer it that way."

Winslow stands up. "I guess I'll see you at the funeral."

"It's so tragic. Her time was up far too soon."

"Yeah. But now it's your time."

<>

Booth and Everest, both with hands on hips and digging their shoes into the dirt, are waiting outside the container office in Beeliar when Huntley and Aphra arrive in the Landy.

"This better be very good," Everest says, after they get out. "We're swamped today."

"How did you get here so quick?" Huntley asks. "I didn't expect you to beat us."

Everest thumbs towards Booth's orange off-roader. "Justin can drive as fast as he wants. Family benefit."

Huntley looks at Booth disdainfully. "I guess you can also park anywhere you want."

"Police work is always urgent," Booth says. "Now, why did you drag us here? Are you here to confess?"

Huntley laughs. "Wow, you are so far behind on this investigation. I think we better talk inside. It feels suspicious that we're all out here like this. Maybe someone's watching."

"Who would be watching?" Everest asks.

Huntley looks at Aphra and gestures at the container. "Can you open this?"

"If the code's still the same." Aphra goes to the door and punches in the code. It works. "No one's changed it yet."

The first inside, Huntley goes straight for the catering cart. He takes a bottle of water and drinks from it. "Bloody hot in here," he says.

Aphra sits down. "The air-con's on a timer. I don't know how to access it."

"Surely you're used to hot containers, Huntley," Everest says.

"At least mine has a fan."

"Huge perk. So? Let's have it."

Huntley has another drink, grins and says, "We think we know who it was."

"Who what was? And who's we?"

"Me and Aphra. We have an idea who killed the violinist, and who garnished Chandice Cowdrey's salad with sweet oleander."

"What's that?" Booth asks.

"You didn't read the medical report? Good thing someone did. The same guy also put jimsonweed in Lance Ford-Brackman's water bottle, I'm sure of it. Maybe he took out Blair Blake-Stendahl as well. Damn, all these hyphens are so pretentious."

"Lance was suicide," Booth says. "Cowdrey was food poisoning. Blair died of natural causes."

"You're a character in the wrong story, mate." Huntley looks at Everest. "You don't believe all that, do you? I bet you my caravan there's something poisonous in Blair's system. Have you checked?"

Everest pauses, then says, "That investigation is ongoing."

"No, it isn't." Booth folds his arms. "There won't be a, you know, thing where they cut the body open."

"Autopsy," Aphra says.

"Right. That's not happening to someone of Blair's calibre. Those three cases are all closed."

Huntley is stunned. "Closed? What do you do all day? Screw that. We've done the work for you. Even without those three, we can still give you the guy who killed Ekaterina."

"Last time I checked, you were the main suspect," Booth says.

Everest holds up a hand. "Justin, let him talk. Who is it, Huntley?"

"His name is Purvis Irving. He lives in Success, on the other side of the park. That's why we called you here."

"Irving? I know that name."

"Did you see it on my student lists? I can't remember him exactly, but I had a student who wrote poetry with a fountain pen. I'm pretty sure it was him. He's an aspiring poet now. Plus the fountain pen connection. And to top it off, we've got marijuana deals linking him to Lance."

"Slow down. What are you talking about? What's this about drugs?"

"Purvis is dealing weed vapes," Aphra says. "To schoolkids. And others."

Everest and Booth share a look.

"How do you know that?" Everest asks.

"Yeah," Booth chimes in. "Where's the proof?"

"There's a box full of vapes at Lance's place," Huntley says.

"What box? You said you didn't find anything there. Why did you lie about that?"

"I didn't lie. I just failed to mention the box. I took a vape, had it tested, and there was dope inside. Then, Aphra got lucky …"

"That's a stretch," Aphra says.

"… And bought the same vape from Purvis Irving just this morning."

"How do you know they're the same?" Booth asks.

Aphra takes out the vape. "There's a snake on the side. That's the brand. Furina."

"The kids call it Fuzz Buzz." Huntley points at the vape and adds, "That little thing has blown this case wide open. We can get this guy on drug dealing, then see what else he has to say."

Booth scoffs at this. "We? Who the fuck do you think you are?"

"I'm the guy doing all your work."

Everest takes out her phone. "Everyone quiet down." She puts the phone to her ear. "Deedee? It's Elenore ... Yeah ... No, thanks for that. Look, there's a file I found last night. I left it on top of one of the filing cabinets ... The cat woman ... Can you check her name? And see if there's an address ... Right. Thanks. Take a photo and send me a copy."

"What cat woman?" Huntley asks. "Does Purvis have a record?"

"Not him. Wendy Irving. I found a report on her last night, when I was looking for poison-related crimes. Apparently, she killed a whole lot of neighbourhood cats."

"What neighbourhood?"

"Success."

"Using wild arum?"

"Aloe vera." When Everest sees Huntley's incredulous reaction, she adds, "I know. Unbelievable. What's good for humans is bad for cats."

"Living at home with his crazy mum perfectly fits this character's profile and back story." Huntley finishes the bottle and drops it in the bin. "Let's get this guy."

"You and Ms Massey are staying here."

"No fucking way. I'm seeing this to the end. We've given you everything. You owe us."

"It's too dangerous."

"What's he gonna do, throw a fern at us? You can't cut us out now. We can just as easily get the address and beat you there."

"Huntley, you need to stay out of this."

"You'll have to cuff me to this table."

"Stop it," Booth shouts. "Stop fighting like this."

"He's right," Aphra says. "This is getting us nowhere."

"I agree," Huntley says. "We're wasting time arguing about this."

Aphra goes to the door. "I'll ride with Huntley in his car. You two take that orange monstrosity and we'll follow you. When we get there, I'll make sure we keep our distance and stay in the car."

Everest nods.

They all head outside.

"I do all the work," Huntley says to Everest, "only for you to swoop down and steal the glory."

"You should be more focused on clearing your name," Booth says.

Everest stops. "Change of plans. I'll ride with Huntley. Justin, you take Ms Massey and follow us."

"Why?" Booth asks.

"Because I said so."

They split up and go to their respective vehicles. Booth really slams the door when he gets in his off-roader.

With Huntley driving, Everest directs him onto Beeliar Drive, Booth following close behind.

"Is Wendy Irving still alive?" Huntley asks.

"I don't know. I didn't check the records. I didn't think too much of it, except now with this connection, it kind of means everything."

"Yeah, mother and son in the poison plant business."

"And possibly the drug trade."

"There's no possibly about it. He must grow it. Somewhere."

Everest is quiet for a moment, then says, "I'm sorry I shouted at you back there."

"It's all right. I get it."

"Another story?"

"Sure. Hmm. Let's see. Once upon a scorching morning, there was a detective full of yearning. She had to pander to an idiotic partner, who got everything from his worthless father."

Everest shakes her head in disbelief. "How do you do that?"

"It's a party trick, even if the metrics are all wrong. Rhymes aside, I know you're not the one closing these cases. You want to solve this just as much as me."

"More so. You wouldn't believe how much gets swept under the rug, just to protect the police force's reputation."

"I don't want to know."

"How does my story end?"

"All the plot lines point towards the idiotic partner getting promoted, while the better, harder-working senior detective winds up on filing duty, and still full of yearning."

"I hope not."

"But, there's a twist ending." Huntley gives Everest a big smile. "The detective tells all the cops to go fuck themselves and makes a massive comeback doing the one thing she truly loves. She plays music at night, but also is a private detective during the day with a local poet."

Everest laughs. "You're letting your imagination get the best of you there, Huntley. Is that what you're going to do? Become some sort of PI?"

"I hadn't thought about it, but now you suggest it. Yeah. Why the hell not? That I have a knack for this caper surprises no one more than me. If someone had asked me a week ago this is where I'd be on the next Thursday, I'd have laughed all the way to Ravensthorpe."

"A caravan has to be the best office for a struggling PI."

"I could always ask Giorgie and go bigger. She's bought land here. She wants to build an arts centre, with a creative writing section. I could quietly make that my detective's office."

Everest points to the right and Huntley turns onto Hammond Road.

"You also sound convinced this development will go ahead," she says.

"There's another story, and there's nothing poetic about it. Once upon a colonial time, this whole city was bushland, very important to those who had lived there for thousands of years. The invaders built then and they'll build now. Nothing is sacred in this town. Blair dying and Chandice in a coma won't stop the locals from trying to make a buck. Where am I going?"

"Down Branch Circus. Next right."

Huntley makes the turn and leans forward to look out the windscreen. "God, look at this place. Suburbia really gives me the creeps, even in the daytime."

"Why?"

"All these gates and garages and locked doors. Guard dogs behind every fence. All these secrets stashed away. All these stories. Who knows what loonies are living out here?"

"Like these Irvings."

"Yep. Like these Irvings. I mean, what lunatic poisons cats?"

Everest raises a hand, to make Huntley slow down.

"Do you trust Booth?" he asks.

"I have to. I can't ask you to be my backup."

"Probably not. I only brought a pen to this gunfight."

Everest points. "That's it. No, don't pull into the driveway. Keep going. Park on the verge. Over there. In front of that van."

Huntley does so and turns the engine off. He moves the side mirror to look at the driveway in the reflection. "No cars. No action."

"Hard to see anything."

The house is the last one on Branch Circus, with bushland opposite. There is a six-foot-high corrugated metal fence all around the property, and a mesh gate securing the driveway.

"Out of interest," Huntley says, "as I'm not yet well-versed in law and order, but if he's not there, can you go in anyway and search the place?"

"I think so. It's a bit sketchy, but the drug angle should give us probable cause. Technically, we would need to have you and Ms Massey on the record first, your testimonies, but we don't have time for that. We should be all right. The police have dropped the ball this week, with these murders, but they love a good drug seizure."

"I bet. Put it all on the table. Get all high and mighty about saving the kids from drugs."

Everest wonders if she might be about to jeopardise her own weed supply. "It's the PR holy grail for us."

Huntley checks the side mirrors, seeing Booth and Aphra get out of the car, parked behind the van. They walk towards the Landy.

Everest opens the passenger door. "Stay here."

"Yes, ma'am. Good luck."

Once Everest is out, Aphra climbs in. They watch Booth and Everest go to the driveway gate, which turns out not to be locked.

"Shouldn't they have their guns out?" Aphra asks.

"That would be a pretty big giveaway that they're police. Right now, they can pretend to be Mormons going door-to-door. Or something."

"They don't look like Mormons."

"Jehovah's?"

"They look like police, even without guns."

Huntley tries to sit up higher, to see over the fence. "What are you going to do, now that your tour of duty with the WAR Party is over?"

"I was never in the party."

"You certainly wore their colours, with or without a membership card. Where does your career go from here?"

"Not sure yet."

Huntley watches Everest knock on the door. She steps back from it, right hand at her side.

"He's not here," he says.

"What makes you think that?"

"He knows we're onto him. Everest is trying to open the door. It's locked. He's gone."

"You're jumping to conclusions."

"It's because you bought the vape from him. You don't look anything like the drug-taking type. Plus, if he's been following you around, in sleazebag fashion, the last thing you would then do is take drugs from him. You'd be worried he'd give you something hard to knock you out and pile you into his van."

"How do you know he has a van?"

"Just hazarding a guess. Maybe because I'm parked in front of one. Does he have one?"

"So he said. I never saw it. What's happening now?"

Huntley sits up again. "They're splitting up, to go around each side of the house. Still no guns."

"I've taken plenty of drugs, I'll have you know. He was completely convinced."

"Maybe." Huntley checks the rearview mirror. "Something just moved. There's someone in the van behind us."

Aphra turns to look. "I don't see anyone."

"I'm going to check it out."

"Wait."

"He's been waiting for us to come. This is what he wanted. My attention."

"Everest told us to stay here."

"It's probable cause," Huntley says. "He's probably in that van, waiting to cause trouble. Lock the doors when I get out."

He closes the door and waits for the click of the locks, then sneaks along the side of the Landy. Once at the van, his heart starts to race; the last time it pounded like this was when he crept around the Edwards farm in the blackest of night, in search of a ram lamb. At the driver's window, he has a look inside. Everything is clean and organised. He takes out the fountain pen and grips it like a dagger, feeling ridiculous doing so. The van's side is fully panelled. He uses the pen's nib to tap on the metal as he moves along. When he reaches the back, the rear doors are flung open and a man jumps out.

"Purvis?"

He's already over the low fence and running into the bushland of Beeliar.

"Everest!" Huntley shouts.

Not as agile as the younger Purvis, Huntley needs longer to get over the fence. He also can't keep pace on the dirt tracks. Purvis tears off, kicking up dust. Huntley lasts about 100 metres before he has to stop, put his hands on his knees, and suck in air. Aphra appears next to him.

"Where did he go?"

"I ... didn't ... was it him?"

"Was he kind of skinny, like a healthy junkie?"

"Healthy junkie? What a great image that is. Yeah. He looked like that. Too quick for me."

"He could be anywhere."

"Don't worry. He won't go far."

"Why? Because you're here and you'll give him the attention he so desperately wants?"

Huntley straightens. "No need for sarcasm, Aphra. He'll come back because this is all he has."

Everest jogs up to them. "What happened?"

"He was in the van," Aphra says.

"We should've checked that first." Everest thumbs back towards the road. "There is a massive greenhouse in the backyard. It almost takes up a whole block."

"Did you go inside?" Huntley asks.

Everest nods. "It's full of dope."

"What's the bet you'll find some poisonous plants in there? Tucked away in a corner."

"Did you lose him? Which direction did he go?"

"He's not running," Huntley says. "This is his backyard. He wants to save it. He won't ever abandon it. This is what it's all about. Well, part of it."

Everest and Aphra share a confused look.

"The development," he says, bending down to take a handful of grainy, camel-coloured sand that he lets fall through his fingers back onto the ground. "The Everglades. He wanted to stop the development. The violinist was something else, but he poisoned Lance and Chandice specifically to protect his backyard. Blair too, I'd say. He considers himself the guardian of this land. He'll probably go after Winslow next."

"If this is his backyard," Everest says, "he would have a place here he would go to."

Huntley nods. "That's good narrative logic. A place he built, that only he knows about. A hut, or something."

"He lived in the trees here once," Aphra says. "It was part of the protest, when the idea for developing this land was first floated."

"That's it. That's where he is. In the trees."

"How do we find it?" Everest asks.

Aphra starts walking. "I think I know where it is. At least, the general vicinity."

Huntley follows her. He gestures for Everest to come as well. She does so, taking out her phone as she walks.

"Justin? We're pursuing Irving on foot into the bushland. Stay at the house and secure the scene … No, don't. Leave your father out of this. We can't let anyone get a whiff of this yet. A greenhouse like that will be a media circus. We need to do this right."

"A media circus on Branch Circus at Purvis Irving's greenhouse address in Success," Huntley says. "Dr Seuss, eat your heart out."

With Aphra leading the way, they walk single-file down the track, deeper into the bushland. Aphra breaks off a small, leafy branch from a tree, to use as a sunshade and swish the flies away. Everest does the same.

<>

After calling his father to give him a detailed update and receive instructions, Booth uses his phone to take lots of photos of the rows of marijuana plants, all of them in pots. When the door creaks open, he groans, because he thinks he'll be forced to share the credit for this fabulous bust.

He emerges from behind a row of lush dope expecting to see Everest, but there's a rifle pointed at him. The old lady holding it is wearing a frilly nightgown, with a purple robe over the top that's open and revealing a little too much splotchy skin. She has yellow curlers in her hair. She holds the rifle with the steady hands of someone accustomed to using one.

Booth raises his hands and tries not to stare at the exposed skin.

"You better have a very good reason for being in here, boy," she says, wrinkled eyes narrowed over the rifle's sights.

"Wendy Irving?"

"Who wants to know?"

"I'm Detective Justin Booth?"

"Booth?"

"Please, lower the gun."

"Sorry, copper. But, no."

"We have the house surrounded. Let's not escalate this any further than necessary. There's no escape."

"I didn't hear any sirens. There's a couple of four-wheel-drives out front, but no police cars."

"The orange one is mine."

"Good for you."

Booth starts to lower his hands, but Wendy gestures with the rifle for him to keep them up.

"Why didn't you answer the door?" he asks, hands above his head again. "We knocked."

"I never answer the door. Too many idiots wanting to talk to me about God. Or sell me something."

"I'm not here for that."

"What are you selling then?"

"I'm not selling anything. I'm Detective Booth. From the WA Police."

"Police? I didn't hear any sirens."

Booth, realising the old woman's not all there in the head, changes track. "I'm looking for Purvis."

"Why?"

"We, uh, work together." Booth tilts his head towards the marijuana plants. "I help him move his product."

"Lance does that."

"Yeah. Lance died, unfortunately. A few days ago. I'm stepping in."

"Lance died?"

"Swimming incident. Purvis didn't say anything?"

"He didn't. That's a real shame. I liked Lance. You better come inside."

"Where's Purvis? I was supposed to meet him here."

"I don't know where he is. Didn't come home last night. You can wait for him in the house."

"Okay." Booth thinks he should be able to overpower the old woman in the close confines of the house, once she puts the rifle down. "Sure."

"Come on. I'll make you some tea."

She holds the greenhouse door open, keeping the rifle raised, and Booth goes through it.

Inside the house, Booth is surprised to find it tidy and sparsely furnished, having assumed a senile old lady's living space would reflect the chaos in her head. But it's neat and comfortable, and it smells of flowers. There's a dog asleep in a basket in the hallway.

In the kitchen, Wendy stands the rifle against the counter and puts the old-fashioned kettle on the gas stove.

"What's your name again?" she asks.

"Justin Booth."

"Right. Sorry. The old head's not as effective as it once was. Sit down."

Booth, deciding to be patient, takes a chair at the kitchen table.

They stare at each other as the kettle comes to a boil and starts whistling. Wendy pours the tea.

"I hope you like herbal," she says. "It's all I've got."

"That's fine. Thanks. When will Purvis be back?"

"It's loose tea. The good stuff. None of that processed tea bag garbage."

Booth takes the cup. "Thanks, Mrs Irving."

"Call me Wendy."

Booth smells the tea, which has a sweet aroma. He blows on it, then sips. "Hmm. How much sugar did you put in this?"

"None. What you're tasting is caramel."

He drinks some more. "It's very tasty."

"It's important to put lots of caramel in." Wendy picks up the rifle again. "To mask the bitterness of hemlock."

"Of what?"

"Hemlock. Very powerful stuff."

Booth looks inside the cup. His stomach convulses, but despite wanting to throw the tea up, his body keeps everything down.

"It killed Socrates," Wendy adds.

"The Brazilian soccer player?"

"The Greek philosopher."

Booth puts the cup down and reaches for his gun.

Wendy is quick to raise the rifle. "No. Don't do that. Put your gun on the table, slowly, and push it away."

Booth does so. Wendy steps forward and picks it up, placing it on the counter behind her.

"And keep on drinking. It takes a while to have an effect. In the meantime, you can tell me what you're doing here."

"I said this already. I'm looking for Purvis. We work together."

"Stop it. I'm not demented. What kind of training do they give you idiots? You're not even a match for an old faker like me."

Booth sneers at Wendy. "Purvis is in trouble."

"No, he isn't. You didn't see anything out the back. Because you're a Booth, in the police. I'm guessing you're related to Mitch Booth."

"He's my father."

"Good. Very good. That'll make everything a lot easier. We should've established that before I poisoned you. I could've just paid you off instead."

"Excuse me?"

"I'm just assuming, like father, like son."

"What are you talking about? He's not corrupt. How dare you say that."

"Kiddo, you don't climb to the top of Perth's police tree without buying a few boxes to stand on along the way."

"That's bullshit. My grandfather broke the Claremont case."

"Sure he did. All by himself. Your father's anything but clean. He worked this area, a few decades back. Did he ever tell you about that?"

"You're lying."

"Believe what you want. You'll be dead soon enough."

"Why not just shoot me then?"

"Too loud. The neighbours will complain. They're not the most tolerant bunch."

"Is that why you poisoned all those cats?"

"Those weren't house pets, by that point, but it started that way."

Booth notices that he's not feeling anything from the tea. He almost subconsciously reaches for the cup, to have a drink, but stops himself. "How did it start?"

Wendy leans against the counter, rifle raised, her robe opening some more and revealing aged flesh that Booth can't help but stare at. She crosses a veiny shin over the other. The puppy-themed slippers she's wearing have floppy ears that are ragged from being dragged along the floor all the time.

"The cats went wild," she says. "When all the old houses were torn down to make way for the new development, there were some cats that escaped and went into the bushland. Dogs, too, but they weren't the problem. The owners couldn't find the cats and then they all moved away. The owners, not the cats. They stayed and went feral in the bush. That started to mess with

Beeliar's ecosystem, particularly the birds and rodents. I decided to save Beeliar from those feral cats. If a few pets got caught up in the mess, so what? It was for the greater good."

"You make it sound like you're a hero for doing that."

"Heroine. I am. Others didn't see it that way. Plenty of the cats had collars and tags, meaning some former owner dobbed me in. Good thing Mitch Booth was around to help me out of that, and protect my interests."

"You're making all of this up."

Wendy cackles. "Maybe I lied about the tea too. I could just shoot you and bury you in the backyard. Bodies make excellent fertiliser. But I wouldn't want to rub Mitch the wrong way. We've been through too much together."

Booth makes a move to stand up.

"Don't," Wendy says, holding the rifle right at him. "I will paint this kitchen with your insides if I have to."

Booth sits back down. "What do you want from me? Do you have the antidote for this hemlock stuff?"

"Who knows you're here?"

"I called my dad. I told him what's in the greenhouse."

"So? What did he say?"

"Take photographs and wait for backup."

"That's probably not coming. I told you, Mitch used to work this area. He knows who I am. He also knows that those who took over from him here know who I am. They're all taken care of."

"All the police here are corrupt?"

"Corrupt? 200 dollars for a speeding fine, or whatever it is these days. That's corrupt. And that's just scratching the surface. How about I tell you that the drug trade in this state is pretty much a joint venture with your precious police force and always has been."

"I'm starting to feel dizzy."

"That's anxiety. I'm stunned you don't know all of this, being Mitch's son. He kept it from you. I don't know why. I thought he'd be grooming you to take over."

"You're way off. Crazy. You've poisoned me with tea."

"Hemlock's a slow killer. You'll most likely fall asleep at some point and never wake up. Unless ..."

"Unless what?"

"You call it all off. I'll give you a little hush money on top. How about that?"

"You can't buy me off."

"Your choice. You're already in a corrupt organisation, and a corrupt family. Might as well join in. You can either live with the extra cash, or die here from hemlock poisoning."

Out of options, Booth takes out his phone and makes the call. "Dad? False alarm ... Just exotic plants ... Yeah, we're still on for that. The weather looks good for tomorrow. No wind ... Right."

When the call has ended, Wendy says, "Good lad. But Mitch never called anyone. They would've been here by now."

"He knows where I am?"

"He knows exactly where you are."

Booth slouches in the chair, angry he's been outsmarted – and poisoned – by this old lady with curlers in her hair and puppy slippers on her feet.

"How does five grand sound to you?" she asks.

Booth shrugs. "I've never been bribed before. Is that a lot?"

"It's a good number to start testing the water. Plus, you get the antidote for free."

"Fine. Give it to me. The money and the cure."

Wendy cackles again. "God, you are so gullible. It's just tea, kiddo."

Booth looks in the cup, then at the woman, wondering how she can be so horrible.

"I had to be sure you're on the right side," she says.

"According to you, drug dealers and police are on the same side."

"They are. Would you like to know why that is?"

"How can I be sure you won't lie about that too?"

"Good question. You ask a lot of them."

"My dad always taught me to have more questions than answers."

More laughter. "What a load of bollocks," Wendy says. "Mitch Booth is not someone to be taking life advice from. But he's a great starting point. Because going way back, it was always the guys like him who were easily corrupted. The greedy ones. Think about booze and how in the old days, pubs and hotels closed early. That led to a huge industry of secret distilleries and breweries."

"Like in America, during Prohibition?"

She takes a finger off the rifle and points it at the floor. "My granddad had a distillery on this property. Everyone knew about it, including the cops, who were loyal customers and easy to buy off. Back then, every suburb had its own local liquor supply, and it was protected. Nothing was going to stop people from drinking."

"But that's alcohol. How does that explain all the dope out back?"

"Don't interrupt the story. It's a good one. After the Second World War, drinking became more socially acceptable and the pubs were open for longer. The private liquor business died. A lot of the families who were doing it, because it was always a family business, turned to the cannabis trade in the 60s. Same deal, different stuff. The cops were happy to take some cash, buy themselves fancy utes and look the other way. There was also the thinking, and I was told this by a local cop years ago, that they preferred people getting high rather than drinking. Because if you're stoned, you're less likely to commit a crime, so he said, or wrap a car around a tree. Alcohol seems to bring out the violence in us, especially men. Frustrated middle-aged men beat their wives when drunk. But dope is calmer, and it's always been tolerated. I'm sure you know the consumption numbers."

"One in ten. Last I heard."

"That's what goes on the record. You can double that. Maybe triple it, with all the medical applications now. Cannabis has always been good to my family and me. There's a whole other industry of harder stuff, crystal meth and ecstasy and what-not. We've stayed away from that. The Ford-Brackmans have that covered all over the south and in most of Perth. The Duval family runs things north of the river and in the country towns out that way. I'll stick with cannabis. Meth and ecstasy aren't natural. It's chemistry and it fucks with you."

"If everyone's working together on this, how does that explain the busts and arrests over the years? There's been some big ones."

"The police definitely need to look like they're fighting the drug war. But take a closer look and you'll see that those who are caught and sent to jail are usually dealers and sellers. Low-level, small-time crooks. The suppliers never get touched."

"I can't believe it."

"I can't believe you don't know it, especially given your father could've told you all this as bedtime stories. There's a whole industry in place here, going back just about to colonial times. You're not the first ambitious young cop to set foot in someone's greenhouse or distillery or meth lab and think you could bring the whole thing down. You can't. This is way bigger than you. It's bigger than me. It's the economy. It's the way things have always been done. Plus, trying to bring me down would end up putting your father and a lot of his mates in jail."

"How does this work then? You give me the cash and I leave?"

"I'll make sure the cash and your gun get sent to your place tonight. Do you still live with Mitch in that huge house in Trigg?"

Booth wonders how much dirty money helped pay for the house he grew up in. "I moved out."

"I bet he had a tidy sum to support you buying a bachelor pad out that way. Write down where it is."

Resigned to his situation, Booth takes a pen from a cup full of them on the table and gets ready to write. "You know, we weren't here just for the drugs."

"Pardon?"

"Your son. He ..." Booth writes down his address. "He's a suspect in a murder case."

Wendy shakes her head. "You've got nothing on him. He's involved in the family business, but that's it."

"A girl was found on Monday morning. Ekaterina Valoskiya. Third violin of the Perth Symphony Orchestra. She died from wild arum poisoning."

"No. No. My boy's not a murderer." Wendy gestures with the rifle. "Time for you to leave, before you say something that might result in a different delivery to your house tonight. Remember, you're mine now. You're in the business. You've probably even had a hit or two from my greenhouse. I happen to know someone in your HQ is doing a very good trade in our vapes."

Booth stands up. "Okay. I'm going."

"Don't ever forget your place in all this."

"I won't."

Booth leaves the kitchen and walks down the hall. Wendy follows him, rifle still raised. Booth has to manipulate three large locks to get the front door open. Wendy pushes him through it with the rifle's barrel.

"Tell your father Wendy Irving sends her regards."

<>

Aphra stops at the lake that's dried up even more than when she first saw it two days ago. She looks around, then up at the trees.

Everest, phone in hand, says, "That's weird."

Huntley sweeps a finger across his forehead to remove the sweat. "Not really. It's been a while since we had a decent rainfall."

"I don't mean the water level, such as it is. I just tried to call Justin. He's not answering."

"Are we out of range?"

"What year do you think it is? There's network coverage everywhere."

"Maybe he's too busy coordinating this big drug seizure and taking all the credit for it."

Aphra shields her eyes with her tree branch as she scans the trees. "Can you two be quiet? He's around here somewhere."

"How do you know?" Huntley asks.

"I was here a few days ago. He came out of nowhere. Like he dropped down from a tree."

"What are we looking for?"

"Some kind of platform, big enough to sleep on. With protection, like a small roof or a plastic tarp."

Everest points to a tree about 50 metres from the track. "Do you mean something like that?"

"That was easy," Huntley says.

"You get the feeling this guy likes a bit of attention?"

The three of them start walking through the bush towards the tree.

Spotted, Purvis stands up on the platform and waves to them. "I'm only talking to Huntley," he shouts.

Everest and Aphra look at Huntley.

"I'm not climbing up there," he says. "He might be waiting to poison me."

"I just want to talk," Purvis calls out.

"That sounds sincere," Everest says. "Go speak with him. Get him down from there."

"How is that my job? You're the one trained to talk crazies down from a ledge."

"What happened to wanting to solve this case? This is your chance. Go get him."

"What do I get in return?"

"The endings," Aphra says.

Everest nods. "Plus my gratitude. And it will fully exonerate you."

Huntley scoffs at this. "How about you get my parking tickets out of the system?"

"I can wait all day up here," Purvis shouts.

"Parking tickets? How many do you have?"

"I don't know. A few. Don't look so surprised. When it comes to ticketing, the police never sleep."

"I can't just press delete on those tickets, Huntley. Is that how you think it works?"

"Well, I can't just climb a tree for you."

They reach the tree and stand in its shade, the platform high above them.

"Everyone wants something," Everest says.

"I want to be able to park in peace, like Booth does."

Aphra looks upwards. "He probably wants something too." Then she points at Huntley. "From you. That's why he's asking for you. It's something only you can give him."

"This is ridiculous. I suggest we cut down the tree."

"We can't do that," Everest says. "This is a protected area."

"For now," Aphra adds.

"We have probable cause," Huntley says.

Everest laughs a little. "That doesn't apply to tree-felling."

"Pretty soon all of this will be cleared."

"No, it won't," Purvis says from up above. "You're cutting down this tree over my dead body."

"Surely that can be arranged," Huntley says.

Aphra tosses her branch to the ground. "Just climb the tree, before we get eaten by snakes out here."

At the trunk of the tree, Huntley tries to see how he can climb up.

"There's a makeshift ladder." Purvis's head appears from the side of the platform. "It's painted the same colour as the tree. Clever, right?"

Huntley moves. "These are just planks nailed into it. Will they hold?"

"Come on. Be brave. It's worth the view, I promise."

Everest gets close to Huntley, who has one foot on the first plank. "Get him to come down," she says. "I'll cuff him."

"Give me the cuffs. I'll put them on him up there."

"How will he climb down?"

"I'll push him and you two can catch him."

Aphra laughs.

"What's so funny?" Purvis asks. "What's taking you so long?"

"I'm girding myself."

"Nice to see your pretty face, Aphra," Purvis says, his head appearing again. "I still have that wonderful image of you at the beach this morning in my head."

Aphra looks up. "Why don't you jump, Purvis? I'll be sure to try and catch you."

"Hah. You love it."

Huntley starts climbing. "Will you stop aggravating him?"

"Sounds like she's turning him on," Everest says.

Some of the planks move under Huntley's hands and feet while he climbs. He takes them one at a time, not looking down. He quickly learns that the areas closest to the nails are the most firm, and he soon makes it to the platform, where Purvis helps him onto it.

Huntley stays on his hands and knees, and looks up at Purvis, now recognising his former student, though he looks old enough to have university well in his past.

"You can stand up, Mr Huntley. It's safe. Can I call you Quintus? Or Quin? How about Q? Yeah, Q. That's good."

No fan of heights, Huntley sits on the platform while Purvis paces around. It affords a view over the trees that has the effect of making the platform seem even higher.

"How old are you?" he asks.

"Why does that matter?"

"I'm just trying to get my year right."

Purvis appears disappointed. "I'm 27."

Huntley remembers the off-kilter rodent face and the ink-splotched poetry, but not much else. He decides it's best to fake it, because Purvis was after his attention all along, and admitting now to have little remembrance of his former student could make him fly off the handle.

"Your poetry was always hard to read," he says. "Because of the ink. It was all smudged."

"You said you liked it. The fountain pen made my presentation unique. You told me to keep doing it, as long as it worked for me."

"Yeah. Writers can be superstitious. They stick with whatever method works best."

"You said I had potential. You liked my work." Purvis stops pacing and stands over Huntley, who's sitting cross-legged, close to the trunk. "But it took me years to figure out what I wanted to say. I had all the words, but never the stories."

Huntley uses his hand to shield the light, so he can look at Purvis. "Stories are precious gifts. You never know when you're going to receive one. If ever."

"It took me by complete surprise. Out of nowhere. Bam. I got the story. This gift, as you say. Then it flowed like it was always meant to be. "

"Do you want me to read it? Is that why you got me up here? To get my feedback?"

"Enjoy the view, first of all. Beeliar. My country."

"Mate, this is not your country. Don't use the word like that."

This makes Purvis angry. "It's mine," he says, stamping the platform, making it shake.

"All right, all right." Huntley looks over the trees and bushland, trying to see it all for what it is, and not for the development it will be. He briefly wonders where the proposed arts centre will be located. "It's your ... country."

"Always was. Always will be."

"Oh, no. That's ... you..." Huntley decides to give up arguing the point.

Purvis sits down opposite, also cross-legged. He pats the platform with a palm. "I built this when I was a kid. I once spent 49 days up here. During the protest against the development."

"How was that?"

"Challenging. Very elemental. Wet, hot, dry, cold."

"Windy, I bet."

"Yes. It made it hard to write on paper, with ink. I wrote a lot of poetry, but none of it was any good. It was all very nature-focused."

"How did you get this story to flow then?"

"I followed your lead." Purvis smiles like they're old friends. "Back at uni, you always said to live what you write and write what you live."

"Gawd, that old line."

"There's no substitute for lived experience. Your words. It's pure. Real. You're there. Inside it. Breathing it. Smelling it. Living it."

Huntley doesn't like where this is going.

"If I was ever going to write something of substance," Purvis continues, "something with body, and with a body, I had to go through it first."

"You killed the girl to get inspired?"

"That Russian tease deserved everything she got."

"Ukrainian."

"Whatever. She had it coming."

"That's really not for you to decide."

"She played with me. That slut. But her death had a purpose. She didn't die for nothing. Oh, no. She'll be immortalised forever in verse. Like Lenore, and, and, and Juliet. And all the others."

"Are those the only two you can think of?"

Purvis laughs. "You were always quick with a line."

"Was the Ukrainian the first?"

Purvis stands up, to pace his small stage. Huntley looks down, squinting at the wooden planks. He notices some of the planks have been written on; poetry, in different coloured pens that have faded over time, and at various angles, the way someone in an insane asylum might write all over the padded walls. Rhymes on every line, terrible structure, amateurish wordplay. It's more catchy ranting than poetry; stuff for a toilet wall. One area is devoted to dumb limericks.

"Trust me, Q. I'm eternally grateful to the violinist. She saved me from the eternal pessimist. From inside of me, she unlocked a bountiful creativity."

Huntley thinks: the idiot even talks in awful rhymes.

"She was the first," Purvis adds. "But if I had known this was the key to finding my flow, I would've acted much sooner."

"Thanks for sharing that. But no one will want to read about this."

"They read yours."

"That was almost all fiction. Anyway, what has all that got to do with me? Why put my book in the violin case?"

"Because you showed me the way. Your book. That work of completely lived experience."

"Slow down. You're reading far too much into it. The whole reality thing with my book, this true crime angle, which was all the rage at the time, it was just part of the marketing."

Purvis nods. "Yes. Sure. I get it. I'll need to say the same thing. People will think I'm crazy otherwise. But you and I both know the truth. You taught me this too. The power of the secret. Keep everyone wondering if it's really you or not."

"You just said it was you. You killed Ekaterina with wild arum in a fountain pen. You stalked her. She rejected you. And she paid the price with her life."

"That's not how it happened. She wanted me. Then she gifted me this story. She's gifted this story to the world. That's her legacy, and it's amazing. I honour her by writing the story, and everyone will honour her by reading it."

"I'm not sure I can help you, Purvis." Huntley starts edging towards the steps. "It's time to come down and give yourself up. Or stay up here, I don't care."

"If you're not going to help me, I will stay up here."

"Good luck with that. It won't be long. The whole area's going to be razed. You'll get razed right along with it."

"I stopped that. Again. For good this time. I removed those pieces from the board."

Huntley is about to start climbing down, then stops. "Is that why you killed Lance Ford-Brackman? To prevent the Everglades project from going ahead?"

"I didn't kill Lance. I could never do that."

"Right. Because you were in this vape business together. Partners. Or did you want to cut him out and make all the money yourself?"

"It wasn't about money. Look around you."

Huntley stares at Purvis, putting it all together. He casts his eyes over the bushland, and ends up back at Purvis. "Holy shit. You didn't know. All that time, you did this drug business, and you didn't know he was planning this project. Using the drug money you earned together to bribe people to get the project approved that will wipe out your … hah … your country."

"I liked Lance. I would never kill him. We went to school together."

"He didn't go to school in Mandurah?"

"He was expelled, and he was thrown out of his house. He moved to Port Kennedy and bussed it to Hammond Park each day."

"Port Kennedy? He grew up with Niranda Stone?"

"I never liked her."

Huntley stands up and gestures towards the trees. "How could you not know Lance was going to destroy all this?"

"He never said anything."

"How did you find out?"

"He visited on Monday. He was in a great mood and I asked him why. He said his brother had been offered a place in the Perth Symphony."

"Marcus Ford-Brackman."

"Ah, you know about that? At the time, it was hard to keep from telling him I made that happen. Anyway, I was loading his car with boxes of vapes and I saw the brochures on the back seat. He was an idiot to let me see them."

"Maybe he wanted you to know. Maybe he wanted to cut you in."

"The brochures were so fresh. Just printed."

"Why didn't you kill him then? Another fountain pen to the neck?"

"Like I said, I could never kill Lance. I decided to mess with him, as a warning. I put a little jimsonweed in his water, just to freak him out. Then, I wanted to confront him and threaten worse, to get him to stop the development. But he went off and died, all on his own."

"High as a freaking kite because of you. All this talk about liking him, you know, going to school together, but you don't seem sad about helping to kill him."

"Well, when I heard about it, I was fully triggered. Pages and pages of sublime rhymes, digging far into Lance's story and the family that threw him out for being gay."

Huntley gets it now. The whole story is right there. He also knows that trying to argue with Purvis or make him see reason won't work. Purvis is too far gone to be reasoned with. What he needs to do, to get Purvis down from this platform, is pander to his ego; and crank up the empathy.

"The muse is fickle," he says. "When she touches you, grab her with both hands."

"Yes. Yes, Q. I knew you would understand."

"The Everglades was just a subplot, right? From then on. The B story. Targeting the people involved was part of it, but it was the inspiration that you wanted. With Chandice Cowdrey."

Purvis nods.

"Blair Blake-Stendahl."

Another nod.

"You must've got some great work out of that. But it's over, for now."

"It hasn't even started yet," Purvis says. "I'm not going to jail. There's no proof I've done any of this."

"You just confessed to all of it."

"I told you stories." Purvis's smile is boastful and proud. "I told you about my forthcoming, fictional, poetry collection. I pitched it to you. None of it's real, right? I'm just an observer, like you. I never participated. I asked you up here because I want you to be my editor."

Huntley looks at Purvis, dumbfounded.

"Lydette's against it," Purvis continues. "But I don't want anyone else. I need the genius with the ragged claws. Because only you know where I'm coming from. You know what it means to dig and get your hands dirty."

Huntley wonders how much Everest and Aphra have heard. "If I say yes, will you come down from here?"

"Of course."

"There's a detective down there. She's going to arrest you."

"She'd be stupid if she did. Because of the drug business." Purvis holds out his hands, as if to be cuffed. "But I'll play along, as a formality. Though I seriously doubt I'll do any time."

"You'll go to prison for murder."

Purvis shakes his head. "They won't find a trace of me in that girl's apartment."

"That explains why you didn't touch her."

"My mother will vouch for me at every turn. It's easy to get away with a crime, isn't it, Q? When the right people support you. Influential people."

"What are you talking about?"

"It's so sad your marriage didn't work out. But it worked out for a while. Right? Long enough for you to get everything you wanted."

Purvis walks across the platform, gets to the trunk and starts descending.

"He's coming down," Huntley shouts.

"Don't shoot," Purvis says, jokingly. "I'm an innocent, unarmed poet."

Huntley stands on the platform, looking over the bushland, wondering how much Purvis knows about him. He feels bereft, having received all the endings he needed, but with a new, unexpected ending being forced on him.

Doubt, that evil spectre, crawls its way forward in his brain.

It's all terrible, he thinks. The new poems. They're rubbish. No one wants to read about murders.

He takes out the poem he wrote that morning in Henrikson's bookstore and reads through it, his heart sinking. He scrunches it up and shoves it in his pocket. It may be rubbish, but he's not littering this beautiful bushland with it.

<>

On the drive from the Surfing Lizard in Coogee to the Claremont Football Club, Winslow works the phone; calling in favours and trying to drum up some last-minute support for the afternoon's private sales event. With nothing to lose and every bridge worth burning, he makes plenty of promises, lies flowing through his teeth.

Once he reaches the carpark, outside the football club's glossy function centre, he pulls into a spot in the shade, looking down on the swimmers pounding laps in the Claremont outdoor pool. The final call he makes is to his accountant.

"Hi, Gary ... yeah, good, good ... It's about to start ... Very excited. Look, I need you to do something for me, just so we're on the safe side ... Hear me out. There's going to be a lot of money coming in this afternoon. I need you to transfer all the funds from the company account to my offshore account in the Bahamas ... No, it's not suspicious at all. We need to put that money somewhere for safekeeping, just until we get the go-ahead. Away from prying eyes. You know what this town is like ... Right. At midnight. Thanks, mate."

He checks his reflection in the mirror. As he straightens his tie, he wonders if it's too much, but decides to keep it; to maintain an appearance of assured professionalism. Everything above board.

Out of the car, he crosses Davies Road and gears himself up for the task ahead, getting into selling mode.

The gym is busy, but the entrance to the function centre is empty. He assumes everyone is already upstairs, looking at the model buildings, flipping through brochures, partaking of the free booze and seafood platters, and greedily envisioning all the money they will make.

On the stairs, he runs into Giorgina Gifford, who's coming down.

"Nate," she says brightly. "Nice to see you."

"Giorgie." He kisses her on both cheeks. "This is a surprise."

"Where were you this morning? You weren't at your office."

"Sorry. I had an emergency meeting. But someone took care of you, right? The deal got done."

Giorgie nods. "It's really exciting, Nate. This is going to be so great for the community."

Winslow moves his head towards the function room on the first floor. "If you're not here for the land sale, why are you here?"

"I didn't know about that. I just stopped by to have a look at the rooms, as a potential location for an exhibition and art sale."

Winslow worries if Giorgie may have seen something. "And? What do you think?"

"It's good, for a temporary showing. There's a full house up there. They seem to be enjoying the catering."

"Fancy a drink?"

"Too early for me. But I will come up for a bit."

"It's just a boring business thing. You don't want to see it."

"Nonsense. I already saw a few people I know, and they saw me. I really should say hello to them. You know how it is."

"Where are you going then?"

"Dashing to the bathroom."

"Hah. A different kind of business."

"I'll be glad just to sit down. I've been rushing around all morning."

"You look great, by the way. I like the jeans jacket."

"Thanks. See you in a bit."

Winslow watches her go gracefully down the stairs, hoping she will forget all about the function room and head off to do other things. It could get very awkward if she finds out her sizeable plot of Beeliar land is about to get sold again.

The function room is buzzing with conversation. Standing just inside the doorway is Leiland Taverton, managing to look dapper in a rumpled cream linen suit, like a lawyer from Christmas Island. He has glasses of champagne in both hands.

"I thought you'd never get here."

"Enjoying yourself, Lee?"

"Cheers to you. The wet bar is fabulous. Half of the buyers in here are already well-sauced."

"Thanks for your help, to fill this room."

"Importantly," Taverton says, sipping champagne, "we have quiet wealth in here. These aren't the nouveau riche, showing off and flaunting it. This is old money. Established families. And they're only too keen to turn their old money into new money."

"Land never loses its value."

"Trust these people know that, as they combine to own a huge chunk of Perth."

"I really appreciate you pulling the strings to get these people here, Lee."

"Be sure to express that gratitude with a donation to the PSO. We've had bad press all week. It would be good to get positive news into our channels."

"Right. The violinist. Sorry about that."

"I found out she was poisoned. Can you believe that?"

"Shocking. With what?"

"Something called wild arum. A common plant. So I was told."

Winslow, scanning the room, finds this interesting. "They catch the person who did it?"

"Not yet. Amazing to think there's someone out there killing people with poison."

"Yeah."

"Time to get to work, Nate." Taverton drains both glasses. "And by that I mean, work the room."

Winslow watches Taverton make a beeline for the bar. The beach-boy bartender isn't Winslow's type, but he knows Taverton can't resist a pretty face. He reminds himself to focus on this moment, because there will be plenty of chances to party, and drop all the charades, once all the deals are done and the money is transferred. Given the level of inebriation he sees, the quality of the property on offer and the amount of money in the room, selling the land seems like a formality.

Still, as he moves into the room, a winning smile on his face, he says to himself, "Make this count."

<>

In the back of the van, its rear doors open to let in the light, Aphra and Huntley, both hunched over, try to get a sense of who Purvis is based on this space. The van is very neat, set up like a mobile office. The narrow desk is bare, except for a glass of fountain pens, their caps on, sunk into a hole in the desk on the right, and a handful of notebooks, neatly stacked, at the left. In lieu of a chair, there's a round, three-legged stool, well padded, like something a drummer might sit on. There's also a pull-down bed on the opposite side of the van.

"This is completely not what I expected," Aphra says.

"Yeah. I guess his crazy is the obsessive type of crazy."

"I'd say tidiness is a good kind of crazy, wouldn't you?"

"Depends on how it's applied and to what."

"Agreed. What are we looking for?"

"Some kind of manuscript. His poetry collection." Huntley looks at the notebooks, but all the pages are blank. "He said I'll know it when I find it."

"There's no computer."

"Not even a typewriter."

Aphra moves the stool aside, then pulls out a box from underneath the desk. "Look. These notebooks are full. All this smudged ink. I can barely read it."

Huntley peeks in the box. "They look too old. This is stuff he's been writing this week. It's fresh. Check the front seat."

Aphra crabs to the back of the van, walks around the side and climbs into the cab.

"I once had a caravan set up like a writing space. I loved it. But I'm not a fan of this writing space."

"Why not?"

"No windows."

"I think it's because you know him and know what he's done. We're kind of inside his brain, right now."

"Awake in this horrid dream."

"I wonder if the house is the same," Aphra says, searching the front. "No clutter. Everything in its place."

"Everest told us not to go in there."

"She also told us not to search the van. But here we are. Okay. I think I've found it."

Huntley leans over the front seat. Aphra holds up a stack of four black notebooks, tied together with string.

"Same as the number of poisonings," he says.

"Purvis said they'll never put this on him." Aphra unties the string. "Before the detectives put him in the car and drove off, he said, 'I'm innocent.' And he said it with total conviction."

"He's lying. But he could be right that there's not enough evidence, especially if his mother gives him an alibi."

"Putting him back on the street."

"Yep. Where anything could happen to him. Couldn't it?"

"Like an old four-wheel-drive knocking him over?"

"Or something untoward."

Aphra starts flipping through a notebook. Huntley reaches over and grabs one as well.

"What if he comes after you?" Huntley asks.

"I think I'm safe for now. He's focused on you."

"This belief that I'm going to apply my magic touch to all this and help the collection get published. It's mad."

"Not to forget that Lydette Gifford will be throwing her power and prestige behind it as well."

"I don't want to be his editor."

Aphra looks up from the notebook. "Everything in this notebook is written in the third person, as far as I can tell."

"Same with this one. I'd say he's created the murderer as a character, to distance himself from it."

"Meaning the narrator is witnessing it all. You used the same method, didn't you? It's a bit cowardly."

Huntley wonders if Aphra is taking a dig at him, but says nothing. He moves back from the front seat and sits on the stool, which sinks a little under his weight. He reads some of the verse written about Lance Ford-Brackman, thinking it marginally better than the juvenile scribbles on the platform's wood.

"How are you finding it?" Aphra asks.

"Ordinary. You?"

"What I can make out, it's nothing special. Graphic isn't clever. Who wants to read this? By the way, I didn't mean to imply you're a coward. You pick the point of view you think is right for the story."

"To be honest, I didn't really know what I was doing, back then." Huntley closes the notebook he's holding. "I can't do anything with this. He writes about plants like they're people. His friends."

"I guess that's the writing that comes naturally to him."

"Seriously? We're doing puns now?"

"Well, Purvis is. I think he considers it wordplay. I'm just copying him." Aphra watches Huntley toss a notebook aside. "You can't give up that quickly. This is your chance."

"My chance at what?"

"Redemption. Maybe even a way to get out of that container."

"I'm not putting my name on this ... doggerel. I only played along before to get him to confess. Getting justice for your friend is the only thing that matters right now."

"How do we do that?"

"There's something really wrong with the world when a guy kills three and a half people, admits it, then gets to walk free."

"And he's a drug supplier."

Huntley picks up the notebook again and looks at it. "I need to edit these, or at least look like I am. I need to play along."

"Agreed. Keep him on side. And get someone to type this stuff up."

"I'm sure Lydette has that kind of slave-for-hire in her contacts list."

Aphra gets out of the van and shuts the door. Huntley does the same, closing the back doors once he's out.

"Hey, Aphra. You have to see this."

She joins him at the back and they look at the personalised IRVAN license plate.

"That just about says it all." Aphra looks at Huntley. "How did we miss that before, when we parked here?"

"There was a lot going on. We were all focused on the house."

"I need to get away from here." Aphra looks at the Irving house. "It feels like we're being watched."

"It does."

"Can you take me to Freo?"

Huntley smiles. "Sure."

They walk to the Landy. Once inside, Aphra gestures towards the bushland.

"You know. My parents have bought into this."

"I believe my ex-wife has as well. Could be a smart investment. Wrong on many ethical fronts, but a potential earner for them."

"Yeah. Now I'm here and I look at it, something feels off. It should be left alone."

"This entire city is made up of subdivisions of a subdivision. They won't leave Beeliar out of that."

"You sound like you hate it here."

"I have a complicated relationship with Perth, but I love this town."

"Same here."

Huntley fires up the Landy and they drive all of the way to Fremantle in silence. On Henry Street, Huntley parks near the bookstore and puts the parking ticket from this morning back under the windscreen wiper.

Aphra gets out and starts walking for her Vespa.

"Hey, Aphra? You all right?"

She nods a few times, then puts on her helmet. As she rides off, looking straight ahead, Huntley resolves to find a way to prove Purvis killed Ekaterina, even if it means editing all that rubbish verse.

In the bookstore, there is a handful of people scattered around, perusing the shelves. An old woman is asleep in a chair, a book open on her lap.

"How'd it go?" Henrikson asks.

"Oh, it went," Huntley says.

"Was that Aphra I saw outside?"

"Yeah. She needs a bit of space, I think. Everything got very weird, out in the suburbs."

"What happened?" Henrikson leans forward and lowers his voice. "Did you catch him?"

"Yes. And no." Huntley drops the stack of notebooks on the counter. "Got any rum? I'm calling a time-out on this dry week. I think a hot toddy is in order."

"Let's go into the office. These folks look more like readers than buyers."

"One of them's a sleeper."

"That's Elise. She's welcome to sleep here anytime she wants. My wife's best friend."

"Ah."

Huntley picks up the notebooks and follows Henrikson into the office, where a few hours earlier the poetry had flowed out of the fountain pen, only for him, in the meantime, to completely doubt its merit. And, as always, with doubt comes thirst. He takes the scrunched-up piece of paper from his pocket and drops it on the desk.

"Quin, I'm going to be tough here and give you just a regular cup of tea."

"That's mean. I can take my business elsewhere."

"Please don't. I think you need to stay lucid."

"Why? Doubt's the thirsty devil, not me."

Henrikson busies himself with the kettle and cups. "So, Purvis got away?"

"No. He was arrested. For the dope. With the murders, he confessed everything, then denied it all. Not sure how long they can hold him for the drugs. He seemed really confident he would walk."

"What's with the notebooks?"

"Each is dedicated to one of the four poisonings. This is his opus. It makes difficult reading."

"Why do you have them?"

"He wants me to edit."

"What about your work? You've been covering the same stories."

Huntley stares at the balled-up piece of paper. "That's a poisoned well."

"You need to stop doing that. I've seen the way you write. Deep down, you believe, but something at your surface is making you doubt yourself."

"If you had rum, I'd be more inclined to listen to you. And believe you."

Henrikson shakes his head. "You have to do better than this. What about Purvis? What's he like?"

"Awful. Rodential. The way he looks. The way he talks. The way he moves. A stalker. A killer. And now, a poet, supposedly."

The kettle boils. Henrikson makes the tea. Then, from a lower cupboard, he takes out a bottle of rum and adds some to the cups.

"Henrikson, marry me." Huntley takes the cup and has a long sip. "Ooh, that's good."

"Keys on the table."

"Come on. One won't hurt."

"It remains to be seen if you can stop at one, especially with the frame of mind you're in."

"My car'll get covered in parking tickets if I leave it there. Speaking of which, can you hack into the whatever police records and wipe my slate clean? Fuck knows where they've been sending the reminders for these things. Gifford manor, I guess."

"Sounds like a challenge, for when I get home. How many do you think?"

"A few." Huntley has another sip; the drink is fast disappearing. "Okay. More than a few."

"You're lucky you're still driving at all."

Huntley throws his keys on the desk. "I need another toddy."

Henrikson fills the kettle and puts it on.

"I envy the way you sip yours," Huntley says. "Like you're really enjoying it."

"I am enjoying it. You look like you're trying to fill a hole with it."

"Accurate."

Henrikson takes the ball of paper and flattens it.

"You can burn that," Huntley says, draining his cup.

After reading it, Henrikson says, "You need to stop questioning yourself. I bet you could write a poem right now. In fact, I challenge you to. Write me a poem and I'll give you another hot toddy."

"What am I, Pavlov's dog? Train me and reward me?"

"I'm just trying to get you to see the talent you have. Still have. Just let go and write. It's clearly the one thing you love doing the most. Don't worry if it turns out to be rubbish."

Huntley gestures at the paper. "So, you agree that one's rubbish?"

"I didn't give it an opinion. It needs some work, but it could be something."

"Blunt. It just so happens I have a pen handy." Huntley takes out the fountain pen. "I'll perform for you, but only because I'm thirsty."

He uses the reverse side of the flattened paper. Bereft, he thinks of Purvis's vehicle and writes IRVAN at the top of the page. Then:

Cruel van man
True Q fan
Green pen stain
Grew dope plain
New rhyme claim
Do kill sane
Drove unseen in
The verse machine

He puts down the pen. "Writing with this thing really hurts. It presses right against the top joint of my middle finger."

Henrikson holds up his right hand. "When you grow up with it, you get a groove right in that spot, so the pen sits in it. The benefits of a private school education, long ago."

"I see it. Gnarly. So, here's my submission, sir." Huntley slides the paper towards Henrikson. "Is it worth a liquid reward?"

Henrikson makes the hot toddy and gives it to Huntley, all without looking at the poem. "I don't need to read it. I just wanted you to write and be aware of how easily it comes to you. What you're missing is the required work ethic."

Huntley sips. "I can see why you were a teacher. A real taskmaster, I bet."

"Only with the students I believed in. The rest were just making up the numbers."

Smiling, Huntley says, "My Landy'll probably get towed."

"It won't. Why would they remove a vehicle they can keep ticketing?"

They both laugh.

"Don't worry," Henrikson says. "I'll solve that for you."

"You make it sound easy."

"It'll depend on whether they've improved their online security or not. When I got my first electric, I was hit with a bunch of speeding tickets. It took me a while to adapt to not hearing the engine. Because it made no sound, I wasn't aware how fast I was going."

"Electric vehicles. The silent earner."

"It didn't take long," Henrikson says. "To get in and clear my name. It's all just data."

"And money."

"Five tickets was about a grand. I'd say that's serious money."

"I don't want to know how much these parking tickets amount to. Harland Gifford's probably had great pleasure burning the reminders."

"You can bet it's high. WA Police Incorporated."

Again, they both laugh.

"Hang on," Huntley says. "If you can get that deep into the system, could you access other stuff?"

"Like what?"

"The street cameras."

"Do you mean traffic control?"

"Yeah. But also the security cameras. You know, the ones they set up after what happened in Claremont. They might have them around Stirling Highway too. In Cottesloe, around the bars there. I think that fruitcake worked that area as well. Napoleon and Station Street. Maybe the entrance to Leake."

"What are you looking for?"

Huntley points at IRVAN written at the top of the paper. "That's his license plate. A white van. If we can get that van on camera, going down Stirling Highway on Sunday night, we can prove he was there. Around the time the violinist was killed."

Henrikson downs his hot toddy in one go. "I'll close the store."

<>

Booth is on the phone, just listening, his face unusually grim, as he and Everest escort the cuffed Purvis Irving to one of the interrogation rooms. Once in there, Everest pulls out a chair for Purvis. He sits, smiling off to one side of his face.

When the call ends, Booth says to Everest, "My father wants to see you in his office."

"Now?"

"Yeah. Now."

"Word spreads fast," Purvis says. "Can you get these bracelets off me?"

Everest, aware the balance of power between her and Booth has somehow shifted since they left Success, watches him take the cuffs of Purvis.

"Thank you, Detective Booth," Purvis says. "You're very good at your job. Can I get a coffee?"

"No," Everest says.

"I wasn't asking you."

Booth looks steadily at Purvis. "Give us a minute."

"How about pen and paper? So I can put this otherwise wasted time to good use. A fountain pen, if you've got one."

"We have a broken one, downstairs in a sealed bag," Everest says.

"That's of no use."

"Because you broke it."

Purvis laughs a little. "Not me. I'll take any old pen, to pass the time."

"You should be asking for a lawyer."

"Only the guilty scream for lawyers. I haven't done anything wrong. What's the problem with growing my own medicine?"

"Is that what you're calling it?"

"Hey, Detective Booth," Purvis says. "Get your sassy underling in line."

"Sassy?" Everest echoes.

"Saucy too. Lose that ponytail and let down your hair. You'd be prettier that way."

Everest grunts with disgust and leaves the room. Booth follows and closes the door.

"What happened at the house?" she asks him. "Did you call for backup?"

Booth wipes a hand across his forehead, unable to look Everest in the eyes. "The house was empty. I told you that."

"What about the greenhouse?"

"Dad said it'll be handled by Narcotics. I told you that too."

"And I told you not to call your dad. Anyway, this is a murder case, first and foremost."

Booth thumbs behind him. "He said he didn't do it. Unless we get a DNA or print match from the apartment, or some witness comes forward, we've got nothing on him. We can't hold him."

"For the drugs we can."

"Which he called medicine, and which isn't our case. If you have a problem with that, talk to my dad. He's waiting for you, and he doesn't like to be kept waiting."

Everest looks at Booth questioningly. "Is something up between you two? You sound like you're angry with him."

"I'm not angry."

"You're also not telling me everything." Everest starts to walk away. "You're entering dangerous territory, Justin."

Her anger quickens her step, but when she reaches Mitch Booth's office, she's forced to wait outside, until the two men in there leave. As they go through the door, both in tight suits, they nod at her.

"Elenore, come in," Booth says. "Shut the door."

"Who were those guys? I didn't recognise them."

When the door is closed, Booth says, "Comms department. Very high up. They're trying to get ahead of anything related to Blair Blake-Stendahl. Just to be on the safe side."

"What if I said I've got her killer in one of the rooms here?"

"I'd say you're banging the wrong drum." Booth chuckles a little, then adds, "She died of natural causes."

Everest feels bile rise in her throat. "I guess that case is closed as well," she says, immediately regretting saying this so sardonically.

"It is." Booth gives her a steely look. "But it's still high profile. We need to get our stories straight."

"Stories? You mean facts, don't you?"

"We're being very careful about what we're sharing with the media. We don't want this at any point to come back and bite us on the bum."

"So, I shouldn't start blaring from the speakers that her killer's in a room down the hall?"

"Pull yourself together, detective. I've already told you there is no case."

Everest goes to sit down, then grips the back of the chair with her hands and stays standing. "What about the tea I found at her house? Has that been tested yet?"

"Seriously, Elenore? Tea? Are you listening to yourself? Imagine if that story got out. That's exactly the kind of nonsense we're trying to avoid."

"But, boss ..."

"Picture the headline. 'Idiot investigators waste taxpayers' money testing dead politician's tea.' The public would eat us alive. We'd be a laughing stock."

"More than we already are?"

"Watch that tone, detective."

"Sir, we arrested the suspect in the Valoskiya case. I believe he's also responsible for the other bodies that surfaced this week, including Lance Ford-Brackman and ..."

"Stop this," Booth says, interrupting. "You're making a fool of yourself. I know who you arrested. Justin is sorting that out. Purvis Irving's mother has already vouched for his whereabouts on Sunday evening. He has a rock-solid alibi."

"But he confessed to it. I heard it."

Booth pretends to search his desk. "And where exactly is that signed confession? Where's the recording of it? You're reaching, and there's nothing to reach for. I have to say, I'm disappointed in you, detective."

"You and your son both seem very keen to see Purvis Irving walk out of here."

"What the fuck are you implying with that?"

"I'm just trying to do my job."

"You're failing at it."

"What about Chandice Cowdrey?" Everest asks. "We believe ..."

"We? Who's we? Don't put Justin in that box. He doesn't believe any of this. Cowdrey woke up this morning, right as rain. Word is she's very happy, as she lost a couple of kilos while in a coma."

"That's news to me."

"You're proving to be very badly informed."

"I know that Purvis Irving has been growing dope for vapes sold to school kids. How about that?"

"Still reaching, and getting nothing. There isn't anything remotely wrong with the contents of that tiny greenhouse."

"Tiny?"

"Wendy has a condition that requires treatment with medicinal cannabis. She has all the right documents. If the Irvings have the knowledge and means to grow what they need for their own purposes, I'd say there's no justice in sending them to jail for that."

"So, it's Wendy now?"

"Mrs Irving."

"You're on a first-name basis with a drug seller. Think of the headlines. Sir."

Booth's bald head is getting shiny with sweat. "You're on very thin ice."

"I just want to solve the Valoskiya case."

"It wasn't Irving. Let that go. Where are you with that Russian lead?"

Everest just manages to keep herself from groaning. "No progress. What about the vapes? The ones with the snake on the side?"

"Lance Ford-Brackman was responsible for that. We found a box at his place."

Everest realises she can't tell Justin anything anymore. "Wow. One whole box?"

"I'm really not liking your sarcasm. Leave the Irvings alone. Do the work you're supposed to do."

"Is that another order?"

"No. I was just thinking out loud. Of course it's a fucking order. Now, get out."

Everest leaves the office and really slams the door on the way out. This causes a few colleagues to look in her direction.

"Sorry," she says. "Someone must've over-oiled the hinges. You know, greased the wheels."

Everest considers going downstairs to ask Deedee again about Russians, then decides to go back to the interrogation room. She finds it empty.

"What the fuck is going on?"

She tries calling Booth, then sees him coming out of the men's room, tucking his shirt into his pants.

"What happened? Where's Irving?"

"He was moved into holding, for now. Just while I clear a few things up."

"At least he's still here."

"What does that mean?"

"Nothing. It doesn't matter. Get your stuff. I want to take another look at the Valoskiya apartment."

"Why?"

"Just a hunch." Everest moves, but Booth doesn't follow. "Hey? Let's go. I need your help with this."

"Sorry. I ... you don't ... look, I've been transferred."

"What? Just now? You got promoted in the bathroom?"

"Earlier. You didn't see the email?"

"Let me guess. Narcotics."

"You did see it."

Everest folds her arms. "What happened at the house, Justin? You're not really the same guy you were this morning."

Booth looks ready to tell Everest the truth, then extends his hand. "It's been a good experience working with you, detective."

Everest leaves Booth standing there with his hand out and goes down the stairs. She wonders if she should talk with Irving. Get him alone in a room and press his buttons; maybe even loosen her ponytail and flirt with him, to see if that hits a nerve. But she decides it would all be a waste of time. She needs evidence.

In the basement, Deedee puts her book down on seeing Everest. "How did it all go?"

"Don't ask."

"You want something to take the edge off?"

Everest is tempted. "No. I'm done with that. My partner, former partner, would probably try to arrest me for it."

"Right. Booth junior's joined the drug boys. I got the email."

"Seems everyone did, except me." Everest drags a chair from the corner and sits down, suddenly exhausted. "Can you tell me anything about Russians? Give me something to get Booth senior off my back."

Deedee smiles. "I'm flattered you think I have my finger still squarely on the pulse of the underworld."

"Hit me with it."

"First up, you're not hearing any of this from me." Deedee gets some background music playing, then rolls her chair next to Everest. "Just in case anyone's listening."

"Someone probably is."

"I asked around. It just so happens an ex-boyfriend of mine is high up in a certain biker gang down south. Word is there's a Russian family in Bunbury running a string of craft breweries across the southwest. Beer's not the only thing they're serving up down there. Apparently, the hops cover up the smell of the meth they're cooking."

"Meth?"

"It might explain the rising popularity of craft beers from down that way. The meth maybe getting into the brew, a bit, making everyone a little high, as well as drunk."

"That territory is already controlled."

Deedee nods. "The Ford-Brackmans. There's a fight coming, you can bet on that. Those folks won't let someone just take their turf."

"That's interesting to know. But I don't see how it connects to the Ukrainian violinist. Why would a Russian drug family from Bunbury want to kill her?"

"No idea. But you asked about Russians, and that's what I know now about Russians."

"I appreciate it. Maybe keep it to yourself, for the moment, until I figure out what to do with it."

"Sure."

"Thanks, Deedee." Everest stands up. "I owe you."

"Again. So, no vape?"

"I'm done with that."

<>

It's no fun rolling with the heavy traffic on Canning Highway, but she eventually makes it to Applecross and turns left onto Cunningham Street. Arriving at the house on Dunkley Avenue, she's surprised to see a gleaming purple caravan taking up much of the front driveway. Not surprising is the "For Sale" sign hammered into the front lawn.

She scoots up to the door, gets off and plugs the Vespa in to charge. Her mother opens the door before she can knock.

"Aph? This is a nice surprise. What are you doing here?"

She takes off her helmet and gives her hair a shake. "Hey, Mum. Are spontaneous visits still allowed?"

"Always. Is everything okay?"

"I was in the area. Sort of. Thought I'd stop by. What's with the eggplant-coloured home on wheels?"

"We got it just this morning. Isn't she gorgeous? Top of the line. All the mod-cons."

"Ready to hitch up and drive to Tassie?"

"Yes, indeed. Do you want to see it?"

As she's not keen to enter into any debates with her father, Aphra says, "Love to."

"Don't be fooled by the size," her mother says, coming out of the house and closing the door. "It's very spacious inside."

"What about all your stuff?"

They walk to the caravan.

"We'll get it shipped. We've already had two offers for the house. Asking too far below, but the interest is good."

In the caravan, they leave the door open to catch the breeze and sit at the tight kitchen table, opposite each other. Strangely, Aphra finds this caravan far more claustrophobic than Huntley's. There's so much plastic inside, Aphra thinks cleaning the caravan would take five minutes with a high-pressure hose.

"It's nice," she says. "I'm sure you two will have some fun adventures in this."

"We've already started packing. We need your help with that. There's a lot of your old stuff in there."

Aphra notices the table still has a film of protective plastic on it, in a light shade of purple. She's also picking up a strange scent, which she decides is new-caravan smell.

"Come on, Aph. I know you're here with a purpose. What's going on?"

"This land you've bought, after the mining redundancy."

"What about it?"

"Any chance you can pull out of it? Get your money back?"

"Why on earth would we do that? We stand to make millions."

"But you'll bank all the money from the house sale, right? The mortgage is paid off."

"It is. Look, what's this all about? You sound worried."

"I've got a bad feeling about it. Maybe I'm wrong. I was there today, at Beeliar."

"Your dad's really excited. That's why we bought this. To celebrate."

"Good move. This is bricks and mortar, on wheels. It's always worth something."

"The same with land. You're worrying for nothing, Aph."

"I'm happy for you. Really. You can see the country on your way home. That feels weird, calling Tassie home."

"For us, that's how it is. Going home."

In the silence that follows, the caravan creaks a little, as the breeze blows in.

Aphra thinks they're so close at this table that they should be arm-wrestling, or playing chess on a really small board. She moves her legs into the middle section, to stretch them out and get some distance from her mother.

"I saw the news. I'm sorry about your boss."

"She wasn't my boss, even though she acted that way. But it's still awful news."

"What do you think will happen?"

"With the party? I guess she'll be replaced."

"By who?"

Aphra shrugs. "Blair was a one-woman cyclone. There isn't really anyone groomed to take her place. No second-in-command, or whatever. They'll have to bring in an outsider, as a ready-made replacement."

"Perhaps that person will be more moderate."

"Or more extreme."

"What does it mean for you?"

Aphra considers telling her mother that Blair fired her, as what must have been close to her last act as head of the WAR Party. She decides to say nothing, because there's always the chance the next person might want her skillset. Smart, she thinks, would be to go to the funeral and do some quiet networking there.

"Aph?"

"Oh, sorry, Mum. Just lost in my thoughts. I guess the messaging and speechwriting for the next party leader could fall into my lap."

"Do you want to go back outside?"

"I'm all right. It's just a little cramped. And a bit hot."

"You never liked camping, or roughing it. You like luxury."

"I think holidays should be relaxing and enjoyable, not exercises in survival."

Her mother laughs. "Even when you were really small, you had that figured out. Any more holidays planned this year?"

"I haven't thought about it. You know I love Europe. Italy's always worth it. Maybe I'll stay here and work on some of my own projects."

"Are you writing poetry again?"

Aphra thinks about how she can ruin Purvis Irving's life, and write about it. The way she did with Jay Palmer. Because if he walks free, he will likely continue to inch his way into her life. Show up at the beach and claim coincidence, or worse, destiny. Stand in front of her condo, smiling his ratty smile. Follow her in that van he transports drugs with and writes poetry in illegible ink. He will lurk and loiter unless she does something drastic about it. Doing it right requires more thought and planning, but even now, she thinks it's a worthwhile endeavour she'd gladly throw her energy into.

"Yeah," she says, hoping it will lead to another collection she can publish. "Writing poetry."

<>

Huntley, in a hurry, helps Henrikson up the stairs. They both stop on the first-floor landing and look at Everest, trying to pick the lock to apartment 10.

"Have you switched sides?" Huntley asks.

"Oh, hey, Huntley. I need to get in here. To have another look around."

"Why?" Henrikson unlocks the door to his apartment. "A new tenant's moving in tomorrow."

"Already?"

"Perth's housing crisis and blah, blah. You won't find anything. It's been cleaned, top to bottom."

"I just want to stand in there. You know, feel it. Huntley, you get that, right?"

"Sure. Give her the keys, mate. She wants to do a visualisation exercise. A bit like I did. Envision the crime being committed, maybe even place herself in one of the roles and act it out. To see if it surfaces anything."

"Like holding a fountain pen and getting inspired," Henrikson says.

"Yeah. Similar."

"Fine. Just don't touch anything, detective. And take your shoes off. The carpet was steam-cleaned."

"Thanks," Everest says.

Henrikson goes inside to retrieve the keys.

"You look like you lost a fight with a rooster," Huntley says. "How did it go with Purvis?"

"Don't ask."

"That bad. Hah. I bet he's a game cock to fight with. But you're here, looking for more, maybe even clutching at straws, which means you don't have enough. Purvis will be let out, just like he said."

"You should've recorded that conversation up in the tree."

"How was I to know he would confess, then deny it all?"

"Well, he's denying everything now. Even saying the dope is medicinal, for his mother's unspecified condition."

"Crafty fella."

"His mother also gave him an alibi for Sunday, and for every day of the week."

"She's lying."

"They all are. My bullshit radar has been going off all day. I'm certain the Irvings know some of my colleagues."

"Oh, not little Justin."

Everest nods. "I think so. A few too many changes today."

"Just when I was starting to like him."

"Yeah. Me too."

"Is there enough dope in the greenhouse to keep all the local schoolkids stoned?"

"I think they'd need more greenhouses. Plus somewhere to make the vapes."

Henrikson comes out and hands Everest the keys. "Sorry I took so long. I had to take my pills."

"I promise I won't touch anything."

"Take your time. Have a cup of tea with us when you're done."

"We might have something to show you," Huntley says.

"Is it a video of Irving stabbing Valoskiya with a pen?" Everest asks.

"Not that compelling, but it could be useful, nonetheless."

"Anything would be helpful. Right now, I have nothing."

"Maybe you'll visualise something, and turn it into poetry."

Henrikson laughs a little.

Huntley closes the door. "Don't make fun of her. She's having a rough day. A rough week."

"You made the joke."

"I was being serious. I really hope she visualises something. Anyway, we have other things to take care of."

"What do you want to do first?"

"I'd say have a hot toddy, but I have a feeling this apartment's dry."

"There's a fair bit of drinkable medicine."

"Pass. Let's do the important stuff first." Huntley writes down his license plate on a piece of paper. "Here. That's my Landy."

"Right. Can you make us some coffee while I see what I can find?"

"That's probably wise. It could be a long night. How's your stamina, Henrikson?"

"Don't worry about that. I used to do my marking at midnight, when everyone in the house was asleep."

In the kitchen, Huntley looks at some of the photos. "Your children have certainly been fruitful."

"It seems to be in the genes," Henrikson says, working at his laptop. "There are a lot of births to cover in my family history."

"The seed of convict loins." Huntley takes the used filter out of the coffee machine and lines it with a new one. He fills it with ground coffee, tops up the machine with water, and switches it on. "I can repay you in coffee, if you get rid of those tickets. My brother's growing beans down south. I've tried it already. It's very good."

"You don't owe me anything, but I won't say no to free coffee. So expensive these days."

As the coffee machine starts gurgling, Huntley goes to the fridge to get milk. He stops to get a closer look at the photos on the fridge door, under various magnets: smiling children, family get-togethers, a shot of a young Henrikson and his very pretty wife in outlandish 70s attire and both with lots of hair leaning against a pale blue VW Beetle. He tries to just look at these snaps, but can't help it when each photo sets off a story train in his mind.

"Milk? Sugar?" he asks.

"Just milk, generously."

Huntley checks the cupboards for suitable cups. Again, he's impressed with how orderly the old man keeps his living space. Not obsessive; just neat. He stands at the kitchen counter, trying to look over Henrikson's shoulder without being intrusive. The laptop's screen is black, with streams of white data flowing down it.

"How's it going?" he asks, making no sense of what's on the screen.

"I'm done already with the tickets. I'm looking for the cameras now."

"That was quick."

"Nothing's been updated. I used the same back door as last time, like they left it open for me."

"You'd think the police would have tighter security for their own systems."

"That costs money," Henrikson says. "This is what happens when public services are run by bean counters. They will save money any way they can."

"It just cost them however much I had to pay in parking fines."

"Well over two grand."

Huntley laughs incredulously. "I think I owe you more than a bag of coffee."

"For now, I'll settle for a cup."

Huntley passes him one. Henrikson hits a couple of buttons and clicks his mouse a few times. The laptop's screen fills with four boxes, each displaying grainy camera footage of cars, roads and footpaths.

"Is that live?"

Henrikson nods. "This is Stirling Highway. The cameras are positioned outside the Albion Hotel."

"Can you move them?"

"Probably, but I'm not going to. That might set off some kind of alarm. We're piggy-backing the stream, and we should just keep it to that."

"He would've turned at Leake Street."

"That's the intersection there." Henrikson points at the top right box. "I just need to figure out how to go back to Sunday night."

"Without that triggering an alarm."

"Right. Do you know her time of death?"

Huntley sips his coffee, wishing he could add a splash of rum or whiskey to it. "The detective next door would know that."

"You want to ask her?"

"You want her to see what you're doing right now? You've hacked the police. Again."

"Do you trust her?"

"She cried a river on my caravan's table. Yes, I trust her."

"I don't need the time." Henrikson works at the laptop. "I can set a start time and the footage will play from there. I can't fast-forward it. We'll have to watch it through."

"That's all right. Set it from 7pm. I bet Purvis waited for the cover of darkness, or near darkness."

Henrikson types. The screen flickers and changes. The four boxes now show roads under streetlights.

"That's a lot of traffic," Huntley says, watching.

"We just need to focus on the vans. That narrows it down."

"It's Sunday." Huntley pulls a chair to the desk and sits down. "Mostly family cars heading home from days out."

They both sip, watching the footage.

"How was it?" Henrikson asks. "Meeting him?"

"I wasn't scared, if that's what you mean. He's not intimidating or unhinged. Maybe that makes it all worse. He's just a sort of regular guy. He was trying to stop the development."

"This Everglades thing?"

"Aphra thinks it won't go ahead now, without Blair Blake-Stendahl. Or maybe she hopes that."

"What do you think?"

"I think this is Perth, where they built an Olympic-sized swimming pool right at Scarborough Beach. If powerful people want to see Beeliar razed, it will happen."

"What did he say about Ekaterina?"

"She deserved it, according to him. She must've rejected him and he couldn't take it. Yet she opened the door for him, let him in, and played for him."

"I don't recall hearing the violin that night."

"No? Could you normally hear it? Through the walls?"

"Yes. Faintly. She played beautifully."

Huntley watches the cars go past in the camera footage. Most are SUVs, with solo drivers, or families returning to their suburban enclaves.

"I'm starting to get the sense she died for nothing. Purvis twisted it, trying to give her death meaning. But really, she just fell into the path of an angry screw-up who killed her because she wanted to have nothing to do with him."

"What about the others? The developer and Cowdrey?"

"That was to stop the development. But they were also convenient targets. Because he knew the poisoning was sparking his creativity. It was the best stuff he'd written, so he thinks, and he wanted to keep tapping it."

"It's now your job to edit it."

Huntley puts his cup on the desk and takes the four notebooks strung together from his jacket pocket. "I'm going to try, but just to keep him in my corner."

"To trap him?"

Placing his van near the crime scene isn't going to be ironclad evidence. I need to get him to confess to me, and record it."

"You're playing a dangerous game, Quin. You could become a target if he gets a whiff you're not genuine."

"I'll be fine. It's Aphra I'm worried about." Huntley yawns and stands up. "Can you watch on your own for a bit? The coffee made me sleepy."

"It did?"

"Wake me in an hour and I'll take over."

"Make yourself comfortable on the sofa."

"Thanks, mate. Of everything that's happened this week, making your acquaintance has been far and away the best thing."

Henrikson smiles and nods.

Huntley lopes to the sofa, lies down and quickly falls asleep.

At the desk, Henrikson eyes the stack of notebooks. He puts down his cup and tugs at the string.

<>

Only the staff remain, collecting glasses and wiping surfaces with the slow deliberation of people paid by the hour. A man is operating a vacuum cleaner at the far end of the function room, pushing it back and forth like he's gently rocking a baby to sleep.

Winslow sits at a table near the big windows, looking down on the football field. He sips champagne, picks at the remains of a seafood platter and reflects. It all happened fast during the afternoon, making it hard to keep track of the sales, but he thinks it must be close to nine figures. Add that to the payouts from the mining companies and the other sales done on the sly, and he is seriously wealthy. All that remains is to ensure that Gary transfers the money, then put him out of action for a bit.

He has an overnight bag and his passport.

It was supposed to be him and Lance, but now it's just him.

Lance, he thinks, drinking down the hurt.

The lights come on to illuminate the football field, where a dozen kids are kicking a footy around, overseen by an adult who's on his phone. Claremont Oval has changed dramatically from when Winslow came here as a kid; those Saturday afternoons with his father and brother, at the footy, eating meat pies and supporting the Tigers. Back then, there weren't the apartment blocks surrounding the field. It was concrete steps and grass areas, where kids could have a kick and try to emulate the stars on the field. The Tigers' fans, despite this being the affluent western suburbs, were rabid and vocal, cursing with every second word and sending vitriol towards every umpire. During the breaks between the quarters, the kids would all jump the boundary fence and get various kick-to-kick groups going, as balls flew everywhere and everyone tried to take a speccy. The adults lingered around the edges of the Tigers' team huddle, arms folded, to hear the coach spray the players or jeer them up for the next quarter. The seasons came and went, defined by wins and losses. Later, as a teenager, he was a promising footballer with a scrappy style and a liking for close contact, always keen to mix it physically and not afraid of taking a hit. At 16, he joined the Colts team, where his brother Marlon was already established, as the 18-year-old pretty-boy forward who never got his hands or jumper dirty. It only took half of that first season for Nate to establish himself as the Winslow to watch, and the team's barometer, first picked every week and always in the best three at every post-match presentation night. Even then there was talk of him joining the Seniors side, and a few former players turned scouts and agents, watching from the sidelines, touted him as a potential draft pick for the national league. But Marlon, sent back to amateurs after a string of poor games, didn't respond well to his younger brother's rise. He was the one who started the "Nate's a poof" rumour, hinting that Nate relished the on-field contact just a bit too much. As it can do in a sports team's dressing room, the rumour soon established itself as an assumed fact, which resulted in awkward situations at training when Nate would tackle a teammate and that teammate would bounce up and push Nate away, not wanting to be touched by him. After this happened a few times, the Colts coach took Nate aside and confronted him about his sexuality, claiming Nate could talk candidly and everything would be tolerated and accepted. Despite Nate's vehement denials, the coach decided to drop Nate for "mental health" reasons, which was how it was written on the injury list. Marlon soon took the vacated spot and proceeded to play far better in the absence of his brother. This all caused problems at home, as Nate became bitter and closed off, while his father stopped speaking to him. Once released by the Claremont Colts,

Nate tried to play footy elsewhere, but Perth can be a ridiculously small place, and the rumours of his "mental health" issues followed him everywhere he went. Nothing was ever said outright. The coaches stuck to the standard lines of "You're not right for the team" and "You're too selfish a player" and "We're focusing on giving the local boys a chance." It was at that time that Nate's parents got divorced, with Marlon staying with his father in Dalkeith and Nate moving with his mother to Salter Point. This was actually good for Nate, getting away from the western suburbs and the nasty rumours he couldn't shake. He reinvented himself at Aquinas College, studying hard in year 12 and earning a place at Curtin University. He dated girls, younger and older than him, having decided the best way to extinguish any rumours was to stay away from footy, act fully hetero and fuck everything he could.

This worked.

He went on to study business and development at Curtin, got a job in real estate after graduating, thanks to friends of Leiland Taverton's parents, another Aquinas connection, then started his own property company when he was 28. He married Daniela, his first secretary, and this union was a step towards reconciliation with his father. But not with Marlon, who wasn't invited to the wedding. His two daughters are now both at university and making their own way. The last time he and Daniela had sex was when their youngest daughter was still in primary school.

His whole life, Nathaniel Winslow suppressed every inclination he had towards his attraction to men, as it was better, so he told himself, to struggle alone with this suppression than live with the consequences of giving into it. His character and personality evolved to be overtly masculine. He was flirtatious and sexist. He hit on women at every chance and even had several affairs in the early years of his marriage, before deciding that keeping all that going in secret was too much effort. Any frustration he had over the years was passive-aggressively directed at Daniela, who soldiered on and took it all. Once their children were old enough to perceive disharmony, Nate and Daniela came to the unspoken understanding that their marriage existed to raise their daughters and to provide a solid, respectful and conservative reputation for Winslow Properties.

But when Nate was partnered for a round of golf at Lake Karrinyup Country Club with Lance Ford-Brackman, everything changed.

He finishes the champagne and takes out his phone. He calls Gary.

"Evening, mate ... Yeah, superb, though you probably got wind of that ... What do you need my authorisation for? You have it already. You can make the transfer ... Okay. I'm just finishing up here. I can be there in an hour ... Yes, champagne is in order. I'll bring it."

He pockets his phone and goes to the bar.

"Do you have a bottle of champagne?"

The bartender Leiland had tried to pick up earlier says, "You drank us dry. I got this, about half full. That's it."

"Can you cap it?"

The bartender takes a mushroomed-out cork and cuts the top off with a knife. He then flips it over and jams it into the bottle.

"Clever," Nate says.

The bartender hands Winslow the bottle. "Look, I'm just about finished here, if you want to share that with me."

"Sorry, mate." Winslow raises his hand to show his wedding ring. "Happily married with two daughters."

"Ah. Right."

"No worries. I'm flattered. Thanks for all your work today."

The bartender nods and goes back to his cleaning.

Winslow gives the field one last look. He's glad he chose this function room as the location for his sales drive. He feels like he's closing the circle, going back to when things went wrong, while also fleecing some of Claremont's wealthy set of their inherited money. He can now venture off to be the person he's meant to be.

He takes the bottle downstairs. Outside, as he crosses Davies Road to the carpark, he thinks Perth's evening air has never felt so good, like he's breathing normally for the first time in his life.

<>

Upon opening her front door, Fozzie comes rushing to meet her. It's exactly the kind of tongue-waggling, floppy-eared welcome Aphra needs. Unconditional love. She scratches the dog's ears and closes the door, securing the deadlock. Her helmet gets hung from a coat hook, then she and her dog go through the rooms of her condo, checking all the closets and storage spaces. Satisfied she's alone, she feeds Fozzie and pours a glass of Chardonnay for herself. She sniffs it, savouring this quiet moment, while also wondering what troubles await. But before she can sip, there's a knock at the door.

"He's here already?" she asks herself.

She puts the glass down and goes to the door, where she looks through the spyhole.

It's Niranda Stone.

This takes Aphra by surprise. She opens the door.

"Niranda? What are you doing here?"

"I'm sorry to just show up like this," Niranda says with a friendly smile.

"How do you know where I live?"

"The party knows. I know people in the party. May I come in?"

"First tell me what this is about."

"It's about Blair, and me, and you, and the past, and the future."

"That's a lot."

"Specifically, how you and I might work together."

Aphra gives Niranda a searching look, wondering how much she knows. "Go on."

"I'd much rather we talk inside. The wind is messing up my hair."

"Sure. Be warned, my dog isn't a fan of visitors."

"I come in peace. I swear."

Aphra steps aside to let Niranda in, then deadlocks the door.

"That's heavy-duty," Niranda says. "You have the full-sized one. There's no getting through that."

"Just to be safe. You never know who might be calling by."

"I admire the way you look after yourself." Niranda's heels click on the wooden floor. "Have you had problems in the past, with unwanted visitors?"

"Probably no more than any woman."

"Yes, well, rest assured. Gender and safety will be at the top of my agenda."

"What agenda is that?"

They end up in the kitchen. Niranda picks up the bottle of wine and looks at the label.

"Good to see you're drinking local," she says. "Margaret River plonk."

"The store was all out of Mandurah wine."

"Thank God. Vile stuff."

"Would you like a glass?"

"Yes. Very much so."

There are two stools at the end of the kitchen counter. Niranda pulls one out and perches herself on it. There's a clatter as her kicked-off heels hit the floor.

"I hope you don't mind, my feet are killing me. Where's this vicious attack dog of yours?"

"Sleeping off his anger." Aphra pours the glass and slides it across to Niranda.

"Thanks. Cheers."

They clink glasses and sip. Aphra remains standing.

"I hear Blair fired you yesterday."

"She did."

"May I ask why?"

"Call it creative differences."

Niranda smiles. "That's neatly put. She went too far on TV. Word is she sent a whole swathe of emails last night, to journalists and reporters, going even further than the garbage she spouted on the news. Fortunately, the media hasn't dishonoured her by publishing any of it today. It'll come out at some point though."

"The party can just deny it all. Say she was acting outside the party's remit."

"You are clever, Aphra. I've always liked that about you. What are you planning to do with this cleverness, now that you're free?"

"I haven't really had the chance to think about it."

"That was a brave move, by the way, speaking to my nephew. He's a very sensitive boy."

"That had nothing to do with the party or work."

"I know. The violinist." Niranda sips, then adds, "Your close friend, so I hear."

"You certainly hear a lot, Niranda."

"People talk a lot. I listen."

"Look, we can dance around each other until the bottle's empty, or you can tell me why you're here."

"That's good. You're honest. Clear. I need this from you."

"For what?"

Niranda looks around a bit, then says, "It's a carefully guarded secret, for now, but I've been asked to replace Blair as head of the WAR Party. My first order of business will be changing the name to the WA Party."

"Smart."

"Not just because the acronym is terrible, but to change the direction of the party. Focus less on making the state a republic and more on making the state great again."

"That wording will need some work," Aphra says, smiling.

"See? You already know what's best for me. Of course, I want WA to be its own country, but that's further down the road. It will be an evolutionary step once the state gets on the right path."

"Make the state strong. Make the locals proud. Make them parochial. Get them to the point they're the ones who want the republic."

"Precisely. It's a popular movement, rather than something a leader, like Blair, tries to force on them. No doubt you know how resistant people here are to change. It has to be slow, and it has to seem like the people themselves are in charge of it."

"And in control."

"Which will need some very structured and targeted narratives."

"I'm getting rehired the day after I was fired?"

Niranda shakes her head. "You were let go by the WAR Party. You're going to be under contract with the WA Party. New agreement. New deal. New salary."

"Presumably higher."

"Much. And no more freelancing. This will be your sole focus. You'll also get a sizeable bonus when I'm elected premier."

Aphra grabs the bottle and tops up their glasses. "Sounds like we have something to celebrate," she says, easing herself onto a stool.

<>

On the sofa, Huntley stirs in his sleep. He rolls over and falls off the sofa, which shocks him awake. When he looks up, he sees Everest, glasses on, staring intently at the laptop screen.

"I give you five points for the dismount," she says.

"Out of what?"

"Ten. You slept gracefully, but didn't land that way."

"The Australian judge, always the hardest to impress." Huntley sits up. "Where's Henrikson?"

"I sent him to bed."

"What time is it? On the camera?"

"Nearly nine."

"I was out for two hours?" Huntley gets to his feet, using the sofa for leverage. "Did he tell you what we're looking for?"

"He did."

"And did he also tell you how we're getting to see this footage?"

Everest nods, keeping her eyes on the screen. "Reviewing the footage myself was on my ever-growing list of things to do. You two only expedited the process."

"Well, until today, we didn't know what vehicle we were looking for. Any coffee left?"

"I made a fresh pot. I'm on my third cup."

In the kitchen, Huntley rinses the cup he used earlier and pours himself a coffee. "Can I refresh you?"

"I'm good. Thanks."

"May I say, you look even more rock'n'roll with your hair down and wearing glasses."

"Like Buddy Holly?"

"Nah. More like Janis Joplin. Big rose-tinted, circular glasses. Like the tops of snare drums."

"I'll take that."

Huntley has black coffee this time. He sits at the desk, next to Everest. They both sip, looking at the screen. Predictably, there's a lot less traffic at this time of night.

"Where are the notebooks?" Huntley asks.

Everest tilts her head towards the closed bedroom door, where there's a slither of light under the door. "He took them to bed."

"Nightmare fuel. Anything come to you next door?"

"No. That kind of thing isn't in my skillset."

"I suggest you take some creative writing classes."

"How will that help?"

"You'll start to see stories, which would help with envisioning crimes. The downside is that you start to see stories everywhere and you can't turn it off."

"That's fiction. I work with facts."

"Did you get any facts interrogating Purvis?" Huntley asks.

"There was no interrogation. His case was moved. To Narcotics. And Justin moved with it."

"Moved or promoted?"

"I don't care."

Huntley sips his coffee and grimaces. "Fucking nepotism. Perth would be lost without it."

"When it's done here, it's networking."

"Doors open left, right and centre for my ex-wife, and ex-sister-in-law. They basically earn a monthly salary on the strength of the Gifford name alone, and always have."

"Your daughter will get that too."

"Already. She wouldn't have been accepted into Methodist otherwise."

Everest laughs a little.

"What?" Huntley asks.

"Oh, you know, I find it fascinating, and funny, that I can love this place as much as I hate it."

"Go on. There's more to it than your partner getting a leg up."

"There is. I'm very proud to say I earned my way into Perth College, but I was surrounded by the daughters of privilege. That's how Salty Lemonade started. The four of us were part of a very small group all there on scholarships. We had come from different schools and didn't know anyone. So we got to know each other. We were outsiders too, at PC. Wearing our uniforms on stage was meant as a royal fuck you to the private school system."

"I thought that was just a gimmick. Like Angus Young dressing as a schoolboy."

"Nuh. Chrissy Amphlett was our hero. Deborah Harry. Patti Smith. Courtney Love. We set out to be the punks of Perth College. I'm guessing Methodist is similar, in terms of tiers and hierarchy. At PC, you can forget about grades and years. The school was defined by class. There were four levels, and there probably still are. At the top, you have the celeb-daughters, from wealthy and prominent families. Real snobs, and nasty too. Walking around like they own the place. Then you've got the boarders, also rich and daughters of former students, coming in from country towns. Something that was still kind of new when I was there was the third class. The fresh money. Families paying top dollar to get their daughters into a school they could never have imagined going to. At the bottom of the heap were the scholarship girls, the ones smart enough to have earned a good education."

"Excellent training for life, this microcosm of the world we live in."

"I think it was worse. I really hope it's more progressive now, and they've got the bullying under control. But when I was there, finding a husband and marrying well were the top priorities."

"Sounds like a century ago. But, I will say that Verity absolutely hates etiquette class. It's rejigged under a different title, but it's all about which fork is for fish and which glass is for white wine, and how to laugh politely and all that."

"They probably get made to walk around balancing books on their heads."

"Yeah. She's complained about that. But Salty Lemonade. You guys fucking rocked."

A week ago, Everest would have been quick to steer the conversation, and her thoughts, away from the band and Charlene, but now she finds herself wanting to talk with Huntley about her. To confide and share. She's about to tell him the truth when on the screen a van stops at the traffic light, waiting to turn onto Leake Street.

"That's him," she says, pointing to the license plate IRVAN.

"It is."

Everest's fingers are poised over the keyboard. "How do I make this stop?"

"Henrikson," Huntley calls out. "He must be asleep."

Everest and Huntley lean towards the screen, their heads almost touching, trying to see who's driving the van.

"Is it him behind the wheel?" Everest asks.

"I can't tell. Note the time. Quarter past nine. Maybe the actual footage is better quality."

"I'll check it later. I bet there's footage of him turning back onto Stirling Highway as well."

"Which would place him at the scene."

"If we can't see who it is, at least it places his van in the area."

"Is that enough?"

"Depends on how he responds."

On the screen, the van turns and drives out of the shot.

"He'll need some kind of story," Huntley says. "You could play it coy. Just say you have footage of him on Stirling Highway on the night of the murder. Let him fill in the rest of it. He might realise he's done and fess up. If he asks, you can show him this footage."

"It's an idea. Importantly, it should be enough evidence to keep him locked up for now."

"Unless he's already been released."

"I need to get this done." Everest stands up. "Thanks for this. Really good initiative."

"You need to thank Henrikson."

"I don't think I'll do that, considering how he got this footage."

"Understood. Get this guy, detective. I want to see him put away. Aphra does too. And somewhere, the violinist wants to see this fucker fry. Aphra said Ekaterina was a scholarship girl. Like you. She earned everything she got."

"She didn't earn the ending she got."

"No. She didn't."

"But that's motivating. Thanks, Quin."

"Hey, first name. I'm honoured. What shall I call you?"

Everest takes off her glasses and sets her hair in a ponytail. "Ellie."

The Problem with Rats

He's leaving, scurrying away
Tail between legs
Goodbye, sinking ship
Escaping the lab
Out of the race
Wet and armed with
Suitcases full of cheese
Abandoning the pack
Self-made, now mature

So, scurry on
Succumb to the thing
The dangerous yearning
That gnawed at him
And gnawed at him
And gnawed at him
That others saw in him
Live now in extremus
Rattus norvegicus

Still foggy with sleep, Everest arrives at the Winslow Properties office in Cockburn and knocks on the glass door. The cleaner, who's surprisingly young and cutting a nice figure in her blue smock, opens it.

"Are you Detective Everest?" she asks in accented English.

"I am. Where is he?"

The cleaner points. "End of the hallway. He was there all night. Tied up."

"Did you touch him?"

"I'm sorry to call so early."

"You said on the phone he was poisoned."

With a shrug, the cleaner says, "I think so. He was asleep. I couldn't wake him."

"Does he smell?"

"Yes. I think he," the cleaner makes a downward pushing motion with her hands, "did himself. In his pants."

"Is there anyone else here?"

"Just me. I tried calling Mr Winslow. No answer. Then I called Shandorah, also no answer."

"Maybe they're all getting ready for work. Or they're driving here. Who's Shandorah again?"

The cleaner points at the front counter. "Receptionist. I found your card on her desk. She ... isn't very nice."

"Maybe she dreamt of bigger things than answering the phones in here."

"Yes." It appears the cleaner also dreamt of bigger things than cleaning up after the Shandorahs of the world. "Maybe."

"I didn't mean ..."

"It's okay. Everyone does the best they can."

Everest nods, then moves down the hall. When she gets halfway, she hears a vacuum cleaner start whirring.

The office at the end of the hall has Gary Lawrence written on a small nameplate on the almost closed door. Everest puts some plastic gloves on and edges the door open. The smell in the small office is rank. There is a single window, high up near the ceiling, prison-cell style, and Everest flips the lever to tilt it open. With the neck of her shirt over her nose, she starts to inspect the scene. Lawrence is tied to a chair with a white extension cable, in improvised fashion. His head is hanging slightly forward and there's a strip of grey tape over his mouth. His breathing is laboured, his nose whistling and squeaking. Like the cleaner, he's surprisingly young, perhaps not long out of university. His white shirt sleeves are rolled up, his tie undone, hinting at a late night of work, while his colourful suspenders seem incongruous enough with the rest of his look to be somehow quirky and daring. On the desk, which has all the accoutrements of old-fashioned bookkeeping, including thick ledgers and a big calculator with a roll of paper in it, is a bottle of champagne, almost empty. The one glass next to it is also empty, but has a pale, sandy film at the bottom and around the rim.

Drugged, she thinks, by the champagne. It's so obvious, it's almost too easy, and too neat, in this week full of creatively administered exotic toxins. Wild arum, jimsonweed and sweet oleander, plus hemlock, which she found out last night, having bribed the pathologist $200, was in the Santorini Sunset tea she lifted from Blair Blake-Stendahl's kitchen; though the pathologist wouldn't say if hemlock was the cause of death, and would only divulge the information if Everest ponied up another $200 and agreed to buy him dinner, which she politely declined.

She gently removes the tape from the accountant's mouth. He immediately starts to mouth-breathe, but remains asleep. She checks his pulse. It's strong.

She has no idea who's done this, and doesn't really want to get involved. It couldn't have been Purvis Irving, as she spent much of the night with him, listening to him spin a variety of stories about Sunday drives in vans, and how it couldn't possibly have been him in the Peppermint Grove street-level footage, which was too blurred and shadowed to be conclusive. Irving finally settled on the story of his van being stolen on Sunday evening and kindly returned to him by the thief, who even parked it outside his house, which was beyond ridiculous and which even Irving found amusing.

Back down the hall, Everest sees that Shandorah has arrived.

"Can you call an ambulance please?" Everest asks.

Shandorah picks up the phone. "Is Gary okay?"

"He should be fine. Looks like sleeping tablets."

"I can't believe he tried to kill himself. Here. In our office. Just when business is absolutely booming."

"Where's Nathaniel Winslow?"

"He hasn't arrived yet." Shandorah is holding the phone, but still hasn't dialled. "He's normally first here. So dedicated."

"Is he at a meeting, offsite somewhere?"

Shandorah slowly shakes her head. "Not that I know of. He was out all day yesterday."

"Can I wait in his office?"

Thumbing towards the hallway, the receptionist says, "Go ahead."

Everest edges towards Winslow's office, which has no name on the door, but is clearly the largest office. The door is closed, but not locked. Once inside, the scene tells the entire story: the flung open wall safe, and everything else left exactly where it is. The Southern Everglades, an elaborate scam.

"He's gone," she says to herself, with a smidgen of admiration.

<>

Huntley lies in bed, hands behind his head, listening to the hum of cars on Stirling Highway, a sound he's grown to find soothing over the years. The caravan's loft doesn't have much headroom, which is why his father fixed a holder to the ceiling to put an e-reader in, so he could just lie and read.

Huntley misses his old man.

The holder is still there, but he has no idea where the e-reader is. It's in the caravan somewhere, or he gave it to Orville. Maybe he broke it in a hot toddy daze. He can't remember.

There's far too much about the last decade that he can't remember.

"A horrid dream," he says to himself. "But I'm awake now."

He moves the blankets aside and shimmies forward, far enough for his legs to dangle over the edge and he can drop down. He splashes water on his face from the kitchen sink and runs a comb through his matted hair. He needs a shave, the flecks of grey in his beard making him look old, but he can't be bothered. He pulls on fresh clothes, then starts piling his dirty clothes into a white laundry basket. There's enough to warrant a trip to the laundromat, so he opens the door to take the basket outside. Sitting in one of the fold-out chairs, drinking coffee from a fancy disposable cup, is Aphra.

"Good morning," she says brightly.

"Morning. This is a ..."

"Surprise?"

"A welcome one. I thought yesterday maybe you'd crossed me off for good. Blacklisted me. Because of this editor business."

Aphra looks at the basket. "Having a domestic day?"

Huntley places the basket on the ground. "What brings you here, so bright and early?"

"I woke up at dawn with the realisation that if I'd stayed at the Mangy Mongrel on Monday night to hear Purvis read, he could well have read out the poem he wrote after killing Katie."

"Would he really have read that one, to a room full of people?"

"I could've nabbed him right there. Maybe Lance would still be alive."

"If we're rolling with this conjecture, then Blair as well."

"Yes. Blair as well."

Huntley laughs.

"What's so funny?"

"You don't sound terribly disappointed that Blair has passed from this mortal coil."

"Of course, I'm sad about someone dying. But, it's possibly a blessing in disguise."

"For who?"

"For three-quarters of the electorate."

"It still doesn't explain why you're here."

"I normally go to the beach in the morning," Aphra says. "I'm working at changing my schedule. The less you stick to a routine, the harder it is for people to follow you."

"Are you worried Purvis has unfinished business with you?"

"Has he been released?"

Huntley shrugs. "No idea. I hope not."

Aphra sips, looking at him. "I get the feeling you have some idea."

"Ellie, Detective Everest, was looking into something rather compelling last night. I don't know how far she got with it."

"You don't have to tell me if you don't want to. It doesn't matter. He'll get released."

"Even if he does, I imagine he'll lay low. He won't do anything to bring attention to himself. There are too many eyes on him now."

"He doesn't scare me. I've handled guys like him before."

"He should be behind bars."

"Life doesn't always work out like you need it to."

Huntley finds it interesting Aphra said "need" rather than "want".

He says, "Lydette is sure to come bulldozing in at some point. No doubt she'll have a plan to profit from all this. Not with these poems, but with something else. Turn Purvis into some kind of bad-boy poet. Spin a story of how cutting-edge he is, pushing the envelope and being so daringly modern and all that garbage. You know what I mean. You could do this better than me."

"As a muckraker or a mudslinger?"

"As a storyteller. You have that gift. Or do you have something new to focus on?"

"I'll tell you mine if you tell me yours."

"What makes you think I have anything good to share?"

Aphra sips, then says, "Your ears are almost coming off your head, like a dog on alert."

"Very sharp. Give me the rest of your coffee, and it might loosen my tongue."

"How is that a fair trade?"

"I'm in need of caffeine, and my brother hasn't shown up this morning, like he usually does."

"Brother? He lives here too?"

"Half-brother, to be exact." Huntley points towards the security office. "He works here. Sometimes, he waddles over to my van with his thermos. But not this morning."

"Waddles? That's brutal."

"Said with undying love and total affection."

Aphra hands Huntley her coffee. "I find myself very interested in your family background, to know how you became who you are. So unpredictable, yet weirdly reliable."

"The best thing to do is to come with me next weekend to Ravensthorpe, for the reunion. You can meet the whole clan."

"Are you asking me on a date?"

"It's the kind of anti-routine move that will throw Purvis right off your scent. You can go country, with me and Verity. Every year, we have a reunion at the commune. It's a big party. All weekend. It's fun."

"Maybe we should establish some trust first, through sharing."

Huntley sips. "Oh, very good. Yes. Trust. Verity likes you."

"I like her. She's a bit annoying though."

"I think that's the SOP of every 13-year-old."

Aphra laughs. "I was hellish at that age."

"Well, let me be the first to say you haven't changed at all." Huntley smiles as Aphra slaps him on the shoulder. "It's a good thing. A way to stay young at heart. You can always behave like a hellish 13-year-old around me."

"Stop it," Aphra says, grinning. "I think it's a shame you don't have a proper place where Verity can spend more time with you. She clearly adores you."

"Yeah?" Huntley is touched by this. "This was my father's caravan. I love it. Verity loves it too, even if she won't admit it. Besides, any place I get will be nothing compared to the Gifford castle."

"This reunion. Is it just to see everyone? Or does it have a deeper purpose?"

"Why do you ask that?"

"The storytelling thing. I'm assuming there's a story behind the reunion."

"Well, you're right. Yeah, it has meaning, even if we never talk about it. My father started it the year after I left to come up here for uni. I thought then it was just about getting me home to visit, but it evolved into something more purposeful."

"What? Come on. Let's build trust."

Huntley finishes the coffee, then says, "We all hoped, still hope, that our mother might show up for it."

"Was she never around?"

"That's a whole other story for a whole other time. I'll just say that me and my siblings all share the same mother, but none of us really know her. She rocked up at the commune, pregnant each time, had the baby, and left. My father took care of all of them."

"What a good man."

"A really good man."

"Is he still around?"

"His caravan is, so that's why I can be precious about it. I leave next Friday for Ravensthorpe. There's room in the Landy for you. The distance is too much for your mo-ped."

"Don't you mock my wheels. Where is your car anyway?"

"In Freo, decorated with a collage of fresh parking tickets, I'm sure."

"I've never been to Ravensthorpe."

"It's a total bucket-list place. Right up there with Florence and Berlin and Niagara and the pyramids. Have to see it before you die."

Aphra laughs again. Huntley thinks she has a beautiful laugh, sweet and musical, and rarely shared. A laugh that's a gift.

"But back to this trust thing," he continues. "The compelling stuff Everest has is footage of Purvis Irving's van turning towards your friend's apartment on the night she was killed."

This makes Aphra sit up straight. "That's it. They've got him."

"Slow down. They've got the van, but not necessarily him driving it. Given he's full-on denying everything, he'll find a way to deny that too. Say he lent his van to a mate, or something like that. All that we have is circumstantial so far. Nothing really concrete to nail him with."

"What about the drugs?"

"He's wheedled his way out of that too, according to Ellie. Something about medicinal purposes. Not enough to convict him. Booth has been moved into the drug division. The deals have been done. Purvis will walk."

"Are you implying that Justin's corrupt? He seems too placid for that. And I have to say, too nice."

"His dad's high up in the cop shop, so likely it runs in the family. Again, circumstantial. A sketchy plot outline. That's all I have. Your turn."

Aphra, quietly glad Purvis might be let out, so she can make him her project, says, "Niranda Stone is going to take Blair's place."

"Hah. Surprising, yet not really. How do you know that?"

"I got it from the mare herself."

"Did she kick you with her hind legs?" Huntley looks at Aphra, and gets it. "Ah, bloody hell. She's hauled you in. This is why you can afford expensive coffees. Are you seriously going to help her take power?"

"I don't know what history you have with her, but I think she's a better alternative to Blair. The whole republic thing will be toned down."

"No more war? Probably a good thing."

"There certainly won't be the racist overtones that Blair was so fond of."

"Undertones instead?"

"Niranda will be good for this state, if only for us to finally have another woman in charge. She'll be the next premier."

"With your help."

"I'm excited by the challenge," Aphra says.

"Spoken like a true politician. Tread carefully with her. She may be a Stone on the outside, but chisel through that and you'll find a Ford-Brackman underneath. She'll use that hyphen as a dagger at some point. They're people not to be messed with."

"Noted. This feels good. Sharing. I much prefer that we're honest with each other rather than sparring all the time."

"Agreed."

They're both quiet for a while, the hum of cars filling the silence. Then Huntley says, "I'm missing something. It was him. The van. The fountain pen collection. The greenhouse. The confession up in the tree. The poems. It's all there. How is it not enough?"

"Stop obsessing. It's unhealthy."

"He put my book in the violin case. I'm the one he wants. All along, it was me. What will he do if I pull out? Or, how will he react if I tell him the poetry's no good?"

"That would be a really stupid move."

"This is the mistake he's making," Huntley says, energised by this train of thought and pacing around a little. "Do you see? He's so deluded, this is the ending he hasn't planned on. This is the twist. Me, not playing my role. The story's supposed to be about him and how he changes, from nobody poet to lauded man of literature. The rest of us are just bit players, helping to drive his plot forward. He's the one who changes. We all stay the same."

"I've changed."

"Have you? You started the week as a speechwriter for a politician, and you're still that. Even losing your friend hasn't really changed you."

"I miss her. And it hurts."

"Yes. Of course. Sorry."

"What are you getting at?"

"We have to stop him from changing. We have to keep him as a nobody poet. As a small-time pusher of drugs and habitual predator."

"By telling him his poetry is rubbish?"

Huntley snaps his fingers. "Exactly. I mean, it is rubbish. Not only that, I tell him that he's rubbish. He's nothing and won't ever be anything. I provoke him and reject him the way Ekaterina did. That's what this is. He's been stalking me, all this time. We need to get him to reveal his true, unchanged self."

"How?"

"Through a grand gesture, a confrontation." He points at the Vespa. "Can we both get on that thing?"

"Never tried it with two. Do you have a helmet?"

"Does a hard-hat count? I'm sure Orv's got one in his office."

"Better than nothing. Where do you want to go?"

"Where do you think? Success."

"Assuming he's already been let out."

Huntley grabs the flag of Italy helmet and tosses it to Aphra. "Call Ellie and check."

"You and the detective are getting pretty close. Has that gone beyond professional?"

"Don't be jealous. I'm a fan."

"I'm not jealous. What are you a fan of? Her police work? It's ordinary, at best."

"She's hogtied by the people she works with. I'm a fan of her band. Salty Lemonade. She was the drummer."

"No way. That's her? I saw them with my mum. I think I was nine."

"Call her. Find out if Purvis is still being held. Just in the interest of your own safety. We don't want her knowing we're going there. If we all rock up together, it'll look suspicious. But with just you and me, it's about the poetry."

"And the stalking," Aphra says, taking out her phone.

"That too."

Huntley starts jogging towards the security office.

<>

Kwinana Freeway, southbound, is relatively bare. On the other side, direction downtown, the cars creep forward like they're being pushed from behind. Even when Booth reaches

Beeliar Drive and turns off, the northbound side is still gridlocked, and extends as far south as Booth can see.

"Awful," he says.

Purvis, his sneakers perched on the generous dashboard of Booth's off-roader, says, "If you're going to drive during peak hour, that's what you get."

"Put your feet down."

"No."

Booth grits his teeth, his grip on the steering wheel tightening.

"Go left down there." Purvis points. "That's Branch Circus."

"I'm tempted to let you out here and make you walk."

"Bad idea. You're part of the team now. We're almost family."

Booth seethes as he stops at the gate of the Irving house. "I'm not happy about this."

"Be happy you're still alive. That was a massively stupid move, trying to take on my mum like that. She could've blown you to bits and buried you in the backyard."

"You make it sound like she's done that before."

"Consider yourself lucky."

"I had it under control." Booth turns the engine off. "I didn't know what you're up to."

"Now you do, and now your pockets are lined with drug money. Trust me. It's the best kind of money there is. It's like, free money. The kind you win from lotto, or at the casino. A gift."

"You can't be selling vapes to school kids. That's wrong."

"Lance was behind the vapes and that's the market he aimed at. It's huge, by the way. I only supplied the product for him. I can just as easily go back to selling it online."

"The dark web?"

"Justin, you can sell this stuff on eBay. Interior plants that can improve your personal health and well-being. Something like that. People know what you're talking about if you word it right."

"That's bullshit."

"Time to get up to speed," Purvis says brightly. "You're working Narcotics now. There's some new deal I've heard about. People buying craft beer online, but it's actually a front for selling meth. Of course, you didn't hear that from me."

"Are the Ford-Brackmans involved?"

"Ha. Look at you. Super keen to make your first big bust, with some clandestine help. If I tell you this, be warned, it'll dig you deeper in debt with us."

"You got a name?"

"Only the beer."

"What is it?"

Purvis takes his sneakers down from the dashboard, leaving dirty scuff marks. "Are you sure you want to do this?"

"Say the name and get the fuck out of my car."

"Watch your tone, mate. You don't get to talk to me like that." Purvis opens the passenger door.

"Wait." Booth takes a deep breath. "I'm sorry."

"Not good enough. You need to apologise for that apology. No feeling whatsoever. How about this? I'll give you the name, and you can give me that money back."

"What kind of deal is that?"

"A very good one, if you crack that case and become a star in your first week in Narcotics. Think of what it'll mean for your career. How proud your dad will be."

"I don't need his approval. I can find out the name myself."

"You're not that clever," Purvis says. "Don't ever try to out-captain the captain."

"What do you want from me?"

"Nothing. I'm just having fun with you. It's way too easy, mate. Look. Keep the money. But know that when I need something, you better be ready to come running."

"I'm not your servant."

Purvis gets out of the car. "You are now. Belykrysa."

"What?"

"That's the name you want."

"Is that a family?"

"It's the craft beer. It's Russian."

As Purvis shuts the door and goes to the gate, Booth takes out his phone and calls his father.

<>

Huntley jumps off the Vespa before Aphra has brought it to a complete stop. He yanks off the bicycle helmet, which was all he could find in Orville's office, and just manages to keep from hurling it over the fence into the Beeliar bushland.

Aphra takes off her helmet and slings the straps over the handlebars. "All right?"

"That Italian thing was killing me. Like trying to balance myself on a moving stack of books."

"I told you to hold on to me. Gripping the rails is useless. It puts too much weight on the back."

Huntley rubs his lower back. "I didn't think that would be proper. I was trying to be a gentleman."

"We could've stopped at Freo on the way, to get your car, but you shouted at me to keep going."

"Time is of the essence. I've got classes later."

Aphra gets off the Vespa. "I'm amazed you can even think about teaching with all this going on."

"Currently, it's my only gainful employment. Have you got your phone ready?"

"Do you really think this will work?"

"I'm betting on Purvis being vain and delicate enough to not handle criticism."

"Takes one to know one?"

"Easy. I'm not like that. The harshest critic has always been myself, but I'm working on that."

"Get a job in politics. It'll make you immune to criticism." Aphra taps at her phone, then puts it in the pocket of her jacket. "What makes you think he's vain?"

"Most chasers are. You'd think your basic stalker would have major insecurity issues, but the opposite's true."

"No, it isn't."

"Hear me out. Giorgie, my ex-wife. Stop-traffic beautiful when we met, and even more beautiful now, if you can believe that. She told me at the start that men have always followed her around. I said then it must be because they have such a low opinion of themselves. But she said it was the other way. They had high opinions of themselves and ridiculously inflated egos. The problem being that they couldn't handle it, or even understand it, when someone isn't interested in them. So, they keep forcing themselves onto their target, because with each rejection, their vanity takes a hit."

"Interesting. I've just recorded that. Detective Everest will hear everything. You're officially on the record."

"Good. Then take this as well. When I had Giorgie on my arm and we were at some event or party or whatever, I felt like I'd have to fight all the men outside in the carpark. Because me being there didn't stop these pricks from hunting her. Let that be a message to vain men everywhere, on this recording, to back the fuck off and change themselves into humble gentlemen. You ready?"

"No."

"I thought he didn't scare you. I'll be honest. A house like this normally scares the bejesus out of me. But we're in this together, and we're just here to talk poetry."

"Okay."

Huntley takes out the stack of notebooks strung together. "Let's keep the focus on this. Don't let him rattle you."

"What's my role?"

"You're Aphra Massey, award-winning poet, brought on board as a consultant, by me, lead editor."

Aphra nods.

"Don't worry," Huntley continues. "I'm certain you can do this. Look at what you did to Jay Palmer."

"How do you know about that?"

"Verity told me, after you told her. Watch out what you reveal to a teenage girl. I kind of knew it anyway."

"That was meant as a warning. For her to be careful, and cautious. Plenty of guys out there aren't to be trusted, no matter how charming they might seem."

"I've had that conversation with her, but no harm in having her hear it from you as well. Thanks for that."

Huntley pushes the gate open and they walk towards the front door.

"I'm glad you reminded me of him. I've forgotten how exciting this stuff is."

"Were you planning to make Purvis your new Jay?"

"Only if it came to that. It's worrying how calm you seem."

"I hate the suburbs, but after the ride here, everything seems tame by comparison."

They reach the door. Huntley knocks gently.

"Do you think he's even here?" Aphra asks.

"If Ellie says he's been released, I believe her. Where else would he go? This is his ... oh, boy ... his country."

The door is opened by an old woman in a dressing gown and slippers.

"Mrs Irving?"

"What do you want? You're not God people, are you?"

"No, no. I'm Quintus Huntley. I've taken on the task of editing your son's book." Huntley smiles and holds up the notebooks as proof. Then he points at Aphra and adds, "This is Aphra Massey. She'll be helping with the project. Always beneficial to have another set of eyes. We're here to talk to Purvis about the next steps."

"Call me Wendy." She smiles and steps aside to allow them both in. "I'm very impressed, to have the man behind that Ravensthorpe lark and the girl who wrote about killing a rapist both here to help my son."

"Lark?"

"Wonderful," Aphra says. "You're familiar with our work."

"I thought his was okay," Wendy says as Huntley and Aphra enter. "But he tried too hard to be clever. He was showing off too much."

"Showing off? I barely knew what I was doing."

Wendy closes the door and looks at Aphra. "But yours was brilliant. So visceral. I could only read it during the day. If I read it before bed, I had dreams of killing that boy myself."

"Not such a bad thing," Aphra says.

Wendy cackles. "I like you."

As the three of them go deeper into the house, Wendy adds, "It's fabulous you're on Purvis's team. I guess that's what happens when you don't produce more work of your own."

"What happens?" Huntley asks.

"You help the next generation."

"Well, writing can be ..."

"That's right," Aphra interjects. "We're honoured to work with your son and we both find it very rewarding to help new voices get heard."

"That's the spirit. Come on in. Purvis just got home from some business in the city. He's in the shower."

Huntley and Aphra follow Wendy through the very orderly house and into the very orderly kitchen.

"Would you like some tea? It's all-natural, grown here."

"Ah," Huntley says. "I think I'm good. Thank you."

"Me too," Aphra says. "I just had breakfast."

"Don't mind me if I water myself." Wendy puts the kettle on. "Please, sit down."

As they both sit, Huntley puts the stack of notebooks on the table.

"So, that's it? Purvis is normally very guarded about his work. Out there in his van for days at a time, never letting me see any of it."

"He probably wants to get it right," Huntley says. "Poetry is a challenging thing. Doubt can be ... problematic."

"What do you mean?"

Huntley clears his throat. "Well, he's written this stuff, and he's very excited about it, but if someone was to express some, uh, misgivings, this could create some doubt in his mind and get him second-guessing everything."

Wendy draws her dressing gown around her and folds her arms. "Is that what happened to you?"

The way the old woman looks at him, in such a caring fashion, makes him want to tell her everything, then have her hug him for a long time.

"Not just him," Aphra says. "It's the kind of thing that happens to many writers."

"Let's hope my boy is spared. I think he's good enough to rise above it."

"I'm certain Purvis knows the demands of the profession."

"But," Huntley says, tapping the top of the notebook stack, "there's always room for improvement. A first draft is normally very rough. Too rough. It needs a lot of revising and polishing."

"First draft?" Purvis stands in the kitchen doorway, in a t-shirt and shorts, his hair still wet. "What's wrong with a first draft? Kerouac wrote *On the Road* in one hit, didn't he? On one long roll of paper."

"That's a great example," Huntley says, turning to Purvis. "It would've benefited no end from a rewrite. It's littered with mistakes and inconsistencies."

The kettle boils. Wendy starts making tea, setting up cups for all of them.

"I don't know," Purvis says. "I never read it. The bent generation was shit."

"Beat generation," Aphra says.

"Whatever." Purvis sits at the table, taking the chair next to Aphra and moving it close to her. "I'm really happy to see you, Aphra."

"We're here to discuss your book," Huntley says.

"What about it?"

Aphra leans back in her chair, putting as much distance as she can between herself and Purvis. "Mrs Irving, perhaps it's better we do this in private. We wouldn't want to ruin the experience for you when you read the final collection."

"Understandable." She takes one of the cups. "If you need me, I'll be in the greenhouse."

"Don't over-water anything," Purvis says. "Keep to the schedule." When she's gone, he adds, "She has the bad habit of watering too much. Every plant has specific hydration needs. You have to get it right."

"A bit like with people," Huntley says.

"No. Plants are more advanced. People consume just any old thing, whenever they want. Plants need far more attention and care. They need balance."

"How thirsty is wild arum? What does that plant like?"

"What kind of question is that?"

"It's poetry-related," Aphra says. "The kind of detail that's missing from your work."

"Don't you worry your pretty head about that. Everything is in there that needs to be in there."

"She makes a good point, Purvis," Huntley says, feeling the tension level rising in the kitchen. "Don't get me wrong. You write well. You compose well."

Purvis stares blankly at Huntley. "But."

Huntley decides to stop wasting time and go for it. "You need to take another run at it. It's missing authenticity. We talked about this, up in the tree. The importance of lived experience, transferring that to the page. I'm not getting it from this. I'm not there. It feels made up. I'm not in the room, holding the fountain pen. It's all too superficial."

"Superficial? Is that a joke?"

The smarmy look on Purvis's ratty face makes Huntley wonder if Purvis knows what they're doing. He decides to take a more empathetic track.

"Let me tell you how it was for me."

"In Ravensthorpe?"

"Yeah. I'm not ashamed to say this. My book, and what I did back then to get the material, it was all about impressing a girl. Sure, my father was already hatching plans to steal a ram lamb and I helped him do it. Man, that was fun. What I didn't know was how inspired that would make me. The combination of crime and passion. I think you know how that feels. The verse that came out of me was meant to win this girl and hopefully win her forever."

"But you failed. You didn't win her forever."

"Inspiration, like love, can wear off. You can try to find it again, but I guess my relationship with that girl peaked during that time in Ravensthorpe. Perhaps even more honestly, I peaked at that time. Which is why I did a few nasty things to ensure the families continued feuding with each other, to keep the inspiration going. That version of me, the good and bad parts, was something I never thought I'd be. It sounds vain, but I really loved myself back then. Who am I kidding? I was vain and I got complacent, and that's the worst thing a writer can be. There is always a way to make the work better."

"What are you trying to say? You're really babbling. You want me to write it all again, and put in more details?"

"A second draft, typed, would be the first step. But you also need to make some hard decisions." Huntley leans forward, across the table, trying to get closer to Purvis and make him feel they're in this together. "Look, no one reads poetry anymore. Hell, people don't really read books anymore. If you want to grab readers, and maybe even get thousands of people reading poetry again, you've got to give them an experience that they can't have anywhere else. You've got to put the reader into the story. Transport them there, living this."

"Give me an example."

Aphra holds up a hand to Huntley. "Maybe I can help. You're using the third person singular, and in a work like this, it comes across as cowardly. You need to be brave. If you don't write in the first person, readers will dismiss you as weak. And with it, they'll think your imagination is weak."

"I'm not a coward."

"Then take the hard line," Aphra continues, glad she's hit him where it hurts. "There's too much distance, the way it is now. It's not intimate. It falls flat."

"I disagree. It's powerful as it is. If I change it to 'I filled the pen with poison and I jammed that pen into her neck,' how does that make it any better?"

Huntley sits back. "I think you just answered your own question. Listen to those lines. They land so much harder. Each one like a knife to the heart. Or a pen to the neck, so to speak. The reader needs to be convinced they're getting a first-hand account. That the narrator did poison that girl."

"Well, I did, so I fucking know what I'm talking about. If you want details, I can give you all the details." Purvis reaches across the table and picks up the stack of notebooks. "This is my opus. It will go down in history as one of the greatest works of poetry ever written."

Huntley struggles to keep himself from smiling. "So, take the risk and make it even better. Make it even more memorable."

"For art's sake," Aphra adds. "Every poet should commit to making their work better."

Purvis nods at her. "For you, I'll do it. Leave it with me. I'll experiment with the point of view and add more gory details. Really dig into it. Get gritty."

"The emotion is just as important as the violence," Aphra says. "Perhaps more so. How it all feels."

Huntley decides to amp it up. "Look, Purvis. This is far better than anything I've done. And the incredible thing is, it can be even better. It takes courage to reach inside yourself and go to places you might not want to go."

"Yeah. Okay. Definitely. I'm all over it. The water bottle. The flower salad. The Greek tea. I can give you everything. I know it, because I was there."

"Tremendous," Huntley says. "It's the hallmark of a great writer that they're open to feedback and willing to do the hard yards to improve their work. We just want to see the best book published. You can be sure your secrets will be safe with us. I'll ask Lydette to draw up an NDA."

Aphra's eyes go wide. Huntley feels cold metal at the base of his skull.

"Those secrets will be safe all right," Wendy says. "Nothing keeps a secret better than a corpse."

Across from him, Aphra raises her hands, and Huntley does the same. His hands shake a little.

"I don't know what's going on here," Huntley says. "We're just here about the poetry."

"Mum, what are you doing? They're on my side. Put the rifle down. He's my editor and she's the girl I'm going to marry."

Huntley thinks that last part scares Aphra more than the rifle. "We're all about the book," he says. "Let's not escalate things. I say that selfishly, because this book will also get our careers going again. We need it just as much as he does. We wouldn't do anything to jeopardise that."

"I don't believe you," Wendy says.

"Mum, don't ruin this for me. I worked too hard to get to this point. Let me have this. I trust both of them."

"Empty your pockets." Wendy pushes the barrel against Huntley's head. "Phones. On the table."

"Is that really necessary?" Huntley asks.

"Do it. Slowly."

"We don't have any weapons," Aphra says.

"Words are weapons." Wendy moves into the kitchen, rifle still raised at Huntley. "The truth is a weapon. Promises are weapons. And trust is the most dangerous weapon of them all. Now, empty your pockets."

"Mum, I trust them. Really, I do."

"You shouldn't. They can earn my trust by putting everything on the table. I didn't raise you to be a killer, Purvis."

"It's just poetry," Purvis says. "None of it's real."

Huntley nods at Aphra. She takes out her phone and places it face down on the table.

"Where's your phone?" Wendy asks.

"Not on me," Huntley says. "I left it in the caravan. I'm always forgetting it."

"Caravan?" Purvis looks confused. "You live in a caravan, Q? You're not mega-rich?"

"There's no money in poetry, mate," Huntley says. "I would've thought you knew that. And definitely no money if your editor gets killed by the writer's mother, as poetic as that sounds."

Wendy points the rifle at Aphra. "Turn that phone over, girlie."

"Mum, don't point the gun at her. That's my girlfriend."

"I'm not your girlfriend." Aphra reaches forward and flips the phone, to show that not only is it recording, but it's recording a call between her and Everest.

"Oh, very smart," Huntley says.

Purvis jumps up from his chair. "No, no, no, no, no."

At that moment, the front door comes crashing down. Wendy turns and fires in that direction, causing Huntley to duck to the floor, hands on his ears, as the rifle was incredibly loud. Wendy moves towards the door, rifle raised to her shoulder. Another shot rings out, higher pitched than the rifle. Wendy falls backwards into the kitchen. Her head thumps against the floor and blood oozes from a hole in her forehead. Purvis screams. He leaps forward to get the rifle from the floor, but Huntley grabs his leg and pulls him to the floor, reaching an arm around his neck to try and put him in a headlock. They wrestle on the floor. Purvis bites Huntley on the hand, causing him to scream, before Aphra brings down a vase of exotic flowers on Purvis's still-wet head. The water and flowers spill all over Huntley, and Purvis collapses on top of him, unconscious.

"Thanks," Huntley says to Aphra.

Everest appears in the doorway, gun up, standing over Wendy. "You all right?"

"Tell me you got everything," Huntley says.

Everest lowers her gun. "We did."

Huntley tries to move out from under Purvis. "Get this piece of shit off me."

<>

Classes finished, Huntley drives from UWA to Doubleview as the sun is setting, the sky awash with colour and birds chattering in the trees. It's the kind of ludicrously glorious evening that Perth bungs on about once a week to quietly remind everyone that natural beauty is worth way more than any six-figure salary or riverside double-acre mansion, and they should all be grateful just to be living here.

He's buzzing, not from the morning's success, nabbing his first criminal, in Success, but from the afternoon's classes, which were the best they've ever been. So good, the students had to tell him the time was over and they wanted to leave. He'd forgotten how the creative energy of a classroom can be so uplifting.

He resolves to decline Giorgie's offer to join the Beeliar Arts Centre and instead throw himself into teaching at UWA; be so good they can't ignore him, and work his way out of the container and into the main Humanities building.

At Stockdale Crescent, he parks half on the verge and carries the bottles up the stairs.

There's not a breath of wind. The parakeets are making an absolute racket.

He knocks. The door is opened by Aphra.

"Yeah, Huntley. At last."

"Looks like I'm just in time."

"You're late," Aphra says, swaying a little.

"You're drunk."

"Ha-ha. We've been celebrating."

"With gusto."

"And you've brought more. Good man."

Huntley holds up his two bottles, like trophies. Red wine and rum. "You don't arrive at a celebration empty-handed."

"You have some catching up to do," Aphra says, stepping aside to let Huntley in, then accidentally slamming the door. "Oops. The champagne has flowed."

"Clearly."

From a short hallway, Huntley finds himself in the U-shaped kitchen, where Everest is stirring a pot on the stove, champagne glass in hand. With her pigtails and cut-off jeans shorts, she looks like a teenager.

"Quin. You made it." Everest raises her glass. "You clever bastard."

"What happened? Tell me everything."

"Relax, pumpkin. He's toast."

Huntley puts the bottles on the counter. "He confessed?"

"Of course he did. We found the plants in the greenhouse, not to mention piles of dope. But that's Booth's glory to enjoy. Now. Junior and senior. He's going away until he dies."

"Superb."

"We did it," Aphra says, a little too celebratory. She pours Huntley a glass of champagne, spilling it and finding it funny.

Huntley picks up the glass and clinks it with Aphra's and Everest's. "Well done."

They all drink.

"You were right," Aphra says. "To target his vanity."

"I don't know whether to call you brave or stupid," Everest adds.

"How about both?" Huntley asks. "Look, we had to do something. We couldn't let him get away with it." He turns to Aphra. "You can go back to your routines. Without Purvis bothering you."

Aphra waves him off. "Someone else will. Too many men don't know when to quit."

"Oh, tell me about it," Everest says. "So many guys hit on me at work, it's become a form of office small talk. I think they're running some kind of betting pool."

"That's wrong," Huntley says. "Tell them all to fuck off back to their caves."

"Or caravans?" Aphra adds.

"Hey, come on. I'm not like them. We've only just met, but surely you know that about me already."

"I'm just kidding."

"We can make that kind of joke because we know you're not like that," Everest says, trying not to slur her words.

"Well, thank you, I guess." Huntley sips the champagne, which is the good stuff, really fizzy, the bubbles can-canning on his tongue. "You both need to eat. You're showing all the signs of alcohol on an empty stomach."

"Are you an expert on that?" Aphra asks.

"What's for dinner, Ellie?"

"Soup, of some kind." Everest looks in the pot as she stirs it, not quite sure what she's seeing. "The kitchen is not the room where I shine. I bought a couple of cans of something. I think they were the same. The labels looked the same."

"I had to show her how to work the stove," Aphra says, and she and Everest laugh.

"I just needed reminding."

Huntley thinks the alcohol is nicely oiling the cogs of friendship between two women who struck him as solitary types when he first met them. He moves around the counter and sits at the end of the dining table, so he can watch the action in the kitchen on his left and enjoy the last of the sunset through the broad windows of the living room on his right. Everest and Aphra both take lusty drinks and stand next to each other at the stove, shoulders touching. Huntley wonders if they're flirting.

"Great spot here," he says. "Up on the hill. Your eagle's nest."

"This was my gran's," Everest says. "She moved in when it was first built. I inherited it."

"Hah. A little nepotism just for you. That means you can no longer complain about Booth."

"True. By the way, before I forget, Purvis is adamant that you have to edit his book. He'll send you the revisions. That's what he said."

"I'm not touching that thing. Lydette will find someone else. You can bet she's celebrating right now. More liberally than you two. She can go all-in on his criminal brand. The killer with words. The antihero with the poison pen. The bad-boy poet."

"So bad he's in jail for multiple murders."

"We've only got him for the violinist." Everest moves to the counter and leans against it. "He would be an accessory to Lance Ford-Brackman, but that went in the books as suicide. The councilwoman woke up, happier than before. Blair Blake-Stendahl was ruled natural causes, for PR reasons."

"I guess one will have to be enough," Huntley says. "But we know he did them all."

Behind Everest, the pot starts to bubble over.

"Hey, chef." Huntley points. "Your mystery soup's trying to escape."

Everest moves the pot off the stove, almost dropping it. "I'm terrible at multi-tasking. The only time I could do two things at once was with singing and drumming."

"I'm so amazed you were in Salty Lemonade," Aphra says, with groupie-level adoration.

"That was a long time ago. We caught a killer this morning. That's more amazing. But, incredibly, not the biggest news at HQ today."

"What was bigger than this?" Huntley asks.

"You don't know?" Aphra holds the bowls for Everest, who's still stirring the soup. "You need one of those phone-on-a-rope things. Put it around your neck so you don't forget it."

"Like a little kid with his house key?"

"Yeah. Just like that."

"If I take my phone with me, people will just call me. I like being disconnected, sometimes."

"What if it's important?"

"I'm a country boy. Anything important can wait. If it really matters, they'll visit in person. Like you did this morning. So? What's the bigger news?"

"Her partner ..."

"Not my partner," Everest says.

"He busted a massive drug ring down south."

"Justin did that?" Huntley asks.

"Some Russian family operating in Bunbury under the guise of a craft brewery," Everest says. "They had a rather substantial sideline meth business going on."

"You're telling me Booth figured all that out by himself and caught them? And he's only just joined Narcotics? Come on. I'd say he'd have massive trouble just to spell ketamine."

Everest, gripping the ladle like a drumstick, starts filling the bowls as Aphra holds them. The soup steams in the bowls appetisingly.

"Someone must've tipped him off," Aphra says.

"Probably one of the Ford-Brackmans. They'll definitely be happy any potential competition down south has been taken off the board."

"Yeah," Everest says. "It'll be all over the papers tomorrow, and the next day. The police getting the kind of PR moment they milk completely dry. Drugs on the table and all that. Piles of cash on show."

"Kids with vapes isn't quite as photogenic as meth and cash, and Russians in handcuffs," Huntley says. "What was the name?"

Aphra brings two bowls to the table.

Everest carries the third. "Of what?"

"The family. Any connection to Ekaterina Valoskiya?"

"None. The beer's called Belykrysa."

Huntley looks in the bowl that Aphra places in front of him. The soup does indeed look like a mixture of different types. "This looks great," he says.

Aphra and Everest start eating. Huntley watches for their reactions; they appear to enjoy it, but may both be too drunk to care.

"Belykrysa." He picks up his spoon. "You know that's a kind of condensed way of saying white rat."

"You speak Russian?" Aphra asks. "You're full of surprises."

"Dad taught me. He worked with Russians in Antarctica, and he always wanted to read the great Russian writers in the original. Especially the Cossack stories. He loved them. Sholokhov and the others. He continued to teach himself when back in WA." Huntley finally tests the soup and is amazed at how good it is. "Hmm. Impressive. Anyway, he was an incredible reader. A couple of books a week. He always said that literature, and stories, are what define us, and we have the obligation to know as many stories as we can. He had a caravan full of books, which became the commune's library. For him, the e-reader was the greatest invention since the printing press. He had every single story, right there in his hands."

"White rat?" Aphra asks. "What kind of name is that for a beer?"

"Maybe it was code for crystal meth."

"Speaking of rats," Everest says, "there was another big case today, one which may very well get the headlines tomorrow. In Cockburn. That was why I was able to get to you so fast."

"We owe you for that," Huntley says. "You saved our lives."

"Aphra was smart to make the call to me, and record it. Not only did I hear everything, I knew where you were."

"He wouldn't have let you die," Aphra says to Huntley. "And he basically proposed to me in that kitchen. It was everything I could do to keep from throwing up on the floor. I hate his ratty face."

Huntley nods. "The rodent poet."

"What happened in Cockburn, Ellie?"

"A rat fled a sinking ship," Everest says. "I found the Winslow Properties accountant unconscious in his office."

Huntley's spoon stops short of his mouth. "Accountant?"

"He'd been drugged, but it wasn't Purvis, because he was in holding with us."

"Why drug an accountant?" Aphra asks. "Or was it suicide?"

"Wait." Huntley stares straight ahead. "Accountant. Winslow Properties. Land. Lance. Chandice. Yeah. It was all a scam."

Everest smiles.

"The whole Southern Everglades," Huntley continues, "a money grab. Let me guess. Winslow's gone. He's the rat you're referring to."

Aphra drops her spoon. "What?"

"We believe he's in the Bahamas. The contents of the Winslow Properties accounts were transferred to a bank in the Bahamas last night. We also tracked Winslow to leaving Perth on a red-eye to KL just after midnight."

"He'd already be there by now, his coffers loaded," Huntley says. "Is that it? Can you get him?"

Everest shrugs. "We don't have an extradition treaty with the Bahamas. I learned that today. Even if we catch him, there's no guarantee we can get the money."

"Wow." Huntley looks at Aphra, who's gone very pale. "Are you all right? The soup's not that bad, is it?"

"No, it's good. There was no land sale?"

"Word is," Everest says, "there are documents showing Winslow sold the same sections of land several times. I don't know how he managed that without anyone knowing."

"Sounds like the accountant knows," Huntley says. "Winslow drugged him to stop him raising the alarm, long enough to leave the country."

"It's all gone?" Aphra asks. "How much are we talking about?"

"The transfer was just over 200 million."

"They were in it together," Huntley says. "Winslow and Lance. They were going to run off together. Then Lance died and Winslow decided to take it all for himself."

Aphra bangs the table with a fist.

"Hey, why does this matter so much to you?" Huntley asks.

"My parents bought some of that land."

"That's awful. Sorry, Aphra."

"It was part of their redundancy package, from the mining company they worked for up north. A whole bunch of people have been laid off, mostly those close to retirement age."

"So, not really their money. Giorgie bought land, with her family's money, but I don't care too much about that. The Giffords have more than enough, and that money's basically been passed from one criminal to another. But I don't agree with fleecing common folks of their hard-earned."

"I say we go right now to the Bahamas and catch this guy. Bring him and all of his money back here."

Everest laughs a little.

"There's no chance of that," Huntley says. "He's a ghost. I think there's a very good chance Nathaniel Winslow no longer exists."

"He's right, Aphra. New name. New identity. The Bahamas was probably just a transit point, if he's smart. He could be anywhere by now. And anyone."

"It's not fair. I know people. We can get him."

"Has this already gone to the media?" Huntley asks. "I bet there are some powerful people involved, including my ex-in-laws. There'll be a lynch mob hunting this guy once word gets out."

"The press conference is tomorrow morning," Everest says. "They want to give the drug bust the most attention."

"Don't worry, Aphra. Justice will be done. Some rich person, maybe even Harland Gifford, will put a bounty on Winslow's head. Your parents won't get their money back, but it wasn't their money to start with." Huntley sips his champagne. "It's hugely ironic, isn't it? Or maybe it's just sad. The Perth elites don't give a crap about a violinist being murdered, but if someone takes their money, then there's hell to pay."

"I need to tell my parents."

"Don't do that," Everest says. "Let it all happen the way it's supposed to. Technically, I don't even know about it. You can be sure the mining company will try to save face by paying off the people who lost money to Winslow. They have their own reputation to protect."

"Listen to the drummer, Aphra. She's beating the right rhythm. Everything will be all right. Enjoy this hodge-podge soup." Huntley has a spoonful. "I don't know what's in it, but it's good."

"It'll all work out, for your parents and everyone else who got this redundancy."

Aphra nods. "Maybe Niranda knows something."

"Niranda Stone?" Everest asks. "She's a piece of work."

"My boss now."

"No way."

"Right," Huntley says. "I'm stopping you both there. No politics at the dinner table. That's a rule my father had at the commune, and I'm applying it here. Speaking of which, the reunion is next weekend and you're both invited."

This helps lighten the mood. Aphra and Everest look at each other.

"I'll go if you go," Aphra says.

Everest nods, then looks at Huntley. "I'll go if you tell me the truth about your book."

"Why is everything a trade with you guys?"

"What nasty things did you do to keep those families feuding?"

"I don't know what you're talking about."

"I heard what you said in Purvis's kitchen. It's all in the transcript. You said it was to win Giorgie, but there's more to it than that."

Huntley folds his arms. "Look at you, Ellie. Become a bit of a storyteller yourself this week. It was all filler. I was trying to ingratiate myself with Purvis. Get him to drop his vanity shield."

"Well, now you can ingratiate yourself with us."

"Yeah," Aphra says, readily teaming up with Everest, "earn our trust. Maybe then we'll come to Ravensthorpe with you."

His soup finished, Huntley drops the spoon in the bowl with a clatter. "It stays here?"

Aphra and Everest nod.

"You know, this time, exactly one week ago, I was sitting in my caravan, after my classes, drunk as a goddamn skunk, working my way towards a hot toddy oblivion, wondering what the hell I was doing with my life. It was pathetic. I was miserable. If I'd had a gun, I don't know what I might've done. The only thing stopping me was Verity, and the thought of her being left alone with the Giffords. Now, here I am, a week later, admittedly soon to be drunk as a skunk again, but in the presence of two very fine people who I had the absolute fortune of meeting this week. Add Henrikson to the mix, and that we all combined to catch a killer. This has been the best handful of days in a really long time."

"We should take Henrikson too," Aphra says. "To the reunion."

"Agreed. Something tells me he'll come, without me having to trade anything with him, and he'll want to drive himself. He has an electric. It's brilliant."

"We should all go with him."

"Not if he's one of these seniors who drives achingly slow," Everest says.

"The opposite." Huntley chuckles a little. "He guns it. He even had to hack into your server to delete all his speeding tickets."

"I didn't hear that. But you're avoiding my question. Again. With impressive skill."

"No, I'm not doing that." Huntley stands up. "This is all preamble. A prologue, to set the scene and establish the basis of the character."

"The character as he is now," Aphra observes. "What about who he was 20 years ago?"

"Good point." Huntley goes to the kitchen. "This is going to require a proper drink."

"A male stripper?" Everest asks, and this makes Aphra laugh really loudly.

"Yes." Huntley puts the kettle on and finds the cupboard with tea. "Excellent. You have Earl Grey. Nothing fuels a storytelling fire quite like rum. Do you have lemon and cinnamon, Ellie?"

"There should be lemon juice in the fridge. I think there's cinnamon on the spice rack. Check the date. It was my gran's, there when I moved in."

"Well aged. It's all right. Cinnamon practically lasts forever. Do you both want one?"

"Not me," Everest says. "I've had enough male strippers for this lifetime."

"We'll stick to champagne," Aphra adds. "Now start the bloody story."

While the kettle boils, Huntley opens the rum and takes a swig straight from the bottle. "Aye. Very good." Another swig. "To tell you about *The Ragged Claws of Ravensthorpe* means starting with the story of Nodge Gurney."

"The guy who died," Everest says. "Second poem, wasn't it?"

"Yes. The first was the ram lamb theft, which got it all going." Huntley pours boiling water into a cup and starts lifting the tea bag up and down. "By the way, me telling this story is not going to be a one-way thing. You need to earn my trust as well, by telling a personal story of your own."

"Deal," Aphra says. "I'll tell you what happened with and to Jay Palmer."

"Who's that?" Everest asks.

"You'll find out, once we get through this Nodge saga."

"Ellie? What have you got for us?"

Everest's cat comes inside from the balcony and jumps up onto her lap. She's finding it comforting and therapeutic to have these two in her apartment; they make her home a place where she wants to be. This sensation, of comfort in her surroundings, is something she hasn't felt since living in the band house in

Highgate. And ever since she cried on Huntley's table in his caravan, she's been more willing to talk about Charlene.

She thinks: it's time to let people in and to let Charlene go.

"Yeah, okay," she says. "I'll tell you about the end of Salty Lemonade. Be warned. It's sad."

Huntley adds rum to the tea, then lemon and cinnamon, and more rum. "Thank you both. I like this. Sharing our stories."

Everest nods. "So do I."

"Then let's begin." Huntley has a long sip. "Oh, yes. Sweet nectar of the pirate gods. I like it best without honey."

"Stop delaying, Quin."

"So pushy, detective." Huntley stands in the kitchen, like he's on a stage, with an audience of two. "This is not a pretty story. It's actually quite horrible, because Nodge Gurney was horrible. Really fucking horrible. He was the head of the Gurney family for years. Since he was a teenager, after his father wrapped his ute around a tree near Lake Grace. He married young and had a pile of kids, which seemed to be mandatory at that time. You know, you breed your workforce. My father, who was always very fair when dealing with people, said that Nodge was a good parent. One of those people who's nice to his own and god-awful to everyone else."

"I know people like that," Aphra says.

"Same."

Huntley notices they have moved their chairs together. "The land the commune is on," he continues, "was won in a fight between Nodge and my dad. Seriously. A fist fight. Dad was a lot older than Nodge, but still knocked him out and he got that section of Gurney land which was part of the bet. Yes, these things really do happen in country towns. It's kind of a form of local entertainment. But that's not the story. You see, I knew Winslow's secret immediately. Remember that, Ellie? When he showed up at Lance's place? I'd seen that before. When I was there with Giorgie, the first time, that was spontaneous. We just drove down there, the morning after the night we met. That was amazing. Giorgie wanted to go to Ravensthorpe and I would've gone anywhere with her. So, we got there and Dad told me Nodge was trying to get the land back. I suggested the best solution was to get the Gurneys fighting with the Edwards clan again, and then the commune would be left alone. And that was how me and Orville ended up stealing a ram lamb from the Edwards farm."

"Why a ram lamb?" Everest asks. "That seems so specific."

"Because that's what started the feud years ago. Back when they were first settling and trying to farm, the Gurneys had no ram and couldn't afford one. No ram means no way to increase the number of sheep. So they stole one from the Edwards. Now, this is where the story gets horrid. Because as me and Orv were driving back to the commune, Orv said, with this little lamb on his lap, and just off-hand like, that he really hopes one of the Edwards kills Nodge for this. I asked him why and he wouldn't say. But he didn't have to say anything, because there'd been rumours about Nodge for decades, and the way Orv went into his shell like that, calmly stroking the lamb, it wasn't hard to guess what had happened. I saw the whole story. We got back to the commune and I sat Orville down with my father and we managed to get some of the details. The whole time, Orville had the lamb on his lap. Well, I can tell you my father and I were after blood. But, we decided to wait a few days, for the lamb to be noticed as stolen and for accusations to be thrown around. Then, my father, on the pretext of meeting Nodge to discuss giving the land back, knocked him out and drove him up to Hatter Hill, in Nodge's car. He threw the keys into the bush and started walking back. When it was dark, I drove out and picked him up."

"He left Nodge there?" Aphra asks.

Huntley sips his drink. He adds another splash of rum. "He did."

Everest and Aphra are motionless, except for Everest slowly stroking her cat.

"You're reminding me of Orville when you do that, Ellie," he says.

"I'm pondering what to do about this."

"There's nothing to do. My father's long gone."

"Did Giorgie know?" Aphra asks.

"No one knew. I didn't tell anyone. Orv assumed it, but he never said anything. I think he was glad to bury all of that without ever having to fully address it. The Gurneys were convinced an Edwards family member killed Nodge in retaliation for the lamb, and the two families went at each other until cops came up from Albany to intervene. No one else died. It was mostly property damage and fist-fights. Ravensthorpe even had a curfew for a couple of weeks. When all that dust had settled, I was already back in Perth, living with Giorgie. And I had the *Ragged Claws*."

"Would you consider that a happy ending?" Everest asks.

"Orville's my brother. I love him dearly. So, yes. Plus, it was the beginning of a long chain of plot twists that brought me here, drinking a hot toddy in your kitchen, with you two, with this incredible week behind me. I think I have a bit of a future in solving crimes, or at least helping with your cases."

"Yeah. Maybe. If I let all this go."

Huntley smiles. "It's just a story, right?"

Travel Page (cont.)